SHANGHAI GIRLS

SHANGHAI GIRLS

LISA SEE

ISIS
LARGE PRINT
Oxford

Copyright © Lisa See, 2009

First published in Great Britain 2009
by
Bloomsbury Publishing

Published in Large Print 2009 by ISIS Publishing Ltd.,
7 Centremead, Osney Mead, Oxford OX2 0ES
by arrangement with
Bloomsbury Publishing

British Library Cataloguing in Publication Data
See, Lisa.
    Shanghai girls
    1. Sisters - - Fiction.
    2. Chinese - - United States - - Fiction.
    3. Immigrants - - United States - - Fiction.
    4. Family secrets - - Fiction.
    5. Large type books.
    I. Title
    813.5'4–dc22

ISBN 978–0–7531–8476–9 (hb)
ISBN 978–0–7531–8477–6 (pb)

Printed and bound in Great Britain by
T. J. International Ltd., Padstow, Cornwall

For my cousin Leslee Leong,
my cohort in memory keeping

Author's Note

Shanghai Girls takes place between 1937 and 1957. Readers will find some of what today we would call politically incorrect terms, but they are accurate to the time. I have used the Wade-Giles system of transliteration for Chinese words — whether in Mandarin, Cantonese, or in the Sze Yup and Wu dialects — again in keeping with the era.

Regarding exchange rates: Silver dollars were used in Shanghai before November 1935; Chinese *yuan* were used after 1935. The two were roughly equivalent. I have chosen to stay with dollars and cents because some were still in circulation and they are a more familiar currency to Western readers. The copper-silver exchange rate ranged from 300 to 330 coppers for every silver dollar (or *yuan*).

Part One

FATE

Beautiful Girls

"Our daughter looks like a South China peasant with those red cheeks," my father complains, pointedly ignoring the soup before him. "Can't you do something about them?"

Mama stares at Baba, but what can she say? My face is pretty enough — some might even say lovely — but not as luminescent as the pearl I'm named for. I tend to blush easily. Beyond that, my cheeks capture the sun. When I turned five, my mother began rubbing my face and arms with pearl creams, and mixing ground pearls into my morning *jook* — rice porridge — hoping the white essence would permeate my skin. It hasn't worked. Now my cheeks burn red — exactly what my father hates. I shrink down into my chair. I always slump when I'm near him, but I slump even more on those occasions when Baba takes his eyes off my sister to look at me. I'm taller than my father, which he loathes. We live in Shanghai, where the tallest car, the tallest wall, or the tallest building sends a clear and unwavering message that the owner is a person of great importance. I am not a person of importance.

"She thinks she's smart," Baba goes on. He wears a Western-style suit of good cut. His hair shows just a few strands of gray. He's been anxious lately, but tonight his mood is darker than usual. Perhaps his favorite horse didn't win or the dice refused to land his way. "But one thing she isn't is clever."

This is another of my father's standard criticisms and one he picked up from Confucius, who wrote, "An educated woman is a worthless woman." People call me bookish, which even in 1937 is not considered a good thing. But as smart as I am, I don't know how to protect myself from my father's words.

Most families eat at a round dining table, so they will always be whole and connected, with no sharp edges. We have a square teakwood table, and we always sit in the exact same places: my father next to May on one side of the table, with my mother directly across from her so that my parents can share my sister equally. Every meal — day after day, year after year — is a reminder that I'm not the favorite and never will be.

As my father continues to pick at my faults, I shut him out and pretend an interest in our dining room. On the wall adjoining the kitchen, four scrolls depicting the four seasons usually hang. Tonight they've been removed, leaving shadow outlines on the wall. They aren't the only things missing. We used to have an overhead fan, but this past year Baba thought it would be more luxurious to have servants fan us while we ate. They aren't here tonight and the room is sweltering.

Ordinarily an art deco chandelier and matching wall sconces of etched yellow-and-rose-tinted glass illuminate the room. These are missing as well. I don't give any of this much thought, assuming that the scrolls have been put away to prevent their silken edges from curling in the humidity, that Baba has given the servants a night off to celebrate a wedding or birthday with their own families, and that the lighting fixtures have been temporarily taken down for cleaning.

Cook — who has no wife and children of his own — removes our soup bowls and brings out dishes of shrimp with water chestnuts, pork stewed in soy sauce with dried vegetables and bamboo shoots, steamed eel, an eight-treasures vegetable dish, and rice, but the heat swallows my hunger. I would prefer a few sips of chilled sour plum juice, cold mint-flavored sweet green bean soup, or sweet almond broth.

When Mama says, "The basket repairer charged too much today," I relax. If my father is predictable in his criticisms of me, then it's equally predictable that my mother will recite her daily woes. She looks elegant, as always. Amber pins hold the bun at the back of her neck perfectly in place. Her gown, a *cheongsam* made of midnight blue silk with midlength sleeves, has been expertly tailored to fit her age and status. A bracelet carved from a single piece of good jade hangs from her wrist. The *thump* of it when it hits the table edge is comforting and familiar. She has bound feet, and some of her ways are just as antiquated. She questions our dreams, weighing the meaning of the presence of water, shoes, or teeth as good or bad omens. She believes in astrology, blaming or praising May and me for one thing or another because we were born in the Year of the Sheep and the Year of the Dragon, respectively.

Mama has a lucky life. Her arranged marriage to our father seems relatively peaceful. She reads Buddhist sutras in the morning, takes a rickshaw to visit friends for lunch, plays mah-jongg until late in the day, and commiserates with wives of similar station about the weather, the indolence of servants, and the ineffectiveness of the latest remedies for their hiccups, gout, or hemorrhoids. She has nothing to fret about, but her quiet bitterness and persistent worry infuse every story she tells us. "There are no happy endings," she often recites. Still, she's beautiful, and her lily gait is as delicate as the swaying of young bamboo in a spring breeze.

"That lazy servant next door was sloppy with the Tso family's night-stool and stunk up the street with their nightsoil," Mama says. "And Cook!" She allows herself a low hiss of disapproval. "Cook has served us shrimp so old that the smell has made me lose my appetite."

We don't contradict her, but the odor suffocating us comes not from spilled nightsoil or day-old shrimp but from her. Since we don't have our servants to keep the air moving in the room, the smell that rises from the blood and pus that seep through the bandages holding Mama's feet in their tiny shape clings to the back of my throat.

Mama is still filling the air with her grievances when Baba interrupts. "You girls can't go out tonight. I need to talk to you."

He speaks to May, who looks at him and smiles in that beautiful way of hers. We aren't bad girls, but we have plans tonight, and being lectured by Baba about how much water we waste in our baths or the fact that we don't eat every grain of rice in our bowls isn't part of them. Usually Baba reacts to May's charm by smiling back at her and forgetting his concerns, but this time he blinks a few times and shifts his black eyes to me. Again, I sink in my chair. Sometimes I think this is my only real form of filial piety, making myself small before my father. I consider myself to be a modern Shanghai girl. I don't want to believe in all that obey, obey, obey stuff girls were taught in the past. But the truth is, May — as much as they adore her — and I are just girls. No one will carry on the family name, and no one will worship our parents as ancestors when the time comes. My sister and I are the end of the Chin line. When we were very young, our lack of value meant our parents had little interest in controlling us. We weren't worth the trouble or effort. Later, something strange happened: my parents fell in love — total, besotted love — with their younger daughter. This allowed us to retain a certain amount of liberty, with the result that my sister's spoiled ways are often ignored, as is our sometimes flagrant disregard for respect and duty. What others might call unfilial and disrespectful, we call modern and unbound.

"You aren't worth a single copper coin," Baba says to me, his tone sharp. "I don't know how I'm ever going to —"

"Oh, Ba, stop picking on Pearl. You're lucky to have a daughter like her. I'm luckier still to have her as my sister."

We all turn to May. She's like that. When she speaks, you can't help listening to her. When she's in the room, you can't help looking at her. Everyone loves her — our parents, the rickshaw boys who work for my father, the missionaries who taught us in school, the artists, revolutionaries, and foreigners whom we've come to know these last few years.

"Aren't you going to ask me what I did today?" May asks, her demand as light and breezy as a bird's wings in flight.

With that, I disappear from my parents' vision. I'm the older sister, but in so many ways May takes care of me.

"I went to see a movie at the Metropole and then I went to Avenue Joffre to buy shoes," she continues. "From there it wasn't far to Madame Garnet's shop in the Cathay Hotel to pick up my new dress." May lets a touch of reproach creep into her voice. "She said she won't let me have it until you come to call."

"A girl doesn't need a new dress every week," Mama says gently. "You could be more like your sister in this regard. A Dragon doesn't need frills, lace, and bows. Pearl's too practical for all that."

"Baba can afford it," May retorts.

My father's jaw tightens. Is it something May said, or is he getting ready to criticize me again? He opens his mouth to speak, but my sister cuts him off.

"Here we are in the seventh month and already the heat is unbearable. Baba, when are you sending us to Kuling? You don't want Mama and me to get sick, do you? Summer brings such unpleasantness to the city, and we're always happier in the mountains at this time of year."

May has tactfully left me out of her questions. I prefer to be an afterthought. But all her chattering is really just a way to distract our parents. My sister catches my eye, nods almost imperceptibly, and quickly stands. "Come, Pearl. Let's get ready."

I push back my chair, grateful to be saved from my father's disapproval.

"No!" Baba pounds his fist on the table. The dishes rattle. Mama shivers in surprise. I freeze in place. People on our street admire my father for his business acumen. He's lived the dream of every native-born Shanghainese, as well as every Shanghailander — those foreigners who've come here from around the world to find their fortunes. He started with nothing and turned himself and his family into something. Before I was born, he ran a rickshaw business in Canton, not as an owner but as a subcontractor, who rented rickshaws at seventy cents a day and then rented them to a minor subcontractor at ninety cents a day before they were rented to the rickshaw pullers at a dollar a day. After he made enough money, he moved us to Shanghai and opened his own rickshaw business. "Better opportunities," he — and probably a million others in the city — likes to say. Baba has never told us how he became so wealthy or how he earned those opportunities, and I

9

don't have the courage to ask. Everyone agrees — even in families — that it's better not to inquire about the past, because everyone in Shanghai has come here to get away from something or has something to hide.

May doesn't care about any of that. I look at her and know exactly what she wants to say: *I don't want to hear you tell us you don't like our hair. I don't want to hear that you don't want us to show our bare arms or too much of our legs. No, we don't want to get "regular full-time jobs." You may be my father, but for all your noise you're a weak man and I don't want to listen to you.* Instead, she just tilts her head and looks down at my father in such a way that he's powerless before her. She learned this trick as a toddler and has perfected it as she's gotten older. Her ease, her effortlessness, melts everyone. A slight smile comes to her lips. She pats his shoulder, and his eyes are drawn to her fingernails, which, like mine, have been painted and stained red by applying layers of red balsam blossom juice. Touching — even in families — isn't completely taboo, but it certainly isn't accepted. A good and proper family offer no kisses, no hugs, no pats of affection. So May knows exactly what she's doing when she touches our father. In his distraction and repulsion, she spins away, and I hurry after her. We've taken a few steps when Baba calls out.

"Please don't go."

But May, in her usual way, just laughs. "We're working tonight. Don't wait up."

I follow her up the stairs, our parents' voices accompanying us in a kind of discordant song. Mama

10

carries the melody: "I pity your husbands. 'I need shoes.' 'I want a new dress.' 'Will you buy us tickets to the opera?'" Baba, in his deeper voice, beats out the bass: "Come back here. Please come back. I need to tell you something." May ignores them, and I try to, admiring the way she closes her ears to their words and insistence. We're opposites in this and so many things.

Whenever you have two sisters — or siblings of any number or either sex — comparisons are made. May and I were born in Yin Bo Village, less than a half day's walk from Canton. We're only three years apart, but we couldn't be more different. She's funny; I'm criticized for being too somber. She's tiny and has an adorable fleshiness to her; I'm tall and thin. May, who just graduated from high school, has no interest in reading anything beyond the gossip columns; I graduated from college five weeks ago.

My first language was Sze Yup, the dialect spoken in the Four Districts in Kwangtung province, where our ancestral home is located. I've had American and British teachers since I was five, so my English is close to perfect. I consider myself fluent in four languages — British English, American English, the Sze Yup dialect (one of many Cantonese dialects), and the Wu dialect (a unique version of Mandarin spoken only in Shanghai). I live in an international city, so I use English words for Chinese cities and places like Canton, Chungking, and Yunnan; I use the Cantonese *cheongsam* instead of the Mandarin *ch'i pao* for our Chinese dresses; I say *boot* instead of *trunk*; I use the Mandarin *fan gwaytze* — foreign devils — and the

Cantonese *lo fan* — white ghosts — interchangeably when speaking about foreigners; and I use the Cantonese word for *little sister* — *moy moy* — instead of the Mandarin — *mei mei* — to talk about May. My sister has no facility with languages. We moved to Shanghai when May was a baby, and she never learned Sze Yup beyond words for certain dishes and ingredients. May knows only English and the Wu dialect. Leaving the peculiarities of dialects aside, Mandarin and Cantonese have about as much in common as English and German — related but unintelligible to nonspeakers. Because of this, my parents and I sometimes take advantage of May's ignorance, using Sze Yup to trick and deceive her.

Mama insists May and I couldn't change who we are even if we tried. May is supposed to be as complacent and content as the Sheep in whose year she was born. The Sheep is the most feminine of the signs, Mama says. It's fashionable, artistic, and compassionate. The Sheep needs someone to take care of her, so she'll always be sure to have food, shelter, and clothing. At the same time, the Sheep is known to smother others with affection. Good fortune smiles on the Sheep because of its peaceful nature and kind heart, but — and it's a big but, according to Mama — the Sheep sometimes thinks only of itself and its own comforts.

I have a Dragon's striving desire, which can never be properly filled. "There's nowhere you can't go with your big flapping feet," Mama frequently tells me. However, a Dragon, the most powerful of the signs, also has its drawbacks. "A Dragon is loyal, demanding, responsible, a tamer of the fates," Mama has told me, "but you, my Pearl, will always be hampered by the vapors that come from your mouth."

Am I jealous of my sister? How can I be jealous when even I adore her? We share *Long* — Dragon — as our generational name. I am Pearl Dragon, and May is Beautiful Dragon. She's taken the Western spelling of her name, but in Mandarin *mei* is one of the words for *beautiful*, and she is that. My duty as May's elder sister is to protect her, make sure she follows the right path, and indulge her for the preciousness of her existence and place of love in our family. Yes, sometimes I get angry with her: for example, when she wore my favorite pink silk Italian high heels without permission and they were ruined in the rain. But here's the thing: my sister loves me. I'm her *jie jie* — her elder sister. In the hierarchy of the Chinese family, I will always and forever be above her, even if my family doesn't love me as much as they love her.

By the time I get to our room, May has already pulled off her dress, leaving it in a limp heap on the floor. I shut the door behind me, enclosing us in our beautiful-girl world. We have matching four-poster twin beds with white linen canopies edged in blue and embroidered in a wisteria design. Most bedrooms in Shanghai have a beautiful-girl poster or calendar, but we have several. We model for beautiful-girl artists, and we've chosen our favorite images to hang on our walls: May seated on a sofa in a lime green silk jacket, holding a Hatamen cigarette in an ivory cigarette holder; me wrapped in ermine, my knees tucked up under my chin, staring at the viewer from a framed colonnade before a mythical lake selling Dr. Williams's pink pills for pale people (who better to sell those pills than someone who has a naturally pink complexion?); and the two of us perched together in a stylish boudoir, each holding a fat baby son — the symbol of wealth and prosperity — and selling powdered baby milk to show we are modern mothers who use the best modern inventions for our modern offspring.

I cross the room and join May at the closet. This is when our day actually begins. Tonight we'll sit for Z.G. Li, the best of the artists who specialize in beautiful-girl calendars, posters, and advertisements. Most families would be scandalized to have daughters who pose for artists and often stay out all night, and at first my parents were. But once we started making money, they didn't mind. Baba took our earnings and invested them, saying that, when we meet our husbands, fall in love, and decide to get married, we'll go to our husbands' homes with money of our own.

We select complementary *cheongsams* to show harmony and style, while sending the message of freshness and ease that promises to bring spring happiness to all who use whatever product we'll be selling. I choose a *cheongsam* of peach-colored silk with red piping. The dress is tailored so close to my body that the dressmaker cut the side slit daringly high to allow me to walk. Frogs fashioned from the same red piping fasten the dress at my neck, across my breasts, under my armpit, and down my right side. May pours herself into a *cheongsam* of pale yellow silk patterned in subtle white blossoms with red centers. Her piping and frogs are the same deep red as mine. Her stiff mandarin collar rises so high it touches her ears; short sleeves accentuate the slimness of her arms. While May draws her eyebrows into the shape of young willow leaves — long, thin, and sleek — I dab white rice powder on my face to hide my rosy cheeks. Then we slip on red high heels and paint our lips red to match.

Recently we cut our long hair and got permanents. May now parts my hair down the middle and then slicks the curls behind my ears, where they puff out like black-petaled peonies. Then I comb her hair, letting the curls frame her face. We add pink crystal drop earrings, jade rings, and gold bracelets to complete our outfits. Our eyes meet in the mirror. From the posters on the walls, multiple images of us join May and me in the reflection. We hold that for a moment, taking in how pretty we look. We are twenty-one and eighteen. We are young, we are beautiful, and we live in the Paris of Asia.

We clatter back downstairs, call out hasty good-byes, and step into the Shanghai night. Our home is in the Hongkew district, just across Soochow Creek. We aren't part of the official International Settlement, but we're close enough to believe we'll be protected from possible foreign invaders. We aren't terribly rich, but then isn't that always a matter of comparison? We're just getting by, according to British, American, or Japanese measures, but we have a fortune by Chinese standards, although some of our countrymen in the city are wealthier than many foreigners combined. We are *kaoteng Huajen* — superior Chinese — who follow the religion of *ch'ung yang*: worshipping all things foreign, from the Westernization of our names to the love of movies, bacon, and cheese. As members of the *bu-er-ch'iao-ya* — bourgeois class — our family is prosperous enough that our seven servants take turns eating their meals on the front steps, letting the rickshaw pullers and beggars who pass know that those who work for the Chins have regular food to eat and a reliable roof over their heads.

We walk to the corner and bargain with several shirtless and shoeless rickshaw boys before settling on a good price. We climb in and sit side by side.

"Take us to the French Concession," May orders.

The boy's muscles contract with the effort of getting the rickshaw rolling. Soon he hits a comfortable trot and the momentum of the rickshaw eases the strain on his shoulders and back. There he is, pulling us like a beast of burden, but all I feel is freedom. During the day I use a parasol when I go shopping, visiting, or to tutor English. But at night I don't have to worry about my skin. I sit up tall and take a deep breath. I glance at May. She's so carefree that she recklessly lets her *cheongsam* flap in the breeze and open all the way up her thigh. She's flirtatious, and she simply couldn't live in a better city than Shanghai to exercise her skills, her laughter, her beautiful skin, her charming conversation.

We cross a bridge over Soochow Creek and then turn right, away from the Whangpoo River and its dank odors of oil, seaweed, coal, and sewage. I love Shanghai. It isn't like other places in China. Instead of swallowtail roofs and glazed tiles, we have *mo t'ien talou* — magical big buildings — that reach into the sky. Instead of moon gates, spirit screens, intricate latticework windows, and red lacquer pillars, we have neoclassical edifices in granite decorated with art deco ironwork, geometric designs, and etched glass. Instead of bamboo groves gracing streams or willows draping their tendrils into ponds, we have European villas with clean façades, elegant balconies, rows of cypress, and cleanly cut lawns lined with immaculate flower beds. The Old Chinese City still has temples and gardens, but the rest of Shanghai kneels before the gods of trade, wealth, industry, and sin. The city has godowns where goods are loaded and unloaded, courses for greyhound and horse racing, countless movie palaces, and clubs for dancing, drinking, and having sex. Shanghai is home to millionaires and beggars, gangsters and gamblers, patriots and revolutionaries, artists and warlords, and the Chin family.

Our puller takes us down alleys just wide enough for pedestrians, rickshaws, and wheelbarrows outfitted with benches for transporting paying customers, before turning onto Bubbling Well Road. He trots onto the elegant boulevard, unafraid of the purring Chevrolets, Daimlers, and Isotta-Fraschinis that hurtle past. At a stoplight, beggar children shoot into the traffic to surround our rickshaw and pull at our clothes. Each block brings us the smells of death and decay, ginger and roast duck, French perfume and incense. The loud voices of native Shanghainese, the steady *click-click* of the abacus, and the rattle of rickshaws rolling through the streets are the background sounds that tell me this is home.

At the border between the International Settlement and the French Concession, the rickshaw boy stops. We pay him, cross the street, step around a dead baby left on the sidewalk, find another rickshaw puller who has a license for the French Concession, and tell him Z.G.'s address off the Avenue Lafayette.

This puller is even dirtier and sweatier than the last. His tattered shirt barely hides the skeletal protuberances that have become his body. He hesitates before daring his way onto Avenue Joffre. It's a French name, but the street is the center of life for White Russians. Signs in Cyrillic hang overhead. We breathe in the smells of fresh bread and cakes from the Russian bakeries. Already the sounds of music and dancing pour from clubs. As we near Z.G.'s apartment, the neighborhood changes yet again. We pass Seeking Happiness Lane, home to more than 150 brothels. From this street many of Shanghai's Famous Flowers — the city's most talented prostitutes — are elected and featured on the covers of magazines each year.

Our puller lets us out, and we pay him. As we walk up the rickety stairs to the third floor of Z.G.'s apartment building, I pouf the curls around my ears with my fingertips, run my lips together to smooth my lipstick, and adjust my *cheongsam* so that the bias-cut silk falls perfectly over my hips. When he opens the door, I'm struck again by how handsome Z.G. is: a thick mop of unruly black hair, a slight frame, big, round wire-rimmed glasses, and an intensity to his gaze

18

and demeanor that speaks of late nights, artistic temperament, and political fervor. I may be tall, but he's taller still. It's one of the many things I love about him.

"What you're wearing is perfect," he enthuses. "Come! Come!"

We never know exactly what he has planned for our sitting. Young women getting ready to dive into a pool, play mini golf, or pull back a bow to send an arrow across the sky have been extremely popular lately. Being fit and healthy is an ideal. Who best to raise China's sons? The answer: a woman who can play tennis, drive a car, smoke a cigarette, and still look as approachable, sophisticated, and beddable as possible. Will Z.G. ask us to pretend we're about to go out for an afternoon of tea dancing? Or will he compose something entirely fictional, requiring us to change into rented costumes? Will May be Mulan, the great woman warrior, brought back to life to promote Parrot wine? Will I be painted as the fictional maiden Du Liniang from *The Peony Pavilion* to extol the merits of Lux toilet soap?

He leads us to a scene he's set up: a cozy corner with an overstuffed chair, an intricately carved Chinese screen, and a ceramic pot decorated in a never-ending knot pattern from which some sprigs of blooming plum give the illusion of outdoor freshness.

"Today we're selling My Dear cigarettes," Z.G. announces. "May, I'd like you in the chair." Once she sits down, he stands back and stares at her intently. I love Z.G. for the gentleness and sensitivity he shows my sister. She's young after all, and what we're doing isn't

19

exactly something most well-bred girls do. "More relaxed," he directs, "like you've been out all night and want to share a secret with your friend."

After positioning May, he calls me over. He puts his hands on my hips and twists my body until I perch on the backrest of May's chair.

"I love your long lines and the length of your limbs," he says, as he brings my arm forward so that my weight rests on my hand while I balance over May. His fingers spread mine, separating the pinkie from the rest. His hand lingers for a moment, and then he edges back to look at his composition. Satisfied, he gives us cigarettes. "Now, Pearl, lean toward May as though you just lit your cigarette from the tip of hers."

I do as I'm told. He steps forward one last time to move a tendril of hair from May's cheek and tilt her chin so that the light will dance on her cheekbones. I may be the one Z.G. likes to paint and touch — and how forbidden that feels — but May's face sells everything from matches to carburetors.

Z.G. moves behind his easel. He doesn't like us to speak or move when he paints, but he keeps us entertained by playing music on the phonograph and talking to us about this and that.

"Pearl, are we here to make money or have fun?" He doesn't wait for my answer. He doesn't want one. "Is it to tarnish or burnish our reputations? I say neither. We're doing something else. Shanghai is the center of beauty and modernity. A wealthy Chinese can buy whatever he or she sees on one of our calendars. Those who have less money can aspire to have these things. The poor? They can only dream."

"Lu Hsün thinks differently," May says.

I sigh impatiently. Everyone admires Lu Hsün, the great writer who died last year, but that doesn't mean May should be talking about him during our sitting. I keep quiet and hold my pose.

"He wanted China to be modern," May continues. "He wanted us to get rid of the *lo fan* and their influence. He was critical of beautiful girls."

"I know, I know," Z.G. responds evenly, but I'm surprised by my sister's knowledge. She's not a reader; she never has been. She must be trying to impress Z.G., and it's working. "I was there the night he gave that speech. You would have laughed, May. You too, Pearl. He held up a calendar that just happened to be of the two of you."

"Which one?" I ask, breaking my silence.

"I didn't paint it, but it showed the two of you dancing the tango together. Pearl, you were dipping May back. It was very —"

"I remember that one! Mama was so upset when she saw it. Remember, Pearl?"

I remember all right. Mama was given the poster from the store on Nanking Road where she buys napkins for the monthly visit from the little red sister. She cried and railed and yelled that we were embarrassing the Chin family by looking and acting like White Russian taxi dancers. We tried to explain that beautiful-girl calendars actually express filial piety and traditional values. They are given away at Chinese and

Western New Years as incentives, special promotions, or gifts to favored clients. From those good homes, they trickle down to street vendors, who sell them for a few coppers to the poor. We told Mama that a calendar is the most important thing in life for every Chinese, even though we didn't believe it ourselves. Whether rich or poor, people regulate their lives by the sun, the moon, the stars, and, in Shanghai, by the tide of the Whangpoo. They refuse to enter into a business deal, set a wedding date, or plant a crop without considering the auspiciousness of *feng shui*. All this can be found in the borders of most beautiful-girl calendars, which is why they serve as almanacs for everything good or potentially dangerous in the year to come. At the same time, they are cheap decorations for even the lowest home.

"We're making people's lives more beautiful," May explained to Mama. "That's why we're called beautiful girls." But Mama only calmed down after May pointed out that the advertisement was for cod-liver oil. "We're keeping children healthy," May said. "You should be proud of us!"

In the end, Mama hung the calendar in the kitchen next to the phone so she could write important numbers — for the soy-milk vendor, the electrician, Madame Garnet, and the birth dates for all our servants — on our exposed, pale legs and arms. Still, after that incident, we were careful about which posters we brought home and worried about which ones might be given to her by one of the neighborhood tradesmen.

"Lu Hsün said that calendar posters are depraved and disgusting," May picks up, barely moving her lips so she can keep her smile in place. "He said that the women who pose for them are sick. He said this kind of sickness doesn't come from society —"

"It comes from the painters," Z.G. finishes for her. "He considered what we're doing decadent and said it won't help the revolution. But tell me, little May, how will the revolution happen without us? Don't answer. Just sit and be quiet. Otherwise, we'll be here all night."

I'm grateful for the silence. In the days before the Republic, I would have already been sent sight unseen to my husband's home in a red lacquer sedan chair. By now I would have given birth to several children, sons hopefully. But I was born in 1916, the fourth year of the Republic. Footbinding was banned and women's lives changed. People in Shanghai now consider arranged marriages backward. Everyone wants to marry for love. In the meantime, we believe in free love. Not that I've given it freely. I haven't given it yet at all, but I would if Z.G. asked me to.

He'd positioned me so that my face would be angled to May's, but he wanted me to look at him. I hold my pose, stare at him, and dream of our future together. Free love is one thing, but I want us to get married. Every night as he paints, I draw on the great festivities I've been to and imagine the wedding my father will host for Z.G. and me.

At close to ten, we hear the wonton soup peddler call, "Hot soup to bring sweat, cool the skin and the night."

Z.G. holds his brush in midair, pretending to consider where next to apply paint, while watching to see which of us will break our pose first.

When the wonton man is just below the window, May jumps up and squeals, "I can't wait any longer!" She rushes to the window, calls down our usual order, and then lowers a bowl attached to a rope that we've made by tying several pairs of our silk stockings together. The wonton man sends up bowl after bowl of soup, which we eat with relish. Then we retake our places and get back to work.

Not long after midnight, Z.G. sets down his brush. "We're done for tonight," he says. "I'll work on the background until the next time you sit for me. Now, let's go out!"

While he changes into a pin-striped suit, tie, and fedora, May and I stretch to loosen the stiffness from our bodies. We touch up our makeup and run combs through our hair. And then we're back out on the streets, the three of us linking arms, laughing, and striding down the block, as food vendors call out their special treats.

"Hand-burning hot ginkgo nuts. Every one popped! Every one big!"

"Stewed plums besprinkled with licorice powder. Ah, sweet! Only ten coppers a package!"

We pass watermelon hawkers on nearly every corner, each with his own call, each promising the best, sweetest, juiciest, coldest melon in the city. As tempting as the watermelon sellers are, we ignore them. Too many of them try to make their melons sound heavier by injecting them with water from the river or one of the creeks. Even a single bite could result in dysentery, typhoid, or cholera.

We arrive at the Casanova, where friends will be meeting us later. May and I are recognized as beautiful girls and shown a good table near the dance floor. We order champagne, and Z.G. asks me to dance. I love the way he holds me as we spin across the floor. After a couple of songs, I glance back at our table and see May sitting alone.

"Maybe you should dance with my sister," I say.

"If you'd like me to," he answers.

We twirl back to our table. Z.G. takes May's hand. The orchestra begins a slow tune. May rests her head on his chest as though listening to his heart. Z.G. moves May gracefully through the other couples. Once he catches my eye and smiles. My thoughts are so girlish: our wedding night, our married life together, the children we'll have.

"Here you are!" I feel a peck on my cheek and look up to see my school friend Betsy Howell. "Have you been waiting long?"

"We just got here. Sit down. Where's the waiter? We're going to need more champagne. Have you eaten yet?"

Betsy and I sit shoulder to shoulder, touch glasses, and sip our champagne. Betsy's an American. Her father works for the State Department. I like her mother and father because they like me and don't try to prevent Betsy from socializing with Chinese as so many other foreign parents do. Betsy and I got to know each other at the Methodist mission, where she was sent to help the heathens and I'd been sent to learn Western ways. Are we best friends? Not really. May is my best friend. Betsy is a distant second.

"You look nice tonight," I say. "I love your dress."

"You should! You helped me buy it. I'd look like an old cow if it weren't for you."

Betsy's a bit on the chunky side, and she's burdened by one of those practical American mothers who know almost nothing about fashion, so I took Betsy to a seamstress to have some decent clothes made. Tonight she looks quite pretty in a sheath of vermilion satin with a diamond-and-sapphire brooch pinned above her left breast. Blond curls bubble loose on her freckled shoulders.

"Look how sweet they are," Betsy says, nodding to Z.G. and May.

We watch them dance while we gossip about school friends. When the song ends, Z.G. and May come back to the table. He's lucky to have three women in his company tonight, and he does the right thing by dancing with one after the other of us. At close to one o'clock, Tommy Hu arrives. Glowing warmth comes to May's cheeks when she sees him. Mama has played mah-jongg with his mother for years, and they have always hoped for a match between our families. Mama will be thrilled to hear about this encounter.

At two in the morning, we burst back out onto the street. It's July, hot and humid. Everyone's still awake, even children, even the old. It's time for a snack.

"Will you come with us?" I ask Betsy.

"I don't know. Where are you going?"

We all look to Z.G. He names a café in the French Concession known as a hangout for intellectuals, artists, and Communists.

Betsy doesn't hesitate. "Come on then. Let's take my dad's car."

The Shanghai I love is a fluid place, where the most interesting people mingle. Some days Betsy takes me out for American coffee, toast, and butter; sometimes I take Betsy into alleys for *hsiao ch'ih* — little eats, dumplings of glutinous rice wrapped in reed leaves or cakes made from cassia petals and sugar. Betsy's adventurous when she's with me; once she accompanied me into the Old Chinese City to buy cheap holiday gifts. Sometimes I'm nervous about entering parks in the International Settlement, which until I turned ten were prohibited to Chinese other than amahs with foreign children or gardeners who tended the grounds. But I'm never scared or nervous when I'm with Betsy, who's gone into those parks her whole life.

The café is smoky and dark, but we don't feel out of place in our fancy clothes. We join a group of Z.G.'s friends. Tommy and May push their chairs away from the table so they can talk quietly together and avoid a heated argument about who "owns" our city — the British, Americans, French, or Japanese? We hugely outnumber foreigners, even in the International Settlement, yet we have no rights. May and I don't worry about things like whether we can testify in court against a foreigner or if they'll let us into one of their clubs, but Betsy comes from another world.

27

"By the end of the year," she says, her eyes clear and impassioned, "over twenty thousand corpses will have been picked up from the International Settlement's streets. We step over those bodies every day, but I don't see any of you doing anything about it."

Betsy believes in the need for change. The question, I suppose, is why does she tolerate May and me when we so deliberately ignore what happens around us?

"Are you asking if we love our country?" Z.G. asks. "There are two kinds of love, wouldn't you say? *Ai kuo* is the love we feel for our country and our people. *Ai jen* is what I might feel for my lover. One is patriotic, the other romantic." He glances at me, and I blush. "Can't we have both?"

We leave the café at close to five in the morning. Betsy waves, gets in her father's car, and is driven away. We say good night — or good morning — to Z.G. and Tommy, and hail a rickshaw. Once again, we change rickshaws at the border between the French Concession and the International Settlement, and then we clatter down the cobblestones the rest of the way home.

The city, like a great sea, has never gone to sleep. The night ebbs, and now the morning cycles and rhythms begin to flow. Nightsoil men push their carts down the alleyways, calling "Empty your nightstool! Here comes the nightsoil man! Empty your nightstool!" Shanghai may have been one of the first cities to have electricity, gas, telephones, and running water, but we lag behind in sewage removal. Nevertheless, farmers around the country pay premium prices for our nightsoil because it's known to be rich from our diets. The nightsoil men will be followed by the morning food vendors with their porridges made from the seeds of Job's tears, apricot kernels, and lotus seeds, their steamed rice cakes made with rugosa rose and white sugar, and their eggs stewed in tea leaves and five spice.

We reach home and pay the rickshaw boy. We lift the latch to the gate and make our way up the path to the front door. The lingering night dampness magnifies the scent of the flowers, shrubs, and trees, making us drunk on the jasmine, magnolia, and dwarf pines our gardener raises. We climb the stone steps and pass under a carved wooden screen that prevents evil spirits from entering the house — in deference to Mama's superstitions. Our heels sound loud as they hit the parquet floor in the entry. A light is on in the salon to the left. Baba is awake and waiting for us.

"Sit down and don't speak," he says, motioning to the settee directly across from him.

I do as I'm told, then fold my hands in my lap and cross my ankles. If we're in trouble, looking demure will help. The anxious look he's been wearing these past few weeks has turned into something hard and immobile. The words he next speaks change my life forever.

"I've arranged marriages for the two of you," he says. "The ceremony will take place the day after tomorrow."

Gold Mountain Men

"That's not funny!" May laughs lightly.

"I'm not joking," Baba says. "I've arranged marriages for you."

I'm still having trouble absorbing what he said. "What's wrong? Is Mama ill?"

"I already told you, Pearl. You need to listen and you're going to do as I say. I'm the father and you're my daughters. This is how things are."

I wish I could convey how absurd he sounds.

"I won't do it!" May cries indignantly.

I try reason. "Those feudal days are over. It's not like when you and Mama married."

"Your mother and I were married in the second year of the Republic," he says huffily, but that's hardly the point.

"Yours was an arranged marriage nevertheless," I counter. "Have you been answering inquiries from a matchmaker about our knitting, sewing, or embroidery skills?" Ridicule creeps into my voice. "For my dowry, have you bought me a nightstool painted with dragon-and-phoenix motifs to symbolize my perfect union? Will you give May a nightstool filled with red eggs to send her in-laws the message that she will have many sons?"

"Say what you want." Baba shrugs indifferently. "You're getting married."

"I won't do it!" May repeats. She's always been good with tears, and she lets them flow now. "You can't make me."

When Baba ignores her, I understand just how serious this is. He looks at me, and it's as though he's seeing me for the first time.

"Don't tell me you thought you were going to marry for love." His voice is oddly cruel and triumphant. "No one marries for love. I didn't."

I hear a deep intake of breath, turn, and see my mother, still dressed in her pajamas, standing in the doorway. We watch as she sways across the room on her bound feet and sinks into a carved pearwood chair. She clasps her hands and looks down. After a moment, tears fall into her folded hands. No one speaks.

I sit up as straight as I can, so I can look down at my father, knowing he'll hate that. Then I take May's hand. We're strong together, and we have our investments.

"I speak for both of us when I respectfully ask for the money you've put away for us."

A grimace passes over my father's face.

"We're old enough now to be on our own," I continue. "May and I will get an apartment. We'll earn our own way. We plan to determine our own futures."

As I speak, May nods and smiles at Baba, but she's not her usual pretty self. Her tears have turned her face splotchy and swollen.

"I don't want you girls to be on your own like that," Mama finds the courage to whisper.

"It's not going to happen anyway," Baba says. "There is no money — not yours, not mine."

Again, stunned silence. My sister and mother leave it to me to ask, "What have you done?"

In his desperation, Baba blames us for his problems. "Your mother goes visiting and plays games with her friends. The two of you spend, spend, spend. None of you see what's happening right under your noses."

He's right. Just last night I'd thought that a kind of shabbiness had settled over our house. I'd wondered about the chandelier, the wall sconces, the fan, and . . .

"Where are our servants? Where are Pansy, Ah Fong, and —"

"I dismissed them. They're all gone, except for the gardener and Cook."

Of course he wouldn't let them go. The garden would die quickly, and our neighbors would know something was wrong. And we need Cook. Mama only knows how to supervise. May and I don't know how to make a single thing. We've never worried about it. We never expected that skill would be necessary. But the houseboy, Baba's valet, the two maids, and Cook's helper? How could Baba hurt so many?

"Did you lose it gambling? Win it back, for God's sake," I spit out. "You always do."

My father may have a public reputation as an important man, but I've always seen him as ineffectual and harmless. The way he looks at me now . . . I see him stripped to his core.

"How bad is it?" I'm angry — how can I not be? — but I feel a creeping sense of pity for my father and, more important, for my mother. What will happen to them? What will happen to all of us?

His head lowers. "The house. The rickshaw business. Your investments. What little savings I had. Everything is gone." After a long while he looks back up at me, his eyes filled with hopelessness, misery, and pleading.

"There are no happy endings," Mama says. It's as if all her dour predictions have finally come to pass. "You can't fight fate."

Baba ignores Mama and appeals to my sense of filial piety and my duty as the elder daughter. "Do you want your mother begging on the street? And what about the two of you? As beautiful girls you're already this close to becoming girls with three holes. The only question that remains is: Will you be kept by one man or fall as low as the whores who ply Blood Alley looking for foreign sailors? Which future do you want?"

I'm educated, but what skills do I have? I teach English to a Japanese captain three mornings a week. May and I sit for artists, but our earnings don't begin to cover the cost of our dresses, hats, gloves, and shoes. I don't want any of us to become beggars. And I certainly don't want May and me to become prostitutes. Whatever happens, I need to protect my sister.

"Who are these grooms?" I ask. "Can we meet them first?"

May's eyes widen.

"It's against tradition," Baba says.

"I won't marry someone unless I meet him first," I insist.

"You can't think I'll do it." May says the words, but her voice tells us that she's given in. We may look and act modern in many ways, but we can't escape what we are: obedient Chinese daughters.

"They're Gold Mountain men," Baba says. "Americans. They've traveled to China to find brides. It's good news, really. Their father's family comes from the same district as ours. We're practically related. You don't have to go back to Los Angeles with your husbands. American Chinese are happy to leave their wives here in China to care for their parents and ancestors, so they can return to their blond *lo fan* mistresses in America. Consider this merely a business deal that will save our family. But if you decide to go with your husbands, you'll have a beautiful house, servants to do the cleaning and washing, amahs to care for your children. You'll live in *Haolaiwu* — Hollywood. I know how you girls love movies. You'd like it, May. You really would. *Haolaiwu!* Just think of it!"

"But we don't *know* them!" May shouts at him.

"But you've met their father," Baba responds evenly. "You know Old Man Louie."

May's lips twist in revulsion. We have indeed met the father. I've never liked Mama's old-fashioned use of titles, but to May and me the wiry, stern-faced foreign

Chinese has always been Old Man Louie. As Baba said, he lives in Los Angeles, but he comes to Shanghai every year or so to look in on the businesses he maintains here. He owns a factory that makes rattan furniture and another for cheap porcelain ware for export. But I don't care how rich he is. I've never liked the way Old Man Louie looks at May and me, like he's a cat licking us up. I don't mind for myself — I can take it — but May was only sixteen the last time he came to town. He shouldn't have drunk her in like that at his age, which had to be mid-sixties at least, but Baba never said a word, just asked May to pour more tea.

And then it hits me. "Did you lose everything to Old Man Louie?"

"Not exactly —"

"Then to whom?"

"These things are always hard to say." Baba taps his fingers on the table and glances away. "I lost a little here, a little there."

"I'm sure you did to have lost May's and my money too. That must have taken you months . . . maybe even years —"

"Pearl —" My mother tries to stop me from saying anything more, but deep rage roars out of me.

"This loss had to be something very big. Something that would threaten all *this*." I motion to the room, the furniture, the house, everything that my father built for us. "What exactly is your debt and how are you paying it back?"

May stops crying. My mother remains silent.

35

"I lost to Old Man Louie," Baba grudgingly admits at last. "He'll let your mother and me stay in the house if May marries the younger son and you marry the older son. We'll have a roof to sleep under and something to eat until I get work. You, our daughters, are our only capital."

May covers her mouth with the back of her hand, stands, and runs from the room.

"Tell your sister I will set up a meeting for this afternoon," Baba acquiesces. "And be grateful I arranged marriages to a pair of brothers. You'll always be together. Now go upstairs. Your mother and I have much to discuss."

Outside the window, the breakfast sellers have moved on and been replaced by a stream of peddlers. Their voices sing to us, enticing us, tempting us.

"*Pu, pu, pu*, reed root to brighten the eyes! Give to baby and he will be free from all summer rashes!"

"*Hou, hou, hou*, let me shave your face, trim your hair, cut your nails!"

"*A-hu-a, a-hu-a*, come out and sell your junk! Foreign bottles and broken glass exchanged for matches!"

A couple of hours later, I walk into the Little Tokyo area of Hongkew for my noon appointment with my student. Why haven't I canceled? The world falls apart and you cancel things, right? But May and I need the money.

In a daze, I ride the elevator to Captain Yamasaki's apartment. He was on the Japanese Olympics team in

1932, so he likes to relive his glories in Los Angeles. He isn't a bad man, but he's obsessed with May. She made the mistake of going out with him a few times, so nearly every lesson begins with questions about her.

"Where is your sister today?" he asks in English, after we review his homework.

"She is sick," I lie. "She is sleeping."

"Sorry to hear such sad news. Every day I ask you when she will go out with me again. Every day you say you don't know."

"Correction. We see each other only three times a week."

"Please help me marry May. I give you wedding . . ."

He hands me a piece of paper, which lists his marriage terms. I can see he used his Japanese-English dictionary, but this is too much. And today of all days. I glance at the clock. We still have fifty minutes to go. I fold the paper and put it in my purse.

"I will make the corrections and return this to you at our next lesson."

"Give to May!"

"I'll give *it* to her, but please know she is too young to marry. My father will not allow it." How easily the lies pour from my mouth.

"He should. He must. This is a time of Friendship, Cooperation, and Co-prosperity. The Asian races should unify against the West. Chinese and Japanese are brothers."

Hardly. We call Japanese dwarf bandits and monkey people. But the captain often returns to this theme, and he's done a good job of mastering the slogans in English and Chinese.

He stares at me sullenly. "You're not going to give it to her, are you?" When I don't respond quickly enough, he frowns. "I don't trust Chinese girls. They always lie."

He's said this to me before, and I don't like it any more today than I have in the past.

"I don't lie to you," I say, even though I have several times just since we started this tutorial.

"Chinese girls never keep promise. They lie in heart."

"Promises. Their hearts," I correct. I need to turn the conversation to a new subject. Today it comes easily. "Did you like Los Angeles?"

"It was very good. Soon I will go back to America."

"For another swimming competition?"

"No."

"As a student?"

"As a . . ." He switches back to Chinese and a word he knows very well in our language. "A conqueror."

"Really? How?"

"We will march to Washington," he responds, returning to English. "Yankee girls will do our laundry."

He laughs. I laugh. And on it goes.

As soon as the hour's up, I take my meager payment and go home. May's asleep. I lie down beside her, put a hand on her hip, and close my eyes. I long for sleep, but my mind batters me with images and emotions. I thought I was modern. I thought I had choice. I thought I was nothing like my mother. But my father's gambling has swept all that away. I'm to be sold — traded like so many girls before me — to help my family. I feel so trapped and so helpless that I can hardly breathe.

I try to tell myself things aren't as bad as they seem. My father even said May and I won't have to go with these strangers to a city across the world. We can sign the papers, our "husbands" will leave, and life will go on as before, with one big difference. We have to get out of my father's house and make our own living. I'll wait until my husband leaves the country, claim desertion, and get a divorce. Then Z.G. and I will get married. (It will have to be a smaller wedding than I imagined — maybe just a party in a café with our artist friends and some of the other beautiful-girl models.) I'll get a real job during the day. May will live with us until she marries. We'll take care of each other. We'll make our way.

I sit up and rub my temples. I'm stupid with dreams. Maybe I've lived in Shanghai too long.

I gently shake my sister's shoulder. "Wake up, May."

She opens her eyes, and for a moment I see all the gentle and trusting loveliness she's held inside her since she was an infant. Then her eyes turn dark as she remembers.

"We've got to get dressed," I say. "It's almost time to meet the husbands."

What should we wear? The Louie sons are Chinese, so maybe we should wear traditional *cheongsams*. They're also Americans, so maybe it would be better to wear something that shows we're Westernized too. It isn't to *please* them, but we can't ruin the deal either. We slip on rayon dresses with floral patterns. May and I exchange glances, shrug at the uselessness of it all, and leave the house.

We flag down a rickshaw boy and tell him to take us to the place my father has arranged for the rendezvous: the gate to the Yu Yuan Garden in the center of the Old Chinese City. The driver — who has a bald head scarred by ringworm — pulls us through the heat and crowds across Soo-chow Creek at the Garden Bridge and along the Bund, passing diplomats, schoolgirls in starched uniforms, prostitutes, lords and their ladies, and black-coated members of the notorious Green Gang. Yesterday this mingling seemed exciting. Today it looks sordid and oppressive.

The Whangpoo River slinks past us to our left like an indolent snake, its grimy skin rising, pulsing, slithering. In Shanghai, you can't escape the river. It's the dead end for every eastbound street in the city. On this great river float warships from Great Britain, France, Japan, Italy, and the United States. Sampans — hung with ropes, laundry, and nets — cluster together like insects on a carcass. Nightsoil boats jostle for right-of-way through ocean-liner tenders and bamboo rafts. Sweating coolies stripped to the waist clutter the wharves, unloading opium and tobacco from merchant ships, rice and grain from junks that have come from upriver, and soy sauce, baskets of chickens, and great rolls of rattan matting from flat-bottomed riverboats.

To our right rise grand five- and six-story edifices — foreign palaces of wealth, greed, and avarice. We wheel past the Cathay Hotel with its pyramid-shaped roof, the Custom House with its great clock tower, and the

Hong Kong and Shanghai Bank with its majestic bronze lions, who beckon passersby to rub their paws to bring good luck to men and sons to women. At the border of the French Concession, we pay the rickshaw puller and then continue on foot along what becomes the Quai de France. After a few blocks, we turn away from the river and enter the Old Chinese City.

Coming here is ugly and hardly auspicious, like stepping into the past, which is precisely what Baba wants us to do with these marriages. Still, May and I have come, obedient as dogs, stupid as water buffalo. I cover my nose with a lavender-scented handkerchief to help block the smells of death, sewage, rancid cooking oil, and raw meat for sale spoiling in the heat.

Ordinarily I ignore my home city's ugly sights, but today my eyes are drawn to them. Here are beggars with eyes gouged out and limbs burned into stumps by their parents to make them all the more pitiable. Some have putrefying sores and horrendous growths blown up to disgusting size with bicycle pumps. We make our way through alleys strung with drying bound-foot bandages, diapers, and tattered trousers. In the Old Chinese City, the women who wash these items are too lazy to wring them out. Water drips down on us like rain. Every step reminds us where we might end up if we don't go through with these marriages.

We find the Louie sons at the gate to the Yu Yuan Garden. We try English, but they don't seem interested in responding to us in that language. Their father is from the Four Districts of Canton, so naturally they speak the Sze Yup dialect, which May doesn't know, but

I translate for her. Like so many of us, they've taken Western names. The older one points to himself and says, "Sam." Then he gestures to his younger brother and declares in Sze Yup, "His name is Vernon, but the parents call him Vern."

I love Z.G., so no matter how perfect this Sam Louie is, I'm not going to like him. And May's groom, this Vern, is only fourteen years old. He hasn't even begun to grow into manhood. He's still a little boy. Baba neglected to mention that.

We all look from face to face. None of us seems to like what we see. Eyes dart to the ground, to the sky, anywhere. It occurs to me that maybe they don't want to marry us either. If that's the case, we can *all* consider this a commercial transaction. We'll sign the papers and go back to our regular lives, with no broken hearts or hurt feelings. But that doesn't mean it isn't awkward.

"Maybe we should walk," I suggest.

No one responds, but when I start to walk, the others follow, our shoes scuffing along the labyrinthine pathways past pools, rockeries, and grottoes. Willows sway in the hot air, giving the illusion of coolness. Pavilions of carved wood and gold lacquer evoke the deep past. Everything is designed to create a feeling of balance and unity, but the garden has broiled under the July sun all morning, and the afternoon air hangs heavy and viscous with fecundity.

The boy, Vern, runs to one of the rockeries and scampers up the craggy wall. May looks at me, silently asking *Now what?* I don't have an answer and Sam doesn't volunteer one. She spins away, steps down the slope to the foot of the rockery, and begins calling softly to the boy to coax him back down. I don't think he understands what she's saying, because he stays on top, looking a bit like a pirate at sea. Sam and I continue walking until we come to the Exquisite Jade Rock.

"I've been here before," he murmurs tentatively in Sze Yup. "Do you know the story of how the rock came to be here?"

I don't tell him that I usually avoid the Old Chinese City. Instead, trying to be polite, I say, "Let's sit down and you can tell it to me."

We find a bench and stare at the rock, which seems like any other rock to me.

"During the Northern Sung dynasty, Emperor Hui Tsung had a great thirst for curiosities. He sent envoys across the southern provinces to find the best examples in the land. They found this rock and loaded it on a ship. But the rock never made it to the palace. A storm — perhaps a typhoon, perhaps angry river gods — sank the ship on the Whangpoo."

Sam's voice is quite pleasant — not too loud, bossy, or superior. As he speaks, I stare at his feet. He stretches his legs out in front of him with his weight resting on the heels of his new leather shoes. I get my nerve up to look from those feet to his face. He's attractive enough. I'll go so far as to say he's handsome. He's quite thin. His face is long like a rice seed, which seems to exaggerate the sharpness of his cheekbones. His skin tone is darker than I like, but that's understandable. He comes from Hollywood. I've read that movie stars like to bathe in the sunshine until their skin turns brown. His hair isn't pure black. Touches of red catch the sunlight. Here it's said that this color variation comes to those too poor to have a proper diet. Perhaps in America the food is so plentiful and rich that it also causes this change. He's smartly dressed. Even I recognize that his suit has been recently tailored. And he's a partner in his father's business. If I weren't already in love with Z.G., then Sam would seem like a good prospect.

"The Pan family pulled the rock from the river and brought it here," Sam continues. "You can see that it satisfies all the requirements for a good rock. It looks porous like a sponge, it has a handsome shape, and it makes you think of its thousands of years of history."

He falls silent again. In the distance, May circles the rockery, hands on her hips, her annoyance radiating across the garden. She calls up one last time, then looks around to find me. She raises her hands in defeat and begins walking toward us.

Next to me, Sam says, "I like you. Do you like me?"

Nodding seems the best response.

"Good. I will tell my father that we will be happy together."

As soon as we wave good-bye to Sam and Vern, I find a rickshaw. May climbs in, but I don't follow her.

"You go on home," I tell her. "I have something I need to do. I'll catch up to you later."

"But I need to talk to you." Her hands grip the rickshaw's armrests so hard that her knuckles have gone white. "That boy didn't say a word to me."

"You don't speak Sze Yup."

"It's not just that. He's like a little boy. He *is* a little boy."

"It doesn't matter, May."

"You can say that. You got the handsome one."

I try to explain that this is just a business deal, but she won't listen. She stamps her foot, and the puller struggles to keep the rickshaw steady.

"I don't want to marry him! If we have to do it, let me have Sam."

I sigh impatiently. These flashes of jealousy and stubbornness are so like May, but they're as harmless as rain on a summer afternoon. My parents and I know the best way to handle them is to indulge her until they blow away.

"We'll talk about it later. I'll see you at home." I nod to the puller, who gives the rickshaw a heave and trots on his bare feet down the cobblestone road. I wait until they turn the corner and then walk to the Old West Gate, where I find another rickshaw. I give him Z.G.'s address in the French Concession.

When we arrive at Z.G.'s building, I run up the stairs and pound on the door. He answers it wearing a sleeveless undershirt and loose khakis held up with a tie wrapped through the belt loops. A cigarette dangles from his lips. I fall into his arms. All the tears and frustration I've held inside pour out. I tell him everything: that my family's broke, that May and I are to be married to foreign Chinese, and that I love him.

On the ride here, I thought of the different ways he might react. I considered that he might say something along the lines of "I don't believe in marriage, but I love you and want you to live here with me." I thought he might be valiant: "We'll get married. Everything will be fine." I thought he would ask about May and invite her to live with us. "I love her as a sister," he would say. I even considered that he might get angry, rush out to find Baba, and give him the beating he deserves. In the end, Z.G. says the one thing I didn't expect.

"You should marry the man. He sounds like a good match, and you have a duty to your father. When a girl, obey your father; when a wife, obey your husband; when a widow, obey your son. We all know this is true."

"I don't believe in any of that! And I didn't think you did either. That kind of thinking is for my mother, not for you!" I'm hurt, but more than anything I'm angry. "How could you say that to me?" I demand. "We love each other. You don't say things like that to the woman you love."

He doesn't speak, but his expression manages to convey weariness and irritation that he has to deal with someone so childish.

Because I'm bruised, indignant, and too young to know any better, I flee. I make a great show of stomping down the stairs, crying, and making myself look foolish in front of Z.G.'s landlady by acting as spoiled as my sister. It doesn't make sense, but many women — and men too — have acted just as rashly. I think . . . I don't know what I think . . . That he'll rush down the stairs after me. That he'll sweep me into his arms like in the movies. That he'll whisk me away from my parents' home tonight and we'll elope. Even if worse comes to worst, I'll marry Sam and then have a lifelong affair with the person I love, as so many women in Shanghai do these days. That isn't such an unhappy ending, is it?

When I tell my sister what happened with Z.G., her face pales in compassion.

"I didn't know you felt that way about him." Her voice is so soft and comforting, I barely hear her.

She holds me as I weep. Even after I stop crying, I feel sympathetic trembling coming from deep within her. We couldn't be closer. Whatever happens, we'll survive together.

I've dreamed of my wedding to Z.G. for so long, but what I get with Sam is nothing like what I imagined. No Chantilly lace, no veil eight yards long, no fragrant cascades of flowers for the Western ceremony. For the Chinese banquet, May and I don't change into red embroidered gowns and phoenix headdresses that quiver when we walk. There's no big gathering of the families, no gossiping or jokes traded, no small children running, laughing, and hollering. At two in the afternoon, we go to the courthouse and meet Sam, Vern, and their father. Old Man Louie is just as I remembered him: wiry and stern-faced. He clasps his hands behind his back and watches the two couples sign the papers: married, July 24, 1937. At four, we go to the American Consulate and fill out forms for nonquota immigration visas. May and I check boxes verifying that we've never been in prison, an almshouse, or a hospital for the insane, that we're not alcoholics,

47

anarchists, professional beggars, prostitutes, idiots, imbeciles, feebleminded, epileptic, tubercular, illiterate, or suffering from psychopathic inferiority (whatever that is). As soon as we sign our forms, Old Man Louie folds them and tucks them into his jacket. At six, we meet our parents at a nondescript hotel that caters to Chinese and foreigners down on their luck, and then we have dinner in the main dining room: four newlyweds, my parents, and Old Man Louie. Baba tries to keep the conversation going, but what can anyone say? The orchestra plays, but none of us dance. Dishes come and go, but even the rice seems to choke me. Baba tells May and me to pour tea, as is the custom for brides, but Old Man Louie waves away the offer.

Finally, it's time for us to retire to our respective bridal chambers. My father whispers in my ear, "You know what you need to do. Once it's done, all this will be over."

Sam and I go to our room. He seems more tense than I am. He sits on the edge of the bed, hunched over, staring at his hands. If I've spent hours imagining my wedding to Z.G., then I've also spent hours envisioning our wedding night and how romantic it would be. Now my mother comes into my mind, and I realize at last why she always speaks so poorly of the husband-wife thing. "You just do it and then you forget about it," she's often said.

I don't wait for Sam to come to me, hold me in his arms, or soften me with kisses on my neck. I stand in the middle of the room, unbutton the frog at my neck, move my fingers to the one above my breast, and then undo the top one under my armpit. Sam looks up and watches as I open all thirty frogs that go from my armpit down my right side. I let my dress slip off my shoulders. I sway unsteadily, chilled even on this hot night. My courage has brought me this far, but I'm unsure what to do next. Sam stands, and I bite my lip.

It's all very awkward. Sam seems nervous about touching me, but we both do what's expected of us. One burst of pain and it's over. Sam stays on his elbows above me for a moment and looks into my face. I don't meet his gaze. Instead, I stare at the braided sash that holds back the curtain. I was so intent on getting this over with that I didn't close the curtains. Does that make me brazen or desperate?

Sam rolls off me and turns onto his side. I don't move. I don't want to talk, but I can't fall asleep either. Maybe this one night and this one time won't matter out of a lifetime of nights with my real husband, whoever he might be. But what about May?

I get up while it's still dark, take a bath, and dress. Then I sit in a chair by the window and watch Sam sleep. He wakes with a start just before dawn. He looks around, seemingly unsure of where he is. He sees me and blinks. His features are open, raw somehow. I can guess what he's feeling: supreme embarrassment at being in this room and something like panic that he's naked, that I'm sitting a few feet from him, and that he somehow has to get out of the bed and get dressed. As I did the night before, I look away. He slides to what had been my side of the bed, slips out from between the sheets, and pads quickly into the bathroom. The door shuts, and I hear the tap begin to flow.

When we get to the dining room, Vern and May are already seated with Old Man Louie. May's skin has taken on the color of alabaster — white with a green tint hidden beneath the surface. The boy scrunches the tablecloth with his fists. He doesn't look up when Sam and I sit down, and I realize I have yet to hear Vernon speak.

"I've ordered already," Old Man Louie says. He turns his attention to the waiter. "Make sure everything arrives at the same time."

We sip our tea. No one comments on the view or the hotel's decor or what sights these Chinese from America might take in today.

Old Man Louie snaps his fingers. The waiter returns to our table. My father-in-law — the title alone is strange to consider — motions the waiter to lean down and then whispers in his ear. The waiter straightens, purses his lips, and leaves the room. He returns a few minutes later with two maids, each carrying bundled cloth.

Old Man Louie signals one of the girls to approach and takes the bundle from her. As he pulls the fabric through his hands, I realize with absolute horror that he has the bottom sheet from either May's or my bed. The diners around us take this in with varying degrees of interest. Most of the foreigners don't seem to understand what's happening, although one couple does, and they look appalled. But the Chinese in the room — from the customers to the hotel staff — seem amused and curious.

Old Man Louie's hands stop when he comes to a bloody splotch.

"What room did this come from?" he asks the maid.

"Room three hundred seven," the girl answers.

Old Man Louie looks from one son to the other. "Who had that room?"

"It was mine," Sam answers.

The sheet falls from his father's hands. He motions for May's sheet, and he once again begins his nasty pawing. May's lips part. She breathes softly through her mouth. The sheet keeps moving. People around us stare. Under the table, I feel a hand on my knee. It's Sam's. When Old Man Louie comes to the end of the sheet without finding a bloodstain, May leans over and throws up all over the table.

That ends breakfast. A car is ordered, and within minutes May, Old Man Louie, and I are on our way back to our parents' home. Once we arrive, there's no small talk, tea served, or words of congratulation, only recriminations. I keep my arm around May's waist when Old Man Louie begins speaking to my father.

"We had an arrangement." The tone is harsh and doesn't allow room for discussion. "One of your daughters failed you." He holds up a hand to prevent my father from offering an excuse. "I will forgive this. The girl is young and my boy . . ."

I'm relieved — beyond relieved — that Old Man Louie has made the assumption that my sister and Vern didn't do what they were supposed to do last night,

51

instead of that they did it and she wasn't a virgin. The result of that second possibility is almost too gruesome to contemplate: an examination by a doctor. If things were found intact, then we wouldn't be any worse off than we are now. If they weren't, there'd be a forced confession from my sister, the dissolution of her marriage on grounds that May had already done the husband-wife thing with someone else, my father's money problems returned to us and perhaps multiplied, our futures once again unstable, not to mention that May's reputation would be forever marred — even in these modern times — and the chances of her marrying into a good family — like that of Tommy Hu — destroyed.

"Never mind all that," the old man says to my father, but it feels as if he's responding to my thoughts. "What matters is that they are married. As you know, my sons and I have business in Hong Kong. We are leaving tomorrow, but I'm concerned. What guarantee do I have that your daughters will meet us? Our ship sails to San Francisco on August tenth. That's only seventeen days from now."

My insides feel like they've fallen through the floor. Baba lied to us again! May breaks away from me and runs up the stairs, but I don't follow her. I stare at my father, hoping he'll say something. But he doesn't. He wrings his hands, acting as subservient as a rickshaw puller.

"I'm taking their clothes," Old Man Louie announces.

He doesn't wait for Baba to argue or for me to object. When he starts up the stairs, my father and I follow. Old Man Louie opens each door until he finds the room with May crying on her bed. When she sees us, she runs into the bathroom and slams the door. We hear her vomit again. The old man opens the closet, grabs an armload of dresses, and tosses them on the bed.

"You can't take those," I say. "We need them for modeling."

The old man corrects me: "You'll need them in your new home. Husbands like to see pretty wives."

He's cold but unsystematic, ruthless but unknowledgeable. He either ignores our Western dresses or throws them on the floor, probably because he doesn't know what's fashionable in Shanghai this year. He doesn't take the ermine wrap, because it's white, the color of death, but he pulls out a fox stole that May and I bought used several years ago.

"Try these on," he orders, handing me a stack of hats he's pulled from the closet's upper shelf. I do as I'm told. "That's enough. You can keep the green one and that thing with the feathers. The rest are coming with me." He glares at my father. "I'll send people later to pack these things. I suggest that neither you nor your daughters touch anything. Do you understand?"

My father nods. The old man turns to me. Wordlessly, he appraises me from my face to my shoes and then back again.

"Your sister is ill. Be good and help her," he says, and then he leaves.

I knock on the bathroom door and call softly. May opens the door a crack, and I let myself in. She lies on the floor, her cheek against the tile. I sit beside her.

"Are you all right?"

"I think it was the crab from dinner last night," she answers. "It's the wrong season and I shouldn't have eaten it."

I lean against the wall and rub my eyes. How is it that two beautiful girls have fallen so low so quickly? I let my hands drop and stare at the repeating pattern of yellow, black, and turquoise tile that climbs the wall.

Later that day, coolies come to pack our clothes in wooden crates. These are loaded onto the back of a flatbed truck as our neighbors watch. In the midst of this, Sam arrives. Instead of approaching my father, he walks directly to me.

"You are to take the boat to meet us in Hong Kong on August seventh," he says. "My father has booked passage for us to sail together to San Francisco three days later. These are your immigration papers. He says everything is in order and that we'll have no problems landing, but he also wants you to study what's in this coaching book — just in case." What he hands me isn't a book but a few pieces of folded paper held together by hand stitching. "These are the answers you'll need to give the inspectors if we have any trouble getting off the ship." He pauses and frowns. He probably has the same thought as I: Why do we need to read the coaching book if everything's in order? "Don't worry about anything," he goes on confidently, as though I need my husband's reassurance and will be comforted by his tone. "As soon as we're through immigration, we'll take another boat to Los Angeles."

I stare at the papers.

"I'm sorry about this," he adds, and I almost believe him. "I'm sorry about everything."

As he turns to leave, my father — suddenly remembering to be the gracious host — asks, "May I find you a rickshaw?"

Sam looks back at me and answers, "No, no, I think I'll walk."

I watch him until he turns the corner, and then I go inside the house and toss the papers he gave me in the trash. Old Man Louie, his sons, and my father have made a terrible mistake if they think this is going any further. Soon the Louies will be on a ship that will take them thousands of miles from here. They won't be able to push or trick us into doing anything we don't want to do. We've all paid a price for my father's gambling. He's lost his business. I've lost my virginity. May and I have lost our clothes and perhaps our livelihoods as a result. We've been hurt, but we're not remotely poor or wretched by Shanghai standards.

A Cicada in a Tree

Now that this whole upsetting and exhausting episode is over, May and I retreat to our room, which faces east. This usually leaves the room a little cooler in summer, but it's so hot and sticky that we wear practically nothing — just thin pink silk slips. We don't cry. We don't clean up the clothes Old Man Louie threw on the floor or the mess he left of our closet. We eat the food Cook leaves on a tray outside our door, but other than that we do nothing. We're both too shaken to voice what happened. If the words come out of our mouths, won't that mean that we'll have to face how our lives have changed and figure out what to do next when at least for me my mind is in such a turmoil of confusion, despair, and anger that I feel like gray fog has invaded my skull? We lie on our beds and try to . . . I don't even know the word. Recover?

As sisters, May and I share a particular kind of intimacy. May is the one person who'll stand by me no matter what. I never wonder if we're good friends or not. We just are. During this time of adversity — as it is for all sisters — our petty jealousies and the question of which one of us is loved more dissolve. We have to rely on each other.

Once I ask May what happened with Vernon, and she says, "I couldn't do it." Then she begins to weep. After that, I don't ask about her wedding night and she doesn't ask about mine. I tell myself that it doesn't matter, that we've just done something to save our family. But no matter how many times I tell myself it wasn't important, there's no getting around the fact that I lost a precious moment. In truth, my heart is more broken by what happened with Z.G. than by my family losing its standing or by having had to do the husband-wife thing with a stranger. I want to bring back my innocence, my girlishness, my happiness, my laughter.

"Remember when we saw *The Ode to Constancy?*" I ask, hoping the memory will remind May of when we were still young enough to believe we were invincible.

"We thought we could put on a better opera," she answers from her bed.

"Since you were younger and smaller, you got to play the beautiful girl. You *always* played the princess. I always had to be the scholar, prince, emperor, and bandit."

"Yes, but look at it this way: You got to play *four* roles. I only got one."

I smile. How many times have we had this same disagreement about the productions we used to stage for Mama and Baba in the main salon when we were

57

young? Our parents clapped and laughed. They ate watermelon seeds and drank tea. They praised us but never offered to send us to opera school or to the acrobatic academy, because we were pretty terrible, with our squeaky voices, our heavy tumbling, and our improvised sets and costumes. What mattered was that May and I had spent hours plotting and staging in our room or running to Mama to borrow a scarf to use as a veil or begging Cook to make a sword from paper and starch for me to fight whatever ghost demons were causing trouble.

I remember winter nights when it was so cold that May crawled into my bed and we snuggled together to keep warm. I remember how she slept: her thumb resting on her jaw, the tips of her forefinger and middle finger balanced on the edges of her eyebrows just above her nose, her ring finger lightly placed on an eyelid, and her pinkie delicately floating in the air. I remember that in the morning she'd be cuddled against my back with her arm wrapped around me to hold me close. I remember exactly how her hand looked — so small, so pale, so soft, and her fingers as slender as scallions.

I remember the first summer I went to camp in Kuling. Mama and Baba had to bring May to see me, because she was so lonely. I was maybe ten and May only seven. No one had told me they were coming, but when they arrived and May saw me, she ran to me, stopping just in front of me to stare at me. The other girls teased me. Why did I need to bother with this little baby? I knew enough not to tell them the truth: I longed for my sister too and felt like a part of me was missing when we were separated. After that, Baba always sent the two of us to camp together.

May and I laugh about these things, and they make us feel better. They remind us of the strength we find in each other, of the ways we help each other, of the times that it was just us against everyone else, of the fun we've had together. If we can laugh, won't everything be all right?

"Remember when we were little and we tried on Mama's shoes?" May asks.

I'll never forget that day. Mama had gone visiting. We'd sneaked into her room and pulled out several pairs of her bound-foot shoes. My feet were too big for the shoes, and I'd carelessly discarded them as I tried to squeeze my toes into pair after pair. May could get her toes in the slippers, and she'd tiptoed to the window and back, imitating Mama's lily walk. We'd tittered and frolicked, and then Mama came home. She was furious. May and I knew we'd been bad, but we had a hard time suppressing our giggles as Mama tottered around the room, trying to catch us to pull our ears. With our natural feet and our unity, we escaped, running down the hall and out into the garden, where we collapsed in laughter. Our wickedness had turned into triumph.

We could always trick Mama and outrun her, but Cook and the other servants had little patience for our mischief, and they didn't hesitate to punish us.

"Pearl, remember when Cook taught us to make *chiao-tzu*?" May sits cross-legged on her bed across from me, her chin resting on her bunched fists, her

59

elbows balanced on her knees. "He thought we should know how to make something. He said, "How are you girls going to get married if you don't know how to make dumplings for your husbands?" He didn't know how hopeless we'd be."

"He gave us aprons to wear, but they didn't help."

"They did when you started throwing flour at me!" May says.

What began as a lesson turned into a game and then finally into an all-out flour battle, with both of us getting really mad. Cook, who has lived with us since we moved to Shanghai, knew the difference between two sisters working together, two sisters playing, and two sisters fighting, and he didn't like what he saw.

"Cook was so angry that he didn't let us back in the kitchen for months," May continues.

"I kept telling him I was just trying to powder your face."

"No treats. No snacks. No special dishes." May laughs at the memory. "Cook could be so stern. He said sisters who fight are not worth knowing."

Mama and Baba knock on our door and ask us to come out, but we decline, saying we prefer to stay in our room awhile longer. Maybe it's rude and childish, but May and I always deal with conflicts in the family this way — by holing up, and building a barricade between us and whatever has harmed us or we don't like. We're stronger together, united, a force that can't be argued with or reasoned with, until others give in to our desires. But this calamity isn't like wanting to visit your sister at camp or protecting each other from an angry parent, servant, or teacher.

May gets off her bed and brings back magazines, so we can look at the clothes and read the gossip. We comb each other's hair. We look through our closet and drawers and try to assess how many new outfits we can make from what we have left. Old Man Louie seems to have taken almost all our Chinese clothes, leaving behind an assortment of Western-style dresses, blouses, skirts, and trousers. In Shanghai, where appearances are nearly everything, it will be important for us to look smart and not dowdy, fashionable and not last year. If our clothes seem old, not only will artists no longer hire us but streetcars won't stop for us, doormen at hotels and clubs might not let us in, and attendants at movie theaters will double-check our tickets. This affects not only women but men too; they, even if they're in the middle class, will sleep in lodgings plagued by bedbugs so they can afford to buy a nicer pair of trousers, which they put under their pillows each night to create sharp creases for the new day.

Does it sound like we lock ourselves away for weeks? Hardly. Just two days. Because we're young, we're easily cured. We're also curious. We've heard noises outside the door, which we've ignored for hours at a time. We tried not to pay attention to the hammering and thumping that shook the house. We heard strange voices but pretended they belonged to the servants. When we finally open the door, our home has changed. Baba has sold most of our furniture to the local pawnshop. The gardener is gone, but Cook has stayed because he has nowhere else to go and he needs a place to sleep and food to eat. Our house has been chopped apart and walls added to make rooms for boarders: a policeman, his wife, and two daughters have moved into the back of the house; a student lives in the second-floor pavilion; a cobbler has taken the space under the stairs; and two dancing girls have moved into the attic. The rents will help, but they won't be enough to care for us all.

We thought our lives would go back to normal, and in many ways they do. Mama still orders around everyone, including our boarders, so we aren't suddenly burdened with carrying out the nightstool, making beds, or sweeping. Still, we're very aware of how far and how quickly we've fallen. Instead of soy milk, sesame cakes, and fried dough sticks for breakfast, Cook makes *p'ao fan* — leftover rice swimming in boiled water with some pickled vegetables on top for flavor. Cook's austerity campaign shows in our lunch and dinner dishes too. We've always been one of those families who have *wu hun pu ch'ih fan* — no meal without meat. We now eat a coolie's diet of bean sprouts, salt fish, cabbage, and preserved vegetables accompanied by lots and lots of rice.

Baba leaves the house every morning to look for work, but we don't encourage him or ask him questions when he returns at night. In failing us, he's become insignificant. If we ignore him — demeaning him by our inattention and lack of concern — then his downfall and ruin can't harm us anymore. It's our way of dealing with our anger and hurt.

May and I try to find jobs too, but it's hard to get hired. You need to have *kuang hsi*, connections. You have to know the right people — a relative or someone you've courted for years — to get a recommendation. More important, you need to give a substantial gift — a leg of pork, a bedroom set, or the equivalent of two months' salary — to the person who will make the introduction and another to the person who will hire you, even if it's only to make matchboxes or hairnets in a factory. We don't have money for that now, and people know it. In Shanghai, life flows like an endlessly serene river for the wealthy, the lucky, the fortunate. For those with bad fates, the smell of desperation is as strong as a rotting corpse.

Our writer friends take us to Russian restaurants and treat us to bowls of borscht and cheap vodka. Playboys — our countrymen who come from wealthy families, study in America, and go to Paris on vacation — take us to the Paramount, the city's biggest nightclub, for joy, gin, and jazz. We hang out in dark cafés with Betsy and her American friends. The boys are handsome and adamant, and we soak them up. May disappears for hours at a time. I don't ask where she goes or with whom. It's better that way.

We can't escape the sense that we're slipping, dropping, falling.

May never stops sitting for Z.G., but I'm uncomfortable going back to his studio after having made such a scene. They finish the advertisement for

My Dear cigarettes, with May doing double duty, modeling for Z.G. in her original spot and then taking my position on the back of the chair. She tells me this and encourages me to help with another calendar Z.G.'s been commissioned to do. I sit for other artists instead, but most of them just want to shoot a quick photo and work from that. I make money, but not much. Now, instead of getting new students, I lose my only student. When I tell Captain Yamasaki that May won't accept his marriage proposal, he fires me. But that's only an excuse. Across the city, the Japanese are acting strangely. Those who live in Little Tokyo pack up and leave their apartments. Wives, children, and other civilians return to Japan. When many of our neighbors desert Hongkew, cross Soochow Creek, and take temporary quarters in the main part of the International Settlement, I attribute it to the usual superstitious nature of my countrymen, especially the poor, who fear the known and the unknown, the worldly and the unworldly, the living and the dead.

To me, it feels as if everything has changed. The city I always loved pays no attention to death, despair, disaster, or poverty. Where once I saw neon and glamour, I now see gray: gray slate, gray stone, the gray river. Where once the Whangpoo appeared almost festive with its warships from many nations, each flying colorful flags, now the river seems choked by the arrival of over a dozen imposing Japanese naval vessels. Where once I saw wide avenues and shimmering moonlight, I now see piles of garbage, rodents boldly scurrying and scavenging, and Pock-marked Huang and his Green

Gang thugs roughing up debtors and prostitutes. Shanghai, as grand as it is, is built on shifting silt. Nothing stays where it's supposed to. Coffins buried without lead weights drift. Banks hire men to check their foundations daily to make sure that the tonnage of silver and gold hasn't caused the building to tilt. May and I have slid from safe, cosmopolitan Shanghai to a place that's as sure as quicksand.

May's and my earnings are our own now, but it's hard to save. After giving Cook money to buy food, we're left with practically nothing. I can't sleep for all the worry I feel. If things continue this way, soon we'll be subsisting on bone soup. If I'm to save anything, I'll have to go back to Z.G.'s.

"I'm over him," I tell May. "I don't know what I ever saw in him. He's too thin, and I don't like his glasses. I don't think I'll ever marry for real. That's so bourgeois. Everyone says so."

I don't mean a word I say, but May, who I think knows me so well, responds, "I'm glad you're feeling better. I really am. True love will find you. I know it will."

But true love *has* found me. Inside I continue to suffer with thoughts of Z.G., but I hide my feelings. May and I get dressed, then pay a few coppers to ride in a passenger wheelbarrow to Z.G.'s apartment. On the way, as the wheelbarrow pusher picks up and drops off others, I agonize that seeing Z.G. in his rooms, where I held such girlish dreams, will leave me shredded with embarrassment. But once we arrive, he acts as if nothing's happened.

"Pearl, I'm almost finished with a new kite. It's a flock of orioles. Come take a look."

I go to his side, feeling awkward to be standing so close to him. He chats on about the kite, which is exquisite. The eyes of each oriole have been fashioned so that they'll spin in the wind. On each segment of the body Z.G. has attached articulated wings that will flap in the breeze. On the tips are little feathers that will quiver in the air.

"It's beautiful," I say.

"The three of us are going to fly it once it's done," Z.G. announces.

It isn't an invitation, just a statement of fact. I think, if it doesn't bother him that I made a fool of myself, then I can't let it bother me either. I have to be tough to bear my deeper feelings, which threaten to overwhelm me.

"I'd love to do that," I say. "May and I both would."

They smile at each other, clearly relieved. "Great," Z.G. says, rubbing his hands together. "Now let's get to work."

May steps behind a screen and changes into red shorts and a cropped yellow top that ties behind her neck. Z.G. puts a scarf over her hair and ties it beneath her chin. I slip into a red bathing suit decorated with butterflies. It has a little skirt and a belt cinched at the waist. Z.G. pins a red and white bow in my hair. May gets onto a bicycle, one foot on a pedal, the other balancing on the floor. I place one hand over hers on the handlebar. My other hand steadies the bike on the back of May's seat. She glances over her shoulder at me, and I stare at her. When Z.G. says, "That's perfect. Hold it," not once am I tempted to look at him. I stay focused on May, smile, and pretend that I couldn't be happier than to push my sister's bike along a grassy hill overlooking the ocean to promote Earth fly and mosquito spray.

Z.G. recognizes that holding this particular pose is difficult, so after a while he lets us have a break. He works on the background for a time, painting a sailboat on the waves, and then he asks, "May, shall we show Pearl what we've been working on?"

While May goes behind the screen to change, Z.G. puts away the bike, rolls up the backdrop, and then pulls a low chaise to the middle of the room. May returns, wearing a light robe, which she drops when she gets to the chaise. I don't know what's more startling — that she's naked or that she seems utterly at ease. She lies on her side, her elbow bent and her head resting on her hand. Z.G. drapes a piece of diaphanous silk over her hips and so lightly across her breasts that I can see her nipples. He disappears for a minute and returns with some pink peonies. He snips the stems and carefully places the blossoms around May. He then unveils the painting, which has been hidden under a cloth on an easel.

It's almost finished, and it's exquisite. The soft texture of the peony petals echoes that of May's flesh. He's used the rub-and-paint technique, working carbon powder over May's image and then applying watercolors to create a rosy complexion on her cheeks, arms, and thighs. In the painting, she looks as though she's just

67

stepped from a warm bath. Our new diet of more rice and less meat and her paleness from the events of the past days give her an air of languorous lassitude. Z.G. has already dotted the eyes with dark lacquer so they seem to follow the viewer, beckoning, luring, and responding. What's May selling? Watson's lotion for prickly heat, Jazz hair pomade, Two Baby cigarettes? I don't know, but looking from my sister to the painting, I see that Z.G. has achieved the effect of *hua chin i tsai* — a finished painting with lingering emotions — that only the great masters of the past realized in their work.

But I'm shocked, deeply shocked. I may have done the husband-wife thing with Sam, but this seems far more intimate. Yet again, it shows just how far May and I have fallen. I suppose this is just an inevitable part of our journey. When we first sat for artists, we were encouraged to cross our legs and hold sprays of flowers in our laps. This pose was a wordless reminder of courtesans from feudal times whose bouquets had been between their legs. Later we were asked to clasp our hands behind our heads and expose our armpits, a pose used since the beginning of photography to capture the allure and sensuous availability of Shanghai's Famous Flowers. One artist painted us chasing butterflies in the shade of willow trees. Everyone knows that butterflies are symbols for lovers, while "willow shade" is a euphemism for that hairy place on women down low. But this new poster is a long way from any of that and further still from the one of the two of us doing the tango that so upset Mama. This is a beautiful painting;

May has to have lain naked for hours before Z.G.'s eyes.

But I'm not just shocked. I'm also disappointed in May for allowing Z.G. to talk her into this. I'm angry at him for preying on her vulnerability. And I'm heartsick that May and I have to take it. *This* is how women end up on the street selling their bodies. But then this is how it is for women everywhere. You experience one lapse in conscience, in how low you think you'll go, in what you'll accept, and pretty soon you're at the bottom. You've become a girl with three holes, the lowest form of prostitute, living on one of the floating brothels in Soochow Creek, catering to Chinese so poor they don't mind catching a loathsome disease in exchange for a few humping moments of the husband-wife thing.

As disheartened and disgusted as I am, I go back to Z.G.'s the next day and the day after that. We need the money. And soon enough, there I am practically naked. People say you need to be strong, smart, and lucky to survive hard times, war, a natural disaster, or physical torture. But I say emotional abuse — anxiety, fear, guilt, and degradation — is far worse and much harder to survive. This is the first time that May and I have ever experienced anything like this, and it saps our energy. While I find it almost impossible to sleep, May retreats to those numbing depths. She dozes in bed until noon. She takes naps. Some days at Z.G.'s she even starts to nod off as he paints. He lets her out of her pose so she can sleep on the couch. While he paints me, I look at May, her fingers placed just so but still not

69

entirely covering her face, which is pensive even in sleep.

We're like lobsters slowly boiling to death in a pot of water. We sit for Z.G., attend parties, and drink absinthe frappeés. We go to clubs with Betsy, and let others pay for us. We go to movies. We window-shop. We simply don't understand what's happening to us.

The date nears when we're supposed to leave for Hong Kong to meet our husbands. May and I have no intention of getting on that boat. We couldn't even if we wanted to because I threw away the tickets, but our parents don't know that. May and I go through the motions of packing so they won't be suspicious. We listen to Mama's and Baba's travel advice. The night before our scheduled departure, they take us out for dinner and tell us how much they'll miss us. May and I wake up early the next morning, get dressed, and leave the house before anyone else rises. When we return home that evening — long after the ship has sailed — Mama weeps with pleasure that we are still here and Baba yells at us for not doing our duty.

"You don't understand what you've done," he shouts. "There's going to be trouble."

"You worry too much," May says in her lightest voice. "Old Man Louie and his sons have left Shanghai, and in a few days they'll leave China for good. They can't do anything to us now."

Baba's face roils with anger. For a moment I think he's going to hit May, but then he squeezes his hands into fists, marches off to the salon, and slams the door.

70

May looks at me and shrugs. Then we turn ourselves over to our mother, who takes us into the kitchen and orders Cook to make tea and give us a couple of precious English butter cookies he has saved in a tin.

Eleven days later, it rains in the morning, so the heat and humidity are not as bad as usual. Z.G. splurges and hires a taxi to take us to the Lunghua Pagoda on the outskirts of the city to fly his kite. It isn't the most beautiful place. There's an airstrip, an execution ground, and a camp for Chinese troops. We tromp across the field until Z.G. finds a spot to stage the flight. Some soldiers — wearing ripped tennis shoes and faded, ill-fitting uniforms with insignia pinned to their shoulders — abandon a puppy they're playing with to help us.

Each oriole is attached by a hook and separate string to the main line. May picks up the lead oriole and lifts it into the air. With the soldiers' assistance, I add a new oriole and its string to the main line. One oriole after the other takes off, until pretty soon a flock of twelve orioles swoosh, swoop, and dip in the sky. They look so free up there. May's hair flies in the breeze. Her hand shields her eyes as she gazes into the sky. Light glints off Z.G.'s glasses, and he grins. He motions me to him and hands me the control of the kites. The orioles are made from paper and balsa, but the pull of the wind and the sky is strong. Z.G. moves behind me and puts his hands over mine to steady the control. His thighs lie against mine and my back against his torso. I breathe in the sensation of being so close to him. Surely he has to be aware of what I feel for him. Even with him there to hold me, the pull from the kite is so powerful that I think I might be lifted up to fly away with the orioles into the clouds and beyond.

Mama used to tell us a story about a cicada sitting high in a tree. It chirps and drinks in dew, oblivious to the praying mantis behind it. The mantis arches up its front leg to stab the cicada, but it doesn't know an oriole perches behind it. The bird stretches out its neck to snap up the mantis for a midday meal, but it's unaware of the boy who's come into the garden with a net. Three creatures — the cicada, the mantis, and the oriole — all coveted gains without being aware of the greater and inescapable danger that was coming.

Later that afternoon, the first shots are exchanged between Chinese and Japanese soldiers.

White Plum Blossoms

The next morning, August 14, we wake late to the sounds of movement, people, and animals outside our walls. We draw back the curtain and see streams of people passing the house. Are we curious about them? Not at all, because our minds are on how to get the most out of the one dollar we have to spend during the shopping expedition we're planning. This isn't some shallow thing. As beautiful girls, we require fashionable ensembles. May and I have done what we can to mix and match the Western outfits Old Man Louie left behind, but we need to keep current. We aren't thinking about the new fall fashions, because the artists we work for are already creating calendars and advertisements for next spring. How will Western designers modify the dress in the new year? Will a button be added to a cuff, the hem shortened, the neckline lowered, the waist nipped? We decide to go to Nanking Road to look in the windows and try to imagine what the changes will be. Then we'll stop by the notions department in the towering Wing On Department Store to buy ribbons, lace, and other trim to freshen our clothes.

May puts on a dress with a pattern of white plum blossoms against a robin's egg blue background. I wear loose white linen trousers and a navy blue short-sleeved top. Then we pass the morning looking through what's left in our closet. It's in May's nature to spend hours at her toilette, choosing the right scarf to tie at her throat or purse to match her shoes, so she tells me what we should look for and I write it down.

It's late afternoon when we pin on hats and pick up our parasols to protect us from the summer sun. August, as I've said, is miserably hot and humid in Shanghai, the sky white and oppressive with heat and clouds. This day, however, is hot but clear. It might have even passed for pleasant if not for the thousands of people who crowd the streets. They carry baskets, chickens, clothes, food, and ancestor tablets. Grandmothers and mothers with bound feet are supported by sons and husbands. Brothers lug poles across their shoulders coolie-style. In the baskets at the ends are their little brothers and sisters. Wheelbarrows transport the aged, sick, and deformed. Those who can afford it have paid coolies to bear their suitcases, trunks, and boxes, but most of the people are poor and from the country. May and I are happy to get in a rickshaw and separate ourselves from them.

"Who are they?" May asks.

I have to think about it. That's how disconnected I am from what's happening around me. I mull over a word I've never before spoken aloud.

"They're refugees."

May frowns as she takes that in.

If I make this sound like this sudden turbulence has come out of nowhere, that's because it has for us. May doesn't pay much attention to the world, but I know a few things. Back in 1931, when I was fifteen, the dwarf bandits invaded Manchuria in the far north and installed a puppet government. Four months later, at the beginning of the new year, they crossed into the Chapei district across Soochow Creek right next to Hongkew, where we live. At first we thought it was fireworks. Baba took me to the end of North Szechuan Road, and we saw the truth. It was horrible to see the bombs exploding and worse still to see Shanghai-landers in their evening clothes, drinking liquor from flasks, nibbling on sandwiches, smoking cigarettes, and laughing at the spectacle. With no help from the foreigners, who got rich off our city, the Chinese Nineteenth Route Army fought back. Japan didn't agree to a cease-fire for another eleven weeks. Chapei was rebuilt, and we let the incident go out of our minds.

Then last month shots were fired on the Marco Polo Bridge in the capital. The official war began, but no one thought the dwarf bandits would come this far south so fast. Let them take Hopei, Shantung, Shansi, and a bit of Honan, the thinking went. The monkey people would need time to digest all that territory. Only after establishing control and snuffing out uprisings would they consider marching southward into the Yangtze delta. The sorry people who would live under foreign

75

rule would be *wang k'uo nu* — lost-country slaves. We don't grasp that the trail of refugees crossing the Garden Bridge with us extends for ten miles into the countryside. There is so much we don't know.

We view the world very much as peasants in the countryside have for millennia. They've always said the mountains are high and the emperor is far away, meaning palace intrigues and imperial threats have no impact on their lives. They've acted as though they could do whatever they wanted without fear of retribution or consequence. In Shanghai, we also assume that what happens elsewhere in China will never touch us. After all, the rest of the country is big and backward, and we live in a treaty port governed by foreigners, so technically we aren't even part of China. Besides, we believe, truly believe, that even if the Japanese reach Shanghai, our army will beat them back as they did five years ago. But Generalissimo Chiang Kai-shek has a different idea. He wants the fight with the Japanese to come to the delta, where he can arouse national pride and resistance, and at the same time consolidate feelings against the Communists, who have been talking about civil war.

Of course, we have no inkling of that as we cross the Garden Bridge and enter the International Settlement. The refugees drop their loads, lie on sidewalks, sit on the steps of the big banks, and crowd onto the wharves. Sightseers gather in clusters to watch our planes try to drop bombs on the Japanese flagship, the *Idzumo*, and the destroyers, mine-sweepers, and cruisers that surround it. Foreign businessmen and shoppers determinedly step around what's at their feet and ignore what's happening in the air, as though things like this go on every day. The mood is at once desperate, festive, and indifferent. If anything, the bombings are an entertainment, because again the International Settlement — as a British port — isn't under any threat from the Japanese.

Our puller stops at the corner of Nanking Road. We pay the agreed-upon price and join the throng. Each plane that sweeps overhead brings whoops of encouragement and applause, but when every single bomb misses its target and falls harmlessly into the Whangpoo, cheers turn to boos. Somehow it all seems a funny game and eventually a dull one.

May and I stroll up Nanking Road, avoiding the refugees and eyeing Shanghainese and Shanghailanders to see what they're wearing. Outside the Cathay Hotel we run into Tommy Hu. He wears a white duck suit and a straw hat tilted back on his head. He seems thrilled to see May, and she melts into her flirtatious mode. I can't help wondering if they arranged to meet.

I cross the street, leaving May and Tommy with their heads together and hands gently touching. I'm just in front of the Palace Hotel when I hear a loud *rat-a-tat* coming from behind me. I don't know what it is, but I duck instinctively. Around me, others fall to the ground or run for doorways. I look back toward the Bund and see a silver plane flying low. It's one of ours. Antiaircraft fire sprouts from one of the Japanese ships. At first, it seems like the dwarf bandits missed their target, and a few people cheer. Then we see smoke spiral out of the plane.

Crippled by the antiaircraft fire, the plane veers over Nanking Road. The pilot must know he's going to crash, because suddenly he lets the two bombs attached to the wing drop. They seem to take a very long time to fall. I hear whistling and then feel a sickening lurch accompanied by a shattering explosion as the first bomb lands in front of the Cathay Hotel. My eyes go white, my eardrums go silent, and my lungs stop working, as if the explosion has punched out my body's knowledge of how to operate. A second later, another bomb goes through the roof of the Palace Hotel and explodes. Debris — glass, paper, bits of flesh, and body parts — hurtles down on me.

It's said that the worst part of the bombing experience is the seconds of total paralysis and silence that immediately follow the initial concussion. It's as though — and I think this is an expression used in every culture — time stands still. That's how it is for me. I'm frozen in place. Smoke and plaster dust billow. Eventually I hear the tinkle of glass falling from the hotel's windows. Someone moans. Someone else screams. And then total panic engulfs the street as another bomber wobbles through the air above us. A minute or two later, we hear and feel the impact of two more bombs. They land, I find out later, in the intersection of Avenue Edouard VII and Thibet Road near the racecourse, where many refugees have gathered to receive free rice and tea. Altogether the four bombs wound, maim, or kill thousands of people.

My immediate thought is for May. I have to find her. I stumble across a couple of mangled bodies. Their clothes have been ripped, shredded, and bloodied. I can't tell if they were refugees, Shanghainese, or Shanghailanders. Severed arms and legs litter the street. A stampede of hotel guests and staff pushes and shoves through the Palace's doors and pours out onto the street. Most of them are screaming, many of them bleeding. People run over the injured and the dead. I join the panicked scramble, needing to make my way back to where I left May and Tommy. I can't see anything. I rub my eyes, trying without success to rid them of dust and terror. I find what's left of Tommy. His hat is gone and so is his head, but I still recognize the white of his suit. May isn't with him, thank God, but where is she?

I turn back toward the Palace Hotel, believing I missed her in my rush. Nanking Road is carpeted with the dead and dying. A few badly injured men lurch drunkenly down the middle of the street. Several cars burn, while others have had their windows blown out. Inside them are more injured and dead. Cars, rickshaws, trams, wheelbarrows, and the people inside them have been pitted by shrapnel. Buildings, billboards, and fences are spattered with flecks of humanity. The sidewalk is slippery with clotted blood and flesh. Shattered glass glitters on the street like so many diamonds. The stench in the August heat burns my eyes and clogs my throat.

"May!" I call and take a few steps. I keep shouting her name, trying to hear her response through the panic that whirls around me. I stop to examine every injured or dead body. With so many dead, how can she have survived? She's so delicate and easily hurt.

And then, amid all the blood and gore, I see through the crowd a patch of robin's egg blue with a white plum blossom pattern. I run forward and find my sister. She's partially buried in plaster and other debris. She's either unconscious or dead.

"May! May!"

She doesn't move. Fear grips my heart. I kneel beside her. I don't see any wounds, but blood has soaked into her dress from a gruesomely injured woman lying next to her. I brush the debris from May's dress and lean down close to her face. Her skin is as white as candle wax. "May," I say softly. "Wake up. Come on, May, wake up."

She stirs. I coax her again. Her eyes blink open, she groans, and closes her eyes again.

I pelt her with questions. "Are you hurt? Do you feel pain? Can you move?"

When she answers with a question of her own, my whole body relaxes in relief.

"What happened?"

"There was a bomb. I couldn't find you. Tell me you're all right."

She twists first one shoulder and then the other. She winces, but not in agony.

"Help me up," she says.

I put a hand behind her neck and pull her into a sitting position. When I let go, my hand is sticky with blood.

All around us people moan from their injuries. Some cry for help. Some gurgle final, tortured gasps for life. Some scream from the horror of seeing a loved one in pieces. But I've been on this street many times, and there's an underlying silence that's chilling, as if the dead are sucking sound into their dark emptiness.

I put my arms around May and get her to her feet. She sways, and I worry she'll lose consciousness again. With my arm around her waist, we take a few steps. But where are we going? Ambulances haven't arrived yet. We can't even hear them in the distance, but from neighboring streets come people — unhurt and in surprisingly clean clothes. They rush from corpse to corpse, from injured to injured.

"Tommy?" May asks. When I shake my head, she says, "Take me to him."

I don't think that's a good idea, but she insists. When we reach his body, May's knees crumple. We sit on the curb. May's hair is white with plaster dust. She looks like a ghost spirit. I probably look the same.

"I need to make sure you aren't hurt," I say, partly to take May's attention away from Tommy's body. "Let me take a look."

May turns her back to me and away from Tommy. Her hair's matted with already clotting blood, which I take to be a good sign. I carefully part the curls until I find a gash on the back of her head. I'm not a doctor, but it doesn't look like it needs stitches. Still, she's been knocked out. I want someone to tell me it's safe to take her home. We wait and wait, but even after the ambulances come no one helps us. Too many others need immediate attention. As dusk settles, I decide we should go home, but May won't leave Tommy.

"We've known him our entire lives. What would Mama say if we left him here? And his mother . . ." She trembles, but she doesn't cry. Her shock is too deep for that.

Just as furniture vans arrive to take away the dead, we feel the concussion of bombs being dropped and hear the rattle of machine guns in the distance. None of us in the street has any illusions about what this means. The dwarf bandits are attacking. They won't bomb the International Settlement or any of the foreign concessions, but Chapei, Hongkew, the Old Chinese City, and the outlying Chinese areas have to be under fire. People scream and cry, but May and I fight our fear and stay with Tommy's body until it's loaded onto a stretcher and put in the back of one of the vans.

"I want to go home now," May says as the van pulls away. "Mama and Baba will be worried. And I don't want to be out when the Generalissimo puts more of our planes back in the air."

She's right. Our air force has already proven it's inept, and we won't be safe on the streets tonight if they take to the skies again. So we walk home. We're both splattered with blood and plaster dust. Passersby pull away from us as though we're bringing death with every step we take. I know Mama will lose control when she sees us, but I long for her concern and tears, followed by her inevitable anger that we placed ourselves in such danger.

We walk in the door and turn in to the salon. The dark green foreign-style drapes fringed with little velvet balls have been pulled shut. The bombing has disrupted the power lines, and the room is lit by soft, warm, and comforting candlelight. In the craziness of the day, I forgot about our boarders, but they haven't forgotten about us. The cobbler sits on his haunches next to my father. The student hovers over Mama's chair, trying to look reassuring. The two dancers stand with their backs against the wall nervously twisting their fingers. The policeman's wife and two daughters perch on the stairs.

When Mama sees us, she covers her face and begins to cry. Baba pushes his way across the room, puts his arms around May, and half carries her to his chair. People cluster around her, pawing at her to make sure she's unhurt — touching her face and patting her thighs and arms. Everyone chatters at once.

"Are you injured?"

"What happened?"

"We heard it was an enemy plane. Those monkey people are worse than turtles' egg abortions!"

With all attention on May, the policeman's wife and daughters come to me. I see dread in the woman's eyes. The older girl pulls on my blouse. "Our baba hasn't come home yet." Her voice is hopeful and brave. "Tell us you saw him."

I shake my head. The girl takes her little sister's hand and skulks back to the stairs. Their mother's eyes close in fear and worry.

Now that May and I are safe, the day's events tumble through me. My sister's fine and we made it home. The fear and excitement that kept me strong disappear. I feel empty, weak, and dizzy. The others must have noticed, because all of a sudden I feel hands on me, leading me to a chair. I let myself sink into the cushions. Someone brings a cup to my lips, and I sip lukewarm tea.

May, now standing, proudly lists what she considers to be my accomplishments. "Pearl didn't cry. She didn't give up. She looked for me and she found me. She took care of me. She brought me home. She —"

Someone or something pounds on the front door. Baba bunches his hands into balls, as if he knows what's coming. We no longer have a houseboy to answer the door, but no one moves. We're all afraid. Is it refugees begging for help? Have the dwarf bandits already marched into the city? Has the looting begun? Or have some clever souls already figured out they can get rich during the war by demanding protection money? We watch as May walks to the door — her hips swaying lightly — opens it, and then slowly takes several steps backward, her hands held before her as if in surrender.

The three men who enter are not in military uniform, but they're immediately recognizable as dangerous nevertheless. They wear pointed leather shoes, the better to inflict damage with their kicks. Their shirts are made from fine black cotton, the better to hide bloodstains. They wear felt fedoras pulled low to shadow their features. One holds a pistol; another grips a club of some sort. The third carries his menace in his body, which is short but solid. I've lived in

Shanghai almost my entire life and can spot — and then avoid — a member of the Green Gang on the street or in a club, but I never expected to see one, let alone three, in our home. I'll say this: You've never seen a room empty faster. Our boarders — from the policeman's daughters to the student and the dancing girls — scatter like leaves.

The three toughs ignore May and casually stroll into the salon. As warm as it is, I shiver.

"Mr. Chin?" the stocky man asks as he plants his feet in front of my father.

Baba — and I'll never forget this — gulps and swallows, gulps and swallows again, like a fish gasping for air on a slab of hot concrete.

"You have a growth in your throat or what?"

The intruder's mocking tone causes me to avert my eyes from my father's face, and I see worse. His pants darken as his bladder lets go. The stocky man, the apparent leader of this small group, spits on the floor in disgust.

"You have failed to pay your debt to Pockmarked Huang. You cannot borrow money from him over many years to provide an extravagant life for your family and not pay it back. You cannot gamble in his establishments and not pay for your losses."

This couldn't be worse news. Pockmarked Huang's control is so great that it's said if a watch is stolen anywhere in the city, his minions will make sure it's restored to its rightful owner within twenty-four hours — for a price, of course. He's known to deliver coffins to people who have displeased him. He usually kills those who have cheated him in some way. We're lucky we received this visit instead.

"Pockmarked Huang made a good arrangement for you to pay him back," the gangster goes on. "It was complicated, but he was amenable. You had a debt and he was trying to decide what to do with you." The thug pauses and stares at my father. "Are you going to explain this to them" — he motions to us casually, but somehow it still feels threatening — "or shall I?"

We wait for Baba to speak. When he doesn't, the thug shifts his attention to the rest of us.

"There was an outstanding debt that needed to be paid," he explains. "At the same moment, a merchant from America came to us looking to buy rickshaws for his business and wives for his sons. So Pockmarked Huang put together a three-way deal to benefit everyone."

I don't know about Mama and May, but I'm still hoping Baba will do or say something to make this horrible man and his sidekicks leave our home. Shouldn't Baba do that — as a man, a father, and a husband?

The leader leans over Baba menacingly. "Our boss ordered you to fill Mr. Louie's procurement needs by giving him your rickshaws and your daughters. No money would be paid by you, and you and your wife would be allowed to stay in your house. Mr. Louie would pay your debt to us with American dollars. Everyone would get what they needed, and everyone would live."

I'm furious with my father for not telling us the truth, but that's insignificant compared with the terror I feel, because now it's not just my father who didn't do what he was supposed to do. May and I were part of the deal. We too have crossed Pockmarked Huang. The gangster wastes no time getting to that point.

"While it's true that our boss has profited nicely, there remains a problem," he says. "Your daughters didn't get on the boat. What kind of message will this send to others who owe Pockmarked Huang if he lets you get away with this?" The thug takes his eyes from my father and scans the room. He gestures first to me and then to May. "These are your daughters, yes?" He doesn't wait for an answer. "They were supposed to meet their husbands in Hong Kong. Why didn't that happen, Mr. Chin?"

"I —"

It's a sad thing to know your father is weak, but it's terrible to realize he's pathetic.

Without thinking, I blurt, "It's not his fault."

The man's cruel eyes turn to me. He comes to my chair, squats before me, puts his hands on my knees, and squeezes them hard. "How can this be, little girl?"

I hold my breath, petrified.

May darts across the room to my side. She begins to speak. Every statement of fact comes out as a question. "We didn't know our father owed money to the Green Gang? We thought he only owed money to an Overseas Chinese? We thought Old Man Louie was unimportant, just a visitor?"

"Good daughters to a worthless man are a waste," the leader declares conversationally. He stands and strides to the middle of the room. His helpers come to his side. To Baba, he says, "You were allowed to stay in this house as long as you sent your daughters to their new homes. Since you have not done so, this is no longer your home. You must leave. And you must pay your debt. Shall I take your daughters with me now? We will find a good use for them."

Afraid of what Baba will say, I jump in. "It's not too late for us to go to America. There are other ships."

"Pockmarked Huang doesn't like liars. You have already been dishonest, and you are probably lying to me now."

"We promise we'll do what you say," May mutters.

Like a cobra, the leader's hand strikes out, grabs May's hair, and yanks her to him. He brings her face close to his. He smiles and says, "Your family is broke. You should be living on the street. Please, I ask you again, wouldn't it be better to come with us now? We like beautiful girls."

"I have their tickets" comes a small voice. "I'll make sure they leave and the deal you arranged for my husband to honor his debts is completed."

At first I'm not even sure who spoke. None of us are. We all look around until we come to my mother, who has not said a word since the men entered our home. I see hardness in her that I've never seen before. Maybe we're all like that with our mothers. They seem ordinary until one day they're extraordinary.

"I have the tickets," she repeats. She has to be lying. I threw them out, along with our immigration papers and the coaching book Sam gave me.

"What good are those tickets now? Your daughters missed their boat."

"We will exchange them and the girls will go to their husbands." Mama wrings a handkerchief in her hands. "I will see to it. And then my husband and I will leave this house. You tell that to Pockmarked Huang. If he doesn't like it, then let him come here and discuss it with me, a woman —"

The sickening sound of a pistol being cocked stops my mother's words. The leader holds up a hand, alerting his men to be ready. Silence hangs like a shroud over the room. Outside, ambulances scream and machine guns rattle and cough.

Then he snorts lightly. "Madame Chin, you know what will happen if we find you're lying to us."

When neither of our parents says anything, May finds the courage to ask, "How long do we have?"

"Until tomorrow," he growls. Then he laughs roughly as he realizes the near impossibility of his demand. "It won't be easy to leave the city though. If one good thing has come from today's disaster, it is that many of the foreign devils will leave us. They will have first priority on the ships."

His men begin to move toward May and me. This is it. We're going to be the Green Gang's property now. May grabs my hand. Then a miracle: the leader grinds out a new offer.

"I will give you three days. Be on your way to America by then, even if you have to swim. We will return tomorrow — and every day — to make sure you don't forget what you must do."

With the threat laid down and a deadline given, the three men leave, but not before they tip over a couple of lamps and use the club to smash Mama's few vases and trinkets that have not yet been taken to the pawnshop.

As soon as they're gone, May sinks to the floor. None of us move to help her.

"You lied to us," I say to Baba. "You lied to us about Old Man Louie and the reason for our marriages —"

"I didn't want you to worry about the Green Gang," he admits feebly.

This response maddens and exasperates me. "You didn't want us to worry?"

He flinches, but then he deflects my anger with a question of his own. "What difference does it make now?"

There's a long moment of silence as we think about that. I don't know what goes through Mama's and May's minds, but I can think of many things we might have done differently if we'd known the truth. I still believe that May and I wouldn't have gotten on the ship to take us to our husbands, but we would have done *something*: run away, hidden ourselves at the mission, begged Z.G. until he agreed to help us . . .

"I've had to carry this burden too long." Baba turns to my mother and asks pitiably, "What will we do now?"

Mama looks at him with scathing contempt. "We're going to do what we can to save our lives," she says, looping her handkerchief through her jade bracelet.

"Are you going to send us to Los Angeles?" May's voice quavers.

"She can't," I say. "I threw away the tickets."

"I pulled them out of the trash," Mama announces.

I slip down next to May. I can't believe Mama is willing to ship us to America to cure my father's and her problems. But then isn't that the kind of thing Chinese parents have done with worthless daughters for thousands of years — abandoned them, sold them, used them?

Seeing the looks of betrayal and fear on our faces, Mama hurries on. "We're going to trade in your tickets to America and buy passage to Hong Kong for all of us. We've got three days to find a ship. Hong Kong is a British colony, so we don't have to worry about the Japanese attacking there. If we decide it's safe to come back onto the mainland, we'll take the ferry or train to Canton. Then we'll go to Yin Bo, your father's home village." Her jade bracelet hits the side table with a resolute *thunk*. "The Green Gang won't find us there."

Moon Sisters

The next morning, May and I start out for the Dollar Steamship Line's office, hoping to exchange our tickets — from Shanghai to Hong Kong, from Hong Kong to San Francisco, and from San Francisco to Los Angeles — for just four tickets to Hong Kong. Nanking Road and the area around the racecourse remain closed so workers can clear away the mangled corpses and body parts, but this is the least of the city's concerns. Thousands upon thousands of refugees continue to arrive, trying to stay ahead of the advancing Japanese. So many infants have been left to die on the streets by desperate parents that the Chinese Benevolent Association has established a special "baby patrol" to pick up the forsaken remains, pile them onto trucks, and take them to the countryside to be burned.

But for all the people coming into the city, thousands more try to leave. Many of my countrymen take trains back to their home villages in the interior. Friends we've known in the cafés — writers, artists, and intellectuals — make choices that will determine the rest of their lives: to go to Chungking, where Chiang Kai-shek has established his wartime capital, or to Yunnan to join the Communists. The wealthiest families — foreign and Chinese — leave by international steamers, which chug defiantly past the Japanese warships anchored off the Bund.

We wait for hours in a long queue. By five o'clock, we've moved perhaps ten feet. We return home with nothing resolved. I'm worn out; May looks distraught and depleted. Baba spent the day visiting friends, hoping to borrow money to help with our escape, but in these suddenly uncertain times, who can afford to be generous to an ill-fated man? The trio of toughs isn't surprised by our lack of progress, but they're hardly happy. Even they seem unnerved by the chaos surrounding us.

That night the house jumps from explosions in Chapei and Hongkew. Billowing ashes from these neighborhoods mingle with the smoke from the baby fires and the great pyres the Japanese use to burn their own dead.

In the morning, I get up quietly so I won't disturb my sister. Yesterday she accompanied me without complaint. But a few times, when she thought I wasn't looking, I'd caught her rubbing her temples. Last night she'd taken some aspirin and promptly thrown them up. She must have a concussion. I hope it's mild, but how can I know for sure? At the very least, after everything that's happened the last two days, she needs to sleep, because

93

today is going to be another hard one. Tommy Hu's funeral is at ten.

I go downstairs and find Mama in the salon. She motions for me to join her. "Here's a little money." An unusual steeliness has taken over her voice. "Go out and bring back some sesame cakes and dough sticks." This is more than we've eaten for breakfast since the morning our lives changed. "We should eat well. The funeral —"

I take the money and leave the house. I hear the din from naval guns bombarding our shore positions, the incessant rattle of machine-gun and rifle fire, explosions in Chapei, and battles raging in outlying districts. Pungent ashes from last night's funerary fires blanket the city so clothes that were hung out to dry will need to be rewashed, stoops swept, and cars doused. My throat chokes on the taste. Plenty of people crowd the street. War may be happening, but we all have things we need to do. I walk to the corner, but instead of doing Mama's errands I board a wheelbarrow to take me to Z.G.'s apartment. I may have acted girlishly before, but that was one moment out of years of friendship. He has to have some affection for May and me. Surely he'll help us find a way to put our lives back together.

I knock on his door. When no one answers, I go back downstairs and find his landlady in the central courtyard.

"He's gone," she says. "But what do you care? Your beautiful-girl days are over. Do you think we can hold back the monkey people forever? Once they have control, no one will need or want your beautiful-girl calendars." Her hysteria grows. "Those monkey people might want you for something else though. Is that what you want for you and your sister?"

"Just tell me where he is," I say wearily.

"He left to join the Communists," she yaps, each syllable coming out like a bullet.

"He wouldn't leave without saying good-bye," I say, doubtful.

The old woman cackles. "What a stupid girl you are! He left without paying his rent. He left behind his paints and brushes. He left without taking a single thing."

I bite my lip to keep from crying. I have to focus on my own survival now.

Still mindful of my money, I hire a wheelbarrow to take me home, squeezing on with three other riders. As we bump along the road, I make a mental list of people who might help us. The men we dance with? Betsy? One of the other artists we pose for? But everyone has their own worries.

I return to an empty house. I've been gone so long I missed going to Tommy's funeral.

May and Mama come home a couple of hours later. They're both dressed in funeral white. May's eyes are as swollen as overripe peaches from crying, and Mama looks old and tired, but they don't ask where I was or why I didn't go to the memorial. Baba isn't with them. He must have lingered with the other fathers at the funeral banquet.

"How was it?" I ask.

May shrugs, and I don't press. She leans against the doorjamb, crosses her arms, and stares at her feet. "We have to go back to the docks."

I don't want to go out. I'm heartsick over Z.G. I want to tell May he's gone, but what good will it do? I despair over what's happening to us. I want to be rescued. If not that, then I want to go back to bed, lie under the covers, and sob until I have no tears left. But I'm May's older sister. I have to be braver than my emotions. I have to help us fight our bad fates. I take a deep breath and stand. "Let's go. I'm ready."

We return to the Dollar Steamship Line. The queue moves today, and when we get to the front we understand why. The clerk is useless. We show him our tickets, but exhaustion has robbed him of grammar and his temper.

"What you want me do with these?" he demands loudly.

"Can we exchange them for four tickets to Hong Kong?" I ask, sure that he'll see this as a good deal for the company.

He doesn't answer. Instead, he waves to the people behind us. "Next!"

I don't move.

"Can we get on a new ship?" I ask.

He hits the grate that separates us. "You stupid!" It seems everyone feels the same way about me today. Then he grabs the grate and shakes it. "No tickets left! All gone! Next! Next!"

I see in him the same frustration and hysteria I saw in Z.G.'s landlady. May reaches out and puts her fingers on his. Touching between sexes — strangers! — is frowned upon. Her act stuns him into silence. Or maybe he's suddenly calmed by the beautiful girl who speaks to him in a mellifluous voice.

"I know you can help us." She tilts her head and lets a small smile transform her face from desperation to serenity. The effect is immediate.

"Let me see your tickets," the clerk says. He studies them intently and checks a couple of logbooks. "I'm sorry, but these won't help you leave Shanghai," he says at last. He pulls out a pad, fills in a form, and then passes it and our tickets back to May. "If you can get to Hong Kong, go to our office there and give them this. You'll be able to trade your tickets for new berths to San Francisco." After a long pause, he repeats, "*If* you can get to Hong Kong."

We thank him, but he hasn't helped us at all. We don't want to go to San Francisco. We want to go south to escape the Green Gang's reach.

Feeling defeated, we start home. Never has the traffic noise, the smell of exhaust, and the stink of perfume seemed so oppressive. Never has the unscratchable itch for money, the flagrant openness of criminal behavior, and the dissolution of the spirit seemed so forlorn and futile.

We find Mama sitting on the front steps, where once our servants pridefully ate their meals.

"Did they come back?" I ask. I don't have to specify who. The only people we're truly afraid of are the Green Gang thugs. Mama nods. May and I let that sink in. What Mama says next sends a ripple of dread down my spine.

"And your father still hasn't returned."

We sit on either side of our mother. We wait, searching both ends of the street, hoping to see Baba turn the corner. But he doesn't come home. Darkness falls and with it intensified bombardment. The night glows from fires raging in Chapei. Searchlights streak across the sky. Whatever happens, the International Settlement and the French Concession, as foreign territories, will be safe.

"Did he say if he was going somewhere after the funeral?" May asks, her voice as tiny as a girl's.

Mama shakes her head. "Maybe he's looking for a job. Maybe he's gambling. Maybe he's seeing a woman."

Other options flash through my mind, and when I look over Mama's head to May, I see she shares them with me. Has he deserted us, leaving his wife and daughters to deal with the consequences? Has the Green Gang decided to kill Baba before the deadline as a warning to us? Or has anti-aircraft fire or shrapnel fallen to earth and found him?

At about two in the morning, Mama pats her thighs decisively. "We should get some sleep. If your father doesn't come home —" Her voice catches. She takes a deep breath. "If he doesn't come home, then we'll still go ahead with my plan. Your father's family will take us in. We belong to them now."

"But how are we going to get there? We can't change our tickets."

Desperation grips Mama's features as she hastily tosses out an idea. "We could go to Woosong. That's only a few miles from here. I could walk it if I had to. Standard Oil has a wharf there. With your marriage papers, maybe they'll give us space on one of their launches to some other city. From there we could go south."

"I don't think that will work," I say. "Why would the oil company want to help us?"

Mama comes back with another proposal. "We could try to find a boat to take us up the Yangtze —"

"What about the monkey people?" May asks. "There are a lot of them on the river. Even the *lo fan* are leaving the interior to come here."

"We could go north to Tientsin and look for passage on a ship," Mama tries again, but this time she holds up a hand to keep my sister and me from speaking. "I know. The monkey people are there already. We could go east, but how long before those areas are invaded?" She pauses to think. It's as though I can see through her skull and into her brain as she anticipates the dangers of different ways out of Shanghai. Finally, she leans forward and confides in a low but steady voice, "Let's go southwest to the Grand Canal. Once we reach the canal, we ought to be able to get a boat — a sampan, anything — and continue on to Hangchow. From there we can hire a fishing boat to take us to Hong Kong or Canton." She looks from me to May and then back. "Do you agree?"

My head swims. I have no idea what we should do.

99

"Thank you, Mama," May whispers. "Thank you for taking such good care of us."

We go inside. Moonlight streams through the windows. Only when we say good night does Mama's voice break, but then she goes into her room and shuts the door.

In the darkness, May looks at me. "What are we going to do?"

I think the better question is, What's going to happen to us? But I don't ask it. As May's *jie jie*, I have to hide my fears.

The next morning, we hurriedly pack what we consider to be practical and useful: sanitary supplies, three pounds of rice per person, a pot and eating utensils, sheets, dresses, and shoes. At the last minute, Mama calls me to her room. From a dresser drawer she pulls out some papers, including our coaching book and marriage certificates. On her vanity, she's gathered together our photo albums. They'll be too heavy to carry, so I think Mama's going to take a few photos as memories. She pulls one from the black paper. Behind it is a folded bill. She repeats the process again and again until she's put together a small stack of bills. She tucks the cash in her pocket, then asks me to help her move the dresser away from the wall. Hanging from a nail is a small bag, which she takes. "This is all that remains of my bride-price," she tells me.

"How could you have kept these things hidden?" I ask indignantly. "Why didn't you offer to pay off the Green Gang?"

"It wouldn't have been enough."

"But it might have helped."

"My mother always said, 'Keep something for yourself,'" Mama explains. "I knew I might have to use these things one day. Now that day is here."

She leaves the room. I linger, staring at the photos: May as a baby, the two of us dressed for a party, Mama and Baba's wedding photo. Happy memories, silly memories, dance before me. My eyes blur, and I blink back tears. I grab a couple photos, put them in my bag, and go downstairs. Mama and May wait for me on the front steps.

"Pearl, find us a wheelbarrow man," Mama orders. Because she's my mother and we don't have any other options, I obey her — a bound-footed woman who never before had a plan for anything beyond her mah-jongg strategy.

I wait on the corner, watching for a wheelbarrow pusher who looks strong and whose cart appears sturdy and large. Wheelbarrow pushers are below rickshaw pullers and just slightly above nightsoil men. They're considered part of the coolie class — poor enough that they'll do anything to make a little money or receive a few bowls of rice. After several attempts, I find a pusher, so thin the skin on his belly seems to meet his spine, willing to enter serious negotiations.

"Who would try to leave Shanghai now?" he asks wisely. "I don't want to be killed by the monkey people."

I don't tell him that the Green Gang is after us. Instead, I say, "We're going home to Kwangtung province."

"I'm not pushing you that far!"

"Of course not. But if you could get us to the Grand Canal . . ."

I agree to pay double his daily take.

We go back to the house. He packs our bags into the wheelbarrow. We prop the cloth-wrapped satchels filled with our dresses on the back of the wheelbarrow so Mama will have something to lean on.

"Before we go," Mama says, "I want to give you girls these." She loops a tiny cloth pouch hanging from a string around May's neck and another around mine. "I bought them from a diviner. They hold three coppers, three sesame seeds, and three green beans. He said they will keep you safe from evil spirits, illness, and the dwarf bandits' flying machines."

My mother's so susceptible, gullible, and old-fashioned. How much did she pay for this nonsense — fifty coppers apiece? More?

She climbs in the wheelbarrow and wiggles her bottom to get comfortable. In her hands she clasps our papers — the boat tickets, our marriage certificates, and the coaching book — wrapped in a piece of silk and tied with silk tape. Then we take one last look at the house. Neither Cook nor our boarders have come outside to wave good-bye or wish us luck.

"Are you sure we should leave?" May asks anxiously. "What about Baba? What if he comes home? What if he's hurt somewhere?"

"Your father has a hyena's heart and a python's lungs," Mama says. "Would he stay here for you? Would he come looking for you? If so, then why isn't he here?"

I don't believe Mama means to be so callous. Baba has lied to us and put us in a desperate situation, but he's still her husband and our father. But Mama is right. If Baba is alive, he probably isn't thinking about us. We can't worry about him either, if we're going to have any chance at survival.

The pusher grabs the wheelbarrow's handles, Mama grips the sides, and they begin to move. For now, May and I walk on either side. We have a long way to go, and we don't want the boy to tire too quickly. As they say, *there is no light load if one has to carry it for a hundred paces*.

We cross the Garden Bridge. Around us men and women dressed in thickly padded cotton carry everything they own: birdcages, dolls, sacks of rice, clocks, rolled up posters. As we walk along the Bund, I stare across the Whangpoo. Foreign cruisers gleam in the sun, black clouds streaming from their smokestacks. The *Idzumo* and her accompaniment sit on the water — solid, gray, and still undamaged by Chinese fire. Junks and sampans bob on wakes. Everywhere, even now that war is upon us, coolies trudge back and forth, carrying heavy loads.

We turn right on Nanking Road, where sand and disinfectant have been used to clean away the blood and stink of death. Eventually, Nanking Road turns into Bubbling Well Road. The tree-shaded street is busy and hard to navigate all the way to the West Train Station, where we see people loaded onto railroad cars on four levels: the floors, the seats, the berths, and the roofs. Our pusher keeps going. Surprisingly quickly, concrete and granite give way to rice and cotton fields. Mama pulls out snacks for us to eat, making sure to give our pusher a generous portion. We stop a few times to relieve ourselves behind a bush or a tree. We walk through the heat of the day. I look back every once in a while and see smoke billowing from Chapei and Hongkew, and I wonder idly when the fires will burn themselves out.

Blisters form on our heels and toes, but we haven't thought to bring bandages or medicine. When the shadows grow long, the pusher — without asking our opinions — turns down a dirt path that leads to a small farmhouse with a thatched roof. A tethered horse nibbles yellow beans from a bucket, and chickens peck the ground before the open door. As the pusher sets down the wheelbarrow and shakes out his arms, a woman emerges from the house.

"I have three women here," our pusher says in his rough country dialect. "We need food and a place to sleep."

The woman doesn't speak but motions us to come inside. She pours hot water into a tub and points to May's and my feet. We take off our shoes and put our feet in the water. The woman returns with an earthenware jar. She uses her fingers to slather a foul-smelling homemade poultice on our broken blisters. Then she turns her attention to Mama. She helps my mother to a stool in the corner of the room, pours more hot water into a tub, and then stands in such a way that she shields Mama from us. Even so, I can see Mama bend over and begin to unwrap her bindings. I turn away. Mama's care of her feet is the most private and intimate thing she can do. I've never seen them naked, and I don't want to.

Once Mama's feet are washed and wrapped in clean bindings, the woman sets to making dinner. We give her some of our rice, which she pours into a pot of boiling water, and she begins the constant stirring that will turn the two ingredients into *jook*.

For the first time, I allow myself to look around. The place is filthy, and I dread eating or drinking anything in this room. The woman seems to sense this. She puts empty bowls and tin soupspoons on the table along with a pot of hot water. She gestures to us.

"What does she want us to do?" May asks.

Mama and I don't know, but our wheelbarrow pusher picks up the pot, pours it into the bowls, dips our spoons in the hot water, swirls the liquid, and then tosses the water on the hard-packed earthen floor, where it's absorbed. The woman then serves us the *jook*, onto which she floats some stir-fried carrot greens. The greens are bitter in the mouth and sour on swallowing. The woman steps away and returns a moment later with some dried fish, which she drops into May's bowl. Then she stands behind May and kneads her shoulders.

I have a flash of irritation. This woman — poor, obviously uneducated, and a total stranger — gave the wheelbarrow pusher the largest bowl of *jook*, provided Mama with privacy, and now frets over May. What is it about me that even strangers recognize as not being worthy?

105

After dinner, our pusher goes outside to sleep by his wheelbarrow, while we stretch out on straw mats laid on the floor. I'm exhausted, but Mama seems to burn with a deep fire. The petulance that's always been so much a part of her character disappears as she talks about her own childhood and the house where she was raised.

"In the summer when I was a girl, my mama, aunties, my sisters, and all my girl cousins used to sleep outside on mats just like this," Mama remembers, speaking low so as not to disturb our hostess, who rests on a raised platform by the stove. "You've never met my sisters, but we were a lot like the two of you." She laughs ruefully. "We loved each other and we knew how to argue. But on those summer nights when we were out under the sky, we didn't fight. We listened to my mother tell us stories."

Outside cicadas hum. From the far distance comes the concussion of bombs being dropped on our home city. The explosions reverberate through the ground and into our bodies. When May whimpers, Mama says, "I guess you're not too old to hear one now . . ."

"Oh, yes, Mama, please," May urges. "Tell us the one about the moon sisters."

Mama reaches over and pats May lovingly. "In ancient days," she begins in a voice that transports me back to my childhood, "two sisters lived on the moon. They were wonderful girls." I wait, knowing exactly what she'll say next. "They were beautiful like May — slender as bamboo, graceful as willow branches swaying in the breeze, with faces like the oval seeds of a melon.

106

And they were clever and industrious like Pearl — embroidering their lily shoes with ten thousand stitches. All night the sisters embroidered, using their seventy embroidery needles. Their fame grew, and soon people on earth gathered to stare at them."

I know by heart the fate that awaits the two mythical sisters, but I feel Mama wants us to hear the story differently tonight.

"The two sisters knew the rules for maidenly conduct," she goes on. "No man should see them. No man should *stare* at them. Each night, they became more and more unhappy. The older sister had an idea. 'We shall change places with our brother.' The younger sister wasn't so sure, for she had a tiny bit of vanity in her, but it was her duty to follow her *jie jie*'s instructions. The sisters put on their most beautiful red gowns embroidered with dragons dashing through fiery blooms and went to visit their brother, who lived in the sun. They asked to trade places with him."

May, who's always liked this part, picks up the story. "'More people walk the earth by day than by night,' their brother scoffed. 'You will have more eyes on you than ever before.'"

"The sisters wept, much like you used to, May, when you wanted something from your father," Mama continues.

Here I am, lying on a dirt floor in some hovel, listening to my mother trying to comfort us with childhood stories, and my heart wrinkles with bitter thoughts. How can Mama talk about Baba so easily? As bad as he is — was? — shouldn't she be grieving? And, worse, how can she choose this time to remind me that I'm less precious to him? Even when I cried, Baba never gave in to my tears. I shake my head, trying to expel the unkind thoughts I have about my father when I should be worrying about him, and telling myself that I'm too tired and scared to be thinking properly. But it hurts, even in this moment of hardship, to know I'm not as loved as my sister.

"The brother adored his sisters and finally agreed to change places with them," Mama says. "The sisters packed up their embroidery needles and went to their new home. Down on earth, the people looked up and saw a man in the moon. 'Where are the sisters?' they asked. 'Where have they gone?' Now when anyone looks at the sun, the sisters use their seventy embroidery needles to stab at those who dare to stare too long. Those who refuse to turn away go blind."

May lets her breath out slowly. I know her so well. In moments she'll be asleep. From the platform in the corner, our hostess grunts. Did she not like the story either? I ache all over, and now my heart aches too. I close my eyes to keep the tears from falling.

Soaring Through the Night Sky

The next morning, the woman boils water so we can wash our faces and hands. She makes tea and gives us each another bowl of *jook*. She smears more of her country medicine on our feet. She gives us old but clean footbinding cloths to use as bandages. Then she follows us outside and helps my mother back into the wheelbarrow. Mama tries to pay her, but she waves it away, refusing even to look at us again she's so insulted.

All that morning we walk. Mist hovers above the fields. The smell of rice cooking over straw fires wafts to us from the villages we pass. May's green hat and my hat with the feathers — both saved during Old Man Louie's rampage — were carefully packed, so as the day wears on our skin parches and burns. Eventually May and I join Mama in the wheelbarrow. Our pusher never complains, never threatens to abandon us, never asks for more money. He stoically just keeps putting one foot in front of the other.

In the late afternoon, just as the day before, he turns down a pathway toward a farm that seems even poorer than the last one. The wife sorts seeds with a sleeping baby tied to her back. A couple of sickly children do other chores with extreme lassitude. The husband looks us over, calculating how much he should charge. When his eyes find my mother's feet, he grins toothlessly. We pay more than we should for some dry patties made from ground corn.

Mama and May fall asleep before I do. I stare at the ceiling. I listen to a rat skitter along the walls of the room, stopping to gnaw on this and that. My whole life I was spoiled with what I ate, what I wore, where I slept, how I moved from one place to another. Now I think how easy it would be for May, my mother, me, and people like us — privileged and cared for — to die out here on the road. We don't know what it means to get by on almost nothing. We don't know what it takes to survive day to day. But the family that lives here and the woman who took us in last night do. When you don't have much, having less isn't so bad.

The next morning we walk around a village that's been burned to the ground. On the road we see those who tried unsuccessfully to escape: men bayoneted and shot, babies abandoned, and women, wearing only tunics, with the bottom halves of their bodies exposed and their bloody legs splayed at odd angles. Just after noon, we pass dead Chinese soldiers moldering in the hot sun. One is curled into a ball. The back of his hand rests in his mouth as if in his last moments he was biting back pain.

How far have we gone? I don't know. Maybe fifteen miles a day? How far do we have to go? None of us knows that either. But we have to keep going and hope that we don't encounter any Japanese before we reach the Grand Canal.

That evening, our pusher repeats his pattern of turning down a dirt path toward a shack, only this time the people are gone, as though they just stepped out. But all of their belongings seem to be here, including their chickens and ducks. Our pusher rummages through the shelves until he finds a jar of salted turnips. We watch — useless and helpless — as he makes the rice. How is it that after three full days together we still don't know his name? He's older than May and me but younger than my mother. Still, we call him Boy, and he responds with the respect his low position requires. After we've eaten, he looks around until he finds some mosquito incense, which he lights. Then he goes outside to sleep by the wheelbarrow. We go into the other room, which has a bed made from two sawhorses and three wooden planks. Mats stretch across the boards, and a quilt stuffed with cotton batting lies at the foot of the bed. It's too hot to sleep under the quilt, but we roll it out over the mats so we'll have a little padding between our bones and hardness.

That night the Japanese come. We hear the scuffling of their boots, their harsh, guttural voices, and the wheelbarrow pusher's cries for mercy. Whether on purpose or not, his suffering and death give us time to hide. But we're in a two-room shack. Where can we conceal ourselves? Mama tells us to take the planks from the sawhorses and lean them against the wall.

"Slide in behind," she orders. May and I look at each other. *What's Mama thinking?* "Do it!" she hisses. "Do it now!"

Once May and I get behind the planks, Mama reaches in. She holds her bride-price bag and our papers wrapped in silk. "Take these."

"Mama —"

"*Shhh!*"

She grabs my hand and wraps it around the bag and package. We hear her scrape one of the sawhorses across the floor. The planks push up against my sister and me, forcing us to turn our faces to the side. That's how tight a space Mama has made. But we're hardly hidden. It will be only a matter of time before the soldiers find us.

"Stay here," she whispers. "Don't come out no matter what you hear." She grabs my wrist and shakes it. She switches to the Sze Yup dialect, not wanting May to understand. "I mean it, Pearl. Stay here. Don't let your sister move from this place."

We hear Mama leave the room and shut the door. Next to me May takes shallow breaths. Each exhale falls on my face warm and moist. My heart thumps in my chest.

From the other room we hear the door being kicked open, the stomp of boots, loud military voices, and soon enough Mama pleading and bargaining with the soldiers. At one point, the door to this room swings open. Lantern light flickers in from the sides of our hiding place. Mama screams — sharp and shrill — the door shuts, and the light goes away.

"Mama," May mewls.

"You have to be quiet," I whisper.

We hear grunting and laughing, but nothing from our mother. Is she already dead? If she is, then they'll come in here. Don't I have to do something to give my sister a chance? I drop the things Mama gave me, and then I slide to my left.

"No!"

"*Quiet!*"

In our flattened space, May holds on to my arm with one hand.

"Don't go out there, Pearl," she pleads. "Don't leave me."

I jerk my arm, and May's hand falls away. As quietly as possible, I edge out from behind the planks. Without hesitation I walk to the door, open it, step into the main room, and close the door behind me.

Mama's on the floor with a man inside her. I'm struck by how thin her calves are, the result of nearly a lifetime of walking — rather, not walking — on her bound feet. Another dozen or so soldiers in yellow uniforms, leather shoes, and carrying rifles slung over their shoulders stand around, watching, waiting their turns.

Mama groans when she sees me.

"You promised you would stay where you were." Her words are weak with pain and sorrow. "It was my honor to save you."

The dwarf bandit atop my mother slaps her. Strong hands grab me and pull me this way and that. Who will get me first? The strongest? The man in my mother suddenly stops what he's doing, pulls up his trousers, and bullies his way through the others to try to seize me for his prize.

"I told them I was alone," Mama mutters in despair. She tries to stand but gets only as far as her knees.

In the insanity of the moment, somehow I remain calm.

"They can't understand you," I say, coolly, unfazed, not thinking for fear.

"I wanted you and May to be safe," Mama says as she weeps.

Someone pushes me. A couple of the soldiers go back to Mama and hit her on the head and shoulders. They shout at us. Maybe they don't want us talking, but I'm not sure. I don't know their language. Finally one of the soldiers tries English.

"What is the old woman saying? Who else are you hiding?"

I see greed in his eyes. There are so many soldiers and only two women, one of whom is a mother.

"My mother is upset because I didn't stay hidden," I answer in English. "I am her only child." I don't have to pretend to weep. I begin to sob, terrified of what's going to happen next.

There are certain moments when I fly away, when I leave my body, the room, the earth, and just soar through the night sky searching for people and places I love. I think of Z.G. Would he see what I've done as a supreme act of filial piety? I think of Betsy. I even think of my Japanese student. Is Captain Yamasaki nearby, aware that it's me, hoping that May will be discovered? Is he thinking about how he wanted her as a wife but now he could have her as a war trophy?

My mother's beaten, but even her blood and her screams don't stop the soldiers. They unwrap her feet, the bindings swirling through the air like acrobats' ribbons. Her feet look the color of a corpse gone cold — bluish white with shades of green and purple beneath the crushed flesh.

The soldiers pull and prod them. Then they stomp on her feet to try to bring them back into "normal" shape. Her cries are not those of foot-binding or childbirth. They're the deep, anguished screams of an animal experiencing agony beyond comprehension.

I close my eyes and try to ignore everything they're doing, but my teeth itch to bite the man on top of me. In my mind I keep seeing the bodies of the women we passed on the road earlier today, not wanting to see my own legs in those unnatural, inhuman angles. I feel tearing — not like on my wedding night — but something much worse, something searing, as though my insides are being torn apart. The air is thick and gummy with the suffocating smells of blood, mosquito incense, and Mama's exposed feet.

A few times — when Mama's cries are the worst — I open my eyes and see what they're doing to her. *Mama, Mama, Mama*, I want to cry out, but I don't. I won't give these monkey people the pleasure of hearing my terror. I reach out and grab her hand. How can I describe the look that passes between us? We're a mother and daughter being raped repeatedly, for all we know until we both die. I see in her eyes my birth, the endless tragedies of mother love, a total absence of hope, and then somewhere deep, deep in those liquid pools a fierceness I've never seen before.

The whole time I silently pray that May will stay hidden, that she won't make a sound, that she won't be tempted to peek out the door, that she won't do anything stupid, because the one thing I won't be able to bear is for her to be in this room with these . . . men. Pretty soon I don't hear Mama anymore. I lose all awareness of where I am and even what's happening to me. All I feel is pain.

The front door scrapes open, and I hear the sound of more boots tramping on the hard-packed earth. The whole thing is horrible, but this is my worst moment, knowing that there's more to come. But I'm wrong. A voice — angry, authoritative, and as rough as grating gears — bellows at the men. They scramble to their feet. They adjust their trousers. They smooth their hair and wipe their mouths with the backs of their hands. Then they stand at attention and salute. I lie as still as possible, hoping they'll think I'm dead. The new voice yelps out orders — or is it a reprimand? The other soldiers bluster.

The cold edge of a bayonet or a saber presses against my cheek. I don't react. A boot kicks me. Again, I don't want to react — *be dead, be dead, be dead, and maybe it won't begin again* — but my body curls in on itself

116

like a wounded caterpillar. No laughing this time, only terrible silence. I wait for the stab of the bayonet.

I feel a wave of cool air and then the soft settling of cloth over my naked body. The gruff soldier — directly above me, I realize, as he shouts his orders and I hear the shuffling of boots when the others file out — reaches down, adjusts the cloth over my hip, and then leaves.

For a long while, black silence fills the room. Then I hear Mama shift her weight and moan. I'm still afraid, but I whisper, "Be still. They may come back."

Maybe I only think I whisper this, because Mama doesn't seem to pay attention to my warning. I hear her creep closer, and then I feel her fingers on my cheek. Mama, whom I've always thought of as physically weak, pulls me onto her lap. She leans back against the mud wall of the shack.

"Your father named you Pearl Dragon," Mama says, as she smoothes my hair, "because you were born in the Year of the Dragon and the Dragon likes to play with a pearl. But I liked the name for another reason. A pearl grows when a piece of sand lodges in the oyster. I was young, just fourteen, when my father arranged my marriage. That husband-wife thing we have to do was my duty and I did it, but what your father put inside me was as unpleasant as sand. But look what happened. My Pearl came out."

She hums for a while. I feel drowsy. My whole body aches. Where is May?

"There was a typhoon the day you were born," Mama suddenly goes on, switching to Sze Yup, the language of my childhood and the language that keeps secrets from May. "It is said that a Dragon born in a storm will have a particularly tempestuous fate. You always believe you are right, and this makes you do things you shouldn't —"

"Mama —"

"Just listen to me this one time . . . and then try to forget . . . everything." She leans down and whispers in my ear. "You're a Dragon, and of all the signs only a Dragon can tame the fates. Only a Dragon can wear the horns of destiny, duty, and power. Your sister is merely a Sheep. You have always been a better mother to her than I have." I stir, but Mama holds me still. "Don't argue with me now. We don't have time for that."

Her voice sounds beautiful. Never before have I felt her mother love so strongly. My body relaxes in her arms, slowly drifting into darkness.

"You have to take care of your sister," Mama says. "Promise me, Pearl. Promise me right now."

I promise. And then, after what seems like days and weeks and months, blackness comes over my eyes.

Eating Wind and Tasting Waves

I wake once to find a moist cloth wiping my face. I open my eyes and there's May — as pale, beautiful, and tremulous as a spirit. I see the sky above her. Are we dead? I close my eyes again and feel myself lurching and bumping.

The next thing I know I'm on a boat of some kind. I fight hard to stay awake this time. I look to my left and see netting. I look to my right and see land. The boat moves in a steady *pull, pull, pull*. The lack of waves tells me we aren't on the ocean. I lift my head and see a cage just beyond my feet. Inside, a boy of about six — retarded, insane, diseased? — twitches and shimmies. I close my eyes and let myself be lulled by the steady rhythm of the boat as it's rowed through the water.

I don't know how many days we travel. Momentary images tear across my eyes and echo in my ears: the moon and the stars above, the incessant croaking of frogs, the sorrowful sound of a *pi-pa* being played, the splash of an oar, the raised voice of a mother calling to a child, the crack of rifle shots. Into the anguished hollows of my mind, I hear a voice say, "Is it true that dead men float facedown in water but women look to the sky?" I don't know who asked the question or if it was asked at all, but I'd prefer to stare down into an eternity of watery blackness.

Once I lift my arm to block the sunlight and feel something heavy slide toward my elbow. It's my mother's jade bracelet, and I know she's dead. My insides boil with fever, while my skin shivers uncontrollably with cold. Gentle hands lift me. I'm in a hospital. Soft voices say words like "morphine," "lacerations," "infection," "vagina," and "surgery." Whenever I hear my sister's voice, I feel safe. When I don't, I despair.

Finally, I come back from my wandering among the nearly dead. May dozes in a chair by the hospital bed. Her hands are so thickly bandaged that she looks like she has two huge white paws lying in her lap. A doctor — a man — stands over me and puts a forefinger to his lips. He jerks his head in May's direction and whispers, "Let her sleep. She needs it."

When he leans over me, I try to pull away, but my wrists have been tied to the bed rails.

"You've been delirious for some time and you fought us pretty hard," he says gently. "But you're safe now." He puts a hand on my arm. He's Chinese, but a man nevertheless. I fight the urge to scream. He looks into my eyes, searching, and then he smiles. "Your fever's gone. You're going to live."

In the coming days, I learn that May put me in the wheelbarrow and pushed me herself until we reached the Grand Canal. Along the way, she discarded or sold much of what we'd brought with us. Now our sole possessions are three outfits apiece, our papers, and what remains of Mama's dowry. At the Grand Canal, May used some of Mama's money to hire a fisherman and his family to take us on their sampan to Hangchow. I was near death by the time she got me to the hospital. When they took me in for surgery, other doctors worked on May's hands, which were blistered and worn raw from pushing the wheelbarrow. She paid for our treatment by selling some of Mama's wedding jewelry at a local pawnshop.

Gradually May's hands heal, but I require another two surgeries. One day the doctors come in with grim faces to tell me they doubt I'll ever be able to have children. May weeps, but I don't. If having a baby means doing the husband-wife thing again, I'd rather die. *Never again*, I tell myself. *Never ever again will I do that thing*.

After nearly six weeks in the hospital, the doctors finally agree to discharge me. With this news, May disappears to make arrangements for us to go to Hong Kong. On the day she's to pick me up, I step into the bathroom to change. I've lost a lot of weight. The person who stares back at me in the mirror looks no more than twelve years old — tall, gawky, and skinny — but with hollowed-out cheeks and dark circles under the eyes. My bob has grown out, and my hair hangs limp and dull. The days spent under the sun without benefit of an umbrella or a hat have left my skin ruddy and tough. How infuriated Baba would be if he saw me now. My arms are so emaciated that my fingers look overly long, like talons. The Western-style dress I put on hangs on me like loose drapery.

When I come out of the bathroom, May's sitting on my bed, waiting. She takes one look at me and tells me to take off the dress.

"A lot has happened while you've been recovering," she says. "The monkey people are like ants looking for syrup. They're everywhere." She hesitates. She hasn't wanted to talk about what happened that night in the shack, for which I'm grateful, but it hangs between us with every word, every look. "We need to fit in," she goes on with false brightness. "We need to look like everyone else."

She sold one of Mama's bracelets and used the money to buy two changes of clothes: native black linen trousers, loose blue jackets, and kerchiefs to cover our hair. She hands me a set of the rough peasant clothes. I've never had any shyness around May. She's my sister, but I don't think I can bear for even her to see me naked now. I take the clothes and go back into the bathroom.

"And I have one other idea," she calls from the opposite side of the closed and locked door. "I can't say it's my own and I don't know if it will work. I heard it from two Chinese missionary ladies. I'll wait until you get out here to show you."

This time when I stare in the mirror I almost laugh. In the last two months I've changed from a beautiful girl into a pitiful peasant, but when I come out of the bathroom, May doesn't comment on how I look. She just motions me to the bed. She pulls out a jar of cold cream and a tin of cocoa powder and sets them on my night table. From my breakfast tray — she frowns when she sees I haven't eaten anything *again* — she takes the spoon, scoops out some of the cold cream, and drops two big dollops of it on the tray.

"Pearl, pour some of the cocoa powder in here." I look at her quizzically. "Trust me," she says and smiles. I shake the powder into the jar, and she begins to stir the disgusting combination. "We're going to wear this on our hands and faces, so we'll look darker, more country."

It's a clever idea, but my skin is already dark and that didn't save me from the soldiers' madness. Still, from the moment I leave the hospital, I wear May's concoction.

While I was in the hospital, May found a fisherman who's discovered a new and better way of making a fortune than looking beneath the waves by transporting refugees on the waves from Hangchow to Hong Kong. When we board his boat, we join another dozen or so passengers in a small and very dark hold once used for storing fish. Our only light comes from between the slats of the deck above us. The lingering smell of fish is overpowering, but we set to sea, tossing in the tail of a typhoon. It doesn't take long before people get seasick. May has it the worst.

On our second day out, we hear shouts. A woman next to me begins to weep. "It's the Japanese," she cries. "We're all going to die."

If she's right, I won't give them a chance to rape me again. I'll throw myself overboard first. The hold echoes with the sound of heavy boots above us. Mothers hug their babies to their breasts to muffle any sounds. Across from me, an infant's arm jerks desperately as he struggles to take a breath.

May rummages through our bags. She pulls out the last of our cash and divides it into three stacks. One she folds and wedges into the wooden slats of the ceiling. She hands me a few of the bills. I follow her lead as she tucks her money up under her kerchief. Hurriedly, she pulls Mama's bracelet off my wrist, takes off her earrings, and adds them to what's left in Mama's dowry bag. This she jams into a crack between the hull and the platform on which we sit. Finally, she reaches into our travel bag and brings out her cold-cream mixture. We smear an extra coating on our faces and hands.

The hatch opens, and light streams down on us.

"Come up here!" a voice demands in Chinese.

We do as we're told. Fresh, salty air blows on my face. The sea thrums under my feet. I'm too frightened to look up.

"It's all right," May whispers. "They're Chinese."

But these aren't sea inspectors, fishermen, or even other refugees being transferred from one boat to another. They're pirates. On land our countrymen are taking advantage of the war by looting areas under attack. Why should the sea be any different? The other travelers are terrified. They don't yet realize that the theft of money and belongings is nothing.

The pirates search the men and take whatever jewels and money they find. Unsatisfied, the head pirate orders the men to strip. At first they hesitate, but when he shakes his rifle, the men do as they're told. More money and jewels are found tucked into the cracks of rear ends, sewn into the hems or linings of clothes, or hidden in the soles of shoes.

It's hard to explain how I feel. The last time I saw men naked . . . But here are my countrymen — cold, scared, trying to cover their private parts with their hands. I don't want to look at them, but I do. I feel confused, bitter, and strangely triumphant to see men reduced to such weakness.

Then the pirates ask the women to hand over whatever they're hiding. Having seen what happened to the men, the women promptly obey. Without regret, I reach into my kerchief and pull out the bills. Our valuables are gathered, but the pirates aren't dumb.

"You!"

I jump, but he isn't addressing me.

"What are you hiding?"

"I work on a farm," a girl standing to my right says, her voice trembling.

"A farm girl? Your face, hands, and feet deny that!"

It's true. She wears peasant clothes, but her face is pale, her hands pretty, and she wears new saddle oxfords. The pirate helps the girl off with her clothes until all she wears is a napkin and belt. That's when we all know for sure that she's lying. A farm girl can't afford Western-style napkins. She'd use coarse grass paper like any other poor woman.

How is it that in times like these we can't help but look? I don't know, but again I look — partly afraid for myself and May, partly curious. The pirate takes the napkin and slits it open with his knife. He comes away with just fifteen dollars Hong Kong money.

Disgusted by his measly haul, the pirate tosses the napkin into the sea. He looks from woman to woman, decides we aren't worth the bother, and then motions to a couple of his men to search the hold. They return a few minutes later, say a few menacing words, jump back onto their boat, and chug away. People rush to be first to scramble down into the stinky hold to see what's been taken. I stay on the deck. Soon enough, faster than I could imagine, I hear cries of dismay.

A man rushes back up the ladder, takes three giant steps across the deck, and flings himself overboard. Neither the fisherman nor I have a chance to do anything. The man bobs in the waves for a minute or so, and then he disappears.

Every day since waking up in the hospital I've wanted to die, but watching that man sink below the waves, I feel something inside me rise up. A Dragon doesn't surrender. A Dragon fights fate. This is not some loud, roaring feeling. It feels more like someone blew on an ember and found a slight orange glow. I have to hang on to my life — however ruined and useless. Mama's voice comes floating to me, reciting one of her favorite sayings, "There is no catastrophe except death; one cannot be poorer than a beggar." I want — *need* — to do something braver and finer than dying.

I go to the hatch and climb down the ladder. The fisherman clamps and locks the hatch. In the sepulchral light I find May. I sit down next to her. Wordlessly, she shows me Mama's dowry bag, and then she glances up. I follow her gaze. The last of our money is still safe in the crevice.

A few days after we arrive in Hong Kong, we read that the areas surrounding Shanghai have been under attack all this time. The reports are almost too much to bear. Chapei has been bombed and burned to the ground. Hongkew, where we lived, hasn't fared much better. The French Concession and the International Settlement — as foreign territories — are still safe. In a city where there isn't room for another rat, more and more refugees arrive. According to the paper, the foreign concessions' quarter-million residents are flummoxed by the crowding caused by three and a half million refugees living on the streets and in converted movie theaters, dance halls, and racecourses. Those concessions — surrounded as they are on all sides by the dwarf bandits — are now being called the Lonely Island. The terror hasn't been limited to Shanghai. Every day brings news of women being abducted, raped, or killed throughout China. Canton, not so far from us here in Hong Kong, suffers from heavy air raids. Mama wanted us to go to Baba's home village, but what will we find once we get there? Will it be burned to the ground? Will anyone be alive? Will our father's name mean anything anymore in Yin Bo?

We live in a hotel on Hong Kong's waterfront. It's dirty, dusty, and louse-ridden. The mosquito netting is sooty and ripped. The things we ignored in Shanghai are all too vivid here: families crouched on street corners with their worldly goods spread on a blanket before them, hoping someone will stop to buy. Nevertheless, the British act as though the monkey people will never come to the colony. "We aren't involved in this war," they say in their crisp accents. "The Japs dare not attack here." With so little money, we're reduced to eating stewed rice bran, a meal often given to pigs. The bran scratches the throat on the way in and is ruinous on the way out. We have no skills, and no one has need for beautiful girls, because there's no point in promoting beautiful girls when the world's turning ugly.

Then one day we see Pockmarked Huang get out of a limousine and bound up the steps of the Peninsula Hotel. There's no mistaking him. We go back to our hotel and lock ourselves in our room. We try to figure out what his presence in Hong Kong means. Has he come here to escape the war? Has he moved the Green Gang's operations here? We don't know, and we don't have a safe way to find out. But no matter what, his reach his great. If he's here in the south, then he'll find us.

Out of options, we go to the Dollar Steamship Line office, exchange our original tickets, and procure spots in special second class on the *President Coolidge* for the twenty-day voyage to San Francisco. We don't think about what will happen once we get there, finding our husbands, or anything like that. We're just trying to stay out of the Green Gang's net and stay ahead of the Japanese.

On the ship, my fever comes back. I stay in our cabin and sleep for most of the journey. May's plagued with seasickness, so she spends most of her time outside in the fresh air on the second-class deck. She speaks of a young man who's going to Princeton to study.

"He's in first class, but he comes to our deck to see me. We walk and talk, and walk and talk some more," she reports. "I've fallen for him like a ton of bricks." It's the first time I've heard the American phrase, and it strikes me as odd. This boy must be very Westernized. No wonder May likes him.

Sometimes May doesn't come back to the room until very late at night. Sometimes she climbs to the top bunk and goes right to sleep, but sometimes she crawls into the narrow bed with me and wraps her arms around me. She matches her breathing to mine and falls asleep. I lie awake then, afraid to move out of fear of waking her, and worrying, worrying, worrying. May seems very smitten with this boy, and I wonder if she's doing the husband-wife thing with him. But how could she when she's so seasick? How could she, period? And then my thoughts spiral to even darker places.

Many people wish to go to America. Some will do anything to get there, but going to America was never my dream. For me, it's just a necessity, another move after so many mistakes, tragedies, deaths, and one foolish decision after another. All May and I have left is each other. After everything we've been through, our tie is so strong that not even a sharp knife could sever it. All we can do now is continue down the road we're on, wherever it takes us.

Shadows on the Walls

The night before we land, I pull out the coaching book Sam gave me and leaf through it. The book says that Old Man Louie was born in America and that Sam, one of five brothers, was born in China in 1913, the Year of the Ox, during one of his parents' visits to their home village of Wah Hong, which makes him an American citizen because he was born to one. (He'd have to be an Ox, I think dismissively. Mama said that those born under this sign lack imagination and are forever pulling the burdens of the world.) Sam went back to Los Angeles with his parents, but in 1920, the old man and his wife decided to go China again and then leave their son, only seven years old, in Wah Hong with his paternal grandparents. (This is something different from what I'd been led to believe. I had thought Sam came to China with his father and brother to find a bride, but he was already there. I suppose this explains why he spoke to me in the Sze Yup dialect instead of English on the three occasions we met, but why hadn't the Louies told us any of that?) Now Sam has returned to America for the first time in seventeen years. Vern was born in Los Angeles in 1923, the Year of the Boar, and has lived there all his life. The other brothers were born in 1907, 1908, and 1911 — all of them born in Wah Hong, all of them now living in Los Angeles. I do my best to memorize the tiny details — the various birth dates, the addresses in Wah Hong and Los Angeles, and the like — tell May the things I think are important, then put the rest out of my mind.

The next morning, November 15, we get up early and put on our best Western-style dresses. "We're guests in this country," I say. "We should look like we belong." May agrees, and she slips into a dress that Madame Garnet made for her a year ago. How is it that the silk and buttons made it all the way here without being soiled or ruined, while I . . .? I have to stop thinking that way.

We gather our things and give our two bags to the porter. Then May and I go outside and find a spot by the rail, but we can't see much in the rain. Above us, the Golden Gate Bridge is draped in clouds. To our right, the city perches on the shore — wet, dreary, and insignificant compared with Shanghai's Bund. Below us on the open-air steerage deck, what seems like hundreds of coolies, rickshaw pullers, and peasants push and shove against one another in a writhing mass, the smell of their wet and stinking clothes wafting up to us.

The ship docks at a pier. Little family groups from first and second class — laughing, jostling, and happy to have arrived — show their papers and then walk down a gangplank covered to protect them from the rain. When our turn comes, we hold out our papers. The inspector looks them over, frowns, and motions to a crew member.

"These two need to go to the Angel Island Immigration Station," he says.

We follow the crewman through the corridors of the ship and down flights of stairs to where the air is dank. I'm relieved when we step outside again until I see that we're now with the steerage passengers. Naturally, no umbrellas or awnings cover this deck. Cold wind blows rain into our faces and soaks our clothes.

Around us people frantically pore over their coaching books. Then the man next to us tears a page from his book, stuffs it in his mouth, chews for a bit, and swallows it. I hear someone else say that he dropped his book into the waves the night before and another boast that he threw his into the latrine. "Good luck to anyone who wants to look for it now!" Anxiety clenches my stomach. Was I supposed to get rid of the book? Sam didn't tell me that. Now I have no way to get to it, because it's tucked in my hat in our luggage. I take a deep breath and try to reassure myself. We have nothing to be afraid of. We're out of China, away from the war, and in the land of the free and all that.

May and I elbow our way through the smelly laborers to the railing. Couldn't they have washed before we landed? What kind of an impression do they want to give our hosts? May has something else on her mind altogether. She watches the people still filing off the first — and second-class decks, searching for the young man she's been spending time with on the voyage. She grips my arm excitedly when she sees him.

"There he is! That's Spencer." She raises her voice and calls. "Spencer! Spencer! Look up here! Can you help us?"

She waves and calls a few more times, but he doesn't turn to look for her standing at the rail of the third-class deck. Her face tightens as he tips the porters and then strolls with a group of Caucasian passengers into a building to the right.

From deep within the ship, cargo is brought up in big netted bundles and deposited on the pier. From there, most of the cargo goes straight on to the customshouse. Pretty soon, we see those same crates and boxes leave customs and get loaded onto trucks. Duties have been paid and the goods go on their way to new destinations, but we continue to wait in the rain.

Some crewmen hoist another gangplank — this one with no protection from the weather — onto the lower deck, where we are. A *lo fan* in a slicker bounds up the gangplank and climbs onto a crate. "Take everything you brought with you," he shouts in English. "Anything you leave will be thrown away."

People around us mumble, confused.

"What's he saying?"

"Be quiet. I can't hear."

"Hurry up!" the man in the slicker demands. "Chop! Chop!"

"Do you understand him?" a soaked and shivering man next to me asks. "What does he want us to do?"

"Take your belongings and get off the boat."

As we begin doing what we're told, the man in the slicker puts his balled fists on his hips and yells, "And stay together!"

We disembark, with everyone pushing against one another as though it's the most important thing in the world to be the first off the ship. When our feet touch ground, we're marched not into the building to the right, where the other passengers went, but to the left, along the pier, and then across a tiny gangplank and onto a small boat — all without explanation. Once on board, I see that, although there are a few Caucasians and even a handful of Japanese, almost everyone here is Chinese.

The lines are let go, and we pull back into the bay.

"Where are we going now?" May asks.

How can May be so disconnected from what's happening around us? Why can't she pay attention? Why couldn't she have read the coaching book? Why can't she accept what's become of us? That Princeton student, whatever his name is, understood her position perfectly, but May refuses to consider it.

"We're going to the Angel Island Immigration Station," I explain.

"Oh," she says lightly. "All right."

The rain gets heavier and the wind colder. The little boat bobs in the waves. People throw up. May hangs her head over the rail and gulps in wet air. We pass an island in the middle of the bay, and for a few minutes it looks like we're going to chug back under the Golden Gate Bridge, out to sea, and return to China. May

135

moans and tries to stay focused on the horizon. Then the boat veers to the right, curves around another island and into a small inlet, where it pulls up to a wharf at the end of a long dock. Low-slung white wooden buildings nestle on the hillside. Ahead, four stubby palm trees shiver in the wind and the wet flag of the United States slaps noisily against its pole. A large sign reads NO SMOKING. Again everyone pushes to be first off the boat.

"Whites without satisfactory paperwork first!" that same man in the slicker shouts, as though his higher decibels will somehow make the people who don't understand English suddenly fluent, but of course most of the Chinese don't know what he's saying. The white passengers are pulled out of the line and brought forward, while a couple of squat and very solid guards push away the Chinese who've made the mistake of standing at the front of the line. But these *lo fan* don't understand much of what the man in the slicker is saying either. They are, I realize, White Russians. They're lower than the poorest Shanghainese, and yet they're given special treatment! They're led off the boat and escorted into the building. What happens next is even more shocking. The Japanese and Koreans are grouped together and politely led to a different door in the building. "We're ready for you now," the man in the slicker instructs. "When you get off the boat, line up in two lines. Men on the left. Women and children under twelve on the right."

There's a lot of confusion and a lot of manhandling by the guards, but once they line us up the way they want, we're led in the driving rain along the dock to the Administration Building. When the men are sent through one door and the women and children through another — separating husbands from wives and fathers from families — cries of consternation, fright, and worry fill the air. None of the guards shows any sympathy. We are treated more poorly than the cargo that traveled with us.

The separation of Europeans (meaning all whites), Asiatics (meaning anyone from across the Pacific who isn't Chinese), and Chinese continues as we're marched up a steep hill to a medical facility in one of the wooden buildings. A white woman wearing a white uniform and a starched white cap folds her hands in front of her and begins speaking in English in that same loud voice that's somehow supposed to make up for the fact that no one except May and I understands what she's saying.

"Many of you are trying to enter our country with loathsome and dangerous parasitic diseases," she says. "This is unacceptable. The doctors and I are going to check you for trachoma, hookworm, filariasis, and liver fluke."

The women around us start to cry. They don't know what this woman wants, but she's wearing white — the color of death. A Chinese woman in a long white (again!) *cheongsam* is brought in to translate. I've been moderately calm up to now, but as I listen to what these people plan to do to us, I start to tremble. We're to be picked over like rice being prepared for cooking. When we're told to undress, murmurs of distress ripple through the room. Not so long ago I would have snickered with May about the other women's prudishness, because we hadn't been like most Chinese women. We'd been beautiful girls. Good or bad, we'd shown our bodies. But most Chinese women are very private, never exposing themselves publicly and rarely even in private before their husbands or even their daughters.

But whatever looseness I had in the past has disappeared for good. I can't bear to be unclothed. I can't stand to be touched. I cling to May, and she steadies me. Even when the nurse tries to separate us, May stays with me. I bite my lips to keep from screaming when the doctor approaches. I look over his shoulder and out the window. I'm afraid that if I close my eyes I'll be back in that shack with those men, hearing Mama's screams, feeling . . . I keep my eyes wide open. Everything's white and clean . . . well, cleaner than my memories of the shack. I pretend I don't feel the icy chill of the doctor's instruments or the white softness of his hands on my flesh; I stare out across the bay. We face away from San Francisco now, and all I see is gray water disappearing into gray rain. Land has to be out there, but I have no idea how far it is. Once he's done with me, I allow myself to breathe again.

One by one, the doctor makes his examinations while we all wait — shivering from cold and fear — until everyone has given a stool sample. So far we've been separated from other races, then men separated from women, and now we women are separated yet again:

one group to go to the dormitory, one to stay in the hospital for treatment for hookworm, which can be cured, and one for those with liver fluke, to be instantly and without appeal deported back to China. Now the tears really flow.

May and I are in the group that goes to the women's dormitory on the second floor of the Administration Building. Once we're inside, the door is locked behind us. Rows of bunks two across and three high are connected to one another by iron poles attached to the ceiling and floor. There are no "beds" to sleep on, just wire mesh. This means that the frames can be folded up to create more space in the room, but apparently no one wants to sit on the floor. The distance between bunks is barely eighteen inches. The vertical gaps between the bunks are so tight that at first glance I can see I won't be able to extend my arm without hitting the one above. Only the top bunk has enough space to sit upright, but that area is cluttered with drying laundry of the women already here, which hangs on strings tied between the poles at the ends of the bunks. On the floor beneath each occupied tier of bunks are a few tin bowls and cups.

May leaves my side and hurries down the center aisle. She claims two top bunks next to each other near the radiator. She climbs up, lies down, and promptly goes to sleep. No one brings our luggage. All we have with us are the clothes we're wearing and our handbags.

The next morning May and I straighten up as best we can. The guards tell us we're going to a hearing before the Board of Special Inquiry, but the women in the dormitory call it an interrogation. Just the word sounds ominous. One of the women suggests we sip cold water to calm our fear, but I'm not afraid. We have nothing to hide, and this is just a formality.

We're herded with a small group of women into a room that looks like a cage. We sit on benches and stare at one another pensively. We Chinese have a phrase — eating bitterness. I tell myself that, whatever happens with our hearings, it won't be as bad as the physical inspection, and it can't be as bad as what has happened to May and me day after day since the moment Baba announced he had arranged marriages for us.

"Tell them what I told you to say and everything will be fine," I whisper to May as we wait in the cage. "Then we'll be able to leave this place."

She nods thoughtfully. When the guard calls her name, I watch her enter a room and the door close. A moment later, the same guard motions me to another room. I put on a false smile, straighten my dress, and stride in with what I hope is an air of confidence. Two white men — one nearly bald, one with a mustache, and both wearing glasses — sit behind a table in the windowless room. They don't return my smile. At a table set to the side, another white man busily cleans the keys on his typewriter. A Chinese man in an ill-fitting Western-style suit studies a file in his hands, looks at me and then back at the file.

"I see you were born in Yin Bo Village," he says to me in Sze Yup as he passes the file to the bald man. "I am happy to speak to you in the dialect of the Four Districts."

Before I can say that I know English, the bald man says, "Tell her to sit down."

The interpreter motions to a chair. "I am Louie Fon," he goes on in Sze Yup. "Your husband and I share the same clan name and the same home district." He sits to my left. "The bald one before you is Chairman Plumb. The other one is Mr. White. The recorder is Mr. Hemstreet. You don't have to concern yourself with him —"

"Let's get on with it," Chairman Plumb cuts in. "Ask her . . ."

Things go well at first. I know the date and year of my birth in both the Western and the lunar calendars. They ask the name of the village where I was born. Then I name the village where Sam was born and the day we were married. I recite the address where Sam and his family live in Los Angeles. And then . . .

"How many trees are in front of your alleged husband's home in his village?"

When I don't answer right away, four sets of eyes stare at me — curious, bored, triumphant, snide.

"Five trees stand before the house," I answer, remembering what I read in the coaching book. "The right side of the house has no trees. A ginkgo tree grows on the left."

"And how many rooms are in the house where your natal family lives?"

I've been so focused on the answers from Sam's coaching book that I haven't considered they'd ask anything so detailed about me. I try to think what the right answer would be. Count the bathrooms or not? Count before or after the rooms were divided for our boarders?

"Six main rooms —"

Before I can explain myself, they ask how many guests were at my "alleged" wedding.

"Seven," I answer.

"Did you and your guests have anything to eat?"

"We had rice and eight dishes. It was a hotel dinner, not a banquet."

"How was the table set?"

"Western style but with chopsticks."

"Did you serve betel nuts to the guests? Did you pour tea?"

I want to say I'm not a country bumpkin, so under no circumstances would I have served betel nuts. I would have poured tea if I'd had the wedding I'd dreamed of, but that night was hardly festive. I remember how dismissively Old Man Louie waved away my father's suggestion that May and I perform the ritual.

"It was a civilized wedding," I say. "Very Western —"

"Did you worship your ancestors as part of the ceremony?"

"Of course not. I'm Christian."

"Do you have any documentary evidence for your alleged marriage?"

"In my luggage."

"Is your husband expecting you?"

This question momentarily takes me aback. Old Man Louie and his sons know we didn't show up in Hong Kong to take the ship here with them. They certainly notified the Green Gang that we failed to fulfill our part of the contract, but did they tell the Angel Island inspectors any of that? And do the old man and his sons still expect us to arrive?

"My sister and I were delayed in our travels because of the monkey people," I say. "Our husbands long for our arrival."

After the interpreter relays this, the two inspectors speak between themselves, not knowing I understand every word.

"She seems honest enough," Mr. White says. "But her papers claim she's the wife of a legally domiciled merchant *and* the wife of an American citizen. She can't be both."

"This could be an error in past paperwork. Either way, we'd have to let her in." Chairman Plumb grimaces sourly. "But she hasn't proven *either* status. And look at her face. Does she look like a merchant's wife to you? She's so dark. I bet she's worked in rice paddies her entire life."

There it is. The same old complaint. I look down, afraid they'll see the flush creep up my neck. I think of the girl on the boat we took to Hong Kong and how the pirate appraised her. Now these men are doing the same with me. Do I really appear that country?

"But consider how she's dressed. She doesn't look like a laborer's wife either," Mr. White points out.

143

Chairman Plumb thrums his fingers on the table. "I'll let her through, but I want to see her marriage certificate showing she's married to a legitimate merchant or something proving her husband's citizenship." He looks at the interpreter. "On what day are the women allowed to go to the wharf to get things from their luggage?"

"Tuesdays, sir."

"All right then. Let's hold her over until next week. Tell her to bring her marriage certificate next time." He nods to the recorder and begins dictating a synopsis, ending with "We are deferring the case for further investigation."

For five days May and I wear the same clothes. At night we wash our underwear and hang it to dry with the laundry the other women drape above our heads. We still have a little money to buy toothpaste and other toiletries from a small concession stand open during mealtimes. When Tuesday arrives, we line up with women who want to get things from their luggage and are escorted by white missionary women to a warehouse at the end of the wharf. May and I get our marriage papers, and then I check to see if the coaching book is still hidden. It is. No one has bothered to search inside my hat with the feathers. I now pull at the lining and hide it properly. Then I grab fresh undergarments and a change of clothes.

Every morning, embarrassed to be seen naked by the other women, I dress under the blanket on my bed. Then I wait to be called back to the hearing room, but no one comes for us. If we aren't called by nine, then we know nothing will happen that day. When afternoon arrives, a new feeling of anticipation and dread fills the room. At precisely four, the guard enters and calls, "*Sai gaai*," which is a bastardization of one of the Cantonese dialects for *hou sai gaai*, which means *good fortune*. Then he lists the names of those allowed to get on the boat to complete the final leg of their journey to America. Once the guard approaches a woman and rubs his eyes as though he were crying. He laughs when he tells her she's being sent back to China. We never learn the reason for her deportation.

Over the next few days, we watch as the women who arrived the same day we did are allowed to continue to San Francisco. We see new women land, have their hearings, and leave. Still no one comes for us. Every night, after another disgusting meal of pig knuckles or stewed salted fish with fermented bean curd, I take off my dress under the blanket, hang it on the line above me, and try to sleep, knowing I'll be locked in this room until morning.

But the feeling of being locked in and trapped extends far, far beyond this room. In a different time, in a different place, and with more money, maybe May and I could have escaped our futures. But here we don't have choice or freedom. Our whole lives up to now have been lost to us. We know no one in the United States other than our husbands and our father-in-law. Baba had said that if we went to Los Angeles, we'd live in beautiful houses, have servants, see movie stars, so maybe this is the path May and I

145

were supposed to be on all along. We could consider ourselves lucky we've married so well. Women — whether in arranged marriages or not, whether in the past or right now, in 1937 — have married for money and all that it brings. Still, I have a secret plan. When May and I get to Los Angeles, we'll skim money from what our husbands give us to buy clothes and shoes, beautify ourselves, and keep our households running, and use it to escape. I lie on the wire mesh that is my bed, listen to the low, mournful sound of the foghorn and to the women in the room cry, snore, or whisper among themselves, and plot how May and I will leave Los Angeles one day and disappear to New York or Paris, cities we've been told are equal to Shanghai in splendor, culture, and riches.

Two tuesdays later, when we're allowed to retrieve things from our luggage again, May fishes out the peasant clothes she bought for us in Hangchow. We wear them in the afternoons and at night, because it's too cold and dirty in this place to wear our good dresses, which we put on in the mornings in case we're called to finish our hearings. In the middle of the following week, May takes to wearing our travel clothes all the time.

"What if we're called for an interview?" I ask. We sit on our top bunks with a little valley of space separating us and clothes hanging like banners all around us. "Do you think this is so different from Shanghai? Our clothes matter. Those who are well dressed leave sooner than those who look like . . ." My voice trails off.

"Peasants?" May finishes for me. She folds her arms over her stomach and lets her shoulders fall. She doesn't look like herself. We've been here a month now, and it feels like all the courage she showed getting me to safety has somehow been sucked out of her. Her skin looks pasty. She isn't terribly interested in washing her hair, which, like mine, has grown out into a straggly mess.

"Come on, May, you have to try. We won't be here much longer. Take a shower and put on a dress. You'll feel better."

"Why? Just tell me why. I can't eat their terrible food, so I rarely use their toilets," she says. "I don't do anything, so I don't sweat. But even if I did, why would I take a shower where people can see me? The humiliation is so great I wish I could wear a sack over my head. Besides," she adds pointedly, "I don't see you going to the toilets or showers."

Which is true. Sadness and despair overwhelm those who stay here too long. The cold wind, the foggy days, the shadows on the walls, depress and frighten all of us. In just this month, I've seen many women, some who've already come and gone, refuse to take showers during their entire stays, and not just because they don't sweat. Too many women have committed suicide in the showers by hanging or by sharpening chopsticks and driving them through their ears and into their brains. No one wants to go to the showers not only because no one likes to do her private business with others around but because nearly everyone here is afraid of the ghosts of the dead, who, without proper burial rites, refuse to leave the nasty place where they died.

We decide that, from now on, May will go with me to the communal toilets or showers, check to see if they're empty, and then stand outside the door to keep the other women out. I'll do the same for her, although I'm not sure why she's become so modest since arriving here.

At last the guard calls us for our interrogations. I run a brush through my hair, take a few sips of cold water to calm myself, and slip on my heels. I glance back to see May trailing after me, looking like a beggar magically dropped here from a Shanghai alley. We wait in the cage until our turns come. This is our last step and then we'll be transferred to San Francisco. I give May an encouraging smile, which she doesn't return, and then I follow the guard into the hearing room. Chairman Plumb, Mr. White, and the stenographer are there, but this time I have a new interpreter.

"I'm Lan On Tai," he says. "From now on you will have a different interpreter for each hearing. They don't want us to become friends. I will speak to you in Sze Yup. Do you understand, Louie Chin-shee?"

In the old Chinese tradition a married woman is known by her clan name with *shee* attached to it. This practice can be traced back three thousand years to the Chou dynasty and it's still common with farmers, but I'm from Shanghai!

"That is your name, isn't it?" the interpreter asks. When I don't answer right away, he glances at the white men and then back at me. "I shouldn't tell you this, but your case has problems. It's best if you accept what's in your record. Don't change your story now."

"But I never said my name was —"

"Sit down!" Chairman Plumb orders. Even though I pretended not to know English during our last meeting and now, after the interpreter's warning, feel sure I should stick to my feigned ignorance, I obey, hoping that the chairman will believe the tone in his voice scared me. "In your last interview you said you had a civilized wedding, which is why you didn't worship your ancestors as part of the ceremonies. We have your husband's file right here, and he says you did worship your ancestors."

I wait for the interpreter to relay this, then reply, "I told you before, I'm a Christian. I don't worship ancestors. Perhaps my husband worshipped his after we parted."

"How long were you together?"

"One night." Even I know this sounds bad.

"Do you expect us to believe you were married for one day and now your husband has sent for you?"

"Our marriage was arranged."

"By a matchmaker?"

I try to think how Sam would have responded to this question in his interrogation.

"Yes, a matchmaker."

The interpreter gives a subtle nod to let me know I answered correctly.

"You said you didn't serve betel nuts and tea, but your sister says you did," Chairman Plumb says, tapping another file, which I assume covers May's case.

As I look at the bald man before me, waiting for the interpreter to finish the translation, I wonder if this is a trick. Why would May have said that? She wouldn't.

"Neither my sister nor I served tea or betel nuts."

This is not the answer the two men want. Lan On Tai looks at me with a combination of pity and aggravation.

Chairman Plumb moves on. "You said you had a civilized wedding, but your sister says that neither of you wore a veil."

I'm torn between berating myself and May for not being more diligent in working on our stories and questioning why any of this matters.

"We had civilized weddings," I say, "but neither of us wore veils."

"Did you raise your veil during the wedding banquet?"

"I already told you I didn't wear a veil."

"Why do you say only seven people came to the banquet, when your husband, father-in-law, and sister say there were many occupied tables in the room?"

I feel sick to my stomach. What's happening here?

"We were a small party in a hotel restaurant where other guests were dining."

"You said your family home consists of six rooms, but your sister says many more and your husband stated the house is grand." Chairman Plumb's face turns crimson as he demands, "Why are you lying?"

"There are different ways to count the rooms and my husband —"

"Let's go back to your wedding. Was your wedding banquet on the first floor or upstairs?"

And on it goes: Did I take a train after my marriage? Did I ride on a boat? Are the houses where I lived with my parents built in rows? How many houses stood between our house and the main street? How do I know if I was married according to the old custom or the new custom if I had a matchmaker and didn't wear a veil? Why don't my alleged sister and I speak the same dialect?

The questioning continues for eight straight hours — with no break for lunch or to use the toilet. By the end, Chairman Plumb is red-faced and weary. As he recites his synopsis for the stenographer, I boil with frustration. Every other sentence begins "The applicant's alleged sister states . . ." I can understand — barely — how my responses might be taken to mean something different from those given by Sam or Old Man Louie, but how could May have given such completely different answers from mine?

The interpreter shows no emotion as he translates Chairman Plumb's conclusion: "It would appear that there are many contradictions which should not exist, particularly concerning the home the applicant shared with her alleged sister. While the applicant adequately answers the queries concerning her alleged husband's home village, her alleged sister seems to have no knowledge whatsoever of her husband, his family, or his family home, either in Los Angeles or in China. Therefore it is the unanimous opinion of the board that this applicant, as well as her alleged sister, be re-examined until the contradictions can be resolved." The interpreter then looks at me. "Have you understood everything that's been asked of you?"

I answer, "Yes," but I'm furious — with these awful men and their persistent questioning, with myself for not being smarter, but most of all with May. Her laziness has caused us to be detained even longer on this horrible island.

She isn't in the holding cage when I leave the room and I have to sit there and wait for another woman whose interrogation also hasn't gone well. After another hour, the woman is pulled from her hearing room by her arm. The cage is unlocked and the guard motions to me, but we don't go back to the dormitory on the second floor of the Administration Building. Rather, we walk across the property to another wood-framed building. At the end of the hall is a door with a small window covered with fine mesh and ROOM NO. I printed above it. We may feel like we are in jail on this island and in our locked dormitory, but this is the real door to imprisonment. The woman wails and tries to pull away from the guard, but he's far stronger than she could ever be. He opens the door, pushes her into the darkness, and locks her inside.

I'm now alone with a very large white man. I have nowhere to go, nowhere to escape. I shake uncontrollably. And then the strangest thing happens. His contemptuous sneer melts into something resembling compassion.

"I'm sorry you had to see that," he says. "We're just shorthanded tonight." He shakes his head. "You don't understand a word I'm saying, do you?" He gestures back toward the door we entered. "We need to go that way, so I can take you back to the dormitory," he goes on, elongating and exaggerating the words so that his lips stretch into the twisted features of a temple demon statue. "Got it?"

Later, as I walk the length of the dormitory back to May's and my bunks, my emotions are in a frenzy — yes, that's the word — of anger, fear, and frustration. The other women's eyes follow each step as my high heels click on the linoleum floor. Some of us have lived together for a month now and in very close quarters. We're attuned to one another's moods and know when to back off or offer comfort. Now I feel the women ripple away from me, as though I'm a large boulder that's been dropped into a very peaceful pond.

May perches on the edge of her bunk, her legs dangling. She cocks her head in the way she has since she was a small girl and knew she was in trouble.

"What took so long? I've been waiting for you for hours."

"What have you done, May? What have you *done*?"

She ignores my questions. "You missed lunch. But I brought you some rice."

She opens her hand and shows me a misshapen ball of rice. I slap it from her palm. The women around us look away.

"Why did you lie in there?" I ask. "Why would you do that?"

Her legs swing back and forth like she's a child whose feet don't yet reach the floor. I stare up at her, breathing heavily through my nose. I've never been this angry with her. This isn't a pair of muddied shoes or a borrowed blouse that's been stained.

"I didn't understand what they were saying. I don't know that singsong Sze Yup. I only know the northern song of Shanghai."

"And that's *my* fault?" But even as I say it, I realize I share some responsibility for this. I know she doesn't understand the dialect of our ancestral home. Why didn't I think of that? But the Dragon in me is still stubborn and mad.

"We've been through so much, but you couldn't take five minutes on the ship to look at the coaching book."

When she shrugs, a wave of fury sweeps through me.

"Do you want them to send us back?"

She doesn't respond, but the predictable tears form.

"Is that what you want?" I persist.

Now those predictable tears fall and drip onto her baggy jacket, staining the cloth with slowly spreading blue splotches. But if she's predictable, so am I.

I shake her legs. The older sister, who's always right, demands, "What's wrong with you?"

She mumbles something.

"What?"

She stops swinging her legs. She keeps her face tucked low, but I'm looking up at her and she can't avoid me. She mumbles again.

"Say it so I can hear it," I rasp impatiently.

She tilts her head, meets my eyes, and whispers just loud enough for me to hear. "I'm pregnant."

Isle of the Immortals

May rolls over and buries her face in her pillow to stifle her sobs. I look around, and it seems like the other women are either ignoring us or pretending to ignore us. It's the Chinese way.

I kick off my shoes and climb up the bunk's tiers and onto May's bed.

"I thought you didn't do the husband-wife thing with Vernon," I whisper.

"I didn't," she manages to get out. "I couldn't."

A guard comes in and announces it's time for dinner, and the women scurry to be first out the door. As bad as the food is, dinner is more important than an argument between two sisters. If any edible pieces exist in tonight's meal, they want to be first to get them. After a few minutes, we're alone and no longer have to whisper.

"Was it that boy you met on the ship?" I can't even remember his name.

"It was before that."

Before that? We were in the hospital in Hangchow and then the hotel in Hong Kong. I don't see how anything could have happened during that time, unless it was when I was sick, or earlier, when I was unconscious. Was it one of the doctors who took care of me? Was she raped when we were trying to get to the Grand Canal? I've been too ashamed to talk about what happened to me. Has she kept a similar secret all this time? I creep around the topic by asking what seems like a practical question.

"How long has it been?"

She sits up, rubs her eyes with both hands, and then stares at me with sorrow, humiliation, and pleading. She pulls her legs under her so our knees touch, and then she slowly unbuttons the frogs of her peasant jacket and smoothes her hands over her shirt to reveal her belly. She's pretty far along, which explains why she's been hiding under baggy clothes almost from the moment we arrived at Angel Island.

"Was it Tommy?" I ask, hoping it was.

Mama always wanted May and Tommy to marry. With Tommy and Mama dead, wouldn't this be a gift? But when May says, "He was just a friend," I don't know what to think. My sister went out with a lot of different young men in Shanghai, especially in those last days, when we were so desperate to forget our circumstances. But I don't know their names, and I don't want to interrogate her with questions like "Was it that young man that night at the Venus Club?" or "Was it that American Betsy used to bring around sometimes?" Wouldn't that approach be as ridiculous and stupid as what I've gone through today? But I can't keep my tongue from flapping.

"Was it that student who came to live in the second-floor pavilion?" I don't remember much about him other than that he was thin, wore gray, and kept to himself. What did he study? I can't say, but I haven't forgotten how he hovered over Mama's chair the day of the bombing. Did he do that because he was in love with May, as so many young men were?

"I was already pregnant then," May confesses.

A disgusting thought enters my mind. "Tell me it wasn't Captain Yamasaki." If May's going to have a half-Japanese baby, I don't know what I'll do.

She shakes her head, and I'm relieved.

"You never met him," May says in a quavering voice. "*I* barely met him. It was just a thing I did. I didn't think *this* would happen. If I'd had more time, I would have asked an herbalist to give me something to expel the baby. But I didn't. Oh, Pearl, everything's my fault." She grabs my hands and begins to weep again.

"Don't worry. We'll be all right," I say, trying to sound comforting but knowing it's an empty promise.

"How could we possibly be all right? Haven't you thought about what this means?"

To tell the truth, I haven't. I haven't had months to think about May's condition. I've had barely two minutes.

"We can't go to Los Angeles right away." May pauses and stares at me appraisingly. "You understand we have to go there, right?"

"I haven't seen another way. But even forgetting about this" — I point to her belly — "we don't know if they'll want us anymore."

"Of course they will. They bought us! But there's the problem of the baby. At first I thought I'd be able to get away with it. I didn't do the husband-wife thing with Vernon, but he wasn't going to say anything. Then Old Man Louie went through our sheets —"

"You knew even then?"

"You were there when I threw up in the restaurant. I was so scared. I thought someone would figure it out. I thought you would guess."

Now, as I think about it, I realize many people understood what I was too ignorant and blind to see. The old woman whose house we stopped at on our first night out of Shanghai had taken particular care with May. The doctor in Hangchow had been very solicitous, wanting May to sleep. I'm May's *jie jie*, and I've always thought we are as close as can be, but I've been so concerned with my own miseries — losing Z.G., leaving home, being raped, almost dying, getting here — that I haven't paid attention every time May has thrown up these past weeks and months. I haven't noticed whether or not the little red sister has visited May. And I can't even remember the last time I saw her completely undressed. I've abandoned my sister when she needed me most.

"I'm so sorry —"

"Pearl! You aren't paying attention to what I'm saying! How can we go to Los Angeles now? That boy is not the father and Old Man Louie knows it."

158

All this is happening too fast, and it's been a long, hard day. I haven't eaten since the bowl of *jook* at breakfast, and I'm not going to get dinner. But I'm not so tired and worn out that I don't see May has something in mind. After all, she told me she was pregnant only because I'd gotten mad at her because . . .

"You lied to the board on purpose. You did at the first interview."

"The baby needs to be born here on Angel Island," she says.

I'm the smart sister, but my mind races to keep up with her.

"You were already prepared to lie when the ship sailed into San Francisco," I say finally. "That's why you didn't study the coaching book. You didn't want to answer correctly. You wanted to end up here."

"That's not quite right. I hoped Spencer would help me — us. He made promises on the ship. He said he would take care of things so we wouldn't have to go to Los Angeles. He lied." She shrugs. "Does it surprise you after Baba? My next option was coming here. Don't you see? If I have the baby here, they'll never know it was mine."

"They?"

"The Louies," she says impatiently. "You have to take it. I'm giving him to you. You did the husband-wife thing with Sam. The timing is almost right."

I pull my hands from hers and lean away from her.

"What are you saying?"

159

"The doctors said you probably can't have a baby. This could *save* me and *help* you."

But I don't want a baby — not now, perhaps not ever. I don't want to be married either — at least not through an arrangement or to pay my father's debts. There has to be another way.

"If you don't want it, then give it to the missionaries," I suggest. "They'll take him. They've got that Chinese Babies Aid society they're always talking about. They'll keep it separate from diseased women."

"Pearl! This is my baby! What other ties do we have to Mama and Baba? We're daughters — the end of the line. Couldn't my son be the beginning of a new line here in America?"

Of course we assume the baby is a boy. Like Chinese everywhere, we can't imagine a child other than a son, who will bring great happiness to his family and guarantee that the ancestors are fed in the afterworld. Nevertheless, May's plan will never work.

"I'm not pregnant and I can't have the baby for you," I say, pointing out the obvious.

Once again, May shows how much she's been thinking about all this.

"You'll have to wear the peasant clothes I bought for you. They cover everything. Those country women don't want anyone to see their bodies — not to attract a man, not to show they're with child. You didn't notice how big my stomach had gotten, did you? Later, if you need to, you can put a pillow in your pants. Who's going to look? Who's going to care? But we do have to string out our time here."

160

"For how long?"

"Another four months or so."

I don't know what else to do or say. She's my sister, my only living relative as far as I know, and I promised Mama I'd take care of her. And like that, I make a decision that will affect the rest of my life . . . and May's too.

"All right. I'll do it."

I'm so overwhelmed by everything that's happened today that I don't have the sense to ask how she's going to deliver the baby and not have the authorities know about it.

The harsh reality of what we did by leaving China and coming here hits us hard in the coming weeks. Hopeful — stupid — people call Angel Island the Ellis Island of the West. Those who want to keep the Chinese out of America call it the Guardian of the Western Gate. We Chinese refer to it as the Isle of the Immortals. Time passes so slowly it feels as if we're in the afterworld, that's for sure. The days are long and staggered by a routine that is as expected and unremarkable as evacuating our bowels. Everything's regulated. We have absolutely no choice about when or what we eat, when the lights are turned on or off, when we go to bed or get up. When you're in prison, you lose all privileges.

When May's belly gets larger, we move to a pair of adjacent lower bunks so she won't have to climb so high. Every morning we wake up and dress. The guards escort us to the dining hall — a surprisingly small room given that on some days meals are served to over three

hundred people. Like everything else on Angel Island, the dining hall is segregated. The Europeans, Asiatics, and Chinese all have their own cooks, food, and dining times. We have a half hour to eat breakfast and be completely out of the hall before the next group of detainees arrives. We sit at long wooden tables and eat bowls of *jook*, and then the guards escort us back to our dormitory and lock us in. Some women make tea using hot water from a pot kept atop the radiator. Others munch on food sent by family members in San Francisco: noodles, pickles, and dumplings. Most go back to sleep, waking only when the missionary ladies come to talk to us about their one God and teach us how to sew and knit. One matron feels sorry for me: pregnant and stranded on Angel Island. "Let me send a telegram to your husband," she offers. "Once he knows you're here and in the family way, he'll come and sort out everything for you. You don't want your baby to be born in this place. You'll need a proper hospital."

But I don't want that kind of help, not yet anyway.

For lunch, we go to the dining hall for cold rice topped by bean sprouts that have been steamed to a soggy mess, *jook* with slivered pork, or tapioca soup with crackers. Dinner consists of one large dish — dried tofu and pork, potatoes and beef, lima beans and pork knuckles, or dried greens and sand dabs. They sometimes give us course red-grain rice barely fit to eat. Everything looks and tastes like it's been chewed and swallowed once already. Some women take to putting pieces of meat from their bowls into mine. "For your

son," they say. I then have to find a way to transfer these luxuries to May.

"Why don't your husbands come to visit?" a woman asks us one night at dinner. Her given name is Dustpan, but she goes by the married name of Lee-shee. She's been detained even longer than May and I. "They could hire a lawyer for you. They could explain everything to the inspectors. You could leave tomorrow."

May and I don't answer that our husbands don't know we've arrived and that they can't know until the baby's born, but sometimes I have to admit it would be a comfort to see them — even those nearly total strangers.

"Our husbands are far away," May explains to Lee-shee and the other pitying women. "It's very hard for my sister, especially at this time."

Afternoons pass slowly. While the other women write to their families — people can send and receive as many letters as they want, although they have to pass through a censor's hands — May and I talk. Or we look out a window — covered in wire mesh to make sure we don't escape — and dream of our lost home. Or we work on our sewing and knitting, skills our mother never taught us. We sew diapers and little shirts. We try to knit baby sweaters, caps, and booties.

"Your son will be born a Tiger and will be influenced by the Earth element, which is strong this year," a woman returning from a trip to her home village tells me during her three-day stay on Angel Island. "Your Tiger child will bring happiness and worry at the same time. He'll be charming and bright, curious and inquisitive, affectionate and athletic. You'll have plenty of exercise just keeping up with him!"

May usually remains silent during the advice given to us by the women, but this time she can't help herself. "Will he truly be joyful? Will he have a happy life?"

"Happiness? Here in the Land of the Flowery Flag? I don't know if happiness is possible in this country, but the Tiger has special attributes that could be helpful to your sister's son. If he's disciplined and loved equally, then a Tiger will respond with warmth and understanding. But you can never lie to a Tiger, because he will bound and thrash and do things that are wild and daring."

"But aren't those good characteristics?" May asks.

"Your sister is a Dragon. The Dragon and the Tiger will always fight for dominance. She must hope for a son — and what mother doesn't wish for this thing? — because then their deeper positions will be clear. Every mother must obey her son, even if she is a Dragon. If your sister was a Sheep, I'd be concerned. The Tiger will usually protect its Sheep mother, but they are compatible only during good weather and easy times. Otherwise, the Tiger will leap away from the Sheep or he'll tear her apart."

May and I look at each other. We didn't believe these things when Mama was alive. Why should we start now?

I try to be sociable with detainees who speak the Sze Yup dialect, and my vocabulary improves as I remember words from my childhood, but truly, what's the point in making conversation with these strangers? They never stay long enough for us to become friends, May can't participate because she doesn't understand them, and we both think it best if we keep to ourselves. We continue going to the communal toilets and the showers by ourselves, explaining that we don't want to expose my son to the ghost spirits who linger in those areas. This, of course, doesn't make sense. I'm not safer from ghosts when I go to the showers or toilet with just my sister instead of the group, but the women let it pass, agreeing I have the typical worries of an expectant mother.

The only changes in pattern come with our twice weekly excursions out of the Administration Building. On Tuesdays, we're allowed to retrieve things from our bags on the wharf, and even though we never take anything new, it's a relief to be in the fresh air. On Fridays, the missionary ladies lead us on a walk around the grounds. Angel Island is beautiful in many ways. We see deer and raccoons. We learn the names of the trees: eucalyptus, California live oak, and Torrey pine. We walk past the men's barracks, which are segregated by race not only in the wings or floors but in the exercise yard as well. And while fences topped with barbed wire surround the entire Immigration Station, keeping it separated from whatever else is on the island, the men's exercise yard has double fencing to keep them from escaping. But where could they escape to? Angel Island has been designed like Alcatraz, the island we passed on our way here. That too is an escape-proof prison. Those foolish or daring enough to swim for freedom are usually found days later washed up on a shore far from here. The difference between us and the inmates on the neighboring island is that we've done nothing wrong. Except that we have in the eyes of the *lo fan*.

In the Methodist mission school in Shanghai, our teachers talked about the one God and sin, about the virtues of Heaven and the horrors of Hell, but they hadn't been completely forthright about how their compatriots felt about us. Between the women detainees and the interrogators, we learn that America doesn't want us. Not only can we not become naturalized citizens but the government passed a law in 1882 barring the immigration of all Chinese, except those in four exempt classes: ministers, diplomats, students, and merchants. Whether a Chinese in these exempt classes or an American citizen of Chinese descent, you need to have a Certificate of Identity to land. This document needs to be carried at all times. Are the Chinese singled out for this special treatment? It wouldn't surprise me.

"You can't pretend to be a minister, a diplomat, or a student," Lee-shee explains, as we eat our first Christmas dinner in the new land. "But it's not hard to fake being a merchant."

"That's right," agrees Dong-shee, another married woman, who arrived a week after May and me. She's the one who told us the reason we have brittle wire mesh to sleep on instead of mattresses is that the *lo fan* don't think we'll find beds comfortable. "They don't want farmers like us. They don't want coolies or rickshaw pullers or nightsoil collectors either."

And I think, *What country would?* Those people are a necessity, but did we even want them in Shanghai? (See how sometimes I still don't realize my place in the world?)

"My husband bought a spot in a store," Lee-shee boasts. "He paid five hundred dollars to become a partner. He's not a real partner, and he didn't pay the money either. Who has money like that? But he promised the owner he'd work until he paid his debt. Now my husband can claim he's a merchant."

"And that's why they question us?" I ask. "They're looking for fake merchants? It seems like a lot of trouble —"

"What they really want to catch are paper sons."

Seeing the stupid expression on my face, the two women chuckle. May looks up from her bowl.

"Tell me," she says. "Do they have a joke?"

I shake my head. May sighs and goes back to poking at the pig's foot in her bowl. Across the table, the two women exchange knowing looks.

"You two don't know very much," Lee-shee observes. "Is that why you and your sister have been here for so long? Didn't your husbands explain what you needed to do?"

"We were supposed to travel with our husbands and my father-in-law," I answer truthfully. "We got separated. The monkey people —"

They nod sympathetically.

"You can also enter America if you're the son or daughter of an American citizen," Dong-shee goes on. She's barely touched her food, and the heavily starched sauce congeals in her bowl. "My husband is a paper son. Is your husband one too?"

"Forgive me, but I don't know what that is."

"My husband bought the paper to become the son of an American. Now he can bring me in as his paper wife."

"What do you mean he bought a paper?" I ask.

"Haven't you heard of paper sons and paper-son slots?" When I shake my head, Dong-shee puts her elbows on the table and leans forward. "Suppose a Chinese man born in America travels to China to get married. When he comes back to America, he tells the authorities that his wife had a baby."

I'm listening carefully for the loopholes, and I think I've found one. "Did she actually have the baby?"

"No. He only tells them that, and the officials at the embassy in China or here on Angel Island aren't going to go to some village to check if he's telling the truth. So this man, who is a citizen of the United States, is given a paper saying that he has a new son, who is also a citizen because of his father. But remember, this son was never born. He only exists on paper. So now the man has a paper-son slot to sell. The man waits ten years, twenty years. He then sells the paper — the slot — to a young man in China, who adopts his new family name and comes to America. He's not a real son. He's only a paper son. The immigration officials here on

Angel Island will try to trick him into admitting the truth. If he's caught, he'll be sent back to China."

"And if he isn't?"

"Then he'll go to his new home and live as a paper son with false citizenship, a false name, and a false family history. These lies will stay with him for as long as he remains here."

"Who would want to do that?" I ask, skeptical because we come from a country where family names are hugely important and can sometimes be traced back twelve or more generations. The idea that a man would willingly change his family name to come here just doesn't seem plausible.

"Plenty of young men in China would love to buy that paper and pretend to be the son of someone else if it meant they could come to America — the Gold Mountain, the Land of the Flowery Flag," Dong-shee answers. "Believe me, he will suffer many indignities and work hard, but he'll make money, save it, and return home rich one day."

"It sounds easy —"

"Look around! It's not that easy!" Lee-shee interrupts. "The interrogations are bad enough, and the *lo fan* are always changing the rules."

"What about a paper daughter?" I ask. "Do women come here that way too?"

"What family would waste an opportunity so precious on a daughter? We're lucky we can take advantage of our husbands' fake status to come here as paper wives."

The two women laugh until tears gather in the corners of their eyes. How is it that these illiterate peasants know more about these things and are clearer about what has to be done to get into this country than we are? Because they're the targeted class, while May and I shouldn't be here. I sigh. Sometimes I wish we could just be sent back, but how can we go back? China is lost to the Japanese, May's pregnant, and we have no money and no family.

Then, as usual, the talk turns to the foods we miss: roast duck, fresh fruit, and black bean sauce — anything other than the overcooked garbage they feed us.

As May planned, I wear the loose clothes I'd worn to escape from China. Most women aren't here long enough to notice that both May and I seem to be growing plumper by the day. Or maybe they do but are as reticent as our own mother would have been about something so private.

My sister and I grew up in a cosmopolitan city. We acted like we knew a lot, but we were ignorant in many ways. Mama — typical for those days — had been unforthcoming about anything that had to do with our bodies. She never even warned us about the visit from the little red sister, and when it first came I was terrified, thinking I was bleeding to death. Even then Mama didn't explain what was happening. She sent me to the servants' quarters to have Pansy and the others teach me what to do to take care of myself and how a woman could get pregnant. Later, when the little red sister visited May, I told her what I'd learned, but we still didn't know much about pregnancy or the process of giving birth. Fortunately, we're now housed with women who know all about it and have all kinds of hints for me, but I grow to count on Lee-shee's advice.

"If your nipples are small like the seeds of a lotus," she counsels, "then your son will rise in society. If your nipples are the size of dates, then your son will sink into poverty."

She tells me to strengthen my *yin* by eating pears cooked in syrup, but we don't have any of those in the dining hall. When May starts having pains in her abdomen, I tell Lee-shee that I am having these pains, and she explains that this is a common ailment for women whose *chi* is stagnating around the womb.

"The best cure is to eat five slices of daikon radish sprinkled with a little sugar three times a day," she recommends. But I have no way to get fresh daikon, and May continues to suffer. This prompts me to sell the last piece of jewelry from Mama's dowry bag to a woman from a village near Canton. From now on, whenever May needs something, I'll be able to buy it outright at the concession stand or pay a bribe to one of the guards or cooks to get it for me. So, when May develops indigestion, I complain accordingly. The women in our dormitory argue over the best remedy for me, suggesting that I suck on whole cloves. These I procure easily, but Lee-shee isn't satisfied.

"Pearl either has a weak stomach or a weak spleen — both signs of deficiencies in her Earth functions," Lee-shee tells the other women. "Does anyone here have any tangerines or fresh ginger we could use to make a tea for her?"

These items are bought without difficulty and bring May relief, which makes me happy, which in turn pleases the other detainees for being able to help a pregnant woman.

More time grows between our interrogations. This is common practice for those whose hearings have problems. The inspectors think that long hours spent in the dormitory will weaken us, intimidate us into forgetting our memorized stories, and trick us into making mistakes. After all, if you're interrogated only once a month for eight hours straight, how can you remember exactly what you said one, two, six, or eighteen months ago, how that conforms to the coaching book that you destroyed, or what your relatives and acquaintances, who aren't on the island, said about you in *their* hearings?

Husbands and wives remain separated throughout their stays. In this way, they aren't allowed to comfort each other or, more important, share information about their interrogations and the questions asked. On their wedding day, did the sedan chair stop at the front gate or the front door? Was it overcast or drizzling when they buried their third daughter? Who can remember these things when the questions and their answers can be interpreted in different ways? After all, in a village of two hundred people, aren't a front gate and a front door one and the same? Can it matter how damp the weather was when they put that worthless daughter in the ground? Apparently it does to the interrogators, and a family whose answers to these questions don't agree might be detained for days, weeks, and sometimes months.

But May and I are sisters and can compare stories before our hearings. The questions asked of us became increasingly difficult as the files for Sam, Vernon, their brothers, Old Man Louie, and his wife, business associates, and people in the neighborhood — other merchants, the policeman on the beat, and the man who makes deliveries for our father-in-law — are brought in. How many chickens and ducks does my husband's family keep in their home village? Where is the rice bin kept in our home in Los Angeles and in the Louie family home in Wah Hong Village?

If we dawdle with our answers, the inspectors get impatient and shout, "Hurry up! Hurry up!" This tactic works well for other detainees, scaring them into making crucial errors, but we use it to appear as though we're confused and stupid. Chairman Plumb grows increasingly annoyed with me, staring silently at me sometimes for a full hour in an effort to intimidate me into coming up with a new answer, but I'm stalling for a reason, and his attempts to bully and threaten me just make me calmer and more focused.

May and I use the complexity, simplicity, or idiocy of these questions to prolong our stays. To the question "Did you have a dog in China?" May answers yes and I answer no. At our hearings two weeks later, the inspectors for each of our interrogations confront us with this discrepancy. May sticks with our story that we owned a dog, while I explain that we once had a dog but our father killed it so we could eat it for our last meal in China. In the next hearing, the inspectors announce that we're both right: the Chin family owned a dog but it was eaten before our departure. The truth is we never had a dog and Cook never served dog — ours or anyone else's — in our home. May and I laugh for hours about our tiny triumph.

"Where did you keep the kerosene lamp in your home?" Chairman Plumb asks one day. We had electricity in Shanghai, but I tell him that we kept the kerosene lamp on the left side of the table, while May says that it was kept on the right.

Let's just say these are not the brightest men. In our Chinese jackets, they don't notice the baby growing inside May or the pillow and bunched up clothes I shove into my pants. After Chinese New Year, I begin to waddle in and out of the interrogation room and exaggerate my efforts at sitting and rising. Naturally, this brings a new round of questions. Am I sure I got pregnant on the one night I spent with my husband? Am I positive of the date? Mightn't there have been someone else? Was I a prostitute in my home country? Is my baby's father who I say he is?

Chairman Plumb opens Sam's file and shows me a photograph of a boy of seven. "Is this your husband?"

I study the photograph. It's a little boy. It could be Sam when he went back to China with his parents in 1920; it could be someone else. "Yes, that's my husband."

The recorder keeps typing, our files keep expanding, and along the way I learn quite a bit about my father-in-law, Sam, Vernon, and the Louie family's businesses.

"It says here that your father-in-law was born in San Francisco in 1871," Chairman Plumb says as he leafs through Old Man Louie's file. "That would make him sixty-seven years old. His father was a merchant. Are these facts correct?"

From the coaching book, I'd learned everything but the year of Old Man Louie's birth. I take a chance and answer "Yes."

"It says here he married a natural-footed woman in San Francisco in 1904."

"I haven't met her yet, but I've heard she has natural feet."

"In 1907 they went to China, where their first son was born. They left him in the home village for eleven years before bringing him here."

At this, Mr. White leans over and whispers in his superior's ear. They both shuffle through the files. Mr. White then points to something on one of the pages. Chairman Plumb nods and says, "Your alleged mother-in-law has five sons. Why did she have only sons? Why were they all born in China? Doesn't that seem suspicious to you?"

"Actually, the youngest son was born in Los Angeles," I offer helpfully.

Chairman Plumb gives me a look. "Why would your in-laws leave four sons in China before bringing them here?"

I've wondered the same thing, but I recite what I memorized: "My husband's brothers grew up in Wah Hong Village because it was cheaper than Los Angeles. My husband was sent back to China to meet his grandparents, learn the home language and traditions, and make offerings to the Louie family ancestors on his father's behalf."

"Have you met the brothers?"

"Only the one named Vernon. The rest not."

Chairman Plumb asks, "If your in-laws were together in Los Angeles, why did they wait eleven more years to have a last child?"

I don't know the answer to this, but I pat my stomach and say, "Some women don't take the proper herbs, eat the proper foods, or follow the proper rules for their *chi* to accept sons from their husbands."

My backward-village answer satisfies my questioners for the day, but a week later their thoughts turn to my father-in-law's occupation, trying to make sure he isn't in the prohibited class of laborer. During the past twenty years, Old Man Louie opened several businesses in Los Angeles. Currently, he has just one store.

"What's the name of the shop and what does he sell?" Chairman Plumb asks.

I dutifully recite my answer. "It's called the Golden Lantern. He sells Chinese and Japanese goods, including furniture, silks, rugs, slippers, and porcelains, with a value of fifty thousand dollars." Just having that number in my mouth is like sucking on sugarcane.

"Fifty thousand dollars?" Chairman Plumb marvels, equally impressed. "That's a lot of money."

176

Again, he and Mr. White put their heads together, this time to talk about the severity of their country's depression. I pretend not to listen. They check Old Man Louie's file, and I hear them say that, later this year, he plans to move his original store and open an additional two shops, a ride for tourists, and a restaurant. I rub my fake belly and feign disinterest when Mr. White explains the Louie family's situation.

"Our colleagues in Los Angeles visit the Louies every six months," he says. "They've never seen a connection between your father-in-law and a laundry, lottery, lodging house, barbershop, pool or gambling hall, or anything else objectionable. Nor has anyone ever reported seeing him do manual labor. In other words, he appears to be a merchant of good standing in the community."

What I learn in my next interrogation, as Mr. White reads aloud in English portions of Sam's and his father's transcripts, which are translated into Sze Yup by yet another interpreter who's been sent to cover the hearing, absolutely stuns me. Old Man Louie reported to inspectors that his business lost two thousand dollars a year from 1930 through 1933. That was a huge amount of money in Shanghai. Just one year's worth of that money would have saved my family: my father's business, the house, and May's and my savings. Yet Old Man Louie still managed to come to China to buy wives for his sons.

"The family has to be rich with hidden wealth," May says that night.

177

Still, it all seems muddled and deliberately confused and confusing. Is Old Man Louie, whose file is only slightly larger than mine after having passed through this station numerous times, as much of a liar as May and I are?

One day Chairman Plumb finally loses his patience, slams his fist on the table, and demands, "How is it that you're claiming to be the wife of a legally domiciled merchant *and* the wife of an American citizen? These are two different things, and only one is needed."

I've asked myself the same question many times these past months, and I still don't know the answer.

Sisters in Blood

A couple of weeks later, I wake in the middle of the night from one of my bad dreams. Usually May is at my side, comforting me. But she isn't there. I roll over, expecting to see her in the bunk across from mine. She isn't there either. I lie still and listen. I don't hear anyone weeping, whispering protective incantations, or padding across the dormitory floor, which means it has to be very late. Where's May?

Lately, she's had as much trouble sleeping as I do. "Your son likes to kick me as soon as I lie down and there's no room inside me anymore for him and me. I need to go to the toilet all the time," she confided a week ago with such tenderness — as if peeing is such a precious gift — that I couldn't help but love her and the infant she carried for me. Still, we've promised each other that we won't go alone to the toilets. I reach for my clothes and my pillow baby. Even this late at night, I can't risk being seen not looking pregnant. I button my jacket over my fake belly and get up.

She isn't in the toilets, so I move on to the showers. When I enter, my chest freezes and my stomach clenches. The room couldn't look more different from the one in my dreams, but there on the floor is my sister with her pants off, her face white with pain, and her private parts . . . exposed, bulging, frightening.

May reaches an arm out to me. "Pearl —"

I run to her side, slipping on the watery tiles.

"Your son is coming," she says.

"You were supposed to wake me up —"

"I didn't realize things had gone so far."

Many times late at night or when we could separate ourselves just a bit when the missionary ladies took us for our weekly walks around the property, we've discussed what we'd need when the time came. We've made plan after plan and gone over detail after detail. In my mind I tick off the things the women we quizzed had said: you experience pains until pretty soon you feel like you're going to fart a winter melon, you go to a corner, squat, the baby falls out, you clean it, wrap it, and then rejoin your husband in the paddies with your baby tied to you by a long cloth. Of course, all this is very different from how things were done in Shanghai, where for months women retreated from parties, shopping, and dancing before going to a Western-style hospital, where they were put to sleep. When they woke up, they'd be handed their babies. Then, for the next two or three weeks, they'd stay in the hospital, entertaining visitors and being cherished for bringing a son to the family. Finally, they'd go home in time for the one-month party to introduce the baby to the world and receive praise from family, neighbors, and friends. The Shanghai way isn't possible here, but as May has said so many times these past few weeks, "Country women have been having babies by themselves forever. If they can do it, I can too. And we've been through a lot. I haven't had a lot to eat, and what I've eaten, I've thrown up. The baby won't be big. It will come out easily."

We'd talked about where the baby could be born and had settled on the showers as the one place where the other women were most afraid to venture. Even so, women sometimes took showers during the day. "I won't let the baby come out then," May had promised.

Now, thinking back on it, I realize that May has probably been in labor most of the day, resting on her bunk, her knees up, her legs crossed, keeping the baby inside.

"When did the pains start? How long between them?" I ask, remembering that these are clues to how much longer it will be until the baby breathes air.

"They started this morning. They weren't so bad, and I knew I had to wait. Suddenly, I started feeling like I needed to use the toilet. The water came out when I came in here."

That has to be the water soaking my feet and knees.

She clutches my hand when a contraction grips her. Her eyes shut and her face reddens as she swallows her agony. She squeezes my hand, digging her nails into my palm so deeply that I'm the one who wants to scream. When the contraction ends, she takes a breath and her hand relaxes in mine. An hour later, I see the top of the baby's head.

"Do you think you can squat?" I ask.

May whimpers in response. I get behind her and pull her to a wall so she can prop herself against it. I get between her legs. I clasp my hands before me and close my eyes to gather my courage. I open my eyes, look into my sister's pained face, and try to put as much conviction as I can into my voice as I repeat to her what she's said to me so many times these past weeks. "We can do this, May. I know we can."

When the baby slips out, it isn't the son that we talked about. It's a wet, mucus-covered girl — my daughter. She's tiny, even smaller than I expected. She doesn't cry. Instead, she makes little sounds like the plaintive calls of a baby bird.

"Let me see."

I blink and look at my sister. Her hair hangs in wet strings, but all traces of pain have faded from her face. I hand her the baby and stand.

"I'll be right back," I say, but May isn't listening to me. She's wrapped her arms around the baby, protecting it from the shock of cold air and wiping away the goo from its face with her sleeve. I stare at them for a moment. This is all the time they'll have together before I take the baby for my own.

As quickly and quietly as I can, I scurry back to the dormitory. I pull out one of the outfits May and I made, a ball of yarn, a small pair of scissors the missionary ladies gave us to help with our handiwork projects, some sanitary supplies, and two towels we bought from the concession stand. I grab the teapot from atop the radiator and hurry back to the showers. By the time I get there, May has expelled the afterbirth. I tie yarn around the umbilical cord and cut it. Then I dampen one end of the clean towel with hot water from the teapot and hand it to May to clean the baby. I use some of the water and the other towel to clean May. The baby was small, so the tearing isn't all that bad compared with what happened to me down in that area. I hope she'll heal without stitches. But in truth, what else can I do? I barely know how to sew a seam. How can I stitch my sister's private parts?

While May dresses the baby, I wipe the floor and wrap the afterbirth in the towels. When everything's as clean as I can make it, I stuff the soiled things in the trash.

Outside the sky turns pink. We don't have much time.

"I don't think I can get up by myself," May says from the floor. Her pale legs tremble from cold and the exertion she's been through. She scoots away from the wall, and I lift her to her feet. Blood trickles down her legs and spots the floor.

"Don't worry," she says. "Don't worry. Here. Take her."

She gives me the baby. I forgot to bring the blanket May knit, and the baby's arms jerk awkwardly in their sudden freedom. I haven't carried her inside me all these months, but I instantly love her as my own. I hardly pay attention to May as she puts a belt and napkin in place and pulls on her underwear and pants.

183

"I'm ready," she says.

We look around the room. It won't be a secret that a woman gave birth here. What matters is that no one suspect it was anything out of the ordinary, because I won't be able to be examined by the station's doctors.

I'm propped in bed, holding my daughter, with May nestled beside me — dozing lightly, her head on my shoulder — when the other women rise. It takes a while before anyone notices us.

"*Aiya!* Look who's come in the night!" Lee-shee squeals excitedly.

The other women and their small children gather around, gently pushing against one another to get a better look.

"Your son arrived!"

"No son. A daughter," May corrects. Her voice sounds so dreamy from exhaustion that for a second I worry she'll give us away.

"A little happiness," Lee-shee says sympathetically, using the traditional phrase to convey the disappointment in the birth of a girl. Then she grins. "But look around. Almost everyone here is a woman, except for the little boys who need their mothers. We must look at this as an auspicious occurrence."

"It won't remain auspicious if the baby stays dressed like that," one of the women says forebodingly.

I look at the baby. Her clothes are the first May and I ever made. The buttons are crooked and the knit hat is lopsided, but apparently these aren't the problems. The baby needs to be protected from bad elements.

184

The women go away and return with gifts of coins to represent the care of "one hundred friends of the family." Someone ties a red string in her black hair to give her luck. Then, one after the other, the women sew tiny charms depicting the animals of the zodiac onto her hat and the other clothes we made to protect her from evil spirits, bad omens, and sickness.

A collection is taken up, and someone is elected to give the money to one of the Chinese cooks to make a bowl of mother's soup of pickled pigs' feet, ginger, peanuts, and whatever hard liquor he can find. (Shaohsing wine is best, but whiskey will do if that's all he has.) A new mother is depleted and suffers from too much cold *yin*. Most of the soup's ingredients are considered hot and builders of *yang*. I'm told they will help shrink my womb, rid my body of stagnant blood, and bring in my milk.

Suddenly, one of the women reaches over and starts to unbutton my jacket. "You've got to feed the baby. We'll show you how."

I gently push away her hand.

"We're in America now, and my daughter is an American citizen. I will do as the Americans do." *And modern Shanghainese women too*, I think, remembering all the times May and I modeled for companies advertising powdered baby milk. "She will have baby formula."

As usual, I translate the exchange from Sze Yup into the Wu dialect so May will understand.

"Tell her the bottles and the formula are in a package under the bed," May rattles off quickly. "Tell her I

185

don't want to leave you, but if one of them could help us, I'd be grateful."

While one of the women takes a bottle and mixes some of the powdered formula we bought from the concession stand with water from the teapot and places it on the windowsill to cool, Lee-shee and the others discuss the problem of the baby's name.

"Confucius said that if names are not correct, then language and society are not in accordance with the truth of things," she explains. "The child's grandfather or someone of great distinction needs to name your baby." She purses her lips, looks around, and observes theatrically, "But I don't see anyone around here like that. Perhaps it's just as well. You have a daughter. Such a disappointment! You wouldn't want her to be named Flea, That Dog, or Dustpan, like my father named me."

Naming is important, but it doesn't belong to women. Now that we have the opportunity to name a child — a girl at that — we find it's a lot harder than it seems. We can't name the girl after my mother or even use our family name as her given name to honor my father, because these options are considered taboo. We can't name her after a heroine or goddess either, because that's presumptuous and disrespectful.

"I like Jade, because it conveys strength and beauty," suggests a young detainee.

"The flower names are pretty. Orchid, Lily, Iris —"

"Oh, but they're such common names and too frail," Lee-shee objects. "Look where this baby was born. Shouldn't she be named something like Mei Gwok?"

Mei Gwok means *Beautiful Country*, which is the official Cantonese name for the United States, but it doesn't sound melodious or pretty.

"You can't go wrong using a two-character generational name," another woman offers. This appeals to me, since May and I share the generational name *Long* — Dragon. "You could use *De* — Virtue — as the base and then name each daughter Kind Virtue, Moon Virtue, Wise Virtue —"

"Too much trouble!" Lee-shee exclaims. "I named my daughters Girl One, Girl Two, Girl Three. My sons are Son One, Son Two, Son Three. Their cousins are Cousins Seven, Eight, Nine, Ten, and so on. Giving numbers reminds everyone where a child fits in the family."

What she leaves unsaid is, Who wants to be bothered with names when too often children die? I don't know how much of this May follows or how much she understands, but when she speaks the others quiet.

"Only one name is right for this baby," May says in English. "She should be called Joy. We're in America now. Let's not burden her with the past."

When May moves her head to look up at me, I realize that all this time she's been staring at the baby. Even though I cradle Joy, May has managed to be physically closer to her than I have. She draws herself up, reaches around her neck, and takes off the pouch with the three coppers, three sesame seeds, and three green beans Mama gave her to keep her safe. My hand goes to the pouch I still wear. I don't believe it protected me, but I still wear it and the jade bracelet as

187

physical reminders of my mother. May places the leather string around Joy's head and tucks the pouch inside her clothes.

"To keep you safe wherever you go," May whispers.

The women around us weep at the beauty of her words and gesture, calling her a good auntie, but we all know this gift will be taken off Joy to keep her from strangling.

When the missionary ladies come, I refuse to let them escort me to the station's hospital. "It's not the Chinese way," I say. "But if you could send a telegram to my husband, I would be most grateful."

The message is short and to the point: MAY AND PEARL ARRIVED ANGEL ISLAND. SEND TRAVEL FUNDS. BABY BORN. PREPARE ONE-MONTH BIRTHDAY.

That night, the women return from dinner with the special mother's soup. Over the objections of the women who cluster around, I share the soup with my sister, saying that she worked as hard as I did. They tsk-tsk and shake their heads, but May needs the soup far more than I do.

Chairman plumb is thoroughly stumped when I walk into my next hearing wearing one of my prettiest silk dresses and my hat with the feathers — with the coaching book well studied by both May and me hidden inside the lining — speaking perfect English and carrying a baby decorated with charms. I answer every question correctly and without hesitation, knowing that in another room May is doing the exact same thing. But my actions and those of May are irrelevant, as is the whole legally domiciled merchant/wife of an American citizen question. What are the officials going to do with this baby? Angel Island is part of the United States, yet no one's citizenship or status is acknowledged until that person *leaves* the island. It's easier for the officials to release us than for them to deal with the bureaucratic problems Joy presents.

Chairman Plumb gives his usual synopsis at the end of the interrogation, but he's hardly happy when he comes to his concluding words: "The submission of this case has been delayed for over four months. While it is clear that this woman has spent very little time with her husband, who claims to be an American citizen, she has now given birth at our station. After considerable deliberation, we have come to agreement on the essential points. I therefore move that Louie Chin-shee be admitted to the United States as the wife of an American citizen."

"I concur," Mr. White says.

"I also concur," the recorder says in the first and only time I hear him speak.

At four that same afternoon, the guard comes in and calls two names: Louie Chin-shee and Louie Chin-shee — May's and my old-fashioned married names. "*Sai gaai*," he announces loudly in his usual mangling of the phrase that means *good fortune*. We're handed our Certificates of Identity. I'm given a United States birth certificate for Joy, stating that she is "too small to be measured" — which means only that they didn't bother to examine her. I hope these words will be useful in erasing any suspicions about dates and Joy's size when Old Man Louie and Sam see her.

The other women help us pack our things. Lee-shee weeps when she says good-bye. May and I watch the guard lock the dormitory door behind us, and then we follow him out of the building and down the path to the dock, where we pick up the rest of our luggage and board the ferry to take us to San Francisco.

Part Two

FORTUNE

A Single Rice Kernel

We pay fourteen dollars to take the *Harvard* steamship to San Pedro. On the voyage, having learned our lesson at Angel Island, we rehearse our stories for why we missed the ship all those months ago, how hard we tried to get out of China to come to our husbands, and how difficult our interrogations were. But we don't need to tell any stories, real or otherwise. When Sam meets us at the dock, he says simply, "We thought you were dead."

We've seen each other only three times: in the Old Chinese City, at our wedding, and when he gave me our tickets and other traveling papers. After Sam's single sentence, he stares at me wordlessly. I look at him wordlessly. May hangs back, carrying our two bags. The baby sleeps in my arms. I don't expect hugs or kisses, and I don't expect him to acknowledge Joy in an extravagant way. That would be inappropriate. Still, our meeting after all this time is very awkward.

On the streetcar, May and I sit behind Sam. This is not a city of "magical tall buildings" like the ones we had in Shanghai. Eventually, I see one white tower to my left. After a few more blocks, Sam gets up and motions to us. Outside the window to the right is a huge construction zone. To the left stands a long block of two-story brick buildings, some of which have signs in Chinese. The streetcar stops, and we get off. We walk up and around the block. A sign reads LOS ANGELES STREET. We cross the street, skirt a plaza with a bandstand in the center, walk past a firehouse, and then make a left down Sanchez Alley, which is lined by more brick buildings. We step through a door with the words GARNIER BLOCK carved above it, walk down a dark passageway, climb a flight of old wooden stairs, and wend our way along a musty corridor that reeks of cooked food and dirty diapers. Sam hesitates before the door to the apartment he shares with his parents and Vern. He turns and gives May and me a look that I read as sympathy. Then he opens the door and we enter.

The first thing that strikes me is just how poor, dirty, and shabby everything is. A couch covered in stained mauve material leans glumly against a wall. A table with six wooden chairs of no particular design or craftsmanship takes up space in the center of the room. Next to the table, not even tucked into a corner, sits a spittoon. A quick glance shows that it hasn't been emptied recently. No photographs, paintings, or calendars hang on the walls. The windows are filthy and without coverings. From where I stand just inside the front door I can see into the kitchen, which is little more than a counter with some appliances on it and a niche for the worship of the Louie family ancestors.

A short, round woman with her hair pinned into a small bun at the back of her neck rushes to us, squealing in Sze Yup. "Welcome! Welcome! You're here!" Then she calls over her shoulder. "They're here! They're here!" She flicks her wrist at Sam. "Go get the old man and my boy." As Sam slumps through the main room and down a hall, she turns her attention back to us. "Let me have the baby! Oh, let me see! Let me see! I'm your *yen-yen*," she trills to Joy, using the Sze Yup diminutive for grandmother. Then to May and me, she adds, "You can call me Yen-yen too."

Our mother-in-law is older than I expected, given that Vernon is just fourteen. She looks like she's in her late fifties — ancient compared with Mama, who was thirty-eight when she died.

"I am the one who will see the child" comes a stern voice, also speaking in Sze Yup. "Give it here."

Old Man Louie, dressed in a long mandarin robe, enters the room with Vern, who hasn't grown much since we last saw him. Again, May and I expect questions about where we've been and why it took so long to get here, but the old man has no interest in us whatsoever. I hand Joy to him. He sets her on a table and roughly undresses her. She begins to cry — alarmed by his bony fingers, her grandmother's exclamations, the hardness of the table against her back, and the sudden shock of being naked.

When Old Man Louie sees she's a girl, his hands draw back. Distaste wrinkles his features. "You didn't write that the child is a girl. You should have done that. We wouldn't have prepared a banquet if we'd known."

"Of course she needs a one-month party," my mother-in-law chirps. "Every baby — even a girl — needs a one-month party. Anyway, no going back now. Everyone is coming."

"You've planned something already?" May asks.

"Now!" Yen-yen rings out. "You took longer to get here from the harbor than we thought. Everyone is waiting at the restaurant."

"Now?" May echoes.

"Now!"

"Shouldn't we change?" May asks.

Old Man Louie scowls. "No time for that. You don't need anything. You're not so special now. No need to try to sell yourselves here."

If I were braver, I'd ask why he's so deliberately rude and mean, but we haven't even been in his home ten minutes.

"She will need a name," Old Man Louie says, nodding to the baby.

"Her name is Joy," I say.

He snorts. "No good. Chao-di or Pan-di is better."

The redness of anger creeps up my neck. This is exactly what the women on Angel Island warned us about. I feel Sam's hand on the small of my back, but his gesture of comfort sends a ripple of anxiety along my spine and I step away from his touch.

Sensing something's wrong, May asks in our Wu dialect, "What's he saying?"

"He wants to name Joy Ask-for-a-Brother or Hope-for-a-Brother."

May's eyes narrow.

"You will not speak a secret language in my home," Old Man Louie declares. "I need to understand everything you say."

"May doesn't know Sze Yup," I explain, but inside I reel from what he's proposing for Joy, whose cries are shrill in the disapproving silence around her.

"Only Sze Yup," he says, emphasizing his point by sharply rapping the table. "If I hear the two of you speak another language — even English — then you'll put a nickel in a jar for me. Understand?"

He isn't a tall or heavily built man, but he stands with his feet planted as if daring any of us to defy him. But May and I are new here, Yen-yen has edged to a wall seemingly trying to make herself invisible, Sam has barely said a word since we got off the boat, and Vernon stands to the side, nervously shifting his weight from one foot to the other.

"Get Pan-di dressed," Old Man Louie orders. "The two of you brush your hair. And I want you to wear these." He reaches into one of the deep pockets of his mandarin robe and brings out four gold wedding bracelets.

He grabs my hand and locks a solid gold, three-inch-wide bracelet on my wrist. Then he attaches one to the other wrist, roughly pushing my mother's jade bracelet up my arm and out of his way. While he locks May's bracelets in place, I look at mine. They're beautiful, traditional, and very expensive wedding bracelets. Here at last is material evidence of the wealth I expected. If May and I can find a pawnshop, then we can use the money . . .

"Don't just stand there," Old Man Louie snaps. "Do something to make that girl stop crying. It's time to go." He looks at us in disgust. "Let's get this over with."

Within fifteen minutes we've gone around the corner, crossed Los Angeles Street, climbed some stairs, and entered Soochow Restaurant for a combination wedding banquet and one-month party. Platters of hard-boiled eggs dyed red to represent fertility and happiness are set on a table just inside the entrance. Wedding couplets hang on the walls. Thin slices of sweet pickled ginger to symbolize the continued warming of my *yin* after the strain of birth are set on each table. The banquet, while not as lavish as I imagined in my romantic days in Z.G.'s studio, is still the best meal we've seen in months — a cold platter with jellyfish, soy-sauce chicken, and sliced kidneys, bird's nest soup, a whole steamed fish, Peking duck, noodles, shrimp and walnuts — but May and I don't get to eat.

Yen-yen — carrying her new grandchild — takes us from table to table to make introductions. Almost everyone here is a Louie, and they all speak Sze Yup.

"This is Uncle Wilburt. This is Uncle Charley. And here's Uncle Edfred," she says to Joy.

These men in nearly matching suits made from cheap fabric are Sam and Vern's brothers. Are these the names they were born with? Not possible. They're the names they took to sound more American, just as May, Tommy, Z.G., and I took Western names to sound more sophisticated in Shanghai.

198

Since May and I have been married for a while already, instead of the usual wedding banter about our husbands' coming fortitude in the bedchamber or how my sister and I are about to be plucked, the teasing revolves around Joy.

"You cook baby fast, Pearl-ah!" Uncle Wilburt says in broken English. From the coaching book, I know he's thirty-one, but he looks much older. "That baby many weeks early!"

"Joy big for her age!" Edfred, who's twenty-seven but looks a lot younger, chimes in. He's quite emboldened by the *mao tai* he's been drinking. "We can count, Pearl-ah."

"Sam give you son next time!" Charley adds. He's thirty, but it's hard to tell because his eyes are red, swollen, and watery from allergies. "You cook next baby so good he come out even earlier!"

"You Louie men. All same!" Yen-yen scolds. "You think you count so good? You count how many days my daughters-in-law run from monkey people. You think you have hardship here? *Bah!* Baby lucky to be born at all! She lucky to be alive!"

May and I pour tea for each guest and receive wedding gifts of *lai see* — red envelopes embossed with gold good-luck characters and filled with money that will be ours alone — and more gold in the form of earrings, pins, rings, and enough bracelets to climb our arms to our elbows. I can barely wait for us to be alone so we can count the first of our escape money and figure out how to sell our jewelry.

Naturally, there are the predictable comments about Joy being a girl, but most people are delighted to see a baby — any baby. That's when I realize that the majority of the guests are men, with very few wives and almost no children. What we experienced on Angel Island begins to make sense. The American government does everything possible to keep out Chinese men. It makes it even harder for Chinese women to enter the country. And in a lot of states it's against the law for Chinese to marry Caucasians. All this ends in the desired result for the United States: with few Chinese women on American soil, sons and daughters can't be born, saving the country from having to accept undesirable citizens of Chinese descent.

At table after table, the men want to hold Joy. Some of them cry when they take her in their arms. They examine her fingers and toes. I can't help it, but I fairly shine with my new status as mother. I'm happy — not in-the-stars happy but relieved happy. We survived. We made it to Los Angeles. Apart from Old Man Louie's disappointment in Joy — and not in ten thousand years will I ever call her Pan-di — he's arranged this celebration and we're being welcomed. I glance at May, hoping she's feeling what I'm feeling. But my sister — even as she performs her new-bride duties — seems pensive and withdrawn. My heart tightens. How cruel all this is for her, but she didn't push me in a wheelbarrow for miles and nurse me back to health by being weak. Somehow my little sister has found a way to keep going forward.

200

I remember back on Angel Island before the baby was born talking with May about the importance of the special mother's soup and whether or not we should ask someone to see if the chefs would make it for us. "I'll need it to help with my bleeding," May had decided practically, while knowing it would also bring in her milk. So May and I had shared the soup. Then, when Joy was three days old, May went to the showers and didn't return. I left the baby with Lee-shee and went to look for my sister. My fear was great. I worried what May might do if left alone. I found her in the shower, crying not from sorrow but from the agony in her breasts. "It's worse than when the baby came out," she said between sobs. Yes, her womb had shrunk, and even naked she barely looked like she'd had a baby, but her breasts were swollen and hard as rocks from milk that had nowhere to go. The hot water helped, and the milk streamed out, dripping from her nipples and mingling in the water before disappearing down the drain.

Some might say, Well, how stupid could you have been to let her eat a soup that would make her milk come in like that? But remember, we didn't know about having babies. We didn't know enough about the milk or how painful it would be. A few days later, when May discovered that every time the baby cried, milk would start to empty out of her breasts, she moved to a bunk at the far end of the room. "That baby cries too much," she told the others. "How can I help my sister at night if I don't get some sleep during the day?"

Now I watch May pour tea for a table of lonely men and scoop up the red envelopes and tuck them in her pocket. The men do their duty by joking, teasing, and mocking her, and she does hers by putting on a smiling face.

"Your turn next, May," Wilburt hoots when we circle back to the uncles' table.

Charley appraises her up and down, and then says, "You small, but hips good."

"You give the old man the grandson he wants, you'll become his favorite," promises Edfred.

Yen-yen joins in the laughter, but before we move to the next table she hands Joy to me. Then she takes May's arm and begins to walk, rattling off several sentences in Sze Yup. "Don't let all these men bother you. They're lonely for their wives back home. They're lonely for wives they don't even have! You came here with your sister. You helped bring this baby to us. You're a brave girl." Yen-yen stops in the aisle and waits for me to finish translating. When I come to the end, she takes May's hands in her own. "You can be freed from one thing, but that only puts you in a tight spot somewhere else. Understand?"

It's late by the time we get back to the apartment. We're all tired, but Old Man Louie isn't done with us.

"Give me your jewelry," he says.

His demand shocks me. Wedding gold belongs to the bride alone. It's the secret treasure she can draw on to buy herself a special treat without her husband's criticism or use in times of emergency, as our mother did when Baba lost everything. Before I can protest,

May says, "These things are ours. Everyone knows that."

"I think you are mistaken," he asserts. "I'm your father-in-law. I'm the master here." He could say he doesn't trust us, and he'd be right. He could accuse us of wanting to use the gold to find a way out of here, and he'd be right. Instead, he adds, "Do you think you and your sister — smart and clever as you think you are with your Shanghai city ways — will know where to go tonight with that baby girl? Will you know where to go tomorrow? The blood of your father has ruined you both. This is why I can buy you for such a low price, but that doesn't mean I'm willing to lose my goods so easily."

May looks at me. I'm the older sister. I'm supposed to know what to do, but I'm completely confused by what we're seeing and experiencing. Not once has anyone asked why we didn't meet the Louies in Hong Kong on the appointed date, what we've been through, how we survived, or how we got to America. All Old Man Louie and Yen-yen care about is the baby and the bracelets, Vernon is in a world of his own, while Sam seems oddly removed from his family's interactions. They appear to have no concern for us one way or the other, yet it feels as if we've been caught in a fisherman's net. We can wiggle and continue to breathe, but there's no escape that I can see. Not yet anyway.

We let the old man take our jewelry, but he doesn't ask for the money hidden in our *lai see*. Maybe he knows that would be too much. But I feel no sense of triumph, and I can see May doesn't either. She stands in the middle of the room, looking defeated, sad, and very much alone.

Everyone takes a turn going down the hall to the toilet. Old Man Louie and Yen-yen go to bed first. May stares at Vern, who pulls on the ends of his hair. When he leaves the room, May follows.

"Is there a place for the baby?" I ask Sam.

"Yen-yen prepared something. I hope —" He juts his chin and lets out his breath.

I trail after him down the dark hall. Sam's room has no windows. A single bare lightbulb hangs from the center of the ceiling. A bed and a dresser take up most of the space. The bottom drawer has been pulled open and packed with a soft blanket for Joy to sleep on. I lay her down and look around. I see no closet, but a corner has been draped with a piece of cloth to offer a little privacy.

"My clothes?" I ask. "The ones your father took after we were married?"

Sam stares at the floor. "They're already at China City. I'll take you there tomorrow and maybe he'll let you have some things."

I don't know what China City is. I don't know what he means about my maybe being allowed to take my clothes, because my mind is stuck on something else altogether: I have to get in bed with the man who is my husband. Somehow in all of May's and my planning, we didn't think about this part. Now I stand in the room as paralyzed as May had just been.

Even in the cramped space, Sam busies himself. He opens a jar of something pungent, gets on his hands and knees, and pours it into four tin lids wedged under the bed legs. When he's done, he sits back on his haunches, screws the jar shut, and says, "I use kerosene to keep away the bedbugs."

Bedbugs!

He takes off his shirt and belt and drapes them on a hook behind the curtain. He plops on the edge of the bed and stares at the floor. After what seems a long while, he says, "I'm sorry about today." After several more minutes, he adds, "I'm sorry about everything."

I remember how bold I was the night of our wedding. That person was as audacious and reckless as a woman warrior of ancient times, but that girl was defeated in a shack somewhere between Shanghai and the Grand Canal.

"It's too soon after the baby," I manage to say.

Sam looks up at me with his sad, dark eyes. Finally, he says, "I think you'll prefer the side of the bed closest to our Joy."

Once he slips under the covers, I pull the string for the light, take off my shoes, and then lie down on top of the blanket. I'm grateful that Sam doesn't try to touch me. After he falls asleep, I reach into my pockets and finger the *lai see.*

What's the first impression you have of a new place? Is it the first meal you eat? The first time you have an ice cream cone? The first person you meet? The first night you spend in your new bed in your new home? The first broken promise? The first time you realize that no one cares about you as anything other than the potential

205

bearer of sons? The knowledge that your neighbors are so poor that they put only a dollar in your *lai see*, as if that were enough to give a woman a secret treasure to last a lifetime? The recognition that your father-in-law, a man born in this country, has been so isolated in Chinatowns throughout his life that he speaks the most pathetic English ever? The moment you understand that everything you'd come to believe about your in-laws' class, standing, prosperity, and fortune is as wrong as everything you thought about your natal family's status and wealth?

What stays with me most are the feelings of loss, unsettlement, unease, and a longing for the past that cannot be relieved. This isn't just because my sister and I are new to this strange and foreign place. It's as though every person in Chinatown is a refugee. No one here is a Gold Mountain man — rich beyond imagining — not even Old Man Louie. On Angel Island, I learned about his ventures and the value of his merchandise, but they mean nothing here, where everyone is poor. People lost their jobs during the Depression. Those lucky enough to have families sent them back to China, because it was cheaper to provide for them there than to feed and house them here. When the Japanese attacked, those families returned. But no new money is being made and conditions are even more cramped and unsettled than ever, or so I'm told.

Five years ago, in 1933, most of Chinatown was torn down to make room for a new railroad station, which is being built on that huge construction site we saw when Sam brought us here on the streetcar. People were given twenty-four hours to move — far less than what May and I had when we left Shanghai — but where could they go? The law says that Chinese can't own property and most landlords won't rent to Chinese either, so people cram into buildings and squeeze into rooms in the last few buildings of the original Chinatown, where we live, or in the City Market Chinatown, which caters to produce growers and sellers, many blocks and a culture away from here. Everyone — including me — misses their families in China, but when I pin the photographs that May and I brought with us on my bedroom wall, Yen-yen yells at me. "You stupid girl! You want to get us in trouble? What happens if the immigration inspectors come? How are you going to explain who those people are?"

"They're my parents," I say. "And that's May and me when we were little. These things are not a secret."

"Everything is a secret. You see pictures of anyone here? Now take those down and hide them before I throw them away."

That's my first morning, and soon I discover that, although I'm in a new land, in many ways it's as though I've taken a giant step back in time.

The Cantonese word for *wife* — *fu yen* — is composed of two elements. One part means *woman* and the other part means *broom*. In Shanghai, May and I had servants. Now I am the servant. Why just me? I don't know. Maybe because I have a baby, maybe because May doesn't understand when Yen-yen tells her to do something in Sze Yup, or maybe because May isn't perpetually scared that we'll be found out, that we'll be disgraced

207

— she for bearing a child that's not her husband's and I for being unable ever to have babies of my own — and that we'll be discarded in the street. So every morning after Vern goes to his ninth-grade classes at Central Junior High and May, Sam, and the old man go to China City, I stay in the apartment to scrub on a washboard sheets, stained underwear, Joy's diapers, and the sweaty clothes of the uncles, as well as those of the bachelors who stay with us periodically. I empty the spittoon and put out extra containers for the shells of the watermelon seeds my in-laws nibble. I wash the floors and the windows.

While Yen-yen teaches me to make soup by boiling a head of lettuce and pouring soy sauce over it or prepare lunch by taking a bowl of rice, slathering lard on top, and sprinkling on soy sauce to cover the taste, my sister goes exploring. While I shell walnuts with Yen-yen to sell to restaurants or swab the bathtub ring the old man leaves after his daily soak, my sister meets people. While my mother-in-law teaches me how to be a wife and mother — jobs she does with a frustrating combination of ineptitude, good cheer, and fierce protectiveness — my sister learns where everything is.

Even though Sam said he'd take me to China City — a tourist attraction that's being built two blocks from here — I have yet to go. But May walks over there every day to help get things ready for the Grand Opening. She tells me that soon I'll work in the café, the antiques store, the curio shop, or whatever place Old Man Louie has told her that afternoon; I listen with a kind of wariness, knowing that I don't have a choice about

208

where I'll work but that I'll be grateful not to be doing any more piecework with Yen-yen: tying scallions in bunches, separating strawberries by size and quality, shelling those damn walnuts until my fingers are stained and cracked, or — and this is truly disgusting — growing bean sprouts in the tub in between the baths the old man takes. I stay home with my mother-in-law and Joy; my sister returns at the end of every day with tales of people with names like Peanut and Dolly. At China City, she looks through our boxes of clothes. We agreed that if we were going to live in America, then we should dress like Americans, but she stubbornly brings only cheongsams. She picks the prettiest ones for herself. Maybe this is as it should be. As Yen-yen says, "You're a mother now. Your sister still has to make my boy give her a son."

Every day May tells me of her adventures, her cheeks pink from fresh air, her face lit with pleasure. I'm the older sister, and I'm suffering from red-eye disease, envy. I've always been the first to discover new things, but now May's the one who reports about the shops and stores and fun things that are being planned at China City. She tells me that a lot of it is being built from used movie sets, which she describes in such detail that I'm sure I'll recognize them all and know their backstories when I finally see them. But I can't lie. It bothers me that she gets to be a part of the excitement, while I have to stay with my mother-in-law and Joy in the grimy apartment, where the dust floating in the air leaves me feeling suffocated and dizzy. I tell myself this is just temporary, like Angel Island was

209

temporary, and soon — somehow — May and I will escape.

In the meantime, Old Man Louie continues to punish me for having a daughter by ignoring me. Sam mopes about with a sullen look on his face, because I refuse to do the husband-wife thing with him. Every time he approaches, I cross my arms and clasp my elbows. He slinks away as though I've wounded him deeply. He rarely speaks to me, and when he does it's in the Wu dialect of the streets, like I'm beneath him. Yen-yen responds to my obvious unhappiness and frustration with a lesson on marriage: "You must get used to it."

At the beginning of May, after we've been here for two weeks, my sister asks for and receives permission from Yen-yen to take Joy and me outside for a walk. "Across the Plaza is Olvera Street, where Mexican people have little shops for tourists," May says, pointing in the general direction. "Beyond that is China City. From there, if you walk up to Broadway and turn north, you'll feel like you've entered a postcard of Italy. Salami hangs in the windows and . . . Oh, Pearl, it's as foreign and strange as how the White Russians lived in the French Concession." She pauses and laughs to herself. "I almost forgot. There's a French Concession here too. They call it French Town, and it's on Hill Street just up one block from Broadway. They have a French hospital and cafés and . . . Never mind all that for now. Let's just talk about Broadway. If you go south on Broadway, you'll come to American movie palaces and department stores. If you go north through Little

Italy, you'll come to a whole other Chinatown that's being built. It's called New Chinatown. I'll take you there whenever you want to go."

But I don't feel like going right then.

"This isn't like Shanghai, where we were separated by race, money, and power but still saw each other every day," May makes clear the next week, when she takes Joy and me around the block again. "We walked on the streets together, even if we didn't go to the same nightclubs. Here everyone is separated from everyone else — Japanese, Mexicans, Italians, blacks, and Chinese. White people are everywhere, but the rest of us are at the bottom. Everyone wants to be a single rice kernel better than his neighbor. Remember in Shanghai how important it was to know English and how people prided themselves on their American or British accents? Here people are split by whose Chinese is better and where and from whom they learned it. Did you learn it in one of the missions here in Chinatown? Did you learn it in China? You know how it is between Sze Yup and Sam Yup speakers? One won't talk to the other. One won't do business with the other. If that weren't enough, the American-born Chinese look down on people like us, calling us fresh off the boat and backward. We look down on them, because we know that American culture isn't as good as Chinese culture. People stick together by name too. If you're a Louie, you have to buy from a Louie, even if you have to pay five cents more. Everyone knows no help will come from the lo fan, but even a Mock, Wong, or SooHoo won't help a Louie."

211

She points out the filling station, although we have yet to meet anyone who owns a car. She walks me past Jerry's Joint — a bar with Chinese food and a Chinese atmosphere but not owned by a Chinese. Every non-business space is a flophouse of one sort or another: tiny apartments like the one we live in for families, boardinghouses for a few dollars a month for Chinese bachelor-laborers like the uncles, and rooms lent out by the missions, where men truly down on their luck can sleep, eat, and make a couple of dollars a month in exchange for keeping the place tidy.

After a month of these excursions around the block, May takes me into the Plaza. "This used to be the heart of the original Spanish settlement. Did we have Spanish people in Shanghai?" May asks lightly, almost gaily. "I don't remember meeting any."

She doesn't give me a chance to answer, because she's so intent on showing me Olvera Street, which is just opposite Sanchez Alley on the other side of the Plaza. I don't want to see it particularly, but after many days of her complaining and insisting, I cross the open space with her and venture into the pedestrian way filled with colorfully painted plywood stalls displaying embroidered cotton shirts, heavy clay ashtrays, and lollipops shaped like pointed spires. People in lacy costumes make candles, blow glass, and hammer soles for sandals, while others sing and play instruments.

"Is this how people in Mexico really live?" May asks.

I don't know if it's at all like Mexico, but it's festive and vibrant compared with our dingy apartment. "I have no idea. Maybe."

"Well, if you think this is funny and cute, wait until you see China City."

About halfway down the street, she stops abruptly. "Look, there's Christine Sterling." She nods toward an elderly but elegantly dressed white woman sitting on the porch of a house that looks like it was made from mud. "She developed Olvera Street. She's behind China City too. Everyone says she has a big heart. They say she wants to help Mexicans and Chinese have their own businesses during these hard times. She came to Los Angeles with nothing, just like we did. Now she's about to have two tourist attractions."

We reach the end of the block. A flock of American cars trawl and beep their way along the roadway. Across Macy Street, I see the wall that surrounds China City.

"I'll take you over there, if you'd like," May offers. "All we have to do is cross the street."

I shake my head. "Maybe another time."

As we walk back through Olvera Street, May waves and smiles to shop owners, who don't wave or smile back.

While may works with Old Man Louie and Sam is getting things ready in China City, Yen-yen and I do our piecework in the apartment, look after Vernon when he comes home from school, and take turns carrying Joy during the long afternoons when she cries endlessly for who knows what reason. But even if I could go visiting, who would I meet? There's only about one woman or girl here for every ten men. Local girls May's and my age are often forbidden to go out

213

with boys, and the Chinese men living here don't want to marry them anyway.

"Girls born here are too Americanized," Uncle Edfred says when he comes to Sunday dinner. "When I get rich, I'll go back to the home village to get a traditional wife."

Some men — like Uncle Wilburt — have wives back in China they don't see for years at a time. "I haven't done the husband-wife thing with my wife since forever. Too expensive to go to China for that. I'm saving my money to go home for good."

With thinking like this, most girls remain unmarried. During the week, they go to American school and then Chinese-language school at one of the missions. On weekends, they work in their families' businesses and go to the missions for Chinese culture instruction. We don't fit in with those girls, and we're too young to fit in with the other wives and mothers, who seem backward to us. Even if they were born here, most of them — like Yen-yen — didn't even complete elementary school. That's how isolated, guarded, and protected they are.

One evening at the end of May, thirty-nine days after we arrived in Los Angeles and a few days before China City opens, Sam comes home and says, "You can go outside with your sister, if you want. I can give Joy her bottle."

I'm reluctant to leave her with him, but these past weeks I've seen that she responds well to the awkward way he holds her, whispers in her ear, and tickles her tummy. Seeing her content — and knowing that Sam

214

would just as soon have me gone so he won't have to make conversation with me — May and I go out into the spring night. We walk to the Plaza, where we sit on a bench, listen to Mexican music wafting over from Olvera Street, and watch children play in Sanchez Alley, using a paper bag plumped with wadded newspapers and tied with a string as their ball.

At last May is no longer trying to show me things or trying to get me to cross this or that street. We can just sit and — for a few minutes — be ourselves. We have no privacy in the apartment, where everyone can hear everything that's said and everything that's done. Now, without so many listening ears, we're able to talk freely and share secrets. We reminisce about Mama, Baba, Tommy, Betsy, Z.G., and even our old servants. We talk about the foods we miss and Shanghai's scents and sounds, which seem so distant to us now. Finally, we pull ourselves away from the loneliness of lost people and places and force ourselves to focus on what's happening right around us. I know every time Yen-yen and Old Man Louie do the husband-wife thing from the creaking of their mattress. I know as well that Vern and May haven't done anything like that yet.

"You haven't done it with Sam either," May retorts. "You've got to do it. You're married. You have a baby with him."

"But why should I do it when you haven't done it with Vern?"

May makes a face. "How can I? There's something wrong with him."

215

Back in Shanghai, I'd thought she was just being unkind, but now that I've lived with Vern and spent far more time with him than May has, I know she's right. And it's not just that he hasn't begun his growth into manhood.

"I don't think he's retarded," I say, trying to be helpful.

May impatiently waves away the idea. "It's not that. He's . . . damaged." She searches the canopy of tree branches above us, as though she might find an answer there. "He talks, but not much. Sometimes he doesn't seem to understand what's happening around him. Other times he's completely obsessed — like with those model airplanes and boats the old man is always buying for him to glue together."

"At least they take care of him," I reason. "Remember the boy we saw on the boat on the Grand Canal? His family kept him in a cage."

Either May doesn't remember or she doesn't care, because she goes on without acknowledging me. "They treat Vern like he's special. Yen-yen irons his clothes and lays them out for him in the morning. She calls him Boy-husband —"

"She's like Mama that way. She calls everyone by title or rank in the family. She even calls her husband Old Man Louie!"

It feels good to laugh. Mama and Baba had called him that as a sign of respect; we'd always called him that because we didn't like him; Yen-yen calls him that because that's how she sees him.

216

"She has natural feet, but she's far more backward than Mama ever was," I continue. "She believes in ghosts, spirits, potions, the zodiac, what to eat and not eat, all that mumbo jumbo —"

May snorts in disgust and irritation. "Remember when I made the mistake of saying I had a cold and she brewed me a tea of ginger and dried scallions to clear my chest and made me breathe steamed vinegar to relieve my congestion? That was disgusting!"

"But it worked."

"Yes," May admits, "but now she wants me to go to the herbalist to make me more fertile and attractive to the boy-husband. She tells me that the Sheep and the Boar are among the most compatible of the signs."

"Mama always said that the Boar has a pure heart, that it has great honesty and simplicity."

"Vern's simple all right." May shudders. "I've tried, you know. I mean . . ." She hesitates. "I sleep in the same bed with him. Some people would say the boy's lucky to have me there. But he won't do anything, even though he has everything below that he needs."

She lets that hang in the air for me to consider. We're both killing time here in this horrible limbo, but anytime I think things are bad for me, all I have to do is think about my sister in the next room.

"And then when I go to the kitchen in the morning," May says, "Yen-yen asks, 'Where's your son? I need a grandson.' When I came home from China City last week, she pulled me aside and said, 'I see the visit from the little red sister has come again. Tomorrow you will eat sparrow kidneys and dried tangerine peel to strengthen your *chi*. The herbalist tells me this will make your womb welcome my son's vital essence.;"

The way she imitates Yen-yen's high-pitched, squeaky voice makes me smile, but May doesn't see the humor.

"Why don't they make *you* eat sparrow kidneys and tangerine peel? Why don't they send *you* to the herbalist?" she demands.

I don't know why Old Man Louie and his wife treat Sam and me differently. Yen-yen may have a title for everyone, but I've never heard her call Sam anything — not by title, not by his American name, not even by his Chinese name. And except for that first night, my father-in-law rarely speaks to either of us.

"Sam and his father don't get along," I say. "Have you noticed that?"

"They fight quite a bit. The old man calls Sam *toh gee* and *chok gin*. I don't know what they mean, but they aren't compliments."

"He's saying Sam's lazy and empty-headed." I don't spend much time with Sam, so I ask, "Is he?"

"Not that I've seen. The old man keeps insisting Sam run the rickshaw rides when China City opens. He wants Sam to be a puller. Sam doesn't want to do it."

"Who would?" I shudder.

"Not here, not anywhere," May agrees. "Not even if it's just an entertainment for people."

I wouldn't mind talking about Sam a bit more, but May circles back to the problem of her husband.

"You'd think they'd treat him like the other boys around here and have him work with his father after school. He could help Sam and me unpack crates and

218

put merchandise on the shelves for when China City opens, but the old man insists that Vern go straight home to the apartment to do his homework. I think all he does is go to his room and work on his models. And not very well from what I can see."

"I know. I see more of him than you do. I'm with him every day." I don't know if May hears the sourness in my voice, but I do and I hurry to hide it. "Everyone knows a son is precious. Maybe they're preparing him to take over the businesses one day."

"But he's the youngest son! They aren't going to let him do that. It wouldn't be right. But Vern's got to learn how to do something. It's like they want to keep him a little boy forever."

"Maybe they don't want Vern to leave. Maybe they don't want *any* of us to leave. They're just so backward. The way we all live together, the way the businesses are kept within the family, the way they keep their money hidden and protected, the way they don't give us any spending money."

That's right. May and I don't receive a household allowance. Of course, we can't say that we want our own money to escape from this place and start over again.

"It's like they're a bunch of bumpkins from the countryside," May says bitterly. "And the way Yen-yen cooks," she adds almost as an afterthought. "What kind of a Chinese woman is she?"

"We don't know how to cook either."

"But we were never expected to cook! We were going to have servants for that."

219

We sit and think about that for a while, but what's the point of dreaming about the past when it's gone? May looks over to Sanchez Alley. Most of the children have returned to their apartments. "We'd better get back before Old Man Louie locks us out."

We walk back to the apartment arm in arm. My heart feels lighter. May and I are not only sisters but sisters-in-law as well. For thousands of years, daughters-in-law have complained about the hardship of life in their husbands' homes, living under the iron fists of their fathers-in-law and under the calloused thumbs of their mothers-in-law. May and I are very lucky to have each other.

Dreams of Oriental Romance

On June 8, almost two months after we arrived in Los Angeles, I cross the street at last and enter China City for the Grand Opening. China City is enclosed by a miniature Great Wall — although it's hard to call it "Great" when it looks just like cardboard cutouts placed on top of a narrow wall. I pass through the main gate and encounter a thousand or so people grouped together in a big open area called the Court of the Four Seasons. Dignitaries and movie stars give speeches, firecrackers spit and crackle, a dragon parades, and lion dancers frolic. The *lo fan* look glamorous and fashionable: the women in silks and furs, gloves and hats, and shiny lipstick; the men in suits, wing tips, and fedoras. May and I wear *cheongsams*, but as sleek and beautiful as we look in them, I feel we appear outdated and foreign compared with the American women.

"Dreams of Oriental romance are woven like silk threads through the little fabric that is China City," Christine Sterling proclaims from the stage. "We ask

Your Honorable Person to see the brilliant colors of its hopes and ideals and to forget the imperfections in its creation, because these will fade with the passing years. Let those who have peopled the generations of China's existence, who have survived catastrophes of every kind in their motherland, find a new haven, where they can perpetuate their desire for collective identity, follow in the footsteps of their ancestors, and ply the trades and arts of their heritage in all tranquillity."

Oh, brother.

"Leave the new world of rush and confusion behind," Christine Sterling goes on, "and enter the old world of languorous enchantment."

Really?

The shops and restaurants will open their doors for business as soon as the speeches finish, and those who work here — Yen-yen and me included — will need to hurry to take their positions. As we listen, I hold Joy in my arms so she can see what's happening. With the undulating crowds and all the jostling, we get separated from Yen-yen. I'm supposed to go to the Golden Dragon Café, but I don't know where it is. How can I get lost in just one block surrounded by a wall? But with so many blind alleys and narrow paths that twist and turn, I'm completely confused. I walk through doorways only to find myself in a courtyard with a goldfish pond or in a stand selling incense. I press Joy tight against my chest and squeeze up against the wall as the rickshaws — emblazoned with the Golden Rickshaws' logo — haul laughing *lo fan* through the alleys, the pullers calling, "Coming through! Coming through!" These aren't like any rickshaw pullers I've ever seen. They're all dolled up in silk pajamas, embroidered slippers, and brand-new coolie hats made from straw. And they aren't Chinese. They're Mexican.

A little girl costumed like a street urchin — only cleaner — wiggles through the crowd, handing out maps. I take one and open it, looking for where I need to go. The map shows the big sights: the Steps of Heaven, the Harbor of Whangpoo, the Lotus Pool, and the Court of the Four Seasons. At the bottom of the map, two men dressed in Chinese robes and slippers drawn in black ink bow to each other. The caption reads: "If you will condescend your august self to enlighten our humble city, we greet you with sweetmeats, wines, and music rare, and also objets d'art that will delight your noble eyes." Nothing on this map shows any of Old Man Louie's enterprises, each of which has Golden in its name.

China City isn't like Shanghai. It isn't like the Old Chinese City either. It isn't even like a Chinese village. It looks a lot like the China May and I used to see in movies brought to Shanghai from Hollywood. Yes, it's all exactly as May described during our walks together. Paramount Studios has donated a set from *Bluebeard's Eighth Wife*, which has now been converted into the Chinese Junk Café. Workmen from MGM have meticulously reassembled Wang's Farmhouse from *The Good Earth*, right down to the ducks and chickens in the yard. Behind Wang's Farmhouse winds the Passage of One Hundred Surprises, where those same MGM carpenters have converted an old blacksmith shop into ten novelty boutiques, selling jewel trees, scented teas, and fringed and embroidered "Spanish" shawls made in China. The tapestries in the Temple of Kwan Yin are reputed to be thousands of years old, and the statue was supposedly saved from the bombing of Shanghai. In fact, like so many things at China City, the temple was constructed from more leftover sets from MGM. Even the Great Wall came from a movie, although it must have been a western in which a fort needed defending. Christine Sterling's determination to repackage her Olvera Street concept into something Chinese has been matched by her total lack of understanding of our culture, history, and taste.

My brain tells me I'm safe. Too many people mill about for anyone to try to trap or hurt me, but I'm nervous and scared. I hurry down another blind alley. I hold Joy so tightly she starts to cry. People stare at me as though I'm a bad mother. *I'm not a bad mother*, I want to shout. *This is my baby.* In my panic I think, if I can find the front entrance, then I'll be able to find my way back to the apartment. But Old Man Louie locked the door on our way out and I don't have a key. Agitated and apprehensive, I put my head down and shove through the people.

"Are you lost?" A voice addresses me in the pure tones of the Wu dialect of Shanghai. "Do you need help?"

I look up to see a *lo fan* with white hair, glasses, and a full white beard.

"I think you must be May's sister," he says. "Are you Pearl?"

I nod.

"I'm Tom Gubbins. Most people call me Bak Wah Tom — Motion Pictures Tom. I have a shop here, and I know your sister. Tell me where you need to go."

"They want me at the Golden Dragon Café."

"Ah, yes, one of the many Golden enterprises. Anything that's worth five cents around here is run by your father-in-law," he says knowingly. "Come along. I'll take you there."

I don't know this man and May has never mentioned him, but perhaps he's just one of many things she hasn't told me. Still, the sounds of Shanghai coming from his mouth give me all the assurance I need. On our way to the café, he points out the various shops my father-in-law owns. The Golden Lantern, Old Man Louie's original store from Old Chinatown, sells cheap curios: ashtrays, toothpick holders, and back scratchers. Through the window, I see Yen-yen talking to customers. Farther along, Vern sits by himself in a tiny shop, the Golden Lotus, selling silk flowers. I've heard Old Man Louie boast to our neighbors about how little it cost him to open this business: "Silk flowers cost almost nothing in China. Here I can sell them for five times their original price." He scoffed at another family that opened a live-flower stand. "They paid eighteen dollars for the icebox at the secondhand store. Every day they'll spend fifty cents to buy a hundred pounds of ice. They have to buy cans and vases to put the flowers in. Altogether fifty dollars! Too much! Too wasteful! And it isn't hard to sell silk flowers, because even my son can do it."

225

I see the top of the Golden Pagoda before we reach it and know that from now on I can always look up to get my bearings. The Golden Pagoda is housed in a fake pagoda five tiers high. From here, Old Man Louie — dressed in a midnight blue mandarin gown — plans to sell his best merchandise: cloisonné, fine porcelains, mother-of-pearl inlay, carved teakwood furniture, opium pipes, ivory mah-jongg sets, and antiques. Through the window, I see May standing a little to his left, chatting with a family of four, gesturing animatedly, and smiling so broadly I can see her teeth. She looks different and yet very much the sister I've always known. Her *cheongsam* clings to her like a second skin. Her hair swirls around her face, and I realize she's gotten her hair cut and styled. How have I not noticed that before? But it's the old radiance that shines out of her that really surprises me. I haven't seen her like this in a long time.

"She's very beautiful," Tom observes, as if reading my thoughts. "I've told her I could get her work, but she's afraid you won't approve. What do you think, Pearl? You can see I'm not a bad man. Why don't you think about it and talk it over with May?"

I understand his words, but I can't take in their meaning.

Seeing my confusion, he shrugs. "All right then. On to the Golden Dragon."

When we get there, he glances in the window and says, "It looks like they could use your help, so I won't keep you. But if you ever need anything, come see me at the Asiatic Costume Company. May will show you where it is. She visits me every day."

With that, he turns away and melts into the crowd. I pull open the door to the Golden Dragon Café and enter. There are eight tables and a counter with ten stools. Behind the counter Uncle Wilburt, wearing a white undershirt and a paper hat folded from plain newsprint, sweats over a sizzling wok. Next to him Uncle Charley chops ingredients with a cleaver. Uncle Edfred carries a load of dishes to the sink, where Sam rinses dirty glasses under a steaming tap.

"Hey, can we get some help over here?" a man calls out.

Sam wipes his hands, hurries over, hands me a notepad, takes Joy from my arms, and places her in a wooden crate behind the counter. For the next six hours, we work without stop. By the time the Grand Opening officially ends, Sam's clothes are smeared with food and grease, and my feet, shoulders, and arms ache, but Joy's sound asleep in her crate. Old Man Louie and the others come to fetch us. The uncles head to wherever it is Chinatown bachelors go at night. After my father-in-law locks the door, we set out for the apartment. Sam, Vern, and their father walk ahead, while Yen-yen, May, and I stay a proper ten paces behind them. I'm exhausted and Joy feels as heavy as a sack of rice, but no one offers to take her from me.

Old Man Louie told us not to use a language he can't understand, but I speak to May in the Wu dialect, hoping Yen-yen won't tell on us and trusting we're far enough from the men that they won't hear.

"You've been keeping things from me, May."

I'm not angry. I'm hurt. May has been building a new life in China City, while I've been locked in the apartment. She's even gotten a haircut! Oh, how that burns now that I've noticed it.

"Things? What things?" She keeps her voice low — so we won't be heard? So I won't raise mine?

"I thought we decided we would wear only Western clothes once we got here. We said we would try to look like Americans, but all you bring me are these."

"That's one of your favorite *cheongsams*," May says.

"I don't want to wear these anymore. We agreed —"

She slows, and as I pass her she reaches for my shoulder to hold me back. Yen-yen keeps walking, obediently following her husband and sons.

"I haven't wanted to tell you, because I knew you'd be upset," May whispers. She taps her lips hesitantly with three knuckles.

"What is it?" I sigh. "Just tell me."

"Our Western dresses are gone. He" — she nods toward the men, but I know she's referring to our father-in-law — "doesn't want us to wear anything but our Chinese clothes."

"Why —"

"Just listen to me, Pearl. I've been trying to tell you things. I've been trying to show you things, but sometimes you're as bad as Mama. You don't want to know. You don't want to listen."

Her words stun and wound me, but she isn't finished.

228

"You know how the people who work on Olvera Street have to wear Mexican costumes? That's because Mrs. Sterling insists on it. It's in their rental agreements, just as it's in our leases at China City. We *have* to wear our *cheongsams* to work there. They — Mrs. Sterling and her *lo fan* partners — want us to look like we've never left China. Old Man Louie must have known that when he took our clothes in Shanghai. Think about it, Pearl. We thought he had no taste, no discernment, but he knew exactly what he was looking for and he took only what he thought would be useful here. He left everything else behind."

"Why didn't you tell me this before?"

"How could I? You're barely *here*. I've been trying to get you to go places with me, but usually you don't want to leave the apartment. I had to drag you out just to sit in the Plaza. You don't say anything about it, but I know you blame me and Sam and Vern and all of us for keeping you inside. But no one's keeping you inside. You won't go anywhere. I couldn't even get you to cross the street to go to China City until today!"

"What do I care about these places? We aren't going to be here forever."

"But how are we going to escape if we don't know what's out there?"

Because it's easier not to do anything, because I'm scared, I think but don't say.

"You're like a bird that's been freed from a cage," May says, "but doesn't remember how to fly. You're my sister, but I don't know where you've gone in your mind. You're so far away from me now."

We climb the stairs back to the apartment. At the door, she holds me back once again. "Why can't you be the sister I knew in Shanghai? You were fun. You weren't afraid of anything. Now you act like a *fu yen*." She pauses. "I'm sorry. That sounded terrible. I know you've been through a lot, and I realize you have to give all your attention and care to the baby. But I miss you, Pearl. I miss my sister."

From inside we hear Yen-yen coo to her son. "Boy-husband, it's time for you to go to bed. Go get your wife and go to bed now."

"I miss Mama and Baba. I miss our home. And this" — she gestures around the dark hallway — "is all so hard. I can't do it without you." Tears roll down her cheeks. She wipes them away roughly, takes a breath, and enters the apartment to go to her room with her boy-husband.

A few minutes later, I lay Joy in her drawer and get in bed. Sam rolls away from me, as he usually does, and I cling to the edge of the bed as far from him and as close to Joy as I can get. My feelings and thoughts are confused. The clothes are yet another unanticipated blow, but what about the other things May said? I hadn't realized she was suffering too. And she was right about me. I have been afraid: to leave the apartment, to go to the end of Sanchez Alley, to enter the Plaza, to walk down Olvera Street, and to cross the street to China City. These past weeks, May had offered many times: "I'll take you to China City whenever you want to go." But I hadn't gone.

I grab the pouch Mama gave me through my clothes. What's happened to me? How have I become such a scared *fu yen*?

On June 25, just a few blocks away and less than three weeks later, New Chinatown has its Grand Opening. Big traditional Chinese carved gates stand stately and colorful at each end of the block. Anna May Wong, the glamorous movie star, leads the parade. A Chinese all-girl drum corps gives a rousing performance. Neon lights outline gaily painted buildings decorated with all manner of Chinese froufrou on the eaves and balconies. Everything seems bigger and better there. They have more firecrackers, more important politicians to cut the ribbons and make speeches, more sinuous and acrobatic crews to perform the dragon and lion dances. Even the people who've opened shops and restaurants there are considered better, wealthier, and more established than those of us in China City.

People say that the opening of these two Chinatowns is the beginning of good times for Chinese in Los Angeles. I say it's the beginning of hard feelings. In China City, we have to do more and make a better effort. My father-in-law uses his iron fist to make us all work even longer hours. He's relentless and often cruel. None of us disobey him, but I don't see how we'll ever catch up. How can you compete when others have a larger advantage? And with things the way they are, how are we ever going to make our own money to leave this place?

Scents of Home

I should be plotting where May, Joy, and I will go, but I find that nothing drives me to explore more than my stomach, where my loneliness has settled. I miss things like honey-covered dough confections, sugared rose cakes, and spiced eggs boiled in tea. Having lost even more weight from Yen-yen's cooking than I did on Angel Island, I watch Uncle Wilburt and Uncle Charley, the first and second cooks at the Golden Dragon, and try to learn from them. They let me go with them to the Sam Sing Butcher Shop with its gold-leafed pig in the window to buy pork and duck. They take me to George Wong's fish market, which backs up to China City on Spring Street, to teach me to buy only what's still breathing. We cross the street to the International Grocery, and for the first time since being here, I smell the scents of home. Uncle Wilburt uses some of his own money to buy me a bag of salted black beans. I'm so grateful that after that the uncles take turns buying me other little treats: jujubes, honeyed dates, bamboo shoots, lotus buds, and mushrooms. Every few days, if we have a lull in the café, they let me join them behind the counter to show me how to cook a single and very quick dish using these special ingredients.

The uncles come to the apartment for dinner every Sunday night. I ask Yen-yen if she'll let me make the meal. The family eats it. After that, I make every Sunday dinner. Pretty soon I can make dinner in thirty minutes, as long as Vern washes the rice and Sam chops the vegetables. At first, Old Man Louie isn't pleased. "Why should I let you squander my money on food? Why should I let you *out* to buy food?" (This, although he doesn't mind that we walk to and from work, where we cater to total strangers, white ones at that.)

I say, "I don't waste your money, because Uncle Wilburt and Uncle Charley pay for the food. And I don't walk alone, because I'm always with Uncle Wilburt and Uncle Charley."

"This is even worse! The uncles are saving their money to go home. Everyone — including me — has the desire to return to China, if not to live then to die, if not to die then to have his bones buried there." Like so many men, Old Man Louie wants to save ten thousand dollars and return a rich man to his ancestral village, where he'll acquire a few concubines, have more sons, and spend his days sipping tea. He also wants to be recognized as a "big man," which can't be more American. "Every time I go back, I buy more fields. If they won't let me own land here, then I'll own it in China. Oh, I know what you're thinking, Pearl. You're

233

thinking, But you were born here! You're an American! I tell you, I may have been born here, but I'm Chinese in my heart. I will go back."

He's so predictable in his complaints and the way he can turn something about the uncles or anyone else into something about him, but I accept them, because he likes my cooking. He'll never *say* that, but he does something even better. After a few Sundays, he announces, "I will give you money every Monday to buy food for all our meals." Sometimes I'm tempted to put a little aside for myself, but I know how closely he watches every penny and receipt, and that he periodically checks with the people at the butcher, fish market, and dry goods store. He's so careful with his money that he refuses to keep it in a bank. It's all hidden, distributed in separate caches in the various Golden establishments to protect it from disaster and from *lo fan* bankers.

Now that I can go to the stores by myself, the shop owners begin to know me. They like my business — small as it is — and reward my loyalty to their roast duck, live fish, or pickled turnips by giving me calendars. The images are Chinafied, with brash reds, blues, and greens against harsh white backgrounds. Instead of beautiful girls reclining in their boudoirs, sending a feeling of ease, relaxation, and eroticism, the artists have chosen to paint uninspired landscapes of the Great Wall, the sacred mountain of Emei, the mystical karsts of Kweilin, or insipid-looking women wearing *cheongsams* made from shiny cloth in geometric patterns and sitting in poses meant to convey the virtues of moral rearmament. The artists' technique is garish and commercial, with no delicacy or emotion, but I hang the calendars on the walls of the apartment, just as the poorest of the poor in Shanghai hung them in their sad little huts to bring a little color and wishful hoping into their lives. These things brighten the apartment as much as my meals, and as long as they're given free, my father-in-law is satisfied.

Christmas eve morning I wake at five, get dressed, give Joy to my mother-in-law, and then walk with Sam to China City. It's still early but strangely warm. Hot winds blew all night, leaving broken branches, dried leaves, confetti, and other trash from Olvera Street's holiday revelers scattered on the Plaza and along Main Street. We cross Macy, enter China City, and follow our usual route, starting by the rickshaw stand in the Court of the Four Seasons and then edging around the chickens and ducks that peck at the ground in front of Wang's Farmhouse. I still haven't seen *The Good Earth*, but Uncle Charley has told me I should, saying, "It's just like China." Uncle Wilburt also wants me to see the movie. "If you go, watch for the mob scene. I'm in that one! You'll see lots of uncles and aunties from Chinatown in that picture show." But I don't go to the movie and I don't enter the farmhouse, because every time I pass it I'm reminded of the shack outside Shanghai.

From Wang's Farmhouse, I follow Sam down Dragon Road. "Walk next to me," he invites me in Sze Yup, but I don't because I don't want to encourage

235

him. If I make small talk with him during the day or do something like walk next to him, then he'll want to do the husband-wife thing.

Apart from the rickshaw rides, all the other Golden businesses are in the oval, where Dragon and Kwan Yin Roads meet. It's along this route that the rickshaws make their serpentine loop. Only twice in the six months I've worked here have I ventured over to the Lotus Pool or into the covered area that houses a theater for Chinese opera, a penny arcade, and Tom Gubbins's Asiatic Costume Company. China City may be one oddly shaped block bordered by Main, Macy, Spring, and Ord Streets — with over forty shops crammed together with all the cafés, restaurants, and other "tourist attractions" like Wang's Farmhouse — but there are distinct enclaves inside the walls, and the people within them rarely associate with their neighbors.

Sam unlocks the door to the café, flips on the lights, and starts brewing coffee. As I refill the salt and pepper shakers, the uncles and the other workers straggle in and begin their chores. By the time the pies are sliced and put on display, the early-bird customers have arrived. I chat with our regulars — truck drivers and postal workers — take orders, and call them out to the cooks.

At nine, a pair of policemen come in and sit at the counter. I smooth my apron and allow my teeth to show in grinning welcome. If we don't fill their bellies for free, they follow our customers to their cars and give them tickets. These last two weeks have been particularly bad as the police walked from one store to the next, collecting Christmas "presents" until their arms were loaded. A week ago, after they decided they hadn't received enough gifts, they blocked the auto park, preventing customers from coming at all. Now everyone's cowed, obedient, and willing to give whatever the policemen ask for so long as they let us keep our doors open.

Just as the police leave, a truck driver calls out to Sam, "Hey, buddy, get me a piece of that blueberry pie to go, will ya?"

Maybe Sam's still nervous about the policemen's visit, because he ignores the request and continues washing glasses. By now it seems like an eternity ago that I learned from my coaching book that Sam was to be the manager of the café, but actually his position is somewhere between a glass washer and a dish washer. I watch him as I serve eggs, potatoes, toast, and coffee for thirty-five cents or a jelly roll and coffee for a nickel. Someone asks Sam for a coffee refill, but he doesn't go over with the pot until the man taps the edge of his cup impatiently. A half hour later, that same man asks for his bill, and Sam points to me. Not once does he say a word to any of our customers.

The breakfast rush slows. Sam gathers dirty plates and silverware, while I follow after him with a wet cloth to wipe the tables and counters.

"Sam," I say in English, "why don't you talk to our customers?" When he doesn't respond, I go on, still in English. "In Shanghai, the *lo fan* always said that Chinese waiters were surly and bad-mannered. You don't want our customers to think that about you, do you?"

His look fades into nervousness, and he gnaws his lower lip.

I switch to Sze Yup. "You don't know English, do you?"

"I know some," he says. Then he amends this, smiling sheepishly. "A little. Very little."

"How can that be?"

"I was born in China. Why would I know it?"

"Because you lived here until you were seven."

"That was a long time ago. I don't remember the words from then."

"But didn't you study it in China?" I ask. Everyone I knew in Shanghai learned English. Even May, who was a very poor student, knows the language.

Sam doesn't respond directly. "I can try to speak English, but the customers refuse to understand me. And when they talk to me, I don't understand them either." He nods to the wall clock. "You'd better go."

He's always pushing me out the door. I know he goes somewhere in the mornings and in the late afternoons, just as I do. As a *fu yen* it's not my place to ask where he goes. If Sam is gambling or has hired someone to do the husband-wife thing with him, what can I do? If he's one of those womanizer types, what can I do? If he's a gambler like my father, what can I do? I learned to be a wife from my mother and from watching Yen-yen, and I know there's nothing you can do if your husband wants to walk out on you. You don't know where he goes. He comes back when he comes back, and that's it.

238

I wash my hands and take off my apron. As I walk to the Golden Lantern, I think about what Sam said. How can he *not* know English? My English is perfect — and I've learned it's polite to say *Occidental* instead of *lo fan* or *fan gwaytze* and *Oriental* instead of *Chinaman* or *Chink* — but I understand that isn't the way to get a tip or make a sale. People come to China City to be entertained. Customers like me to speak wantee-chopsuey English — and how easy that is, after I've listened to Vern, Old Man Louie, and so many others, who were born here but speak crooked, misshapen English. For me, it's an act; for Sam, it's ignorance — country, and as distasteful to me as his secret dalliances with who knows who.

I reach the Golden Lantern, where Yen-yen sells curios and babysits Joy. Together we polish, dust, and sweep. When I finish, I play with Joy for a while. At 11:30, I once again leave Joy with Yen-yen and go back to the café, where as fast as I can I serve hamburgers for fifteen cents. Our hamburgers aren't as popular as the Chinaburgers at Fook Gay's Café, with their stir-fried bean sprouts, black mushrooms, and soy sauce, but we do well with our bowls of salted fish with pork for ten cents, and plain bowls of rice and tea for five cents.

After lunch, I work at the Golden Lotus, selling silk flowers until Vern arrives from school. Then I go to the Golden Pagoda. I want to talk to my sister about our plans for Christmas Day, but she's busy convincing a customer that a piece of lacquer was painted on a raft in the middle of a lake lest a speck of dust mar the

239

perfection of its surface, and I'm busy sweeping, dusting, polishing, and shining.

Before heading back to the café, I return to the Golden Lantern, pick up Joy, and take her for a short walk through China City's alleys. Much like the tourists, she loves to watch the rickshaws. Golden Rickshaw rides are hugely popular — they're Old Man Louie's most successful enterprise. Johnny Yee, one of the local boys, pulls rickshaws for celebrities or for promotional photographs, but usually Miguel, Jose, and Ramon do the job. They earn tips and a small percentage of the twenty-five-cent fare for each ride. They get a little more if they can persuade a customer to buy a photo for an extra twenty-five cents.

Today a woman passenger kicks Miguel and then swats him with her purse. Why would she do that? Because she can. The way pullers were treated in Shanghai never bothered me. Was it because my father owned the business? Because I was like this white woman — *above* the pullers? Because in Shanghai pullers were barely better than dogs, whereas here May and I are now in their class? I have to say yes, yes, and yes again.

I drop Joy back with her grandmother, kiss my baby good night because I won't see her again until I go home, and then spend the rest of the evening serving sweet-and-sour pork, cashew chicken, and chop suey — all dishes I never saw or even heard of in Shanghai — until closing time at ten. Sam stays to lock up, and I start out for the apartment alone, wending my way through the festive Christmas Eve crowds on Olvera Street rather than walk alone on Main.

I'm ashamed that May and I have ended up here. I blame myself that we work so hard and never receive even one of the *lo fan* dimes. Once when I held out my hand to Old Man Louie and asked for pay, he spit on my palm. "You have food to eat and a place to sleep," he said. "You and your sister don't need any money." And that was the end of that, except that I'm starting to get a sense of what we might be worth. Most people in China City make thirty to fifty dollars a month. Glass washers make only twenty dollars a month, while dish washers and waiters take home between forty and fifty dollars a month. Uncle Wilburt earns seventy dollars a month, which is considered a very good wage.

"How much money did you make this week?" I ask Sam every Saturday night. "Have you put any money aside?" I hope that someday, somehow, he will give me some of those funds to leave this place. But he never tells me what he earns. He just bends his head, cleans a table, scoops Joy off the floor, or goes down the hall to the bathroom and shuts the door.

Looking back, I can see how Mama, Baba, May, and I believed Old Man Louie was wealthy. In Shanghai, our family had been well-to-do. Baba had his own business. We had a house and servants. We thought the old man had to be considerably richer than we were. Now I see things differently. An American dollar went a long way in Shanghai, where everything from housing and clothes to wives like us was cheap. In Shanghai, we looked at Old Man Louie and saw what we chose to

241

see: a man who bragged through money. He made us look and feel insignificant by treating Baba with great disdain during his visits. But it was all a lie, because here in the Land of the Flowery Flag, Old Man Louie is better off than most in China City but poor nevertheless. Yes, he has five businesses, but they're small — minuscule really, at fifty square feet here and a hundred square feet there — and even together don't add up to much. After all, his fifty thousand dollars in merchandise has zero value if no one buys it. But if my family had come here, we would have been at the bottom of the heap with the laundrymen, glass washers, and vegetable peddlers.

On that dreary thought, I climb the stairs to the apartment, strip off my smelly clothes, and leave them in a pile in a corner of the room. I get in bed and try to stay awake to enjoy a few minutes of quiet and stillness with my baby already asleep in her drawer.

On christmas morning, we dress and join the others in the main room. Yen-yen and Old Man Louie repair broken vases that arrived in a shipment from a curio shop in San Francisco that went out of business. May stirs a pot of *jook* on the hot plate in the kitchen. Vern sits with his parents, looking around, hopeful yet forlorn. He's grown up here and goes to American school, so he knows about Christmas. In the last two weeks, he's brought home a few Christmas decorations that he made in art class, but other than these there isn't a single thing to suggest the holiday: no stockings, no tree, and no gifts. Vern looks like he wants to celebrate, but what can he do or say? He's a son in his parents' home and he has to accept their rules. May and I glance at each other, then at Vern, and back at each other. We understand how he feels. In Shanghai, May and I celebrated the birth of the baby Jesus at the mission school, but it wasn't a holiday Mama and Papa acknowledged in any way. Now that we're here, we want to celebrate like *lo fan*.

"What shall we do today?" May asks optimistically. "Shall we go to the Plaza church and Olvera Street? They'll have festivities."

"We don't do things with those people," Old Man Louie says.

"I'm not saying we have to *do* something with them," May responds. "I just think it would be interesting to see how they celebrate."

But by now May and I have learned there's no point in arguing with our in-laws. We just have to be happy that we have a day off from work.

"I want to go to the beach," Vern suggests. He so rarely speaks that when he does we know he really wants something. "Take the streetcar."

"Too far," the old man objects.

"I don't need to see their ocean," Yen-yen scoffs. "Everything I want is right here."

"You stay home," Vern says, startling everyone in the room.

May raises her eyebrows. I can see she really wants to go, but I have no intention of dipping into our wedding money for something so frivolous, and I've never seen

Sam with money in his hands other than at the restaurant.

"We can have a nice time here," I say. "We can walk along the *lo fan* part of Broadway and look in the department store windows. Everything is decorated for Christmas. You'll like that, Vern."

"I want the beach," he insists. "I want the ocean." When no one says anything, he scrapes back his chair, trudges to his room, and slams the door. He emerges a few minutes later with several dollars crushed in his fist. "I will pay," he says shyly.

Yen-yen tries to take the money, telling the rest of us, "A Boar and his money are easily parted, but you shouldn't take advantage of him."

Vern shakes her hands off his and then holds his arm above his head so she can't reach the money. "It is a Christmas present for my brother, May, Pearl, and the baby. Mama and Baba, you stay home."

Not only is it the most I've ever heard him say, but it may be the most any of us have heard him say. So we do as he wants. The five of us go to the beach, stroll on the pier, and dip our toes in the freezing Pacific. We take care not to let Joy get burned by the unseasonably bright winter sun. The water shimmers against the sky. In the distance, green hills roll into the sea. May and I go for a walk by ourselves. We let the wind and sounds of the waves wash away our worries. On the way back to where Vern and Sam sit with the baby under an umbrella, May says, "It's sweet of Vern to do this for us." It's the first nice thing she's said about him.

Two weeks later, a group of women from United China Relief invite Yen-yen to go to Wilmington to picket the shipyards for sending scrap iron to Japan. I'm sure Old Man Louie will say no when she asks permission to accompany them, but he surprises us all. "You can go if you take Pearl and May."

"It will leave you with too few workers," Yen-yen says, hope that this might happen and fear that he will change his mind glossing the edges of her voice.

"No matter. No matter," he says. "I'll have the uncles work extra hours."

Yen-yen would never do anything like smile broadly to let us see how happy she is, but we all hear the lilt in her voice as she asks May and me, "Will you come?"

"Absolutely," I say. I'll do everything I can to raise money to fight the Japanese, who've been brutal and systematic in their policy of "the three alls" — kill all, burn all, and destroy all. It's my duty to help women who are being raped and killed. I turn to May. Surely she'll want to join us, if for nothing else than that she'll get out of China City for a day, but she shrugs off the invitation.

"What can we do? We're only women," she says.

But it's because I'm a woman that I dare to go. Yen-yen and I walk to the meeting place and board a bus to drive us to the shipyards. The organizers hand us printed placards. We march, we shout our slogans, and I experience a sense of freedom, which I owe entirely to my mother-in-law.

"China is my home," she says on the bus back to Chinatown. "It will always be my home."

After that day, I keep a cup on the counter in the café for people to put their change. I wear a United China Relief pin on my dress. I picket to stop those scrap-iron shipments and join other demonstrations to stop the sale of aviation fuel for the monkey people's planes. I do all this because Shanghai and China are never far from my heart.

Eating Bitterness to Find Gold

Chinese new year arrives. We follow all the traditions. Old Man Louie gives us money to buy new clothes. I put together an outfit for Joy that will celebrate her Tiger sign: a pair of baby slippers shaped like Tiger cubs and an orange-and-gold baby hat with little ears on top and a tail made from twisted embroidery thread coming out the back. May and I pick out American cotton dresses in floral prints. Then we have our hair washed and styled. At home, we take down the picture of the Kitchen God and burn it in the alley, so he'll travel to the afterworld to report on our activities during the past year. We put away knives and scissors to make sure we won't cut our good fortune. Yen-yen makes offerings to the Louie ancestors. Her wishes and prayers are simple. "Bring a son to Boy-husband. Make that wife of his pregnant. Give me a grandson."

In China City, we hang red gauze lanterns and couplets in red and gold paper. We arrange for dancers, singers, and acrobats to entertain children and their parents. We search out special ingredients to make holiday dishes in the café that will be Chinese in feeling but appeal to Occidental palates. We expect big crowds, so Old Man Louie hires extra help for his various enterprises, but he needs even more people to assist with what he anticipates will be the most profitable business on New Year's Day: the rickshaw rides.

"We have to beat the people in New Chinatown," he tells Sam on New Year's Eve. "How can we do that if I have Mexican boys pulling my rickshaws on the most Chinese day of the year? Vern's not strong enough, but you are."

"I'll be too busy in the café," Sam says.

My father-in-law has asked Sam to pull rickshaws other times, and he always has some excuse not to do it. I can't say what it will be like on New Year's, but I know how busy we've been on other festival days. We've never been so overwhelmed that I haven't been able to follow my usual routine of working in the café, the flower shop, the curio shop, and the antiques store. I know Sam's lying, and so does Old Man Louie. Ordinarily my father-in-law's anger would be great, but this is New Year's, when no harsh words should be spoken.

On New Year's morning, we dress in our new clothes, putting Chinese custom above Mrs. Sterling's rules about wearing costumes to work. These things are factory-made, but it's wonderful to have something fresh and Western on our skins again. Joy, who's eleven months old, looks adorable in her Tiger hat and slippers. I'm her mother, so of course I think she's beautiful. Her face is round like the moon. White as clean as new snow circles the black of her eyes. Her hair is wispy and soft. Her skin is as pale and translucent as rice milk.

I didn't believe in the Chinese zodiac when Mama talked about it, but the more time that's passed since her death, the more I understand that the things she said about May and me might have been true. Now when I hear Yen-yen talk about a Tiger's traits, I see my daughter very clearly. Like a Tiger, Joy can be temperamental and volatile. One minute she's brimming over with giddiness; the next she can dissolve into tears. A minute later, she might try to climb up her grandfather's legs, wanting and getting his attention. She may be a worthless girl in his eyes — forever Pan-di, Hope-for-a-Brother — but the Tiger in her has pounced into his heart. Her temper is greater than his. I think he respects that.

I know the exact moment when New Year's Day starts to turn rotten. While May and I fix each other's hair in the main room, Yen-yen has Joy on her back on the floor, tickling her stomach, building anticipation by zooming in and out with her fingers and by raising and lowering her voice, only the words that come out of her mouth do not match her happy actions.

"*Fu yen* or *yen fu?*" Yen-yen asks, as Joy squeals in expectation. "Would you rather be a wife or a servant? Women everywhere would rather be a servant."

Joy's giggles do not have their usual melting effect on her grandfather, who watches sourly from a chair.

"A wife has a mother-in-law," Yen-yen trills. "A wife has the despair of her children. She must obey her husband even when he is wrong. A wife must work and work but never receive a word of thanks. It's better to be a servant and the mistress of yourself. Then, if you want, you can jump in the well. If only we had a well . . ."

Old Man Louie pushes himself away from the table. Wordlessly, he gestures to the door, and we leave the apartment. It's still early morning, and already ill-omened words have been spoken.

Thousands of people come to China City, and the festivities are great. The firecrackers are loud and plentiful. The dragon and lion dancers wiggle and squirm from shop to shop. Everyone wears such bright colors it's as if a great rainbow has come to earth. In the afternoon even more people come. Whenever I look out the window, another rickshaw rushes past. By evening, the Mexican pullers look exhausted.

During dinner, the Golden Dragon is completely full, and perhaps two dozen people stand just inside the door, waiting for a table to become free. Around 7:30, my father-in-law enters and pushes his way through the clustered customers.

"I need Sam," he says.

I look around and spot Sam setting a table for eight. Old Man Louie follows my glance, strides across the room, and speaks to Sam. I can't hear what he says, but Sam shakes his head no. Old Man Louie says something else, and Sam shakes his head again. At the third refusal, my father-in-law grabs Sam's shirt. Sam pushes his hand away. Our customers stare.

The old man raises his voice, spitting the Sze Yup dialect out of his mouth like phlegm. "Don't disobey me!"

"I told you I won't do it."

"*Toh gee! Chok gin!*"

I've been working at Sam's side for months now, and I know he's neither lazy nor empty-headed. Old Man Louie yanks his son across the room, bumping past tables and through the crowd by the door. I follow them outside, where my father-in-law shoves Sam to the ground.

"When I tell you to do something, you do it! Our other pullers are tired, and you know how to do this."

"No."

"You're my son and you'll do as I say," my father-in-law pleads. His face quavers, and then his moment of weakness hardens. When he next speaks, his voice sounds like grinding rocks. "I've promised everything to you."

This is not one of the pretty dramas with singing and dancing that are happening elsewhere in China City as part of tonight's festivities. The tourists don't understand what's being said. Still, this is a captivating and entertaining spectacle. When my father-in-law begins to kick Sam down the alley, I trail along with the others. Sam doesn't fight or cry out. He just takes it. What kind of man is he?

When we reach the rickshaw stand in the Court of the Four Seasons, Old Man Louie looks down at Sam and says, "You're a rickshaw puller and an Ox. That's why I brought you here. Now do your job!"

Fear and shame wash the color from Sam's face. Slowly he gets to his feet. He's taller than his father, and for the first time I see that this is as distressing to the old man as my height was to Baba. Sam takes a step toward his father, looks down at him, and says in a trembling voice, "I won't pull your rickshaw. Not now. Not ever."

Then it's as though both men become aware of the silence around them. My father-in-law brushes at his mandarin robe. Sam's eyes dart about uncomfortably. When he sees me, his whole body cringes. Then he takes off, sprinting through the gawking tourists and our curious neighbors. I run after him.

I find him in our windowless room in the apartment. His fists are bunched. His face is red with anger and hurt, but his shoulders are back, his posture upright, and his tone defiant.

"For so long I've been embarrassed and ashamed before you, but now you know," he says. "You married a rickshaw puller."

In my heart I believe him, but my mind thinks otherwise. "But you're the fourth son —"

"Only a paper son. Always in China people ask, 'Kuei hsing?' — What's your name? — but really it means, 'What is your precious family name?' Louie is just a chi ming — a paper name. I'm actually a Wong. I was born in Low Tin Village, not far from your home village in the Four Districts. My father was a farmer."

I sit on the edge of the bed. My mind spins: a rickshaw puller and a paper son. This makes me a paper wife, so we're both here illegally. I feel sick to my stomach. Still, I recite the facts from the coaching book: "Your father is the old man. You were born in Wah Hong. You came here as a baby —"

Sam shakes his head. "That boy died in China many years ago. I traveled here using his papers."

I remember Chairman Plumb showing me a picture of a little boy and thinking that it didn't look all that much like Sam. Why hadn't I questioned that more? I need to hear the truth. I need it for me, for my sister, and for Joy. And I need him to tell me *everything* — without having him close up and slump away as he usually does. I use a tactic I learned from my weeks of interrogations at Angel Island.

"Tell me about your village and your real family," I say, hoping my voice doesn't shake too much from the emotions I feel and believing if he talks about these comfortable things, then maybe he'll tell me the truth about how he came to be a paper son to the Louies. He doesn't answer right away. He stares at me in the way he has so many times since the first day we met. Always I've seen that look as sympathy for me, but maybe he's been trying to show compassion for our shared troubles and secrets. Now I try to match his expression. The funny thing is, I mean it.

"We had a pond in front of our house," he murmurs at last. "Anyone could throw fish in it and raise them. You could dip a crock in the water, pull it out, and there'd be fish in your crock. No one had to pay. When the pond ran dry, you could pick up fish sitting in the mud. Still, no one had to pay. In the field behind our house, we grew vegetables and melons. We raised two pigs a year. We were not rich, but we were not poor either."

It sounds poor to me. His family had lived from dirt to mouth. He seems to sense my understanding as he goes on haltingly.

"When the drought came, my grandfather, father, and I worked hard, trying to make the ground yield to our desires. Mama went to other villages to earn money by helping others plant or harvest rice, but those places also suffered from no rain. She wove cloth and took it to market. She tried to help our family, but it wasn't enough. You can't live on air and sunshine. When two of my sisters died, my father, my second brother, and I went to Shanghai. We wanted to earn enough to go back to Low Tin Village and farm again. Mama stayed home with my youngest brother and sister."

In Shanghai, they found not promise but hardship. They didn't have connections, so they couldn't get factory jobs. Sam's father took work as a rickshaw puller, while Sam, who'd just turned twelve, and his brother, who was two years younger, scavenged for small jobs. Sam sold matches on street corners; his brother ran after coal trucks to pick up pieces that fell from the beds to sell to the poor. They ate watermelon rinds plucked from trash pits in summer and watered down *jook* in winter.

"My father pulled and pulled," Sam continues. "At first he drank tea with two lumps of sugar to restore his strength and cool his skin. When money ran low, he could only afford cheap tea made from dust and stems and no sugar. Then, like so many pullers, he began smoking opium. Not real opium! He couldn't afford that! And not for pleasure either. He needed it for stimulation, to keep pulling in the hottest weather or if there was a typhoon. He bought the dregs left over from the rich and sold by servants. The opium gave my father false vigor, but his strength was eaten and his heart shriveled. Pretty soon he began to cough blood. They say that you never see a rickshaw puller reach age fifty and that most pullers are already past their best days by the time they turn thirty. My father died when he was thirty-five. I wrapped him in a straw mat and put him on the street. Then I took his place, selling my sweat by pulling a rickshaw. I was seventeen and my brother was fifteen."

As he talks, I think about all the rickshaws I've ridden in and how I never really thought about the men who pulled them. I hadn't considered pullers actual people. They'd seemed barely human. I remember how many of them had not owned shirts or shoes, the way their spines and shoulder blades had protruded from their skin, and the sweat that had oozed from their bodies even in winter.

"I learned all the tricks," Sam goes on. "I learned I could get an extra tip if I carried a man or woman from my rickshaw to the door during typhoon season so they wouldn't ruin their shoes. I learned to bow to women and men, invite them to ride in my *li-ke-xi*, call them *Mai-da-mu* for *Madame* or *Mai-se-dan* for *Master*. I hid my shame when they laughed at my bad English. I made nine silver dollars a month, but I still couldn't afford to send money home to my family in Low Tin. I don't know what happened to them. They're probably dead. I couldn't even take care of my brother, who joined other poor children helping to push rickshaws over the arched bridges at Soochow Creek for a few coppers a day. He died of the blood-lung disease the next winter." He pauses, his mind back in Shanghai. Then he asks, "Did you ever hear the rickshaw pullers' song?" He doesn't wait for me to answer but begins to sing:

"To buy rice, his cap is the container.
To buy firewood, his arms are the container.
He lives in a straw hut.
The moon is his only lamplight."

The melody comes back to me, and my mind is transported to Shanghai's streets and rhythms. Sam is talking about his hardship, but I feel loneliness for my home.

"I listened to riders who were Communists," he continues. "I heard them complain that since ancient times poor men have been urged to find contentment in poverty. That was not my life. That was not why my father and brother died. I wish I could have changed their fates, but once they were gone all I could think about was my own mouth. I thought, if the leaders of the Green Gang got their starts pulling rickshaws, then why couldn't I? I had no schooling in Low Tin. I was a farmer's son. But even pullers understood the importance of education, which is why the rickshaw guild sponsored schools in Shanghai. I learned the Wu dialect. I learned more English — not the ABCs but some words."

The more Sam talks, the more my heart opens to him. When I first met him in the Yu Yuan Garden, I hadn't thought he was so bad. Now I see just how hard he's tried to change his life and how little I've understood. He speaks Sze Yup fluently and the Wu dialect of the streets, while his English is practically nonexistent. He's always looked uncomfortable in his clothes. I remember the day we met noticing his shoes and suit were new. They must have been the first he owned. I remember the red tinge to his hair and mistakenly believing it had something to do with the fact that he was from America and not recognizing it as the well-known sign of malnutrition. And then there is his manner. He's always been deferential to me, treating me not as a *fu yen* but as a customer who must be pleased. He's always bowed down to Old Man Louie and Yen-yen — not because they're his parents but because he's like a servant to them.

"Don't feel sorry for me," my husband says. "My father would have died anyway. Farming is not a good life when you have to carry a two-hundred-fifty-*jin* load on a bamboo pole balanced on your shoulders or you have to stoop in the rice fields all day. The only riches I've earned have come from working with my hands and feet. I started out as so many rickshaw pullers, not knowing what to do, my bare feet slapping the road like a pair of palm fronds. I learned to hold my stomach in, expand my chest wide, raise my knees high, and stretch my head and neck forward. As a rickshaw puller, I earned an iron fan."

I'd heard my father use the term about his best pullers. It suggested a hard, straight back and a chest as wide, spread open, and strong as a fan made from iron. I also remember what Mama said about being born in the Year of the Ox: that the Ox is capable of great sacrifices for his family's welfare, that he'll pull his own load and more, and that — while he may be as plain and serviceable as the beast of burden he emulates — he is forever worth his weight in gold.

"If I could make forty-five coppers from a fare, I was happy," Sam goes on. "I would exchange those coppers for fifteen cents. I would keep turning my coppers into silver coins, and my silver coins into silver dollars. If I could pocket an extra tip, I was happier still. I thought, if I could save ten cents a day, I would have one hundred dollars in a thousand days. I was willing to eat bitterness to find gold."

"Did you work for my father?"

"At least I didn't have that humiliation." He touches my jade bracelet. When I don't flinch, he loops a forefinger through the bracelet, his flesh barely grazing mine.

"Then how did you find the old man? And why did you have to marry me?"

"The Green Gang owned the largest of the rickshaw businesses," he answers. "I worked for it. The gang often served as matchmaker between those who wanted to become paper sons and those seeking to sell paper-son slots. In our case, they acted as a traditional matchmaker too. I wanted to change my fate. Old Man Louie had a paper-son slot to sell —"

"And he needed rickshaws and brides," I finish for him, shaking my head at the memories all this brings back. "My father owed the Green Gang money. All he had left to sell were his rickshaws and his daughters. May and I are here. My father's rickshaws are here, but that still doesn't explain how you ended up here."

"For me, the price to buy the paper was one hundred dollars for each year of my life. I was twenty-four, so the coast was twenty-four hundred dollars for boat passage, plus room and board once I got to Los Angeles. I would never be able to earn that amount at nine dollars a month. Today I work to pay off the old man — not only for myself but for you and Joy too."

"Is this why we're never paid?"

He nods. "He's keeping our money until my debt is paid. This is why the uncles aren't paid either. They're paper sons too. Only Vern is a blood son."

"But you're different from the other uncles —"

"That's right. The Louies want me as a true replacement for the son who died. This is why we live with them and why I'm the manager of the café, even though I know less than nothing about food or business. If the immigration people ever discover I'm not who I say I am, they could put me in jail and deport me. But I might have a way to stay, because the old man made me a paper partner too."

259

"But I still don't understand why you needed to marry me. What does he want from us?"

"Only one thing: a grandson. That's why he bought you and your sister. He wants a grandson one way or another."

My chest tightens. The doctor in Hangchow said I'd probably never be able to have children, but to say that to Sam would mean I'd have to tell him why. Instead I ask, "If he wants you as his true son, then why do you have to pay him back?"

When he takes my hands, I don't pull away, even though I'm terrified I'm about to be caught.

"Zhen Long," he intones earnestly. Even my parents rarely called me by my Chinese name — Pearl Dragon. Now I hear it as an endearment. "A son must pay his debts, for himself and his wife and child. Back in Shanghai, when I was considering this whole arrangement, I thought, When the old man dies I will become a Gold Mountain man with many businesses. Then I came here. There were days in the beginning when I just wanted to go home. Passage only costs a hundred and thirty dollars in steerage. I thought I could make that by hiding my tips, but then you and Joy came. What kind of a husband would I be if I left you here? What kind of a father would I be?"

From the moment May and I arrived in Los Angeles, we've been thinking of ways to escape. If only we — I — had known Sam felt the same way.

"I began to think you, Joy, and I could go home together, but how could I allow our baby to travel in steerage? She could die down there." He squeezes my hands in his. He stares directly into my eyes, and I don't look away. "I'm not like the others. I don't want to go back to China anymore. Here, I suffer every day, but it's a good place for Joy."

"But China's our home. The Japanese will tire eventually —"

"But what is there for Joy in China? What is there for any of us? In Shanghai, I was a rickshaw puller. You were a beautiful girl."

I hadn't realized he'd known this about May and me. The way he says it strips me of the pride I've always felt for what we'd done.

"I don't care to hate anyone, but I can hate my fate — and yours too," he says. "We can't change the people we are or what's happened to us, but shouldn't we try to change our daughter's fate? What road awaits her in China? Here, I can pay back the old man and eventually earn our freedom. Then we will give Joy a proper life — a life of opportunities that you and I will never have. Maybe she could even go to college one day."

He speaks to my mother's heart, but the practical part of me that survived my father losing everything and my body being torn apart by monkey people doesn't see how his dreams can become real.

"We'll never be able to break away from this place and these people," I say. "Look around. Uncle Wilburt has worked for the old man for twenty years and he still hasn't paid his debt."

"Maybe he's paid his debt and is saving his treasure to return home a wealthy man. Or maybe he's happy where he is. He has a job, a place to live, a family to have dinner with on Sunday nights. You don't know what it's like to live in a village with no electricity or running water. Maybe you have one room for the whole family, maybe two. You eat only rice and vegetables, unless there's a festival or a celebration, but even that takes great sacrifice."

"All I'm saying is that one man by himself is barely able to support himself. How are you going to help the four of us?"

"Four? You mean May."

"She's my sister, and I promised my mother I'd take care of her."

He considers that for a moment. Then he says, "I'm patient. I can wait and I can work hard." He smiles shyly and then says, "In the morning when you go to the Golden Lantern to help Yen-yen and see Joy, I work at the Temple of Kwan Yin, where I have an extra job selling incense to the *lo fan* to stick in the big bronze burners. I'm supposed to say, 'Your dreams will come true, for the blessings of this graceful deity are limitless,' but my mouth can't form those words in English. Still, the people seem to take pity on me and buy my incense."

He gets up and walks to the dresser. He's such a sadly thin man, but I don't know how I didn't recognize his iron fan before this. He rummages through the top drawer and then returns to the bed with a sock that bulges at the toe. He turns the sock upside down, and nickels, dimes, quarters, and a few dollar bills spill on the mattress.

262

"This is what I've saved for Joy," he explains.

I run my hands over the money. "You are a good man," I say, but it's hard to imagine this pittance changing Joy's life.

"I know it isn't much," he admits, "but it's more than I made as a rickshaw puller, and it will add up. And maybe, in another year or so, I can become a second cook. If I learn to be a first cook, I might make as much as twenty dollars a week. Once we can afford to go out on our own, I will become a fish peddler or maybe a gardener. If I'm a fish peddler, then we can always eat fish. If I'm a gardener, then we can always eat vegetables."

"My English is good," I offer tentatively. "Maybe I could look for a job outside Chinatown."

But honestly, what makes either of us think Old Man Louie will ever release us? And even if he does, don't I have to tell Sam the truth too? Not the part about Joy not being his! That secret belongs to May and me, and I'll never reveal it, but I have to tell him what the monkey people did to me and how they killed Mama.

"I've been smeared with mud that I'll never be able to wipe clean," I tentatively begin, hoping that what Mama said about the Ox is true: that he won't abandon you in times of trouble, that he'll stick by you faithfully, and that he is charitable and good. Don't I have to believe her now? Still, the emotions that play across his face — anger, disgust, and pity — don't make it easy for me as I tell my story.

When I'm done, he says, "You went through all that and still Joy came out perfectly. She must have a precious future." He puts a finger to my lips to keep me from saying anything more. "I would rather be married to broken jade than flawless clay. And my father used to say that anyone can add an extra flower to brocade, but how many women will fetch the coal in winter? He was talking about my mother, who was a good and loyal woman, just as you are."

We hear the others enter the apartment, but neither of us moves. Sam leans close and whispers in my ear. "On the bench in Yu Yuan Garden, I said I liked you and I asked if you liked me. You only nodded. In an arranged marriage this is more than we can hope for. I never expected happiness, but shouldn't we try to look for it?"

I turn to him. Our lips nearly touch as I whisper, "What about more children?" As close as I feel to him now, I find it hard to tell him the whole truth. "After Joy came out, the doctors at Angel Island told me I'd never be able to have another baby."

"As boys, we are told that if we don't have a son by age thirty, we are unlucky. The worst insult you can yell on the street is 'May you die sonless!' We are told that if we don't have a son, we should adopt one to carry on the family name and care for us when we become ancestors. But if you have a son who is . . . who has . . . who can't . . ." He struggles, as May and I often have, to put a name to Vernon's problem.

"You buy a son, as Old Man Louie bought you," I finish for him, "so that you can care for him and Yen-yen when they become ancestors."

"And if not me, then the son we might give them one day. A grandson would ensure them a happy existence here and in the afterworld."

"But I can't give them that."

"They don't have to know, and I don't care. And who knows? Maybe Vern will give your sister a son, and all debts and obligations will be paid."

"But, Sam, I can't give *you* a son."

"People say a family is incomplete without a son, but I am happy with Joy. She is my heart's blood. Every time she smiles at me, grasps my finger, or stares at me with her black eyes, I know I'm lucky." As he speaks, I bring his hand to my cheek, and then I kiss his fingertips. "Pearl, you and I may have been given bad fates, but she is our future. With just one child, we can give her everything. She can have the education I didn't have. Maybe she will be a doctor or . . . These things don't matter so much, because she will always be our consolation and our joy."

When he kisses me, I kiss him back. We're sitting on the edge of the bed, so all I have to do is put my arms around him and bring him with me as I lie down. Even though people are in the apartment and even though they hear every squeak of the bed and stifled moan, Sam and I do the husband-wife thing. It isn't easy for me. I keep my eyes squeezed shut and terror clenches my heart. I try to concentrate on the muscles that labored in the fields, pulled rickshaws through my home city, and so recently cradled our Joy. For me, the husband-wife thing will never bring great feelings of enjoyment, the release of clouds and rain, the taste of ecstasy of a hundred years, or any of the things the poets write about. For me, it's about being close to Sam, the loneliness we feel for our home country, the way we miss our parents, and the hardship of our daily lives here in America, where we are *wang k'uo nu* — lost-country slaves, forever living under foreign rule.

After he finishes and a proper amount of time has passed, I get up and go into the main room to get Joy. Vern and May have already gone to their room, but knowing glances pass between Old Man Louie and Yen-yen.

"You bring me a grandson now?" Yen-yen asks as she hands me Joy. "You're a good daughter-in-law."

"You'd be a better daughter-in-law if you told your sister to do her job," the old man adds.

I don't respond. I just take Joy back to our room and lay her in her drawer in the bottom of the dresser. Then I reach around my neck and take off the pouch Mama gave me. I open the top drawer and tuck the pouch together with the one that May gave Joy. I don't need it anymore. I close the drawer and turn back to Sam. I take off my clothes and slip naked back into the bed. As his hand runs up my side, I find the courage to ask one more question.

"Sometimes you disappear in the afternoons too," I say. "Where do you go?"

His hand stops on my hip. "Pearl." My name comes out long and soft. "I didn't go to those places in Shanghai, and I'll never go to them here."

"Then where —"

"I go back to the temple, but this time it's to make offerings to my family, to your family, and even to the Louie ancestors —"

"To *my* family?"

"You just told me how your mother died, but I knew she had to be gone, and your father too. You wouldn't have come here to us if they'd still been living."

He's smart. He knows me well and he understands me.

"I also made offerings to our ancestors after we were married," he adds.

I nod to myself. He'd answered the Angel Island interrogators honestly about that.

"I don't believe in these things," I confess.

"Maybe you should. We've done them for five thousand years."

As we do the husband-wife thing again, sirens sound in the distance. In the morning we wake to learn that a fire has swept through China City. Some people say it was an accident that flared in the smoldering firecracker remains behind George Wong's fish market, while others insist it was arson set by people in New Chinatown who don't like Christine Sterling's idea of a "native Chinese village" or by people in Olvera Street who don't like the competition. The gossips will go on and on, but no matter who started the fire, a good part of China City has been destroyed or damaged.

Even the Best of Moons

The fire god is indiscriminate. He lights lamps, he makes fireflies glow, he reduces villages to ash, he burns books, he cooks food, and he warms families. All people can hope for is that a dragon — with its watery essence — will douse unwanted fires when they come. Whether you believe in these things or not, making offerings is probably wise. As Americans would say, it's better to be safe than sorry. In China City, where no one has insurance, no offerings are made to appease the Fire God or inspire a dragon to be benevolent. These are not good omens, but I tell myself that people in America also say lightning never strikes twice.

It will take almost six months for the parts of China City damaged by smoke and water to be repaired and the destroyed sections to be rebuilt. Old Man Louie is in an even worse position than most, since not only did some of the cash he'd hidden in his various enterprises burn but some of his real wealth — his merchandise — turned to ash. No money fills the family pot, but plenty goes out for the rebuilding effort, to order new goods from his factories in Shanghai and from antiques emporiums in Canton (and hope that they can leave those cities on foreign ships and pass safely through the Japanese-infested waters), and to feed, house, and clothe his household of seven, as well as support his paper partners and paper sons, who live in bachelor boardinghouses nearby. None of this sits well with my father-in-law.

Although he insists that May and I stay with our husbands and work at their sides, there's nothing for us to do. We don't know how to use a hammer or saw. We have no merchandise to unpack, polish, or sell. There are no floors to sweep, windows to wash, or customers to feed. Still, May, Joy, and I walk over to China City every morning to see how construction is progressing. May isn't unhappy with Sam's plan to stay together and save our money. "They feed us here," she's told me, finally, it seems to me, showing some maturity. "Yes, let's wait until the four of us can leave together."

In the afternoons, we often visit Tom Gubbins in the Asiatic Costume Company, which escaped fire damage. He rents props and costumes, and acts as an agent for Chinese extras to movie studios, but otherwise he's a bit of a mystery. Some say he was born in Shanghai. Some say he's a quarter Chinese. Some say he's half and half. Some say he doesn't have a single drop of Chinese in him. Some call him Uncle Tom. Some call him Lo Fan Tom. We call him Bak Wah Tom, Motion Pictures Tom, which is how he introduced himself to me at China City's Grand Opening. From Tom, I learn that mystery, confusion, and exaggeration can build your reputation.

He helps a lot of Chinese — buying them clothes, buying *their* clothes, finding them rooms, getting them jobs, making arrangements for expectant mothers at hospitals unfriendly to Chinese, sitting for interviews by the immigration inspectors, who are always on the lookout for paper merchants and paper sons — but few like him. Maybe it's because he once worked as an interpreter at Angel Island, where he'd been accused of getting a woman pregnant. Maybe it's because he has a fondness for young girls, although others say he has a fondness for young men. All I know is that his Cantonese is near perfect and his Wu dialect is very good. May and I love to hear the sounds of our home dialect coming from his mouth.

He wants my sister to work as an extra in the movies; naturally, Old Man Louie objects, saying, "That's a job for a woman with three holes." He can be so predictable, but in this he's just voicing the sentiments of many old-timers who believe that actresses — whether in operas, plays, or motion pictures — are little better than prostitutes.

"Keep talking to your father-in-law," Tom instructs May. "Tell him that one out of every fourteen of his neighbors works in the movies. It's a good way to make extra income. I could even get him a job. I promise he'll make more money in a week than he did in three months sitting in his antiques shop." The idea makes us laugh.

270

People in Chinatown are often called "acting conscious." When the studios realized they could hire Chinese for as little as "five dollars a Chink," they used our neighbors for crowd scenes and to fill all kinds of nonspeaking roles in films like *Stowaway, Lost Horizon, The General Died at Dawn, The Adventures of Marco Polo*, the Charlie Chan series, and of course *The Good Earth*. The Depression may be receding, but people need money and will work for it in any way possible. Even people in New Chinatown, who are wealthier than we are, like to work as extras. They do it because they want to have fun and see themselves on the silver screen.

I don't want to work in *Haolaiwu*. Not for any old-fashioned reasons but because I understand I'm not beautiful enough. My sister is, though, and she wants this badly. She idolizes Anna May Wong, even though everyone around here talks about her as though she's a disgrace, because she always plays singsong girls, maids, and murderers. But when I see Anna May on the screen, I think back to the way Z.G. used to paint my sister. Like Anna May, May glows like a ghost goddess.

For weeks Tom begs us to sell him our *cheongsams*. "I usually buy clothes from people who bring them back after a visit to China, because they've gained too much weight at home. Or I buy them from people who've come here for the first time, because they've lost so much weight on the ship and on Angel Island. But these days no one's going home because of the war, and those lucky enough to make it out of China have usually left everything behind. But you two are different. Your father-in-law looked out for you and brought your clothes."

I don't mind selling our clothes — I chafe at having to wear them for the sake of China City's tourists — but May doesn't want to part with them.

"Our dresses are beautiful!" she cries indignantly. "They're part of who we are! Our *cheongsams* were made in Shanghai. The material came from Paris. They're elegant — more elegant than anything I've seen here."

"But if we sell some of our *cheongsams*, then we can buy new dresses — American dresses," I say. "I'm tired of looking unfashionable, of looking like I'm fresh off the boat."

"If we sell them," May inquires shrewdly, "what will happen when China City reopens? Won't Old Man Louie notice that our clothes are gone?"

Tom waves away that worry as inconsequential. "He's a man. He won't notice."

But of course he will. He notices everything.

"He won't care as long as we give him a portion of what Tom pays us," I say, hoping I'm right.

"Just don't give him too much." Tom scratches his beard. "Let him think you'll make more money if you keep coming back here."

We sell Tom one *cheongsam* apiece. They're our oldest and ugliest, but they're splendid compared with what he has in his collection. Then we take the money and walk south on Broadway until we come to the Western department stores. We buy rayon dresses, high heels, gloves, new undergarments, and a couple of hats — all from the sale of two dresses, with enough left over that our father-in-law isn't angry with us when we put the remaining money in his palm. That's when May begins her campaign, teasing him, cajoling him, and, yes, even flirting with him, trying to get him to surrender to her desires just as our father did in the past.

"You like us to keep busy," she says, "but how can we keep busy now? Bak Wah Tom says I can make five dollars a day if I work in *Haolaiwu*. Think how much that will be in a week! Add to that the extra I'll make if I wear my own costume. I have plenty of costumes!"

"No," Old Man Louie says.

"With my beautiful clothes, I might get a close-up. I'll earn ten dollars for that. If I get to say a line — just one single line — I'll make twenty dollars."

"No," Old Man Louie says again, but this time I can practically see him counting the money in his mind.

Her lower lip trembles. She crosses her arms. Her body shrinks into itself, making her appear pitiful. "I was a beautiful girl in Shanghai. Why can't I be a beautiful girl here?"

The mountain crumbles one grain at a time. After several weeks, he finally gives in. "Once. You may do it once."

To which Yen-yen sniffs and walks out of the room, Sam shakes his head in disbelief, and blood rushes to my face in pleasure that May's beaten the old man just by being herself.

I don't catch the title of May's first movie, but since she has her own clothes, she gets to play a singsong girl

273

instead of a peasant. She's gone for three nights and she sleeps during the days, so I don't hear about her experience until the shoot ends.

"I sat in a fake teahouse all night and nibbled on almond cakes," she recalls dreamily. "The assistant director called me a cute tomato. Can you imagine?"

For days she calls Joy a cute tomato, which doesn't make much sense to me. The next time May works as an extra, she comes back with a new phrase: "What in the H," as in "What in the H did you put in this soup, Pearl?"

Often she comes home bragging about the food she's eaten. "They give us two meals a day, and it's good food — American food! I have to be careful, Pearl, truly I do or I'm going to get fat. I won't fit into a *cheongsam* then. If I don't look perfect, they'll never give me a speaking part." After that, she takes to dieting — dieting for someone so tiny, for someone who knows what it means not to eat because of war, poverty, and ignorance — before Tom sends her out for a job and then for days afterward to lose the imagined weight she's gained. All this in hopes that a director will give her a line. Even I know that — except for Anna May Wong and Keye Luke, who plays Charlie Chan's Number One Son — speaking parts go only to *lo fan*, who wear yellow makeup, have their eyes taped back, and affect chop-suey English.

In June, Tom comes up with a new idea, May gobbles it and then spits it out to our father-in-law, who embraces it as his own.

"Joy's a beautiful baby," Tom tells May. "She'll make a perfect extra."

"You can make more money from her than you can from me," May relays to Old Man Louie.

"Pan-di is lucky for a girl," the old man confides to me. "She can earn her own way and she's only a baby."

I'm not sure I want Joy spending so much time with her auntie, but once Old Man Louie sees he can make money from a baby, well . . .

"I will let her do it on one condition." I can make a requirement because, as Joy's mother, only I can sign the paper allowing her to work all day and sometimes at night under the supervision and care of her aunt. "She will keep everything she makes."

Old Man Louie doesn't like this. Why would he?

"You will never again have to buy her clothes," I press. "You will never again pay for her food. You will never again pay one single penny for this Hope-for-a-Brother."

The old man smiles at that.

When may and Joy aren't working, they stay in the apartment with Yen-yen and me. Often, in the long afternoons as we wait for China City to reopen, I think back to stories Mama told me about when she was a girl and confined to the women's chambers in her natal home with her bound-footed grandmother, mother, aunts, cousins, and sisters. They'd been trapped to maneuver for position, harbor resentments, and snipe at one another. Now, in America, May and Yen-yen fight like turtles in a bucket about anything and everything.

"The *jook* is too salty," May might say.

"It isn't salty enough" comes Yen-yen's predictable reply.

When May twirls through the main room in a sleeveless dress, stockingless legs, and open-toed sandals, Yen-yen complains, "You shouldn't be seen in public like that."

"Women in Los Angeles like bare legs and arms," May counters.

"But you aren't a *lo fan*," Yen-yen points out.

But nothing and no one is better to fight over than Joy. If Yen-yen says, "She should wear a sweater," May responds with "She's roasting like corn on a fire." If Yen-yen observes, "She should learn to embroider," my sister argues back, "She should learn to roller-skate."

More than anything Yen-yen hates that May works in motion pictures and exposes Joy to such low-class activities, and she blames me for letting it happen.

"Why do you let her take Joy to those places? You want your girl to marry one day, don't you? You think anyone will want a bride who puts her shadow self in trash stories?"

Before I can say anything — and I'm probably not meant to anyway — my sister comes back with her objection: "They aren't trash stories. They just aren't for people like you."

"The only real stories are the old ones. They tell us how to live."

"Movies tell us how to live too," May retorts. "Joy and I help tell stories of heroes and good women that are romantic and new. They aren't about moon maidens or ghost girls languishing for love."

"You're too simple," Yen-yen chides. "That's why it's a good thing you have your sister to look out for you. You need to learn from your *jie jie*. She understands that those way-back stories have something to teach us."

"What does Pearl know about it?" May asks, as though I'm not in the room. "She's as old-fashioned as our mother."

How can she call me old-fashioned? How can she compare me with Mama? I admit that, in my longing for home, for the past, and for our parents, I've become like Mama in many ways. All those old ideas about the zodiac, food, and other traditions give me comfort, but I'm not the only one looking backward for consolation. May is bright, effervescent, and undeniably exquisite at twenty, but her life — even though she gets to go to movie sets and dress up — is not what she envisioned back when we were beautiful girls in Shanghai. We both have our disappointments, but I wish she could show me a little more sympathy.

"If your movies teach you to be romantic, then why is it that your sister, who stays with me every day, has done a much better job at this than you?" Yen-yen asks.

"I'm romantic!" May fights back, haplessly falling into Yen-yen's trap.

My mother-in-law smiles. "Not romantic enough to bring me a grandson! You should have a baby already . . ."

I sigh. These kinds of arguments between mother-in-law and daughter-in-law are as old as humankind. With conversations like this, I'm happy that most days May and Joy are on a film set and I'm alone with Yen-yen.

On Tuesdays, after delivering lunch to our husbands in China City, Yen-yen and I go door to door to every boardinghouse, apartment, and business along Spring Street, where people buy their groceries, and even over to New Chinatown to raise money for United China Relief and national salvation. We've gone beyond picketing. Now we carry empty vegetable cans and use them as beggars' bowls, walking down Mei Ling, Gin Ling, and Sun Mun Ways, agreeing that we can't go home until our cans are at least half full with pennies, nickels, and dimes. People are starving in China, so we also visit groceries and make the owners donate imported Chinese food, which we pack and send back to where it came from: China, home.

Doing this work, I meet people. Everyone wants to know my natal family name and which village I'm from. I meet more Wongs than I can count. I meet lots of Lees, Fongs, Leongs, and Moys. Through it all, Old Man Louie never once complains that I'm traipsing from Chinatown to Chinatown or that I'm meeting strangers day after day, because I'm always with my mother-in-law, who begins to confide in me not as a despised daughter-in-law but as a friend.

"I was kidnapped from my village as a small girl," she tells me one Tuesday as we walk back from New Chinatown along Broadway. "Did you know that?"

"I didn't know. I'm sorry," I say, which doesn't begin to cover what I feel. I was expelled from my home, but I can't imagine being taken from it forcibly. "How old were you?"

"How old was I? How can I know? I don't have anyone to tell me that. Maybe I was five. Maybe I was older, maybe younger. I remember I had a brother and a sister. I remember there were water chestnut trees along the main road to my village. I remember a fishpond, but I guess every village has one of those." She pauses before going on. "I left China long ago. I long for it every day and suffer when she suffers. That's why I work so hard to raise money for China Relief."

No wonder she doesn't know how to cook. She wasn't taught by her mother, just as I wasn't taught by mine — but for different reasons. Yen-yen has no desire for something better to eat, because she doesn't have memories of shark's fin soup, crisp Yangtze River eel, or braised pigeon in lettuce leaves. She's grabbed on to old traditions — outdated traditions — in the same way I latch on to them now: as a means of soul survival, as a way to hang on to ghost memories. Perhaps it's better to treat a cough with winter melon tea than by putting a mustard plaster on your chest. Yes, her way-back stories and her old ways are sinking into me, changing me, instilling more "Chinese" into me, as surely as the flavor of ginger seeps into soup.

"What happened after they took you?" I ask, my heart in a great sympathy of understanding.

Yen-yen stops on the sidewalk, bags filled with donations hanging from her hands. "What do you think

279

happened? You've seen unmarried girls without families. You know what happens to them. I was sold as a servant in Canton. As soon as I was old enough, I became a girl with three holes." She juts her chin. "Then one day, maybe I was thirteen, I was bundled in a sack and put on a boat. The next thing I knew I was in America."

"What about Angel Island? Didn't they ask you questions? Why weren't you sent back?"

"I came before Angel Island opened. Sometimes I look in the mirror and I'm surprised by what I see. I still expect to see that girl, but I don't like to remember those days. What do they matter to me now? You think I want to remember being a wife to many men?" She shuffles down the street, and I hurry to keep up with her. "I've done the husband-wife thing too many times. People make such big talk about it, but why worry so much? The man goes in. The man goes out. As women, we stay the same. Do you know what I mean, Pearl-ah?"

Do I? Sam's different from those men in the shack, that I know. But have I stayed the same? I remember all the times I've seen Yen-yen sleeping on the couch. Usually some new bachelor — an immigrant from China, who appears on Old Man Louie's partnership list until his debt is paid by someone who needs a laborer at a cheap price — sleeps there. But whenever they aren't there, Yen-yen can be found in the main room in the morning, folding blankets and reciting one excuse or another: "That old man snores like a water buffalo." Or "My back hurts. This place is more comfortable." Or "That old man tells me I move around in the bed like a mosquito. He can't sleep. If he doesn't sleep, then everyone is unhappy the next day, no?" Now I understand that her reasons for sleeping on the couch are the same ones I had when I wished I could escape Sam's bed. Too many men did things to her that she doesn't want to remember.

I put a hand on her arm. Our eyes meet and something passes between us. I don't tell her what happened to me. How can I? But I think she understands . . . something, because she says, "You're lucky you have Joy and that she's healthy. My boy . . ." She sucks in a long, deep breath and lets it out slowly. "Maybe I spent too long in that business. I'd worked almost ten years by the time the old man bought me. There were so few Chinese women here back then — maybe less than one for every twenty men — but he got me for a cheap price anyway because of my job. I was happy, because I finally left San Francisco and came here. But even then he was like he is now — old and stingy in heart. All he wanted was a son, and he worked hard to give me one."

She nods to a man sweeping the sidewalk before his business. He looks the other way, afraid we'll ask him for a donation.

"When the old man went back to his home village to see his parents, I went with him," Yen-yen continues. I've heard her say this before, but this time I hear it differently. "When he traveled around China to buy merchandise, he left me behind. I don't know what he thought: that maybe I would stay in the house for the

281

weeks he was gone with his essence inside me, my legs up, waiting for a son to grab hold. But as soon as he left, I walked from village to village. I speak Sze Yup. My home village has to be in the Four Districts, right? Every day I looked for a village with chestnut trees and a fishpond. I never found it, and I didn't have a son. I got pregnant, but the babies all refused to breathe the air of this world. Every trip back to Los Angeles, we reported that I had had a son in China and left him with his grandparents. This is how we brought in the uncles. Wilburt was my first paper son. He was eighteen, but we said he was eleven to match the papers we filed claiming he was born one year after the San Francisco earthquake. Charley came next. He was easy. We'd gone back to China the next year, so I had a certificate for a son born in 1908, and Charley was born that same year."

My father-in-law had had to wait a long time for his investment — his crop — to ripen, but it had worked for him, providing cheap labor for his enterprises and easily lining his pockets.

"And Edfred?" Yen-yen smiles in amusement. "He's Wilburt's son, you know."

No, I didn't know. Until recently I had thought all these men were Sam's brothers.

"We had a paper for a son born in 1911," Yen-yen continues, "but Edfred wasn't born until 1918. Edfred was only six when we brought him here, but his paper said he was thirteen."

"And no one noticed?"

"They didn't notice that Wilburt wasn't eleven either." Yen-yen shrugs at the stupidity of the immigration inspectors. "With Edfred, we said he was small and undeveloped for his age, that he'd been starving in the home village. The inspectors appreciated the idea that he hadn't benefited from "proper nutrition." They assured me he would "plump up" now that he was in his proper country."

"It's all so complicated."

"It's *supposed* to be complicated. The *lo fan* try to keep us out with their changing laws, but the more complicated they make them, the easier it is for us to trick them." She pauses to let that sink in. "I had only two sons of my own. My first son was born in China. We brought him here and we had a peaceful life. We took him back to the home village when he turned seven, but he had an American stomach, not a village stomach. He died."

"I'm sorry."

"Long time ago now," Yen-yen says, almost matter-of-factly. "But I tried and tried and tried to have another son. Finally, *finally*, I got pregnant. The old man was happy. I was happy. But happiness doesn't change your fate. The midwife came to catch Vernon. She could tell right away something was wrong. She said this happens sometimes when a mother is old. I must have been over forty when he was born. She had to use —"

She stops before a shop that sells lottery tickets and sets down her packages so she can shape her hands into claws. "She pulled him out of me with these things. His head was bent when he came out. She squeezed on this side and then the other to make it into a better shape, but . . ."

She picks up her bags again. "When Vern was a tiny baby, the old man wanted to go back to China to get one more paper son. We had the certificate, see? Our last one. I didn't want to go. My Sam died in the home village. I didn't want my new baby to die too. The old man said, "Don't worry. You'll nurse the baby the whole time." So we went to China, picked up Edfred, got on a boat, and brought him back here."

"And Vern?"

"You know what they say about marriage. Even a blind man can get a wife. Even a man with no sense can get a wife. Even a man with palsy can get a wife. All those men have one duty and one duty alone. To have a son." She looks up at me as pathetic as a bird but with a will as strong as jade. "Who will take care of the old man and me in the afterlife if we don't have a grandson who will make offerings to us? Who will take care of my boy in the afterworld if your sister doesn't give *him* a son? If not her, Pearl, then it has to be you, even if he is just a paper grandson. This is why we keep you here. This is why we feed you."

My mother-in-law steps into the dry goods store to buy her weekly lottery ticket — the eternal hope of the Chinese — but I'm filled with great concern.

I can barely wait for May to come home. As soon as she walks in the door, I insist that she go with me to China City, where Sam is working on the rebuilding effort.

The three of us sit on crates, and I tell them what I learned from Yen-yen. They aren't surprised by anything I say.

"Then either you didn't hear me or I didn't tell it the right way. Yen-yen said they used to go back to the old man's home village to see his parents. He always says he was born here, but if his parents lived in China, then how could that be?"

Sam and May look at each other and then back at me.

"Maybe his parents lived here, had the old man, and then retired to China," May suggests.

"That's possible," I say. "But if he was born here and lived here for almost seventy years, why isn't his English better?"

"Because he's never left Chinatown," reasons Sam.

I shake my head. "Think about it. If he was born here, then why is he so loyal to China? Why did he let Yen-yen and me out to picket and raise money for China? Why does he always say he wants to retire 'home'? Why is he so desperate to keep us close? It's because he's not a citizen at all. And if he's not a citizen, then the consequences for us —"

Sam stands. "I want to know the truth."

We find Old Man Louie at a noodle shop on Spring Street, having tea cakes and tea with his friends. When he sees us, he gets up and comes to the entrance.

"What do you want? Why aren't you working?"

"We need to talk to you."

"Not now. Not here."

But the three of us aren't going anywhere without answers. Old Man Louie motions us to a booth far enough from his friends that they won't hear the conversation. It's been months since the New Year's Day fight, but Chinatown's gossips haven't stopped murmuring about it. Old Man Louie has tried to be more congenial, but an awkwardness lingers between him and Sam, who doesn't waste time with niceties.

"You were born in Wah Hong Village, weren't you?"

The old man's lizard eyes narrow. "Who told you that?"

"It doesn't matter who told us. Is it true?" Sam asks.

The old man doesn't respond. We wait. Around us, we hear laughing, chatting, and the sounds of chopsticks against bowls. Finally, the old man grunts.

"You're not the only ones here on a lie," he says in Sze Yup. "Look at the people in this restaurant. Look at the people who work in China City. Look at the people on our block and in our building. Everyone has a lie of some sort. Mine is I wasn't born here. When the earthquake and fire in San Francisco destroyed all birth records, I was here and thirty-five years old by American counting. Like many others, I went to the authorities and told them I was born in San Francisco. I couldn't prove I was, and they couldn't prove I wasn't. So now I am a citizen . . . on paper, just as you are my son on paper."

"What about Yen-yen? She also came here before the earthquake. Does she claim to be a citizen too?"

The old man's eyebrows furrow in disgust. "She's a *fu yen*. She's bad at telling lies and she can't keep a secret. Obviously. Or you wouldn't be here."

Sam rubs his forehead as he absorbs the implications of all this. "If someone finds out you aren't a real citizen, then Wilburt, Edfred —"

"Yes, all of us, including Pearl here, will be in trouble. This is why I hold you like this." He closes his hand into a tight fist. "There can be no mistakes, no slips, eh?"

"What about me?" May asks, her voice tentative.

"Vern was born here, so you, my May, are the wife of a true citizen. You came legally and you are forever safe. But you need to watch your sister and her husband. One bad report from someone and they'll be sent back. We could all be sent back, except for you, Vern, and Pan-di — although I'm sure the baby would go back to China with its parents and grandparents. I trust you, May, to help make sure that doesn't happen."

May pales at his words. "What could I ever do?"

A slight smile curls the corners of Old Man Louie's lips, but for the first time I don't see it as heartless. "Don't worry too much," he says. He turns to Sam. "Now you know my secret, and I know yours. Like a true father and son, we are bound together forever. The two of us not only protect each other but we also protect the uncles."

"Why me?" Sam asks. "Why not one of them?"

"You know why. I need someone to care for my businesses, take care of my real son when I'm dead, and look after me as an ancestor when I go to the afterworld because Vern won't be able to do that for me. I know you think I'm a cruel man and you probably don't believe me, but I truly did choose you to be my replacement son. I will always look at you as my eldest son, my first son, which is why I'm so hard on you. I'm trying to be a proper father! I'm giving you *everything*, but you have to do three things. First, you must give up your plans to run away." He puts up a hand to prevent any of us from speaking. "Don't bother denying it. I'm not stupid, I know what's happening in my home, and I'm tired of worrying about it all the time." He pauses and then says, "You have to stop working at the Temple of Kwan Yin. That's an embarrassment to me. My son shouldn't need to do that job. And finally, you must promise to care for my boy when the time comes."

Sam, May, and I look from one to the other of us. May sends me a message, almost pleading: *I don't want to keep moving. I want to stay in Haolaiwu.* Sam, whom I still don't know that well, takes my hand: *Maybe this is an opportunity after all. He says he'll treat me as the true first son.* For myself . . . I'm tired of running. I'm not very good at it, and I have a baby to care for. But are we selling ourselves for less than what the old man already bought us for?

"If we stay," Sam says, "you have to give us more freedom."

"This is not a negotiation," the old man shoots back. "You have nothing to bargain with."

But Sam doesn't surrender. "May is already working as an extra. This makes her happy. Now you must do the same for the sister. Let Pearl see what's outside China City. And if you won't let me work at the temple, then you need to pay me. If I am to be your first son, then you must treat me the same as my brother —"

"You two are not the same —"

"That's right. I work much harder than he does. He gets paid from the family pot. I need to get paid too. Father," Sam adds deferentially, "you know this is right."

The old man's knuckles tap on the table, weighing, weighing, weighing. He gives one final decisive rap, and then he stands. He reaches out his hand and squeezes Sam's shoulder. Then he walks back to his tea cakes, tea, and friends.

The next day, I buy a newspaper, circle a classified ad, and walk to a phone booth, where I make a call about a position as a clerk in a refrigerator repair shop.

"You sound perfect, Mrs. Louie," a pleasant voice says on the line. "Please come in for an interview."

But when I get there and the man sees me, he says, "I didn't realize you were Chinese. I thought you were Italian because of your name."

I don't get the job, and variations of this happen again and again. Finally, I put in an application at Bullock's Wilshire Department Store. I'm hired to work in the storeroom, where no one will see me. I make eighteen dollars a week. After my time in China City, moving from the café to the various shops throughout the day, staying in one place is easy. I dress better than the other storeroom clerks and work harder too. One day the assistant manager releases me into the store proper to stack merchandise and keep it in order. After a couple of months — and intrigued by my British accent, which I use because it seems to please my Occidental boss — he promotes me to elevator operator. It can't be easier or more mindless — just up and down from ten in the morning until six at night — and I earn a few dollars more a month.

Then one day the assistant manager has a new idea. "We just got in a shipment of mah-jongg sets," he says. "You're going to help me sell them. You're going to provide atmosphere."

He has me change into a cheap *cheongsam* sent by the game's manufacturer, and then he takes me to the ground floor just inside the main entrance and shows me a table — *my* table. By the end of the afternoon, I've sold eight sets. The following day, I come to work wearing one of my most beautiful *cheongsams* — bright red with embroidered peonies. I sell two dozen mah-jongg sets. When customers announce they want to learn how to play the game, the assistant manager asks me to teach a class once a week — for a fee, of which I receive a percentage. I'm doing so well that I ask the assistant manager if he'll let me take the written test for another promotion. When his boss grades me down because of my Chinese hair, skin, and eyes, I know I've gone as far as I can at Bullock's, even though I sell more mah-jongg sets than the other girls sell gloves or hats.

But what can I do? For now I'm happy with the money I make. I give a third to Father Louie, as we all have called him since he and Sam came to their agreement, for the family pot. Another third is put aside for Joy. And I keep a third to spend as I please.

Six months after the fire, on August 2, 1939, China City has its second Grand Opening, with an opera, dragon parade, lion dance, magicians, devil dancers, and carefully monitored firecrackers. In the months that follow, the fragrances of incense and gardenias perfume the air. Soft Chinese music wafts down the alleyways. Children dart among tourists. Mae West, Gene Tierney, and Eleanor Roosevelt visit. Shriners host events, and fraternities come to rush. Other groups go to the Chinese Junk Café — modeled on the command ship of a pirate fleet led by the greatest pirate in the world, who just happened to be a Chinese woman — "docked" in the Harbor of Whangpoo to eat "pirate chow" and drink "pirate grog" prepared by "an expert mixologist, a man of soft words but loud concoctions." The alleyways are full of Occidentals, but China City will never be what it was.

Perhaps people begin to stay away because many of the original sets that had been a big draw are now reproductions. Maybe they stay away because New Chinatown is seen as more modern and fun. While we were closed, New Chinatown and its neon lights seduced visitors with the promise of late nights, dancing, and amusement, while China City — no matter how much pirate grog you imbibe — is peaceful, quiet, and quaint, with its little alleyways and people dressed as villagers.

I quit my job at Bullock's and resume my old routine of cleaning and serving in China City. This time I'm properly paid for the work I do. May, however, doesn't want to go back to the Golden Pagoda.

"Bak Wah Tom has offered me a full-time job," she tells Father Louie, "helping him find extras, making sure everyone arrives on time for the bus to take them to the studio, and translating on sets."

I listen to this in surprise. I'd be better at that job. I'm fluent in Sze Yup, for one thing — something even my father-in-law understands.

"What about your sister? She's the smart one. She should do this work."

"Yes, my *jie jie* is very smart, but —"

Before she can make her arguments, he tries a different tack. "Why do you want to be apart from the family? Don't you want to stay with your sister?"

"Pearl doesn't mind," May answers. "I've given her plenty of things she would never have otherwise."

Lately, whenever May wants something, she reminds me that she gave me a child and all the many secrets that go with that. Is this meant to be a threat — that if I don't let her do this she'll tell the old man Joy isn't mine? Not at all. This is one of those times when May has thought things through very clearly. This is her way of reminding me that I have a beautiful daughter, a husband who loves me, and a little home for the three of us in our room, while she has no one and nothing. Shouldn't I help her get something to make her life more bearable?

"May already has experience with people from *Haolaiwu*," I tell my father-in-law. "She'll be good at this."

So May goes to work for Tom Gubbins, and I take her place in the Golden Pagoda. I dust from one end of the store to the other. I wash the floor and windows. I make lunch for Father Louie and then scrub his dishes in a tub, throwing the dirty water outside the door as if I'm a peasant's daughter. And I take care of Joy.

Like women everywhere, I wish I were a better mother. Joy is seventeen months old and still in diapers that have to be washed by hand. She often cries in the afternoons, and I have to walk her back and forth for what seems like hours to calm her. It isn't her fault. Because of her filming schedules, she doesn't sleep well at night and she barely naps during the day. She eats American food on the sets and spits out the Chinese food I make for her. I try to hold her, snuggle her, and do all the things a mother's supposed to do, but there's a part of me that still doesn't like to touch or be touched. I love my daughter, but she's a Tiger child and not easy. And then there's May, who now spends a lot of time with Joy. A kernel of bitterness begins to grow, which Yen-yen feeds and nourishes. I shouldn't listen to that old woman, but I can't get away from her.

"That May thinks only of herself. Her beautiful face hides a devious heart. She has just one thing to do and she doesn't do it. Pearl, Pearl, Pearl, you sit here and take care of a worthless girl all day. But where is your sister's child? Why won't she bring us a son? Why, Pearl, why? Because she's selfish, because she doesn't think of helping you or anyone else in the family."

I don't want to believe these things are true, but I can't deny that May is changing. As her *jie jie*, I should try to stop it, but my parents and I didn't know how to do it when May was a little girl and I don't know how to do it now.

To make things more difficult, May often calls me from the set, lowers her voice, and then asks, "How in the H do I tell these people they have to carry their firearms over their shoulders?" Or "How in the H do I tell them to huddle together when they're being beaten?" And I tell her the Sze Yup words, because I don't know what else to do.

By Christmas, our lives have settled. May and I have been here twenty months. Making our own money allows us to slip away for excursions and treats. Father Louie calls us spendthrifts, but we always weigh how to spend our cash. I want a more stylish haircut than I can get in Chinatown, but every time I go to a beauty parlor in the Occidental part of town, they say, "We don't cut Chinese hair." I finally get someone to cut my hair after hours, when white customers won't be offended by my presence. A car would be nice too — we could get a used four-door Plymouth for five hundred dollars — but we have a long way to save for that.

In the meantime, we go to the movie palaces on Broadway. Even if we pay for the best seats, we have to sit in the balcony. But we don't care, because movies perk up the spirits. We cheer when we glimpse May as a fallen woman begging a missionary for forgiveness or Joy as an orphan being handed onto a sampan by Clark Gable. Seeing my daughter's beautiful face on the screen, I'm embarrassed by my dark skin. I take some of my money to the apothecary and buy face cream embellished with ground pearls, hoping to make my face as fair as Joy's mother's should be.

During our time here, May and I have changed from beautiful girls buffeted by fate and looking for escape to young wives not completely happy with our lots — but what young wives are? Sam and I are doing the husband-wife thing, but so are May and Vern. I know because the walls are thin and I can hear everything. We have accepted and adapted to what's safe, and we do our best to find pleasure where we can. On New Year's Eve, we dress up and go to the Palomar Dance Hall, only to be turned away because we're Chinese. Standing on the street corner, I gaze up and see a full moon that looks worn and blurred, dulled by the lights and the exhaust that hang in the air. As one poet wrote, Even the best of moons will be tinged with sadness.

Part Three

DESTINY

Haolaiwu

We are back in Shanghai. Rickshaws clatter past. Beggars squat on the ground, their arms outstretched, their palms open. Barbecued ducks hang in the windows. Street vendors hover over carts, boiling noodles, roasting nuts, frying bean curd. Peddlers sell bok choy and melons from baskets. Farmers have come into the city, carrying bundles of live chickens, ducks, and pig parts hanging from poles slung over their shoulders. Women drift past in skintight *cheongsams*. Old men sit on upturned crates, smoking pipes, their hands tucked into their sleeves for warmth. Thick fog drapes itself around our feet, oozing into alleys and dark corners. Red lanterns hang above us, turning everything into an eerie dream.

"Places! Places, everyone!"

Home vanishes from my mind, and I'm back on the movie set I'm visiting with May and Joy. Bright lights turn on the fake scene. A camera rolls across the floor. A man positions a sound boom overhead. It's September 1941.

"You should be proud of Joy," May says, brushing a loose strand of hair from my daughter's face. "No matter what studio we go to, everyone loves her."

Joy sits on her aunt's lap, looking content but alert. She's three and a half years old and beautiful; "just like her aunt," people always say. And what a perfect auntie May is, getting Joy jobs, taking her to movie sets, making sure she has good costumes and is always in the exact right spot when the director looks for an innocent face on which to focus his camera lens. This past year or so, Joy has spent so much time with her auntie that being with me is like spending time with a bowl of rancid milk. I discipline Joy, and make her eat her supper, dress properly, and show respect to her grandparents, her uncles, and every other person older than she. May prefers to indulge Joy with treats, kisses, and letting her stay up all night on shoots like this.

People have always called me the smart one — even my father-in-law says so — but what seemed like a good idea a couple of years ago has turned out to be a big mistake. When I said May could take Joy to movie sets, I didn't fully understand that my sister was going to provide my daughter with a different world, which was fun and completely separate from me. When I mentioned this to May, she frowned and shook her head. "It's not like that. Come with us and watch what we do. You'll see how good she is, and you'll change your mind." But this isn't just about Joy. May wants to show off her importance, and I'm supposed to tell her how proud of her I am. We've followed this same pattern since we were children.

So today, in the late afternoon, we boarded a bus with neighbors for whom May had also gotten jobs. When we reached the studio, we drove through a gate and straight to the wardrobe department, where women shoved clothes at us with no regard to our sizes. I was handed a filthy jacket and a wrinkled pair of loose trousers. I hadn't worn clothes like these since May and I crept out of China and then languished on Angel Island. When I tried to exchange them, the wardrobe girl said, "You're supposed to look dirty, plenty dirty, understand?" May, who usually plays someone glamorous and naughty, also took a set of peasant clothes so we'd be together in the scene.

We changed in a big tent with no privacy and no heating. Somehow, although I dress my daughter every day, her auntie took charge, slipping off Joy's felt jumper and helping her step into trousers that were as dark, dirty, and loose as the ones May and I wore. Then we went to hair and makeup. They hid our hair under black cloths wrapped tightly around our heads. They tied Joy's hair with several rubber bands until her head looked like it was sprouting exotic black plants. They smeared our faces with brown makeup, bringing back memories of May coating my face with the mixture of cocoa and cold cream. Then we went back outside, so we could be spattered with mud from a spray gun. After that, we waited in the fake Shanghai, our wide black trousers fluttering in the breeze like dark spirits. For those born here, this is as close as they'll ever get to the land of their ancestors. For those born in China, the set

301

allows us a moment to feel as though we've been transported across the water and back in time.

I have to admit I love seeing how much the crew likes my sister and the way the other extras respect her. May is happy, smiling, greeting friends, reminding me of the girl she used to be back in Shanghai. And yet, as the night drags on, I see more and more things that disturb me. Yes, a man sells live chickens, but behind him a group of men squat on their haunches and gamble. In another part of the scene, men pretend to smoke opium — right on the fake street! Nearly all the men have pigtails, even though the story not only takes place after the Republic was formed but has as its background the dwarf bandits' invasion twenty-five years later. And the women . . .

I think about *The Shanghai Gesture*, which May, Sam, Vern, and I saw earlier this year at the Million Dollar. Josef von Sternberg, the director, had spent time in Shanghai, so we thought we might see something that would remind us of our home city, but it was just another one of those stories where a white girl was led into gambling, alcohol, and who knew what else by a dragon lady. We laughed at the movie posters, which read, "People live in Shanghai for many reasons . . . most of them bad." Toward the end of my days in Shanghai, I'd thought that was true, but it still hurt to see my home city — the Paris of Asia — painted in such an evil light. We've seen this kind of thing in movie after movie, and now we're in one.

"How can you do this, May? Aren't you ashamed?" I ask.

She looks genuinely confused and hurt. "About what?"

"Every single Chinese in this film is portrayed as backward," I answer. "We're made to giggle like idiots and show our teeth. They make us pantomime because we're supposed to be stupid. Or they make us speak the worst sort of pidgin English —"

"I suppose, but are you telling me this doesn't remind you of Shanghai?" She looks at me, hopeful.

"That's not the point! Don't you have any pride in the Chinese people?"

"I don't know why you have to complain about everything," she replies. Her disappointment is palpable. "I brought you here so you could see what Joy and I do. Aren't you proud of us?"

"May —"

"Why can't you have a good time?" she asks. "Why can't you take pleasure in watching Joy and me earn money? I admit we don't make as much as those guys over there." She points to a gaggle of fake rickshaw pullers. "I got them a guaranteed seven fifty a day for a week, so long as they kept their heads completely shaved. Not bad —"

"Rickshaw drivers, opium smokers, and prostitutes. Is that what you want people to think we are?"

"If by people you mean *lo fan*, what do I care what they think?"

"Because these things are insulting —"

"To whom? They aren't slurs against *us*, you and me. Besides, this is just part of an evolution for us. Some people" — meaning me, I suppose — "would rather be

303

unemployed than take a job they feel is beneath them. But a job like this gives us a start, and it's up to us to go from here."

"So today those men will play rickshaw pullers and tomorrow they'll own the studio?" I ask skeptically.

"Of course not," she says, finally annoyed. "All they want is a speaking role. There's a lot of money in that, Pearl, as you know."

Bak Wah Tom has been enticing May with the dream of a speaking role for a couple of years now and it still hasn't happened, although Joy has already had a few lines on different films. The bag where I keep Joy's earnings has gotten quite fat, and she's still a small child. In the meantime, Joy's auntie yearns to make her own twenty dollars for a line, any line. By now she'd settle for something as simple as "Yes, ma'am."

"If sitting around pretending all night to be a bad woman offers such opportunity," I say rather pointedly, "then why haven't you gotten a speaking role?"

"You know why! I've told you a thousand times! Tom says I'm too beautiful. Every time the director chooses me, the female star shoots me down. She doesn't want my face to fight with hers because I'll win. I know that sounds immodest, but that's what everyone says."

The crew finishes positioning people and adding a few more props for the next part of the scene. The film we're working on is a "warning" movie about the Japanese threat; if the Japanese can invade China and disrupt foreign interests, shouldn't we all be worried? So far, from my perspective, having spent a couple of hours shooting the same street scene over and over, it has little to do with what May and I experienced on our way out of China. But when the director describes the next scene to us, my stomach tightens.

"Bombs are going to drop," he explains through a megaphone. "They aren't real, but they're going to sound real. Next the Japs are going to rush into the market. You have to run that way. You, over there with the cart, tip it over on your way out. And I want the women to scream. Scream really loud — like you think you're going to die."

When the camera begins to roll, I hold Joy on my hip, give what I think is a pretty good fake scream, and run. I do it again and again and again. Even though I'd had a momentary fear that this would bring bad memories, it doesn't. The fake bombs don't shake the ground. My ears don't go deaf from the concussions. No one loses their limbs. Blood doesn't spurt. It's all just a game and fun in the way it had been years ago when May and I used to put on plays for our parents. And May was right about Joy. She's good at following directions, waiting between shots, and crying when the camera starts rolling, just as she was instructed.

At two in the morning, we're sent back to the makeup tent, where they daub fake blood on our faces and clothes. When we return to the set, some of us are positioned on the ground — legs splayed, clothes twisted and bloody, eyes unseeing. Now the dead and dying lie around us. As the Japanese soldiers advance, the rest of us are supposed to run and scream. This isn't hard for me. I see the yellow uniforms and hear the stomp of boots. One of the extras — a peasant like

305

me — bumps into me, and I scream. When the fake soldiers run forward with their bayonets before them, I try to get away, but I fall. Joy scrambles to her feet and continues to run, tripping over corpses, getting farther away from me, leaving me. One of the soldiers pushes me down when I try to get up. I'm paralyzed with fear. Even though the men around me have Chinese faces, even though they're my neighbors dressed up to look like the enemy, I scream and scream and scream. I'm no longer on a movie set; I'm in a shack outside Shanghai. The director yells, "Cut."

May comes to my side. Her face is etched with concern. "Are you all right?" she asks as she helps me up.

I'm still so upset that I can't speak. I nod, and May gives me a questioning look. I don't want to talk about what I'm feeling. I didn't want to talk about it in China, when I woke up in the hospital, and I still don't. I take Joy from May's arms and hug my baby tight. I'm still shaking when the director saunters over to us.

"That was terrific," he says. "I could have heard you scream two blocks away. Could you do it again?" He eyes me appraisingly. "Could you do it several more times?" When I don't answer right away, he says, "There's extra money in it for you, and the kid too. A great scream is a speaking part as far as I'm concerned, and I can always use a face like hers."

May's fingers tighten on my arm.

"So you'll do it?" he asks.

I push the memory of the shack out of my mind and think about my daughter's future. I could put a little extra money aside for her this month.

"I'll try," I manage to say.

May's fingers dig into my arm. As the director strolls back to his chair, May pulls me away from the others. "You have to let me do this," she implores desperately under her breath. "Please, *please* let me do it."

"I'm the one who screamed," I say. "I want to make something worthwhile come out of this night."

"This could be my only chance —"

"You're only twenty-two —"

"I was a beautiful girl in Shanghai," May pleads. "But this is Hollywood, and I don't have much time left."

"We all have fears of getting older," I say. "But I want this too. Have you forgotten I was also a beautiful girl?" When she doesn't respond, I use the one argument I'm sure will work. "I'm the one who remembered what happened in the shack —"

"You always use that excuse to get your way."

I step back, stunned by her words. "You don't mean that."

"You just don't want me to have anything of my own," she says forlornly.

How can she possibly say that when I've sacrificed so much for her? My resentment has grown over the years, but it has never stopped me from giving May everything she wants.

"You're always being given opportunities," May continues, her voice gathering strength.

Now I understand what's happening. If she can't have her way, she's going to fight me. But I'm not going to give in so easily this time.

"What opportunities?"

"Mama and Baba sent you to college —"

That's going way back in time, but I say, "You didn't want to go."

"Everyone likes you more than they like me."

"That's ridiculous —"

"Even my own husband prefers you to me. He's always nice to you."

What's the point in arguing with May? Our disagreements have always been about the same things: our parents liked one or the other of us more, one of us has something better — whether it's a better flavor ice cream, a prettier pair of shoes, or a more companionable husband — or one of us wants to do something at the expense of the other.

"I can scream just as well as you," May persists. "I'm asking again. Please let me do it."

"What about Joy?" I ask softly, attacking my sister's vulnerable spot. "You know Sam and I are saving for her to go to college one day."

"That's fifteen years away, and you're assuming an American college will take Joy — a Chinese girl." My sister's eyes, which earlier tonight had sparkled with pleasure and pride, suddenly glare at me. For an instant I'm thrown back in time to our kitchen in Shanghai when Cook tried to teach us how to make dumplings. It had started out as something fun for May and me to do and had ended in a terrible fight. Now, all these years later, what was supposed to be an enjoyable outing has turned bitter. When I look at May, I see not just jealousy but hate. "Let me have this part," she says. "I *earned* it."

I think about how she works for Tom Gubbins, how she doesn't have to stay confined in one of the Golden enterprises all day, how she gets to come to sets like these with my daughter and be out of Chinatown and China City for a while.

"May —"

"If you're going to start in with all your grudges against me, I don't want to hear them. You refuse to see how lucky you are. Don't you know how jealous I am? I can't help it. You have everything. You have a husband who loves you and talks to you. You have a *daughter*."

There! She said it. My reply comes out of my mouth so fast, I don't have a chance to think about it or stop it.

"Then why is it that you spend more time with her than I do?" As I speak, I'm reminded of the old saying that diseases go in through the mouth, disasters come out of the mouth, meaning that words can be like bombs themselves.

"Joy prefers being with me because I hug and kiss her, because I hold her hand, because I let her sit on my lap," May snaps back.

"That's not the Chinese way to raise a child. Touching like that —"

"You didn't believe that when we lived with Mama and Baba," May says.

"True, but I'm a mother now and I don't want Joy to grow up to be porcelain with scars."

"Being hugged by her mother won't cause her to become a loose woman —"

"Don't tell me how to raise my daughter!" At the sharp tone in my voice, some of the extras peer at us curiously.

"You won't let me have *anything*, but Baba promised that if we agreed to our marriages I would get to go to *Haolaiwu*."

That's not how I remember it. And she's changing the subject. And she's confusing things.

"This is about Joy," I say, "not your silly dreams."

"Oh? A few minutes ago you were accusing me of embarrassing the Chinese people. Now you're saying it's bad for me but fine if you and Joy do it?"

This is a problem for me and one I don't know how to reconcile in my mind. I'm not thinking properly, but I don't think my sister is either.

"You have everything," May repeats as she begins to weep. "I have nothing. Can't you let me have this one thing? Please? *Please?*"

I shut my mouth and let the heat of my anger burn my skin. I refuse to believe or acknowledge any of her reasons for why she — and not I — should have this part in the movie, but then I do what I've always done. I give in to my *moy moy*. It's the only way for her jealousy to dissipate. It's the only way for my resentment to go back to its hiding place while giving me time to think about how to get Joy out of this business without creating more friction. May and I are sisters. We'll always fight, but we'll always make up as well. That's what sisters do: we argue, we point out

310

each other's frailties, mistakes, and bad judgment, we flash the insecurities we've had since childhood, and then we come back together. Until the next time.

May takes my daughter and my place in the scene. The director doesn't notice that my sister isn't me. To him, it seems one Chinese woman dressed in black trousers, smeared with fake mud and blood, and carrying a little girl is interchangeable with the next. For the next few hours, I listen to my sister scream again and again. The director's never satisfied, but he doesn't replace May either.

Snapshots

On December 7, 1941, three months after my night on the film set, the Japanese bomb Pearl Harbor and the United States enters the war. The very next day, the Japanese attack Hong Kong. On Christmas Day, the British surrender the island. Also on December 8, at precisely 10a.m., the Japanese seize the International Settlement in Shanghai and raise their flag atop the Hong Kong and Shanghai Bank on the Bund. During the next four years, foreigners imprudent enough to have remained in Shanghai live in internment camps, while in this country, the Angel Island Immigration Station is turned over to the U.S. Army to house Japanese, Italian, and German prisoners of war. Here in Chinatown, Uncle Edfred — without giving any of us a chance to weigh in — joins the first group of men to enlist.

"What! Why would you do that?" Uncle Wilburt demands in Sze Yup when his birth son announces the news.

"Because I feel patriotic!" comes Uncle Edfred's jubilant answer. "I want to fight! Number one reason: I want to help defeat our shared enemy — the Jap. Number two reason: If I enlist, I can become a citizen. A real citizen. Down the line, of course." If he lives, the rest of us think. "All the laundrymen are doing it," he adds when he sees our lack of enthusiasm.

"Laundrymen! Bah! Some people will do anything not to be laundrymen." Uncle Wilburt sucks air through his teeth in worry.

"What did you do when they asked about your citizenship status?" This comes from Sam, who's always anxious that one of us will be caught and we'll all be sent back to China. "You're a paper son. Are they going to come looking for the rest of us?"

"I admitted my status straight out. I told them I came over on fake papers," Edfred answers. "But they didn't seem too interested. When they asked anything that I thought might come back to the rest of you, I said, 'I'm an orphan. Now do you want me to fight or not?'"

"But aren't you too old?" Uncle Charley asks.

"On paper I'm thirty, but I'm really only twenty-three. I'm fit and I'm willing to die. Why wouldn't they take me?"

A few days later, Edfred enters the café and announces, "The Army told me to buy my own socks. Where do I do that?" He's lived in Los Angeles for seventeen years, but he still doesn't know where or how to get even the most basic necessities. I offer to take him to the May Company, but he says, "I need to go by myself. I've got to learn to be on my own now." He returns a couple of hours later scraped up and with holes in the knees of his baggy pants. "I bought the socks all right, but when I left the store, some men pushed me in the street. They thought I was a Jap."

While Edfred is at boot camp, Father Louie and I go through the store to check each item, removing stickers that say MADE IN JAPAN and replacing them with new stickers that read 100% CHINESE PRODUCT. He starts to buy curios made in Mexico, which puts us in direct competition with the merchants on Olvera Street. Oddly, our customers don't seem to notice the difference between something made in China, Japan, or Mexico. It's foreign, simple as that.

We too are forever foreign, which makes us suspect. The family associations in Chinatown print up signs that read CHINA: YOUR ALLY for us to hang in the windows of our businesses, homes, and automobiles to announce that we aren't Japanese. They make armbands and badges, which we wear to make sure we aren't attacked in the street or rounded up, stuck on a train, and sent to one of the internment camps. The government, aware that most Occidentals think all Orientals look alike, issues special registration certificates that verify that we're "members of the Chinese Race." None of us can let down our guard.

But when Edfred comes to Los Angeles to visit after his military training, people salute him on the street. "When I wear my uniform, I know I'm not going to be kicked around. It tells folks I have as much right to be here as anyone else," he explains. "Now I have number three reason: in the Army I'm getting a fair chance — one that's based not on my being Chinese but on my being a man in uniform fighting for the United States."

That day I buy a camera and take my first photograph. I still keep my photographs of Mama and Baba hidden for when the immigration inspectors make their periodic checks, but seeing Uncle Edfred go to war is different. He'll be fighting for America . . . and for China. The next time the inspectors come, I'll proudly show my snapshot of Uncle Edfred, forever China-skinny, dressed in his uniform, beaming at the camera, his cap tilted at a jaunty angle, and having just told us, "From now on, just call me Fred. No more Edfred. Got it?"

What the photo doesn't show is my father-in-law, standing a few feet away, looking devastated and scared. My feelings about him have changed the past few years. He has almost nothing here in Los Angeles: he's a third-class citizen, he faces the same discrimination we all do, and he will never break out of Chinatown. Now his adopted country, America, is also fighting Japan. Since the commercial shipping channels are closed, he no longer receives goods from his rattan and porcelain factories in Shanghai or earns money from bringing in paper partners, but he continues to send "tea money" back to his relatives in Wah Hong Village, not only because an American dollar goes a long way in China but because his longing for his home country has never diminished. Yen-yen, Vern, Sam, May, and I have no one to send money to, so Father

Louie's remittances are from all of us — for all the villages, homes, and families we've lost.

"Those who can't fight need to produce," Uncle Charley tells us one day. "You know the Lee boys? They've gone over to Lockheed to build airplanes. They say there's a place for me, and it's not making chop suey. They say every blow I strike in building planes is a blow of freedom for the land of our fathers and for the land of our new home."

"But your English —"

"No one cares about my English as long as I work hard," he says. "You know, Pearl, you could get a job over there too. The Lee boys took their sisters to work with them. Now Esther and Bernice are driving rivets in bomber doors. You want to know how much money they're making? Sixty cents an hour during the day and sixty-five cents an hour for the night shift. You want to know what I'm going to make?" He rubs his eyes, which look particularly painful and swollen from his allergies. "Eighty-five cents an hour. That's thirty-four dollars a week. I tell you, Pearl-ah, those are good wages."

My photograph shows Uncle Charley sitting at the counter, his sleeves rolled up, a piece of pie in front of him, his apron and paper hat discarded on a vacant stool.

"What can my boy do for the war?" my father-in-law asks when Vern, who graduated the previous June from high school, where they didn't want him and didn't bother to educate him, receives his draft notice. "He's better off at home. Sam, go with him and make sure they understand."

"I'll take him," Sam says, "but I'm going to enlist. I want to become a real citizen too."

Father Louie doesn't try to change Sam's mind. Citizenship is one thing and the risks of being questioned can affect many people, but we all know what this war is about. I'm proud of Sam, but that doesn't mean I'm not worried. When Sam and Vern return to the apartment, I know things didn't go well. Vern was turned down for obvious reasons, but, surprisingly, Sam was classified 4-F.

"Flat feet, and yet I pulled a rickshaw through the streets and alleyways of Shanghai," he complains to me when we're alone in our room. Once again, he's been belittled and dismissed as a man. In so many ways, he continues to eat bitterness.

Not long after this, May picks up the camera and takes a photograph. In it, you can see how much the apartment has changed since May, Joy, and I first arrived. Bamboo shades are rolled above the windows, but we can let them down for privacy. On the wall above the couch hang four calendars depicting the four seasons that we received over four years from Wong On Lung Market. Old Man Louie sits on a straight-backed chair, looking cocooned and solemn. Sam gazes out the window. His posture is erect and held up by his iron fan, but his face looks as though he's been punched. Vern — content in the womb of his family — sprawls on the couch, holding a model airplane. I sit on the floor, painting a banner advertising the sale of war bonds in China City and New Chinatown. Joy hovers nearby, building a ball of rubber bands. Yen-yen scrunches used tinfoil into compact lumps. Later that day we plan to take these things over to Belmont High School and deposit them in the collection boxes.

To me, this photograph shows how we sacrifice in big and small ways. We can finally afford to buy a washing machine, but we don't because metal is so scarce. We promote the boycott of Japanese silk stockings and wear cotton stockings instead, using the motto "Be in style, wear lisle," and, sure enough, women all over the city join the Non-Silk Movement. Everyone suffers from shortages of coffee, beef, sugar, flour, and milk, but in the café and in Chinese restaurants all over the city, we suffer even more because ingredients like rice, ginger, tree-ear mushrooms, and soy sauce no longer cross the Pacific. We learn to substitute sliced apple for water chestnuts. We buy rice grown in Texas instead of fragrant jasmine rice from China. We use oleo, squirt yellow food coloring in it, knead it, and press it into bar-shaped molds so it will look like butter when we cut it into pats for the café. Sam gets eggs on the black market, paying five dollars for a case. We save our bacon grease in a coffee can under the sink to take to the collection center, where we're told it will be used in the production of armaments. I stop feeling resentful that I have to spend so much time stringing peas and peeling garlic in the restaurant, because now we're serving our boys in uniform and we need to do everything we can for them. And at home we begin to eat American dishes — pork and beans, grilled Spam sandwiches with cheese and sliced onion, creamed tuna, and casseroles made with Bisquick — that will spread our ingredients the furthest.

SNAP: THE CHINESE New Year Fund-raiser. Snap: Double-ten Fundraiser. Snap: China Night, with your favorite movie stars. Snap: the Rice Bowl Parade, where the women of Chinatown carry a gigantic Chinese flag by its edges and ask bystanders to throw coins onto the flag. Snap: the Moon Festival, where Anna May Wong and Keye Luke serve as the mistress and master of ceremonies. Barbara Stanwyck, Dick Powell, Judy Garland, Kay Kyser, and Laurel and Hardy wave to the crowd. William Holden and Raymond Massey stand around, looking debonair, while the girls in the Mei Wah Drum Corps march in their V for Victory formation. The monies raised buy medical supplies, mosquito nets, gas masks, and other necessities for refugees, as well as ambulances and airplanes, which are sent across the Pacific.

Snap: the Chinatown Canteen. May poses with soldiers, sailors, and flyboys, who leave Union Station during their layovers, cross Alameda, and visit the canteen. These boys have come from all over the country. Many of them have never seen a Chinese before, and they say things like "golly" and "gee whillikers," which we adopt and use ourselves. Snap: I'm surrounded by airmen sent by Chiang Kai-shek to train in Los Angeles. It's wonderful to hear their voices, learn news of our home country, and know that China still fights hard. Snap, snap, snap: Bob Hope, Frances Langford, and Jerry Colonna come to the canteen to put on shows. Girls between sixteen and eighteen years old — wearing white pinafores, red blouses, and saddle shoes with red socks — volunteer as hostesses to jitterbug with the boys, hand out sandwiches, and listen with sympathetic ears.

My favorite photograph shows May and me chaperoning at the canteen just before closing time on a Saturday night. We wear gardenias pinned in our hair, which falls in soft curls around our shoulders. Our sweetheart necklines show a lot of pale flesh but somehow look girlish and chaste. Our dresses are short, and our legs are bare. We may be married women, but we look pretty and cheerful. May and I know what it means to live through war, and being in Los Angeles isn't that.

Over the next fifteen months, many people pass through the city: servicemen going to or coming from the Pacific Theater, wives and children journeying to see husbands and fathers in military hospitals, and diplomats, actors, and salesmen of every sort involved in the war effort. I never think I'll see someone I know, but one day in the café a man's voice calls my name.

"Pearl Chin? Is that you?"

I stare at the man sitting at the counter. I know him, but my eyes refuse to recognize him because my humiliation is instantaneous and deep.

"Aren't you the Pearl Chin who used to live in Shanghai? You knew my daughter, Betsy."

I set down his plate of chow mein, turn away, and wipe my hands. If this man truly is Betsy's father — and he is — he's the first and only person from my past to see just how far I've fallen. I was once a beautiful girl, whose face decorated walls in Shanghai. I was smart and clever enough to be allowed into this man's home. I turned his daughter from a dowdy mess into someone half fashionable. Now I'm mother to a five-year-old, wife to a rickshaw puller, and waitress in a café in a tourist attraction. I paste a smile on my face and turn to look at him.

"Mr. Howell, it's wonderful to see you again."

But he doesn't look so happy to see me. He looks sad and old. I may be humbled, but his grief is elsewhere.

"We came looking for you." He reaches across the counter and grabs my arm. "We thought you were dead in one of the bombings, but here you are."

"Betsy?"

"She's in a Jap camp out by the Lunghua Pagoda."

A memory of flying kites with Z.G. and May flashes through my mind, but I say, "I thought most Americans left Shanghai before —"

"She got married," Mr. Howell says sadly. "Did you know that? She married a young man who works for Standard Oil. They stayed in Shanghai after Mrs. Howell and I left. The oil business, you know how it is."

I come around the counter and sit on the stool next to Mr. Howell, aware of the curious looks Sam, Uncle Wilburt, and the other café helpers shoot my way. I wish they'd stop staring at us like that — their mouths hanging open like they're street beggars — but Betsy's father doesn't notice. I want to say my feeling of disgrace is hard to find, but I'm ashamed to admit it's hidden just beneath the surface of my skin. I've been in this country for almost five years and still haven't been fully able to accept my situation. It's as if in seeing this face from the past all the goodness in my life is reduced to nothing.

Betsy's father probably still works for the State Department, so maybe he's aware of my discomfort. At last he fills the silence between us. "We heard from Betsy after Shanghai became the Lonely Island. We thought she was safe, since she was in British territory. But after December eighth, there was nothing we could do to get her back. Diplomatic channels don't work so well now." He stares into his cup of coffee and smiles ruefully.

"She's strong," I say, trying to bolster Mr. Howell's spirits. "Betsy's always been smart and brave." Is that even true? I remember her as being passionate about politics when May and I just wanted to have another glass of champagne or another twirl around the dance floor.

"That's what Mrs. Howell and I tell ourselves."

"All you can do is hope."

He lets out a knowledgeable snort. "That's so like you, Pearl. Always looking at the bright side. That's why you did so well in Shanghai. That's why you got out before bad things happened. All the smart people got out in time."

When I don't say anything, he stares at me. After a long while, he says, "I'm here for Madame Chiang

Kai-shek's visit. I've been traveling with her on her American tour. Last week we were in Washington, where she appealed to Congress for money to help China in its fight against our common enemy and reminded the men who listened that China and the United States cannot be true allies with the Exclusion Act still on the books. This week she's going to speak at the Hollywood Bowl and —"

"Participate in a parade here in Chinatown."

"It sounds like you know all about it."

"I'm going to the Bowl," I say. "We're all going, and we're looking forward to having her here."

Hearing the word *we*, for the first time he seems to absorb his surroundings. I watch as his cheerless eyes see past his memories of a girl who perhaps never existed. He takes in the grease on my clothes, the tiny wrinkles around my eyes, and my chapped hands. Then his understanding expands as he assesses the smallness of the café, the walls painted baby-shit yellow, the dusty fan spinning overhead, and the wiry men wearing ME NO JAP armbands gawking at him as though he were a creature from beneath the waves.

"Mrs. Howell and I live in Washington now," he says carefully. "Betsy would be angry with me if I didn't invite you to come home with me. I could get you a job. With your language skills, there's a lot you could do to help the war effort."

"My sister's here with me," I respond, without thinking.

323

"Bring May too. We have room." He pushes away his plate of chow mein. "I hate to think of you here. You look . . ."

It's funny how in that moment I see things clearly. Am I beaten down? Yes. Have I allowed myself to become a victim? Somewhat. Am I afraid? Always. Does some part of me still long to fly away from this place? Absolutely. But I can't leave. Sam and I have built a life for Joy. It isn't perfect, but it's a life. My family's happiness means more to me than starting over again.

If in the canteen photos I'm smiling, the one from this day shows me at my worst. Mr. Howell — wearing an overcoat and a fedora — and I are posed next to the cash register, onto which I've taped a handmade sign that reads: ANY RESEMBLANCE TO LOOKING JAPANESE IS PURELY OCCIDENTAL. Usually our customers get a big kick out of that, but no one's showing teeth in the photograph. Even though it's in black and white, I can almost see the redness of shame on my cheeks.

A few days later, the whole family gets on a bus and rides to the Hollywood Bowl. Because Yen-yen and I have worked so hard raising money for China Relief, our family has good seats just behind the fountain that separates the stage from the audience. When Madame Chiang steps on the stage wearing a brocade *cheongsam*, we applaud like crazy people. She's splendid and beautiful.

"I implore the women here today to become educated and take an interest in politics both here and in the home country," she proclaims. "You can churn the wheel of progress without jeopardizing your roles as wives and mothers."

We listen attentively as she asks us and the Americans to help raise money and support for the Women's New Life Movement, but the whole time she speaks we ooh and aah over her appearance. My thoughts about my clothes change once again. I see that the *cheongsam*, which I've had to wear to please the tourists in China City and meet Mrs. Sterling's lease requirements, can be a patriotic, and fashionable, symbol.

When May and I go home, we bring our most precious *cheongsams* out of their chests and put them on. Inspired by Madame Chiang, we want to be as stylish and as loyal to China as possible. Instantly, we're once again beautiful girls. Sam takes our picture, and for a moment it feels as though we're back in Z.G.'s studio. But why, I wonder later, didn't we ask Sam to take a photograph of Yen-yen and me when we were invited to shake Madame Chiang Kai-shek's hand?

Tom gubbins retires and sells his business to Father Louie. It becomes the Golden Prop and Extras Company. Father Louie puts May in charge, even though she doesn't know beans about running a business. She now earns as much as $150 a week as a technical director, supplying extras, costumes, props, translation, and advice. She continues to work in countless films, which are now sent around the world and viewed by millions of people to show how bad the Japanese are. Her parts are small: a hapless Chinese maiden, a servant to some colonel or other, a villager being saved by white missionaries. But May is best known for her screaming roles, and, with the war on, she's played victim after victim in films like *Behind the Rising Sun, Bombs over Burma, The Amazing Mrs. Holliday*, in which an American woman tries to smuggle Chinese war orphans into the United States, and *China*, with its tagline, "Alan Ladd and twenty girls — trapped by the rapacious Japs!" May seems to be well liked by the various studios, especially MGM. "They call me the Cantonese ham," she boasts. She brags that she once earned one hundred dollars in one day for her screaming abilities.

Then May gets the call to supply MGM with extras for the filming of *Dragon Seed*, which will be released next summer in 1944. She contacts the Chinese Cinema Club on Main and Alameda, where members of the Chinese Screen Extras Guild hang out, to hire people, making a commission of ten percent for each extra, and she works in the motion picture herself.

"I tried to get Metro to let Keye Luke play one of the Jap captains, but the studio doesn't want to ruin his image as Charlie Chan's Number One Son," she says. "They have the prize Chinese egg, and they don't want it to go bad. It isn't easy to fill all the roles. I need hundreds of people to play Chinese peasants. For the Jap soldiers, the studio told me to hire Cambodians, Filipinos, and Mexicans."

Ever since my night on the movie set, I've been torn between my distaste for *Haolaiwu* and my desire to put money aside for my little girl. Joy has worked steadily since the war began, and I've made a good start on what I imagine she'll need for an education. My chance to pull her away from that world comes one night when Joy and May return from the set. Joy's crying and goes straight to our room, where she now has a little cot in the corner. May's furious. I've gotten mad at Joy sometimes. What mother doesn't get upset with her children on occasion? But this is the first time I've seen May angry at Joy, ever.

"I had a great role for Joy as Third Daughter," May fumes. "I made sure she got a good costume, and she looked darling. But just before the director called her, Joy went to the toilet. She missed her opportunity! She embarrassed me. How could she do that to me?"

"How?" I ask. "She's five years old. She needed to use the pot."

"I know, I know," May says, shaking her head. "But I really wanted this for her."

Grasping at my opportunity before it disappears, I continue. "Let's have Joy work in one of the stores with her grandparents for a while. That way she'll learn to be more appreciative of everything you do for her." I don't say that I won't let her go back to *Haolaiwu*, that in September Joy will start American school, or that I don't know how I'll save enough for Joy to go to college, but May's so mad she agrees with me.

Dragon Seed remains a highlight of May's career. One of her most precious possessions becomes the photo of her with Katharine Hepburn on the set. They're both wearing Chinese peasant clothes. Miss Hepburn's eyes have been taped back and heavily lined with black. The famous actress doesn't look even a little bit Chinese, but then neither do Walter Huston or Agnes Moorehead, who also star in the picture.

On my dresser, I put a photo of Joy at the orange juice stand we've set up for her outside the Golden Dragon Café. She's surrounded by servicemen, who crouch around her, smiling and giving her a thumbs-up. The photograph captures a single moment but one that's repeated day after day, night after night. The boys in uniform love to see my little girl — wearing cute silk pajamas and her hair in pigtails — squeezing oranges. They get to drink all they want for ten cents. Some of those boys will drink three or four glasses just to watch our Joy, her lips pursed in concentration, squeezing, squeezing, squeezing. Sometimes I look at that photograph and wonder if she knows how hard she's working. Or does she see it as a break from all-night calls and her aunt's demands? An added bonus: if men stop to look at this little Chinese girl — a curiosity — and drink her orange juice, which doesn't poison them, then they might come in for a meal.

In September I get Joy ready for kindergarten. She wants to go to Castelar School in Chinatown with Hazel Yee and the other neighbor kids. But Sam and I don't want her to go to the school that passed Vern from grade to grade even though he couldn't read, write, or do sums. We want her to have a step up in the world. We want her to attend school outside Chinatown, which means Joy has to say she lives in that district. She also has to be taught the official family story. Father Louie's lies about his status were passed to Sam, the uncles, and me. Now those lies go to a third generation. Joy will forever need to be careful when she applies for school, a job, or even her marriage certificate. All that starts now. For weeks we rehearse her as though she's about to go through Angel Island: Where do you live? What's the cross street? Where was your father born? Why did he return to China as a boy? What is your father's job? Not once do we tell her what's true or what's false. It's better if she knows only fake truth.

"All little girls need to know these things about their parents," I explain to Joy as I tuck her in her cot the night before school starts. "Don't tell your teacher anything except what we've told you."

The next day Joy puts on a green dress, a white sweater, and pink tights. Sam takes a photo of Joy and me standing on a step outside our building. She carries a new lunch box with a smiling and waving cowgirl sitting astride her trusty horse. I gaze at Joy with mother love. I'm proud of her, proud of all of us, for having come so far.

Sam and I take Joy by streetcar to the elementary school. We fill out the forms and lie about where we live. Then we walk Joy to her classroom. Sam stretches out Joy's hand to the teacher, Miss Henderson, who stares at it and then asks, "Why can't you foreigners just go back to your own countries?"

Just like that! Can you believe it? I have to respond before Sam works out what she's said. "Because this *is* her home country," I say, imitating the British mothers I used to see walking along the Bund with their children. "This is where she was born."

We leave our daughter with that woman. Sam doesn't say a word as we ride the streetcar back to China City, but when we reach the café, he pulls me to him and speaks to me in a voice ragged with emotion. "If they do something to her, I'll never forgive them and I'll never forgive myself."

A week later, when I go to the school to pick up Joy, I find her crying on the curb. "Miss Henderson sent me to the vice principal's office," she says, tears dripping down her face. "She asked a lot of questions. I answered like you told me, but she called me a liar and said I can't go here anymore."

I walk to the vice principal's office, but what can I do or say to change her mind?

"We keep an eye out for these infractions, Mrs. Louie," the heavyset woman intones. "Besides, your daughter doesn't belong here. Anyone can see that. Take her to the school in Chinatown. She'll be happier there."

The next day I walk Joy the couple of blocks to Castelar School, right in the heart of Chinatown. I see children from China, Mexico, Italy, and other European countries. Her teacher, Miss Gordon, smiles as she takes Joy's hand. She escorts Joy into the classroom and shuts the door. In the weeks and months that follow, Joy — who's been raised to be obedient, and refrain from doing something as wild as ride a bicycle, and been scolded by our neighbors for laughing too much and too loudly — learns to play hopscotch, jacks, and leapfrog. She's happy to be in the same class with her best friend, and Miss Gordon seems like a nice enough person.

We do the best we can at home. For me, this means making Joy speak English as much as possible, because she's going to have to make a living in this country and because she's an American. When her father, grandparents, or uncles speak to her in Sze Yup, she answers in English. Along the way Sam's understanding of English — but not his pronunciation — improves. Still, the uncles constantly tease her about going to school. "Education is only trouble for a girl," Uncle Wilburt cautions. "What do you want to do? Run away from us?" I find an ally in her grandfather. Not so long ago, he threatened May and me, telling us we'd have to put a nickel in a jar if we spoke any language other than Sze Yup in front of him. Now he tells Joy a variation of the same thing: "If I hear you speak something other than English, you will put a nickel in my jar." Her English is almost as good as mine, but I still can't imagine how she'll break out of Chinatown completely.

In late fall we gather around the radio to hear that President Roosevelt has asked Congress to repeal the Chinese Exclusion Act: "Nations, like individuals, make mistakes. We must be big enough to acknowledge our mistakes of the past and correct them." A few weeks later, on December 17, 1943, all exclusion laws are overturned, just as Betsy's father hinted they would be.

We listen to Walter Winchell's broadcast when he announces, "Keye Luke, Charlie Chan's Number One Son, just missed being number one Chinese naturalized U.S. citizen." Since Keye Luke is working in a picture that day, a Chinese doctor in New York becomes the first. Sam commemorates that moment of happiness by taking a picture of his daughter standing with one hand on her hip and her other hand resting on top of the radio. No *cheongsams* for her! Since Joy started school and we gave her that lunch box, she's decided she loves cowgirls and cowgirl dresses. Her grandfather has even bought her a pair of cowgirl boots on Olvera Street, and once she has her outfit on, there's no getting it off. She grins happily. Even though the rest of the family is not in the picture, I will always remember that we all smiled with her.

After that day, Sam and I talk about applying for naturalization, but we're afraid, as are so many paper sons and the wives who squeaked in with them. "I have my fake citizenship from masquerading as Father's real son. You have your Certificate of Identity through being married to me. Why should we risk losing what we have? How can we trust the government when our Jap neighbors are sent to internment camps?" Sam asks. "How can we trust the government after everything it's done to us? How can we trust the government when the *lo fan* look at us funny — like we're Japs too?" May is in a different situation than Sam and I. She's married to a real American citizen, and she's lived in the country for five years. She becomes the first person in our building to become a citizen through the naturalization process.

The war drags on month after month. We try to keep life as normal as possible for Joy, and it pays off. She does so well in school that her kindergarten and first-grade teachers recommend her for a special second-grade program. I work with Joy all summer to get her prepared, and even Miss Gordon — who's taken a continuing interest in our girl — comes to the apartment once a week to help my daughter with her sums and reading comprehension.

Maybe I push Joy too hard, because she gets a bad summer cold. Then, two days after the bomb drops on Hiroshima, her cold takes a turn. Her fever rages, her throat burns red, and she coughs so hard and long that she throws up. Yen-yen goes to the herbalist, who makes a bitter tea for Joy to drink. The next day, when I'm working, Yen-yen takes Joy back to the herbalist, who blows an herb powder into her throat with the cap of a calligraphy brush. On the radio Sam and I hear that another bomb has been dropped — this one on Nagasaki. The broadcaster says that the destruction is terrible and vast. Government officials in Washington are optimistic that the war will end soon.

Sam and I close up the café and hurry to the apartment, wanting to share the news. When we get there, we see that Joy's throat has become so swollen she's starting to turn blue. Somewhere people are rejoicing — sons, brothers, and husbands will be coming home — but Sam and I are so afraid for Joy that we can't think beyond our own fear. We want to take her to a Western doctor, but we don't know one and we don't have a car. We're talking about how to find and hire a taxi when Miss Gordon arrives. In the chaos of the news of the bombs and the anxiety we feel for Joy, we've forgotten about the tutorial. As soon as Miss Gordon sees Joy, she helps me wrap her in a sheet, and then she drives us to General Hospital, where, she says, "They treat people like you." Within minutes of our arriving at the hospital, a doctor cuts a hole in my daughter's throat so she can breathe.

Less than a week after Joy's encounter with death, the war ends and Sam — shaken by almost losing his little girl — takes three hundred dollars of our savings and buys a very used Chrysler. It's old and dented, but it's ours. In our last photograph from the war years, Sam sits in the Chrysler's driver's seat, Joy perches on the fender, and I stand by the passenger door. We're about to go for a Sunday drive, our first.

Ten Thousand Happinesses

"Fifteen cents for one gardenia," a melodious voice rings out. "Twenty-five cents for a double." The little girl standing behind the table is adorable. Her black hair shimmers under the colored lights, her smile beckons, her fingers look like butterflies. My daughter, my Joy, has her own "place of business," as she calls it, and she runs it wonderfully well for a child of ten. On weekend nights she sells gardenias from six to midnight outside the café, where I can keep watch on her, but she doesn't need me or anyone else to protect her. She's a Tiger — brave. She's my daughter — persistent. She's her aunt's niece — beautiful. I have exciting news. I want to get May alone to tell her, but seeing Joy sell gardenias has us entranced and paralyzed.

"Look how precious she is," May coos. "She's good at this. I'm glad she likes it and that she earns a little money. It's a good thing all the way around, isn't it?"

May looks lovely tonight: like a millionaire's wife in vermilion silk. She dresses well, because she can afford to spend the money she earns frivolously. She recently turned 29. Oh, the tears! As if she turned 129. But to me she hasn't changed one bit since our beautiful-girl days. Still, every day she worries about gaining weight and forming wrinkles. Lately, she's been stuffing her pillow with chrysanthemum leaves so she'll wake with her eyes clear and moist.

"China City is a tourist place, so who do you think should be the seller? The smallest and the cutest, that's who," I agree. "And Joy's smart. She watches to make sure nothing's stolen."

"For an extra penny, I'll sing 'God Bless America,'" Joy says to a couple who stop at her table. She doesn't wait for an answer but begins to sing in a clear, high, and earnest voice. At American school, she's learned all the patriotic songs — "My Country, 'Tis of Thee" and "You're a Grand Old Flag" — as well as songs like "My Darling Clementine" and "She'll Be Comin' Round the Mountain." At the Chinese Methodist Mission on Los Angeles Street, she's learned to sing "Jesus Is All the World to Me" and "Jesus Loves Even Me" in Cantonese. Between work, regular school, and Chinese school — which she attends Monday through Friday from 4:30 to 7:30 and Saturdays from 9:00 to 12:00 — she's a busy but happy little girl.

Joy glances at me and smiles as she holds out her hand to the couple. She's learned this trick — getting people to pay for things they may not want — from her grandfather. The husband puts some change in Joy's palm, and she closes her hand around it as fast as a monkey. She drops the change into a can and gives the woman a gardenia. Once done with these customers, Joy moves them along. She's learned this from her grandfather too. Every night she counts the money and then turns it over to her father, who converts the change into dollars, which he then gives to me to hide with Joy's college money.

"Fifteen cents for one gardenia," Joy trills, a serious but endearing look on her face. "Twenty-five cents for a double."

I link my arm through my sister's. "Come on. She's fine. Let's get a cup of tea."

"But not in the café, all right?" May doesn't like to be seen in the café. It isn't glamorous enough for her. Not these days.

"That's fine," I say. I nod to Sam, who's behind the counter in the café, stir-frying an order in a wok. He's the second cook now, but he can keep an eye on our daughter while I visit with May.

My sister and I swing through China City's alleyways toward the costume and prop shop that came to her through Tom Gubbins. It's been ten years since we arrived in Los Angeles, ten years since we stepped into China City. When I first passed through the miniature Great Wall, I felt no connection to this place. Now it feels like home: familiar, comfortable, and much loved. This isn't the China of my past — the busy streets of Shanghai, the beggars, the fun, the champagne, the money — but I see reminders of it here in the laughing tourists, the traditionally costumed shop owners, the smells that come from the cafés and restaurants, and the stunning woman at my side, who happens to be my sister. As we stroll, I catch glimpses of us in the shopwindows and I'm transported to our girlhoods: the way we dressed in our room and stared at our reflections and those of our beautiful-girl images that hung on the walls around us, the way we walked together along Nanking Road and smiled at ourselves in store windows, and the way Z.G. captured and painted our perfect selves.

And yet we've both changed. Now I see myself — thirty-two years old, no longer a new mother but a woman content with herself. My sister is a flower in full bloom. The desire to be looked at and admired still burns from deep within her. The more she feeds it, the more she needs. She'll never be satisfied. This malady is in her bones — from birth, her essential character, her Sheep that wants to be taken care of, petted, and admired. She isn't Anna May Wong and she never will be, but she gets more movie work and more varied roles — as a whimsical cashier, the giggly but ineffectual maid, or the stoic wife of a laundryman — than anyone else in Chinatown. This makes her a star in our neighborhood and a star to me.

May opens the door to her shop and flips on a light, and there we are — surrounded by the silks, embroideries, and kingfisher feathers of the past. She makes tea, pours it, and then asks, "So what's this thing you're so eager to tell me?"

"Ten thousand happinesses," I say. "I'm pregnant."

May clasps her hands together. "Really? Are you sure?"

"I went to the doctor." I smile. "He says it's true."

338

May gets up, comes to me, and hugs me. Then she pulls away. "But how? I thought —"

"I had to try, didn't I? The herbalist has been giving me wolfberry fruit, Chinese yam, and black sesame to put in our soup and other dishes."

"It's a miracle," May says.

"Beyond a miracle. Unlikely, impossible —"

"Oh, Pearl, I'm so pleased." Her joy mirrors mine. "Tell me everything. How far along are you? When is the baby coming?"

"I'm about two months."

"Have you told Sam yet?"

"You're my sister. I wanted to tell you first."

"A son," May says, smiling. "You're going to have a precious son."

Everyone has this desire, and I flush with pleasure just hearing the word — *son*.

Then a shadow crosses May's face. "Can you do this thing?"

"The doctor says I shouldn't be so old, and I have my scars."

"Women older than you have babies," she says, but this isn't the best thing to say given that Vern's problems are often blamed on Yen-yen's age. May winces at the insensitivity of her remark. She doesn't ask about the scars, because we never talk about how I came to get them, so she shifts to more traditional questions about my condition. "Are you sleepy all the time? Are you sick to your stomach? I remember . . ." She shakes her head as if ridding herself of those memories. "They always say that life is extended only by having children." She reaches over and touches my jade bracelet. "Think how happy Mama and Baba would have been." May suddenly grins, and our sad feelings melt. "Do you know what this means? You and Sam have to buy a house."

"A house?"

"You've been saving all these years."

"Yes, for Joy to go to college."

My sister brushes away that worry with a wave of her hand. "You have plenty of time to save for that. Besides, Father Louie will help you with the house."

"I don't see why. We have an arrangement —"

"But he's changed. And this is for his grandson!"

"Maybe, but even if he does decide to help us, I wouldn't want to be separated from you. You're my sister and my closest friend."

May gives me a reassuring smile. "You're not going to lose me. You couldn't even if you tried. I have my own car now. Wherever you move, I'll come and visit."

"But it won't be the same."

"Sure it will. Besides, you'll come to China City every day to work. Yen-yen will want to take care of her grandson. I'll need to see my nephew too." She takes my hands. "Pearl, buying a house is the right thing to do. You and Sam deserve this."

Sam is beyond thrilled. He may have once told me he didn't care if he had a son, but he's a man, and, for all his words, he's needed and wanted a son very badly. Joy hops up and down with excitement. Yen-yen weeps, but my age concerns her. Father Louie, wanting to behave as a patriarch should, tries to capture his emotions in his clenched fists, but he can't stop beaming. Vern stands by me, a kind but small protector. I don't know if my posture is taller and straighter because I'm happy or if Vern is just shy around me, but he seems shorter and thicker — as though his spine is collapsing and his chest broadening. He should have grown out of the slouch of his teen years by now, but I often notice that he will lean over and put his hands on his thighs as though propping himself up from fatigue or boredom.

On Sunday the uncles come for dinner to celebrate. Our family — like so many in Chinatown — is growing. The Chinese population in Los Angeles has more than doubled since we first arrived. This isn't because the Exclusion Act was overturned. We thought that was going to be wonderful when it happened, but only 105 Chinese a year are allowed to enter the country under the new quota. As always, people find ways to get around the law. Uncle Fred brought in his wife under the War Brides Act. Mariko's a pretty girl, quiet, and Japanese, but we don't hold it against her. (The war is over and she's part of our family now, so what else can we do?) Other men have brought in wives through other acts, and when you have men and women together, you're going to get children. Mariko had two babies one right after the other. We love Eleanor and Bess, even though they're half-and-half, even though we don't see them as much as we'd like. Fred and Mariko don't live in Chinatown. They took advantage of the G.I. Bill to buy a house in Silver Lake, not far from downtown.

341

The men wear sleeveless undershirts and drink bottles of beer. Yen-yen — in loose black trousers, a black cotton jacket, and a really fine jade necklace — dotes on Joy and Mariko's daughters. May swishes through the main room in a full-skirted American-style dress of polished cotton belted at the waist. Father Louie snaps his fingers, and we sit down to eat. My family use their chopsticks to snap up the best morsels to drop in my bowl. Everyone has advice. And surprisingly, everyone agrees that we should look for a house in which to raise the Louie grandson. And May was right. Father not only volunteers to help but says he'll match us dollar for dollar as long as his name's on the title too.

"Married people are starting to live away from their in-laws," he says. "It will look strange if you don't have your own home." (Because after ten years he's no longer afraid we'll run away. We're his true family now, just as he and Yen-yen are ours.)

"This apartment — too much bad air," Yen-yen says. "The boy will need a place to play outside, not in an alley." (Which had been fine for Joy.)

"I hope there's room for a pony," Joy says. (She isn't getting a pony, no matter how much she wants to be a cowgirl.)

"With the war over, everything's changed," chimes in Uncle Wilburt, for once wholly optimistic. "You can go to the Bimini Pool to swim. You can sit wherever you want at the movie show. You could even marry a *lo fan* if you wanted to."

"But who'd want to?" Uncle Charley asks. (So many laws have changed, but that doesn't mean attitudes — Oriental or Occidental — have changed with them.)

Joy reaches her chopsticks across the table, looking for a piece of pork. Her grandmother smacks her hand. "Only take food from the dish directly in front of you!" Joy's hand retreats, but Sam dips his chopsticks into the pork dish and fills his daughter's bowl. He's a man — soon to be the father of a precious grandson — and Yen-yen won't correct his manners, but later she'll give Joy a talking-to about being virtuous, graceful, courteous, polite, and obedient, which means, among other things, learning to sew and embroider, take care of the house, and use her chopsticks properly. All this from a woman who barely knows these things herself.

"So many doors have opened," Uncle Fred says. He came back from the war with a box full of medals. His English, which had been pretty good to begin with, improved in the service, but he still speaks Sze Yup with us. We thought he'd return to China City and the Golden Dragon Café to work, but no. "Look at me. The government is helping me with my college tuition and housing." He raises his beer. "Thank you, Uncle Sam, for helping me become a dentist!" He takes a swig, then adds, "The Supreme Court says we can live wherever we want. So where do you want to live?"

Sam runs a hand through his hair and then scratches the back of his neck. "Wherever they'll accept us. If they don't want us, I don't want to live there."

"Don't worry about that," Uncle Fred says. "The *lo fan* are more open to us now. A lot of guys were in the service. They met and fought with people who looked like us. You'll be welcome wherever you go."

Later that night, after everyone goes home and Joy has been tucked into her permanent sleeping place on the couch in the main room, Sam and I talk more about the baby and a possible move.

"With our own place, we could do what we want," Sam says in Sze Yup. Then he adds in English, "In privacy." No single word in Chinese conveys the concept of privacy, but we love the idea of it. "And all wives want to be away from their mothers-in-law."

I don't suffer under Yen-yen's thumb, but the thought of moving out of Chinatown and giving Joy and our baby new opportunities brightens my heart. But we aren't like Fred. We can't use the G.I. Bill to buy a house. No bank will give just any Chinese a loan, and we don't trust American banks because we don't want to owe money to Americans. But Sam and I have been saving, hiding our money in his sock and in the lining of the hat I wore out of China. If we keep our desires modest, then we might just be able to buy something.

But it isn't as easy as Uncle Fred said. I look in Crenshaw, where I'm told we can buy only south of Jefferson. I try Culver City, where the real estate agent won't even show me property. I find a house I like in Lake-wood, but the neighbors sign a petition saying they don't want Chinese to move in. I go to Pacific Palisades, but the land covenants still say that houses can't be sold to someone of Ethiopian or Mongolian descent. I hear every excuse: "We don't rent to

Orientals." "We won't sell to Orientals." "As Orientals, you won't like that house." And the old standby: "On the phone we thought you were Italian."

Uncle Fred — who was in the war and earned his bravery — encourages us not to give up, but Sam and I are not the kind to holler and cry that we've been robbed, beaten, or discriminated against. The only way we can hope to buy a house outside Chinatown is to find a seller so desperate he doesn't mind offending his neighbors, but by now I'm nervous about moving at all. Or maybe I'm not nervous; maybe I'm feeling homesick in advance. After Shanghai, how can I lose what we've built for ourselves in Chinatown?

I work hard to grow my baby the Chinese way. I have the worries of every expectant mother, but I also know that my baby's home environment was once invaded and nearly destroyed. I go to the herbalist, who looks at my tongue, listens to the many pulses in my wrist, and prescribes *An Tai Yin* — Peaceful Fetus Formula. He also gives me *Shou Tai Wan* — Fetus Longevity Pills. I don't shake hands with strangers, because Mama once told a neighbor woman this would cause her baby to be born with six fingers. When May buys a camphor chest for me to store the clothes I'm making for the baby, I remember Mama's beliefs and refuse to accept it, because it resembles a casket. I begin to question my dreams, recalling what Mama said about them: if you dream of shoes, then bad luck is coming; if you dream of losing teeth, then someone in the family will die; and if you dream of shit, then big trouble is about to arrive.

Every morning I rub my belly, happy that my dreams have been free from these bad omens.

During the New Year festivities I visit an astrologer, who tells me my son will be born in the Year of the Ox, just like his father. "Your son will have the purest of hearts. He will be filled with innocence and faith. He will be strong and never whimper or complain." Every day, when the tourists leave China City, I go to the Temple of Kwan Yin to make offerings to assure that the baby will be safe and well. As a beautiful girl in Shanghai, I looked down on those mothers who went to the temples in the Old Chinese City, but now that I'm older I understand that my baby's health is more important than girlish ideas of modernity.

On the other hand, I'm not stupid. No matter what, I'll be an American mother, so I go to an American doctor too. I still don't like that Western doctors dress in white and paint their offices white — the color of death — but I accept these things because I'll do anything for my baby. *Anything* means having the doctor examine me. The only men who have been in that area are my husband, the doctors who repaired me in Hang-chow, and the men who raped me. I'm not happy to have this man feeling around and *looking* in there. And I really don't like what he says: "Mrs. Louie, you will be lucky to carry this baby to term."

Sam understands the dangers, and he quietly goes to each family member to warn them. Immediately, Yen-yen refuses to let me cook, wash dishes, or iron clothes. Father orders me to stay in the apartment, put my feet up, sleep. And my sister? She takes more responsibility for Joy, walking her to American school and Chinese school. I don't know quite how to explain this. My sister and I have fought over Joy for many years. May gives her niece beautiful clothes bought in department stores — a sky blue party dress in dotted swiss, another with exquisite smocking, and a blouse with ruffles — while I sew practical clothes for my daughter — jumpers made with two pieces of felt, Chinese jackets with raglan sleeves made with cotton bought from the remnant bin, and smocks made from seersucker (what we call atomic fabric, because it never wrinkles). May buys Joy patent leather shoes, while I insist on saddle shoes. May is fun, while I'm the maker of rules. I understand why my sister wants to be the perfect auntie; we both do. But right now I don't worry about that, and I let Joy drift away from me and into her auntie's arms, believing I'll never have to compete with May for my son's love.

Perhaps realizing she's stealing Joy from me, my sister gives me Vern. "He'll be with you all the time," she says, "to make sure nothing bad happens. He can take care of simple things, like getting you tea. And if there's an emergency — and there won't be — he can come and get one of us."

Anyone would think May's offer would please Sam, but he doesn't like the idea one bit. Is Sam jealous? How can he be? Vern is a grown man, but as we spend our days together, he seems to shrink while my belly grows. Still, Sam won't let Vern sit next to me at dinner or any other meal. As a family we accept this, because Sam is going to be a father.

We spend a lot of time talking about names. This isn't like when May and I named Joy. Father Louie will have the honor and duty of naming his grandson, but that doesn't mean everyone doesn't have an opinion or try to sway him.

"You should name the baby Gary for Gary Cooper," my sister says.

"I like my name. Vernon."

We smile and say that's a nice idea, but no one wants to name a baby after a person so defective that if he'd been born in China he would have been left outside to die.

"I like Kit for Kit Carson or Annie for Annie Oakley." This of course comes from my cowgirl daughter.

"Let's name him after one of the ships that brought the Chinese to California — Roosevelt, Coolidge, Lincoln, or Hoover," Sam says.

Joy giggles. "Oh, Dad, those are presidents, not boats!"

Joy often makes fun of her father for his poor understanding of English and American ways. At the very least, this should hurt his feelings. At the most, he should punish her for being unfilial. But he's so happy about his coming son that he pays no attention to his daughter's tart tongue. I tell myself I have to stop this trait in our girl. Otherwise she'll end up like May and me when we were young: rude to our parents and flagrantly disobedient.

Some of our neighbors also give suggestions: One named a son after the doctor who delivered the baby.

Another named a daughter after a nurse who'd been particularly kind. The names of midwives, teachers, and missionaries fill cribs throughout Chinatown. I remember how Miss Gordon saved Joy's life, so I suggest the name Gordon. Gordon Louie sounds like a smart, successful, non-Chinese man.

When my fifth month comes, Uncle Charley announces that he's returning to his home village as a Gold Mountain man, saying, "The war's over and the Japanese are gone from China. I've saved enough and I can live well there." We host a banquet, we shake his hand, and we drive him to the port. It seems that for every wife who arrives in Chinatown, another man goes home. Those who've always seen themselves as sojourners are now finding their happy endings. But not once does Father Louie, who always said he wanted to return to Wah Hong Village, bring up the idea of closing the Golden enterprises and taking us back to China. Why would he retire to his home village when at last he's going to get his grandson, who will be an American citizen by birth, venerate his grandfather when he goes to the afterworld, and learn to hit baseballs, play the violin, and become a doctor?

At the beginning of my sixth month, I receive a piece of mail with stamps from China. I eagerly rip open the envelope and find a letter from Betsy. I can't believe she's alive. She survived her time in the Japanese camp by the Lunghua Pagoda, but her husband didn't. "My parents want me to join them in Washington to regain my health," she writes, "but I was born in Shanghai. It's my home. How can I leave it? Don't I owe it to the city of my birth to help with the rebuilding efforts? I've been working with orphans . . ."

Her letter reminds me that there's one person I would like to hear from or about. Even after all these years, Z.G. still comes into my mind. I put a hand on my belly — which protrudes like a steamed bun — feel the baby move inside me, and visit my artist and Shanghai in my mind. I'm not lovesick or homesick. I'm just pregnant and sentimental, because my past is simply that — past. My home is here with this family I've built from the scraps of tragedy. My hospital bag is packed and sitting by the door to our room. In my purse I carry fifty dollars in an envelope to pay for the delivery. Once the baby's born, he'll come home to a place where everyone loves him.

The Air of This World

So often we're told that women's stories are unimportant. After all, what does it matter what happens in the main room, in the kitchen, or in the bedroom? Who cares about the relationships between mother, daughter, and sister? A baby's illness, the sorrows and pains of childbirth, keeping the family together during war, poverty, or even in the best of days are considered small and insignificant compared with the stories of men, who fight against nature to grow their crops, who wage battles to secure their homelands, who struggle to look inward in search of the perfect man. We're told that men are strong and brave, but I think women know how to endure, accept defeat, and bear physical and mental agony much better than men. The men in my life — my father, Z.G., my husband, my father-in-law, my brother-in-law, and my son — faced, to one degree or another, those great male battles, but their hearts — so fragile — wilted, buckled, crippled, corrupted, broke, or shattered

351

when confronted with the losses women face every day. As men, they have to put a brave face on tragedy and obstacles, but they are as easily bruised as flower petals.

If we hear that women's stories are insignificant, then we're also told that good things always come in pairs and bad things happen in threes. If two airplanes crash, we wait for a third to fall from the sky. If a motion-picture star dies, we know that another two will succumb. If we stub a toe and lose our car keys, we know that another bad thing must happen to complete the cycle. All we can hope is that it will be a bent fender, a leaky roof, or a lost job rather than a death, a divorce, or a new war.

The Louie family's tragedies arrive in a long and devastating cascade like a waterfall, like a dam burst open, like a tidal wave that breaks, destroys, and then pulls the evidence back to sea. Our men try to act strong, but it is May, Yen-yen, Joy, and I who must steady them and help them bear their pain, anguish, and shame.

It's the beginning of summer 1949, and the June gloom is worse than usual, especially at night. Damp fog creeps in from the ocean and hangs over the city like a soggy blanket. The doctor tells me that the pains will start any day now, but maybe the weather has lulled my baby into inactivity or maybe he doesn't want to come into a world so gray and cold when he is surrounded by warmth where he is. I don't worry. I stay at home and wait.

Tonight Vern and Joy keep me company. Vern hasn't been feeling well lately, so he's asleep in his room. Joy has just one more week of fifth grade. From where I sit at the dining table, I can see her curled up on the couch and frowning. She doesn't like practicing her times tables or seeing how fast she can complete the pages of long division her teacher has given her to increase her speed and accuracy.

I look back down at the newspaper. Today I've returned to it again and again, believing and then refusing to believe what I've read. Civil war is tearing apart my home country. Mao Tse-tung's Red Army has been pushing across China as steadily and as relentless as the Japanese once did. In April, his troops seized control of Nanking. In May, he grabbed Shanghai. I remember the revolutionaries from the cafés I used to frequent with Z.G. and Betsy. I remember how Betsy used to get more riled up than they did, but for them to take over the country? Sam and I have talked a lot about this. His family were peasants. They had nothing. If they had lived, they would have had everything to gain from a Communist system, but I came from the *bu-er-ch'iao-ya* — bourgeois class. If my parents were still alive, they'd be suffering. Here, in Los Angeles, no one knows what will happen, but we hide our worries behind forced smiles, no-meaning words, and a constant false face presented to Occidentals, who are far more terrified of the Communists than we are.

I go to the kitchen to make tea. I'm standing in front of the sink, filling the teakettle, when I feel a rush of wetness down my legs. This is it! My water's finally

353

broken. Grinning, I look down, but what I see running down my legs and pooling on the floor is not water but blood. The fear that grips me starts somewhere in that down-below area and comes all the way up to my heart, which pounds in my chest. But this is like a small tremor compared with what happens next. A contraction wraps from my back to my belly button and pushes down with such ferocity that I think the baby will fall out in one fast whoosh. That doesn't happen. I don't even know if that *could* happen. But when I reach under my belly and pull up, more liquid gushes down my legs. Squeezing my thighs together, I shuffle to the kitchen door and call to my daughter.

"Joy, go find your auntie." I hope May's in her office and not out with the studio people she entertains to keep her business connections strong. "If she's not in her office, go to the Chinese Junk. She likes to meet people there for dinner."

"Ah, Mom —"

"Now! Go now."

She looks at me. She can see only my head peeking out of the kitchen. For this I'm thankful. Still, my face must betray something, because she doesn't try to fight me as she usually does. As soon as she leaves the apartment, I grab dish towels and press them between my legs. I sit back in my chair and grip the armrests to keep from screaming every time another contraction hits. I know they're coming too fast. I know something is terribly wrong.

When Joy returns with May, my sister takes one look at me, grabs my daughter before she can see anything, and pulls her out of sight.

"Go to the café. Find your father. Tell him to meet us at the hospital."

Joy leaves, and my sister comes to my side. Creamy red lipstick has turned her mouth into an undulating sea flower. Eyeliner widens her eyes. She wears an off-the-shoulder dress of periwinkle satin that hugs her body as closely as a *cheongsam*. I smell gin and steak on her breath. She looks in my face for a moment, then lifts my skirt. She tries not to reveal anything that will be less than a comfort, but I know her too well. Her head tilts as she takes in the blood-soaked towels. She sucks a tiny bit of her lip into her mouth and holds it between her right front tooth and the tip of her tongue. She smoothes my skirt carefully back over my knees.

"Can you walk to my car, or do you want me to call an ambulance?" she asks, her voice as calm as if she's asking if I prefer her pink hat or the blue one with the ermine trim.

I don't want to be any trouble, and I don't like to waste money. "Let's go in your car, so long as you don't mind the mess."

"Vern," May calls. "Vern, I need you." He doesn't answer, and May goes down the hall to get him. They come back a minute or so later. The boy-husband's hair is tousled and his clothes wrinkled from sleep. When he sees me, he starts to whimper.

"You take one side," May instructs, "I'll take the other."

355

Together they help me up, and we walk downstairs. My sister's grip is strong, but Vern feels like he's crumbling under my weight. There's some kind of fiesta on the Plaza tonight, and people pull away when they see me with my hand pressing something between my legs and my sister and Vern holding me up. No one likes to see a pregnant woman; no one likes to see such private business made public. May and Vern put me in the backseat of her car, and then she drives me the few blocks to the French Hospital. She parks in the porte cochere and runs inside for help. I stare out the window at the lights that illuminate the parking area. I breathe slowly, methodically. My stomach sits on my hands. It feels heavy and still. I remind myself that my baby is an Ox, just like his father. Even as a child, the Ox has willpower and inner stamina. I tell myself that my son is following his nature right now, but I'm very afraid.

Another contraction, the worst one yet.

May returns to the car with a nurse and a man, both dressed in white. They shout orders, put me on a gurney, and wheel me into the hospital as fast as they can. May stays by my side, staring down at me, talking to me. "Don't worry. Everything will be fine. Having a baby is painful in order to show how serious a thing life is."

I grasp the metal bars on the sides of the gurney and grind my teeth. Sweat drenches my forehead, my back, my chest, and I shiver from cold.

The last thing my sister says as I'm wheeled into the delivery room is "Fight for me, Pearl. Fight to live like you did before."

My baby son comes out, but he never breathes the air of this world. The nurse wraps him in a blanket and brings him to me. He has long lashes, a high nose, and a tiny mouth. While I hold my son, staring into his lonely face, the doctor works on me. Finally, he stands up and says, "We need to perform surgery, Mrs. Louie. We're going to put you under." When the nurse takes the baby away, I know I'll never see him again. Tears run down my face as a mask is put over my nose and mouth. I'm grateful for the blackness that comes.

I open my eyes. My sister sits by my bed. The remnants of her red lipstick are just a stain. The eyeliner has muddied her face. Her luxurious periwinkle dress looks tired and wrinkled. But she's still beautiful, and in my mind I'm transported to another time when my sister was with me in a hospital room. I sigh, and May takes my hand.

"Where is Sam?" I ask.

"He's with the family. They're down the hall. I can get them for you."

I want my husband badly, but how can I face him? *May you die sonless* — the worst insult you can give.

The doctor comes in to check on me. "I don't know how you carried the baby as long as you did," he says. "We almost lost you."

"My sister is very strong," May says. "She's been through worse than this. She'll have another baby."

The doctor shakes his head. "I'm afraid she won't be able to have another child." He turns to look at me. "You're lucky you have your daughter."

May squeezes my hand confidently. "The doctors told you that before and look what happened. You and Sam can try again."

I think these are among the worst words I've ever heard. I want to scream, *I've lost my baby!* How can my sister not know what I'm feeling? How can she not understand what it is to have lost this person who's been swimming inside me for nine months, whom I've loved with my whole heart, whom I've steeped with so many hopes? But May's words are not the worst I can hear.

"I'm afraid that won't be possible." The doctor covers the horror of his words with his strange *lo fan* cheerfulness and reassuring smile. "We took out everything."

I can't bear to cry in front of this man. I focus my eyes on my jade bracelet. All these years and for all the years after I die, it will remain unchanged. It will always be hard and cold — just a piece of stone. Yet for me it is an object that ties me to the past, to people and places that are gone forever. Its continued perfection serves as a physical reminder to keep living, to look to the future, to cherish what I have. It reminds me to endure. I'll live one morning after another, one step after another, because my will to continue is so strong. I tell myself these things and I tamp steel around my heart to cover my sorrow, but they don't help me when the family comes into the room.

Yen-yen's face sags like a sack of flour. Father's eyes are as dull and dark as lumps of coal. Vern takes the news physically, wilting before the rest of us like a cabbage after a terrible storm. But Sam . . . Oh, Sam. That night ten years ago when he confessed his life to me, he said he didn't need a son, but these last months I've seen how much he wanted — needed — a son who would carry on his name, who would venerate him as an ancestor, who would live all the dreams that Sam has but will never achieve. I'd given my husband hope, and now I've destroyed it.

May pushes the others out of the room so Sam and I can be alone. But my husband — this man with his iron fan, who looks so strong, who can lift and carry anything, who can absorb humiliation upon humiliation — cannot spread open his chest to bear my pain.

"While we were waiting . . ." His voice trails off. He clasps his hands behind him and paces back and forth, struggling to maintain his composure. At last he tries again. "While we were waiting, I asked a doctor to examine Vernon. I told the doctor my brother has weak breath and thin blood," Sam explains, as though our Chinese ideas would mean anything to the doctor.

I want to bury my face in his warm and fragrant chest, absorb the strength of his iron fan, hear the steadiness of his heartbeat, but he refuses to look at me.

He stops at the foot of the bed and stares at a spot somewhere above my head. "I should go back to them. Make the doctors do their tests on Vern. Maybe there's something they can do."

This, even though they couldn't save our son. Sam leaves the room, and I cover my face with my hands. I've failed in the worst way a woman can, while my husband, to bury his grief, has shifted his concern to

359

the weakest member of our family. My in-laws don't come back, and even Vern stays away. This is common practice when a woman has lost a precious son, but it hurts me nevertheless.

May does everything for me. She sits with me when I cry. She helps me to the toilet. When my breasts become painfully swollen and the nurse comes in to squeeze out the milk and throw it away, my sister pushes her out of the room and does the job herself. Her fingers are gentle, loving, and tender. I miss my husband; I *need* my husband. But if Sam has abandoned me when I've needed him the most, then May has abandoned Vern. On my fifth day in the hospital, May finally tells me what's happened.

"Vern has the soft-bone disease," she says. "Here they call it tuberculosis of the bone. This is why he's been shrinking." She's always been loose with her tears, but not this time. The way she fights to keep them inside tells me just how much she's come to love the boy-husband.

"What does this mean?"

"That we're dirty, that we live like pigs."

My sister's voice is as bitter as I've ever heard it. We grew up believing that the soft-bone disease and its sister, the blood-lung disease, were markers of poverty and filth. It was considered the most shameful of all the diseases, more terrible than the ones transmitted by prostitutes. This is even worse than my losing a son, because it is a visual and very public message to our neighbors — and to the *lo fan* — that we are poor, polluted, and unclean.

360

"It usually attacks children, and they die as their spines collapse," she continues. "But Vern's not a child, so the doctors can't say how long he'll live. They only know that his pain will give way to numbness, weakness, and finally paralysis. He'll be in bed for the rest of his life."

"Yen-yen? Father?"

May shakes her head, and her tears break free. "He's their little boy."

"And Joy?"

"I'm taking care of her." Sadness fills my sister's voice. I understand too clearly what my losing the baby means to her. I will return as Joy's full-time mother. Maybe I should feel some sense of triumph about this, but I don't. Instead, I swim in our shared losses.

Later that night Sam comes to talk. He stands at the foot of my bed, looking awkward. His cheeks are gray and his shoulders droop from bearing the weight of two tragedies.

"I thought the boy might be sick. I recognized some of the symptoms from my father. My brother was born with a no-good fate. He never hurt anyone and has only been kind to us, and yet there was no way to change his destiny."

He says these words about Vern, but he could be speaking about any of us.

These twin tragedies bind us together as a family in ways none of us could have imagined. May, Sam, and Father go back to work; sorrow and despair hang around their necks like cangues. Yen-yen stays in the apartment to take care of me and Vern. (The doctor is very much against this. "Vern will be better off in a sanatorium or some other institution," he tells us, but if Chinese are treated badly right on the street, where everyone can see, how can we possibly let him go to a place behind gates and closed doors?) Paper partners fill in for us at China City. But fate is not done with us.

In August, a second fire destroys nearly all of China City. A few buildings survive, but all the Golden enterprises are reduced to charred ruins, except for three rickshaws and May's costume and extras company. Still, no one has insurance. With China enmeshed in a civil war, Father Louie once again can't go back to the home country to replenish his stock of antiques. He could try to buy antiques here, but everything is too expensive after the world war and much of the savings he squirreled away in China City is ash anyway.

But even if we had the resources to restock the shops, Christine Sterling has no desire to rebuild China City. Convinced the fire was the result of arson, she decides she no longer wants to re-create her ideas of Oriental romance in Los Angeles. In fact, she no longer wants to associate with Chinese in any way whatsoever and doesn't want them sullying her Mexican marketplace on Olvera Street. She persuades the city to condemn the block of Chinatown between Los Angeles Street and Alameda to make room for a freeway on-ramp. For now all that will remain of the city's original Chinatown is the row of buildings between Los Angeles Street and Sanchez Alley, where we live. People fight the overall plan, but no one has much hope. We all know the saying that's so popular here in America: We don't stand a Chinaman's chance.

Our home is in jeopardy, but we can't worry about that yet, not when we have to work together to reopen the family businesses. While some people decide to limp along and stay in what remains of China City, Father Louie opens a new Golden Lantern in New Chinatown, stocking it with the cheapest curios he can buy from local wholesalers, who get their goods from Hong Kong and Taiwan. Joy must now spend more time there, selling what she calls "junk" to tourists who don't know any better, giving her grandfather a break so he can nap. The new shop doesn't have much business, but she's a star watcher. And when no one's in the shop, which is most of the time, she reads.

Sam and I decide to start our own business with some of our savings. He looks for a new café location and finds one on Ord Street just a half block west of China City, but Uncle Wilburt won't be coming with us. He decides to take advantage of the *lo fans'* increased interest in Chinese food since the war ended by opening his own chop-suey joint in Lakewood. We're sad to see the last of the uncles leave, even though this means that Sam will be the head cook at last.

We prepare for our Grand Opening, doing renovations, creating menus, and thinking about advertising. The café has a little office behind glass in the back where May will manage her business. She stores the props and costumes in a small warehouse over on Bernard Street, saying that she doesn't need to sit among those things every day and that getting jobs for herself and for other extras is more profitable than the rental business anyway. She encourages Sam to produce a calendar to promote the café. She asks a local photographer to come and take a picture. Even though the restaurant is named after me, the image shows May and Joy standing at the counter next to the pie spinner: EAT AT PEARL'S COFFEE SHOP: QUALITY CHINESE AND AMERICAN FOOD.

At the beginning of October 1949, Pearl's Coffee Shop opens, Mao Tse-tung establishes the People's Republic of China, and the Bamboo Curtain falls. We don't know how permeable this curtain will be or what any of it means for our home country, but our opening is successful. The calendar is popular, and so is our menu, which combines American and Chinese-American specialties: roast beef, apple pie with vanilla ice cream, and coffee, or sweet-and-sour pork, almond cookies, and tea. Pearl's Coffee Shop is clean. The food is fresh and consistent. Day and night a line extends out the door.

Father Louie continues sending money to his home village by wiring funds to Hong Kong and then hiring someone to walk the money into the People's Republic of China and on to Wah Hong Village. Sam warns him against this. "Maybe the Communists will confiscate it. Maybe this will be bad for the family in the village."

I have different fears. "Maybe the American government will call us Communists. That's why most families aren't sending home remittances anymore."

364

And it's true. Many people in Chinatowns across the country have stopped sending money home because everyone is afraid and perplexed. The letters we receive from China confuse us even further.

"We are happy with the new government," writes my father-in-law's cousin twice removed. "Everyone is equal now. The landlord has been made to share his wealth with the people."

If they're so happy, we ask ourselves, then why are so many trying to get out? These are men, like Uncle Charley, who went back to China with their savings. Here in America, they'd suffered and been humiliated as low and unworthy of citizenship, but they'd withstood it, believing that great happiness, prosperity, and respect awaited them in the country of their birth, only to discover bitter fates upon their return to China, which treats them as dreaded landlords, capitalists, and running dogs of imperialism. The unlucky ones die in the fields or in the village squares. The fortunate ones escape to Hong Kong, where they die broken and broke. A few lucky ones come *home* to America. Uncle Charley is one of these.

"Did the Commies take everything from you?" Vern asks from his bed.

"They didn't have a chance," Uncle Charley answers, rubbing his swollen eyes and scratching his eczema. "When I got there, Chiang Kaishek and the Nationalists were still in power. They asked everyone to exchange their gold and foreign currency for government certificates. They printed billions of Chinese *yuan*, but it wasn't worth anything. A sack of rice, which once cost twelve *yuan*, soon cost sixty-three million *yuan*. People took their money in wheelbarrows to go shopping. You wanted to buy a postage stamp? It cost the equivalent of six thousand U.S. dollars."

"Are you saying bad things about the Generalissimo?" Vern asks nervously. "You better not do that."

"All I'm saying is that by the time the Communist soldiers came, I had nothing left."

All those years of labor with the promise of returning to China a Gold Mountain man, and now he's back where he started — working as a glass washer for the Louie family.

I regain my strength and go to work with Sam, which is wonderful in many ways. I get to see my husband, but I also get to be with May every day until five, when I go home to make dinner and she goes to General Lee's or Soochow, which have moved to New Chinatown, to meet with casting directors and the like. Sometimes it's hard to believe we're sisters at all. I cling to memories of our home in Shanghai; May clings to memories of being a beautiful girl. I wear my greasy apron and little paper hat; she wears beautiful dresses made from fabrics the colors of the earth — sienna, amethyst, celadon, and mountain lake blue.

I feel bad about how I look until the day my old friend Betsy — who, now that China's closed, is on her way east to be with her parents — walks through the door of the coffee shop. We're the same age, thirty-three, but she looks twenty years older. She's thin, almost skeletal, and her hair has gone gray. I don't know if this is from her time spent in the Japanese camp or from the hardships of recent months.

"Our Shanghai is gone," she says when I take her to May's office at the back of Pearl's so the three of us can share a pot of tea. "It will never again be what it was. Shanghai was my home, but I'll never see it again. None of us will."

My sister and I exchange glances. We had dark moments when we thought we'd never be able to go home because of the Japanese. After the war ended, we had our hopes revived that one day we might go back for a visit, but this feels different. It feels permanent.

Fear

It's almost noon on the second Saturday in November 1950. I don't have much time before I need to pick up Joy and her friend Hazel Yee at the new Chinese United Methodist Church, where they attend Chinese-language classes. I rush downstairs, get the mail, and then hurry back up to the apartment. I quickly sort through the bills and pull out two letters. One has a postmark from Washington, D.C. I recognize Betsy's handwriting on the envelope and tuck it in my pocket. The other letter is addressed to Father Louie, and it's from China. I leave it and the bills on the table in the main room for him to look at when he gets home tonight. Then I grab my shopping bag and a sweater, go back downstairs, and walk to the church, where I wait outside for Joy and Hazel.

When Joy was little, I wanted her to learn proper written and spoken Chinese. The only place to do it — and you have to admit the missionaries were clever about this — was at one of the missions in Chinatown.

It wasn't enough that we had to pay a dollar a month for Joy's lessons five and a half days a week or that she had to go to Sunday school, but one of her parents also had to attend Sunday services, which I've done regularly for the last seven years. Although many parents grumble about this rule, it seems like a fair exchange to me. And sometimes I rather like listening to the sermons, which remind me of those I heard as a girl in Shanghai.

I open Betsy's letter. It's been thirteen months since Mao took power in China and four and a half months since North Korea — with help from China's People's Liberation Army — invaded South Korea. Only five years ago China and the United States were allies. Now, seemingly overnight, Communist China has become — after Russia — the second most hated enemy of the United States. These last couple of months, Betsy has written several times to tell me that her loyalty has been questioned because she stayed in China so long and that her father is one of many people at the State Department accused of being a Communist and an old China hand. Back in Shanghai, calling someone an old China hand was a compliment; now, in Washington, it's like calling someone a baby killer. Betsy writes:

> My father's in real hot water. How can they blame him for things he wrote twenty years ago criticizing Chiang Kai-shek and what he was doing to China? They're calling Dad a Communist sympathizer, and they reproach him for helping to "lose China." Mom and I are hoping he'll be able

to keep his job. If they end up pushing him out, I hope they let him keep his pension. Luckily, he still has friends at the State Department who know the truth about him.

As I fold the letter and put it back in its envelope, I wonder what I should write back. I don't think it will help Betsy to say that we're all frightened.

Joy and Hazel burst out onto the street. They're twelve years old and have been in sixth grade for all of seven weeks. They think they're practically grown up, but they're Chinese girls and still completely undeveloped physically. I follow behind them as they swing down the street, holding hands and whispering conspiratorially on our way to Pearl's. We make a quick stop at a butcher shop on Broadway to pick up two pounds of fresh *char siu*, the fragrant barbecued pork that's the secret ingredient in Sam's chow mein. The shop is crowded today, and everyone is fearful, as they have been since this new war started. Some people have retreated into silence. Some have sunk into depression. And some, like the butcher, are angry.

"Why don't they just leave us alone?" he demands in Sze Yup of no one in particular. "You think it's my fault that Mao wants to spread Communism? That has nothing to do with me!"

No one argues with him. We all feel the same way.

"Seven years!" he shouts as he whacks his cleaver through a piece of meat. "It's been only seven years since the Exclusion Act was overturned. Now the *lo fan* government has passed a new law so they can lock up

370

Communists if there's a national emergency. Anyone who has ever said one single word against Chiang Kai-shek is suspected of being a Communist." He waves his cleaver at us. "And you don't even have to say anything bad. All you have to be is a Chinese living in this pit of a country! You know what that means? Every single one of you is a suspect!"

Joy and Hazel have stopped chatting and stare at the butcher with wide eyes. All a mother wants to do is protect her children, but I can't shield Joy from everything. When we walk together, I can't always distract her from the newspaper headlines that shout out at us in English and Chinese. I can ask the uncles not to talk about the war when they come for Sunday dinner, but the news is everywhere, and so is gossip.

Joy is too young to understand that, with the suspension of habeas corpus rights, anyone — including her father and mother — can be detained and held indefinitely. We don't know what will make a national emergency either, but the internment of the Japanese is still very much in our minds. Recently, when the government asked our local organizations — from the Chinese Consolidated Benevolent Association to the China Youth Club — to hand over their membership rosters within twenty-four hours, a lot of our neighbors panicked, knowing their names would show up on the list of at least one of the forty groups targeted. Then we read in the Chinese newspaper that the FBI had bugged the headquarters of the Chinese Hand Laundry Alliance and had decided to investigate all subscribers to the *China Daily News*. I've been grateful ever since that Father Louie subscribes to *Chung Sai Yat Po*, the pro-Kuomintang, pro-Christian, pro-assimilation newspaper, and buys only the occasional copy of the *China Daily*.

I don't know where the butcher will go next in his rant, but I don't want the girls listening to it. I'm just about to take them out of there when the butcher calms down enough for me to place my order. As he wraps the *char siu* in pink paper, he confides to me in a more temperate tone, "It's not so bad here in Los Angeles, Mrs. Louie. But I had a cousin up in San Francisco who committed suicide rather than face arrest. He hadn't done anything wrong. I've heard of others who've been sent to jail and are now awaiting deportation."

"We've all heard these stories," I say. "But what can we do?"

He hands me the pork. "I've been afraid for so long, and I'm tired of it. I'm just plain tired of it. And frustrated . . ."

As his voice begins to grow in intensity again, I lead the girls out of the shop. They're silent for the rest of the short walk to Pearl's. Once we get inside, the three of us go straight to the kitchen. May, who's in her office talking on the phone, smiles and waves. Sam's mixing the batter for the sweet-and-sour pork that's so popular with our customers. I can't help noticing that he's using a smaller bowl than he did a year ago, when we opened. This new war has caused much of our clientele to stay away; some businesses in Chinatown have closed completely. While outside of Chinatown, there's so much fear about Chinese in China that many Chinese Americans have lost their jobs or can't get hired.

We may not be getting as many customers as we used to, but we don't have it as rough as some people. At home we've been economizing, making our meals stretch by eating more rice and less meat. We also have May, who still runs her rental business, works as an agent, and appears in the occasional film or television show herself. Any minute now the studios are going to start making films about the threat of Communism. Once that happens, May will be very busy. The money she'll make will go into the family pot, to be shared by all of us.

I hand Sam the *char siu*, and then I put together a tray for the girls that combines Chinese and Western sensibilities about what a snack should be: some peanuts, a few orange wedges, four almond cookies, and two glasses of whole milk. The girls drop their books on the worktable. Hazel sits down and folds her hands in her lap to wait, while Joy goes over to the radio we keep in the kitchen to amuse the staff and turns it on.

I flick my wrist at her. "No radio this afternoon."

"But, Mom —"

"I don't want to argue. You and Hazel need to do your homework."

"But why?"

Because I don't want you hearing any more bad news is what I think but don't say. I hate lying to my daughter, but these last few months I've come up with excuse after excuse for why I don't want her listening to the radio: I have a migraine or her father is in a bad mood. I've even tried a sharp "Because I said so," which seems to work, but I can't use it every day. Since Hazel is here, I try something new:

"What would Hazel's mother think if I let you girls listen to the radio? We want you girls to get straight A's. I don't want to tell Mrs. Yee that I let her down."

"But you always let us listen before." When I shake my head, Joy turns to her father for help. "Dad?"

Sam doesn't bother to look up. "Just do what your mother says."

Joy turns the radio off, goes to the table, and plops down next to Hazel. Joy's an obedient child, and I'm grateful for that, because these last four months have been difficult. I'm a lot more modern than many of the mothers in Chinatown but not nearly as modern as Joy would like me to be. I've told her that pretty soon she'll be getting a visit from the little red sister and what that means in terms of boys, but I can't find a way to talk to her about this new war.

May sweeps into the kitchen. She kisses Joy, gives Hazel a pat, and sits down across from them.

"How are my favorite girls?" she asks.

"We're fine, Auntie May," Joy answers glumly.

"That doesn't sound very enthusiastic. Cheer up. It's Saturday. You're done with Chinese school and you have the rest of the weekend free. What would you like to do? Can I take the two of you to a movie?"

"Can we go, Mom?" Joy asks eagerly.

Hazel, who anyone can see would love to spend the afternoon at the movies, says, "I can't go. I have homework for regular school."

"And so does Joy," I add.

May defers to me without hesitation. "Then the girls had better finish it."

Since my baby died, my sister and I have been very close. As Mama might have said, we're like long vines with entwined roots. When I'm down, May's up. When I'm up, she's down. When I gain weight, she loses weight. When I lose weight, she still stays perfect. We don't necessarily share the same emotions or ways of looking at the world, but I can love her just as she is. My resentments are gone — at least until the next time she hurts my feelings or I do something that irritates or frustrates her so much that she pulls away from me.

"I can help, if you want," May says to the girls. "If we get it done quickly, then maybe we could go out for ice cream."

Joy looks at me, her eyes bright and questioning.

"You can go *if* you finish your homework."

May puts her elbows on the table. "So what do you have? Math? I'm pretty good at that."

Joy answers, "We have to present a current event to the class —"

"About the war," Hazel finishes for her.

Now I really do feel a headache coming on. Why can't the girls' teacher be a little more sensitive about this subject?

375

Joy opens her bag, pulls out a folded *Los Angeles Times*, and spreads it on the table. She points to one of the stories. "We were thinking of doing this one."

May looks at the story and starts to read aloud: "Today the United States government issued orders restraining Chinese students who are studying in America from returning to their home country, fearing that they'll take scientific and technological secrets with them." May pauses, glances at me, and goes back to reading: "The government has also banned all remittances to mainland China and even the British colony of Hong Kong, so that money can no longer be walked across the border. Those caught trying to send funds to relatives in China will be fined up to $10,000 and jailed for up to ten years."

My hand goes to my pocket, and I finger Betsy's letter. If things are dangerous for someone like Mr. Howell, then they could get a lot worse for people like Father Louie, who've been sending tea money back to their families and villages in China for years.

"In response," I hear May reading, "the Six Companies, the most powerful Chinese-American organization in the United States, has mounted a virulent anti-Communist campaign in hopes of halting criticism and curtailing attacks in Chinatowns across the country." May looks up from the paper and asks, "Are you girls scared?" When they nod, she says, "Don't be. You were born here. You're Americans. You have every right to be here. You don't have to be afraid."

376

I agree that they have a right to be here, but they should be scared. I try to match the tone I took when I first warned Joy about boys: steady but serious.

"You need to be careful though. Some people are going to look at you and see girls who are yellow in race and red in ideology." I frown. "Do you understand what I mean?"

"Yes," Joy answers. "We've been talking about that in class with our teacher. She says that because of how we look, some people might see us as the enemy, even though we're citizens."

Hearing her words, I know I have to try harder to protect my daughter. But how? We've never learned how to fight against evil stares or sidewalk ruffians.

"Walk together to and from school like I told you," I say. "Keep doing your classwork and —"

"That's so like your mother," May says. "Worry, worry, worry. Our mama was like that too. But look at us now!" She reaches across the table and takes one of each of the girls' hands. "Everything's going to be fine. Don't ever feel that you have to hide who you are. Nothing good ever comes from keeping secrets like that. Now, let's finish your assignment so we can get some ice cream."

The girls smile. As they work on the project, May keeps talking to them, pushing them to look deeper into the issues brought up in the article. Maybe she's taking the right approach with them. Maybe they're too young to be so scared. And maybe if they do their current events report, they won't be as ignorant about what's happening around them as May and I once were in Shanghai. But do I like it? Not one bit.

That night after dinner, Father Louie opens the letter from Wah Hong Village: "We have no wants. Your money is not needed," it says.

"Do you think it's real?" Sam asks.

Father Louie passes it to Sam, who examines it before passing it on to me. The calligraphy is simple and clear. The paper looks properly worn and tattered, as have the letters we've received in the past.

"The signature looks the same," I say, handing the letter to Yen-yen.

"It must be real," she says. "It traveled very hard to get here."

A week later we learn that this cousin tried to escape, was captured, and then was killed.

I tell myself that a Dragon shouldn't be so afraid. But I am. If something happens here — and my mind reels with the possibilities — I don't know what I'll do. America is our home, and I fear every day that somehow the government will find a way to push us out of the country.

Just before Christmas, we receive an eviction notice. We need a new place to live. Sam and I could continue to save money for Joy and rent a place just for ourselves, but the one thing we have — our strength — comes from the family. It's old-fashioned Chinese, but Yen-yen, Father, Vern, and Sam are the only people May and I have left in the world. Everyone but Vern and Joy chips in, and I'm given the task of finding a new home for all of us.

Not so long ago, filled with optimism about the birth of our son, I'd gone looking for a place for Sam and me to buy and had been turned away by real estate agents who wouldn't show me houses even though the laws had changed. I'd spoken to people who'd bought houses and moved in at night, only to have garbage thrown in their yards. Back then Sam said he wanted to go "wherever they'll accept us." We're Chinese, and we're a family of three generations choosing to live together. I know of only one place that will accept us completely: Chinatown.

I see a small bungalow off Alpine Street. I'm told it has three small bedrooms, a screened porch that can be used for sleeping, and two bathrooms. A low chain-link fence covered with dormant Cecile Brunner roses surrounds the property. A huge pepper tree sways gently in the backyard. The lawn is a dried-out rectangle. Marigolds left over from summer lie shriveled and brown. Some chrysanthemums, which look like they've never been pruned, languish in a wilted heap. Above me, endless blue sky holds the promise of another sunny winter. I don't even have to enter the house to know I've found our home.

By now I understand that for every good thing that happens, something bad will happen too. When we're packing, Yen-yen says she's tired. She sits down on the couch in the main room and dies. Heart attack, her doctor says, because she's been working too hard taking care of Vern, but we know better. She died of a broken heart: her son melting before her eyes, a grandson born dead, most of her family wealth built over too many years turned to ash, and now this move. Her funeral is small. After all, she was not a person of importance, rather just a wife and mother. The mourners bow to her casket three times. Then we have a banquet of ten tables of ten at Soochow Restaurant, where the proper and plainly flavored dishes are served.

Her death is terrible for all of us. I can't stop crying, while Father Louie has retreated into pitiable silence. But none of us has time to spend our mourning period confined, quiet, and playing dominoes, as everyone does here in Chinatown, because the following week we move into our new home. May announces that she can't sleep in the same bed with Vern, and everyone understands. No one — no matter how loving or loyal — would want to sleep next to someone who's plagued by night sweats and a festering abscess on his spine that reeks of pus, blood, and decay the way Mama's bound feet once did. Two twin beds are put on the screened porch — one for my sister, one for my daughter. I hadn't considered this eventuality, and it worries me, but there's nothing I can do about it. May keeps her clothes in Vern's closet, where her rainbow of silk, satin, and brocade dresses bulge through the door, her matching purses spill from a high shelf, and her colorfully dyed shoes litter the floor; Joy is allotted two bottom drawers in the built-in linen closet in the hallway next to the bathroom shared by her, Father Louie, and May, and to deal with Vern's needs.

Now each of us must find a way to help the family. I'm reminded of one of Mao's sayings that has been mocked in the American press: "Everybody works, so everybody eats." We're each given a task: May continues hiring extras for films and the new television shows, Sam runs Pearl's, Father Louie manages the curio shop, Joy studies hard in school and helps her family when she has free time. Yen-yen was supposed to take care of her ailing son, but that job comes to me. I like Vern well enough, but I don't want to be a nursemaid. When I walk into his room, the warm odor of sickly flesh hits my face. When he sits, his spine slides down until he looks like a toddler. His flesh feels soft and heavy, like when your feet go numb. I last one day, and then I go to my father-in-law to appeal the decision.

"When you don't want to help the family, you sound like you live in America," he says.

"I do live in America," I answer. "I care for my brother-in-law very much. You know that. But he's not my husband. He's May's husband."

"But you have a heart inside you, Pearl-ah." His voice chokes with emotion. "You're the only one I can trust to take care of my boy."

I tell myself that fate is inevitable and that the only provable fate is death, but I wonder why fate always has to be tragic. We Chinese believe that there are many ways to improve our fates: sewing amulets onto our children's clothes, asking for help from *feng shui* masters to pick propitious dates, and relying on astrology to tell us whether we should marry a Rat, a Rooster, or a Horse. But where is my fortune — the

381

good that's supposed to come to us in the form of happiness? I'm in a new home, but instead of a baby son to dote on, I have to take care of Vern. I'm just so tired and worn down. And I'm afraid all the time. I need help. I need someone to hear me.

The following Sunday, I go to church with Joy as I usually do. Listening to the reverend, I remember the first time God came into my life. I was a little girl, and a *lo fan* man dressed in black came up to me on the street outside our house in Shanghai. He wanted to sell me a Bible for two coppers. I went home and asked Mama for the money. She pushed me away, saying, "Tell that one-Goder to worship his ancestors instead. He'll be better off in the afterworld."

I went back outside, apologized to the missionary for keeping him waiting, and gave him Mama's message. At that, he gave me the Bible for free. It was my first book, and I was excited to have it, but that night, after I went to sleep, Mama threw it away. The missionary didn't give up on me though. He invited me to the Methodist mission. "Just come and play," he said. Later he asked me to attend the mission's school, also for free. Mama and Baba couldn't turn down a bargain like that. When May was old enough, she began coming with me. But none of that Jesus-thinking sank into us. We were rice Christians, taking advantage of the foreign devils' food and classes while ignoring their words and beliefs. When we became beautiful girls, whatever tendrils of Christianity had wormed their way into us shriveled and died. After what happened to China, Shanghai, and my home during the war, after what happened to Mama and me in the shack, I knew there couldn't be a one-God who was benevolent and kind.

And now we have all of our recent trials and losses, the worst of which was the death of my son. All the Chinese herbs I took, all the offerings I made, all the questioning about the meaning of my dreams, did not, could not, save him, because I was looking for help in the wrong direction. As I sit on the hard bench in the church, I smile to myself as I remember the missionary I met on the street all those years ago. He always said that true conversion was inevitable. Now it has come at last. I begin to pray — not for Father Louie, whose lifetime of hard work is coming to an end; not for my husband, who bears the family's burdens on his iron fan; not for my baby in the afterworld; not for Vern, whose bones are collapsing before my eyes; but to bring peace of mind, to make sense of all the bad things in my life, and to believe that maybe all this suffering will be rewarded in Heaven.

Forever Beautiful

I water the eggplants and the tomatoes, then pull the hose to the cucumber vine that engulfs the trellis by the incinerator. When I'm done, I roll up the hose, duck under the clothesline, and head back toward the porch. It's still early on this Sunday morning in the summer of 1952, and it's going to be a scorcher. I love that American word — *scorcher* — because it makes so much sense in this desert of a city. Shanghai always felt like we were being steamed to death in the humidity.

When we first moved into this house, I told Sam, "I want us to have food to eat, and I also want to bring a little China here." So Sam and a couple of the uncles dug up the lawn and I planted a vegetable garden. I brought back to life the chrysanthemums, which bloomed beautifully last fall, and have nursed some geranium cuttings into thriving plants against the screened porch. During the past two years, I've added pots with cymbidiums, a kumquat tree, and azaleas. I tried peonies — the most beloved of Chinese flowers —

but it never gets cold enough here for them to grow properly. My rhododendrons failed too. Sam asked for a patch of bamboo; now we're forever hacking it back and seeing new shoots come up in places where we don't want it.

I climb the steps and enter the screened porch, where I toss my apron on the washing machine, straighten May's and Joy's beds, and then go to the kitchen. Sam and I are co-owners of the property with the rest of the family, but I'm the eldest woman in the household. The kitchen is my territory, and this room literally holds my wealth. Under the sink are now two coffee cans: one for bacon grease, the other for Sam's and my savings for Joy to go to college. An oilcloth covers the table, and a thermos filled with hot water sits ready to make tea. A wok is set permanently on the stove; in a pot on one of the back burners some herbs boil for a tonic for Vern. I prepare a breakfast tray and take it through the living room and down the hall.

Vern's room belongs to a man forever a small child. Other than the closet with May's clothes — the one reminder that Vern is married — the many models that he's glued together and painted decorate the room. Fighter jets hang from fishing line from the ceiling. Ships, submarines, and race cars line floor-to-ceiling shelves.

He's awake, listening to a radio commentary about the war in North Korea and the threat of Communism, and working on one of his models. I set down his tray, pull up the bamboo shades, and open the window so the glue won't go to his head too much.

"Can I get you anything else?"

He smiles at me sweetly. After three years of the soft-bone disease, he looks like a little boy, staying home sick from school for a day. "Paints and brushes?"

I put them within arm's reach. "Your father will stay with you today. If you need anything, just call and he'll come."

I refuse to worry that something bad will happen if we leave the two of them home alone, because I know exactly what their day will be: Vern will work on his model, eat a simple lunch, mess his pants, and work on his model some more. Father Louie will do light chores around the house, make that simple lunch, avoid his son's messy bottom by walking to the corner to buy his newspapers, and nap until we come home.

I give Vern a wave, and then I go to the living room, where Sam tends the family altar. He bows before Yen-yen's photograph. Since we don't have photographs of everyone who's left us, he's put one of Mama's pouches on the altar and a miniature rickshaw to represent Baba. In a tiny box, there's a clip of my son's hair. Sam honors his entire family with ceramic fruit made in the country style.

I've grown to love this room. I've framed and hung family photos on the wall above the couch. Each winter since we've lived here, we've set up a flocked Christmas tree in the corner and decorated it with red balls. We outline our front windows with Christmas lights so that this room glows with the news of Jesus' birth. On cold nights, May, Joy, and I take turns standing over the heater grate until our flannel nightgowns balloon out like we're snow creatures.

I watch as Joy helps her grandfather to his recliner and serves him tea. I'm proud that Joy is a proper Chinese girl. She defers to her grandfather, the eldest in our family, above everyone else, including her father and me. She understands that everything she does is not only her grandfather's business but also his right to decide. He wants her to learn embroidery, sewing, cleaning, and cooking. In the curio shop after school, she does many of the jobs I once did — polishing, sweeping, and dusting. "Her training as a future wife and mother of my great-grandsons is important," Father Louie says, and we all try to honor that. And even though all hope of returning to China is lost, he still says, "We don't want Pan-di to become too Americanized. We'll all go back to China one day." Sentiments like this tell us he's slipping. It's hard to believe that he once ruled us with such authority or that we were all so afraid of him. We used to call him Old Man, but now he's a very old man, slowly weakening, slowly drifting away from us, slowly losing his memories, his strength, and his connection to the things that have always driven him: money, business, and family.

Joy gives a half bow to her grandfather, and then the two of us walk to the Methodist church for the Sunday service. As soon as the sermon ends, Joy and I go to the Central Plaza in New Chinatown to meet Sam, May, and Uncle Fred, Mariko, and their daughters at one of the district association halls. We've joined a group — a union of sorts — composed of members from the Congregational, Presbyterian, and Methodist churches in Chinatown. We meet once a month. We stand erect and proud, place our hands over our hearts, and recite the Pledge of Allegiance. Then all the families troop out to Bamboo Lane and pile into sedans for the drive to Santa Monica Beach. Sam, May, and I sit together in the front seat of our Chrysler, Joy and the two Yee girls — Hazel and her younger sister, Rose — squeeze together in the backseat, and then we head west in a caravan along Sunset Boulevard. Cars with huge fins shoot ahead of us, their windshields flashing in the summer glare. We go by old-fashioned clapboard houses in Echo Park and pink stucco mansions and rat-proofed palms in Beverly Hills, where we cut over to Wilshire Boulevard and continue west past supermarkets as massive as B-29 hangars, parking lots and lawns as big as football fields, and cascades of bougainvillea and morning glories.

Joy's voice rises as she presses a point to Hazel and Rose, and I smile to myself. Everyone says my daughter has my gift for languages. At age fourteen, her Sze Yup and Wu dialects are as perfect as her English, and her mastery of written Chinese is excellent too. Each Chinese New Year or if someone is celebrating a happy occasion, people ask Joy to write appropriate couplets in her fine calligraphy, which is said by all to be *tong gee* — uncorrupted by adulthood. This praise isn't enough for me. I know Joy can obtain more spiritual growth and learn more about Caucasians by going to church outside Chinatown, which we do once a month.

"God loves everyone," I often remind my daughter. "He wants you to make a good living and have a happy life. This is true about America too. You can do anything in the U.S. You can't say that about China."

I tell Sam things like this too, because the Christian words and beliefs have taken deep root in me. My faith in God and Jesus is also very much a part of the patriotism and loyalty I feel for my daughter's home country of America. And of course, being Christian these days is deeply tied to anti-Communist sentiment. No one wants to be accused of being a godless Communist. When asked about the war in Korea, we say we're against Red China's interference; when asked about Taiwan, we say we support the Generalissimo and Madame Chiang Kai-shek. We say we're for moral rearmament, Jesus, and freedom. Going to a Western church is a practical thing to do, just as my going to a mission in Shanghai was. "You have to be sensible about these things," I've told Sam, but inside I've become a one-Goder and he knows it.

Sam may not like it, but he comes to our church gatherings because he loves me, our family, Uncle Fred and his brood of girls, and these picnics. Our outings make him feel American. In fact, although our daughter has finally grown out of her cowgirl infatuation, almost everything we do makes us feel more American. On days like today, Sam ignores the God aspects and embraces the things he likes: preparing the food, eating slices of watermelon that we don't have to worry have been injected with foul river water, and celebrating

389

family fellowship. He considers these adventures purely social and purely for the children.

Sam pulls into a parking spot by the Santa Monica Pier, and we unload the car. Our feet burn as we cross the sand, roll out blankets, and set up umbrellas. Sam and Fred help the other men dig a pit for the barbecue. May, Mariko, and I assist the other wives and mothers setting out bowls of potato, bean, and fruit salads; Jell-O molds with marshmallows, walnuts, and grated carrots; and plates of cold cuts. As soon as the fire is ready, we give the men trays of chicken wings marinated in soy, honey, and sesame seeds, and pork ribs steeped in hoisin sauce and five spice. The ocean air mixes with the scent of the roasting meat, children play in the surf, the men bend their heads over the barbecue, and the women sit on blankets and gossip. Mariko stands apart from us. She holds baby Mamie on her hip, while keeping a close eye on her other half-and-half daughters, Eleanor and Bess, who are building a sand castle.

My sister, childless, is known as Auntie May to everyone. Like Sam, she isn't a one-Goder. Far from it! She works hard, sometimes staying up late to arrange extras for a shoot or staying out all night on a set herself. At least that's what she says. I honestly don't know where she goes, and I don't ask. Even when she's home and asleep, the phone might ring at four or five in the morning, a call from someone who's just lost all his money gambling and needs a job. None of this, *none of this*, matches well with my one-God beliefs, which is one reason I like to bring her on these excursions to the seashore.

"Look at that FOB," May says, adjusting her sunglasses and big hat. She tips her head delicately toward Violet Lee, who shades her eyes with her long, tapered fingers and peers out to the ocean, where Joy and her friends hold hands and jump over waves. Plenty of women here, including Violet, are fresh off the boat. Now almost forty percent of the Chinese population in Los Angeles is made up of women, but Violet wasn't a war bride or a fiancée. She and her husband came to UCLA to study: she bioengineering, Rowland engineering. When China closed, they were trapped here with their young son. They aren't paper sons, paper partners, or laborers, but they're still *wang k'uo nu* — lost-country slaves.

Violet and I get along well. She has narrow hips, which Mama always said marked a woman with the gift of gab. Are we best friends? I sneak a glance at my sister. Never. Violet and I are good friends, like Betsy and I once were. May will always be not only my sister and my sister-in-law but also my best friend, forever. That said, May doesn't know what she's talking about. While it's true that many of the new women do seem FOB — just as we once did — most of them are exactly like Violet: educated, arriving in this country with their own money, not having to spend even a single night in Chinatown but buying bungalows and homes in Silver Lake, Echo Park, or Highland Park, where Chinese are welcomed. Not only do they not live in Chinatown, but they don't work there either. They aren't laundrymen, houseboys, restaurant workers, or curio-shop clerks. They're the cream of China — the ones who could afford to leave. Already they've gone further than we ever could. Violet now teaches at USC, and Rowland works in the aerospace industry. They come to Chinatown only to go to church and to buy groceries. They've joined our group so their son can meet other Chinese children.

May eyes a young man. "You think that FOB wants our ABC?" She asks suspiciously. The FOB she's speaking of is Violet's son; the ABC is my American-born Chinese daughter.

"Leon's a sweet boy and a good student," I say, watching as the boy dives smoothly into the surf. "He's at the top of his class at his school, just as our Joy is at the top of hers."

"You sound like Mama talking about Tommy and me," May teases.

"It's not so bad if Leon and Joy get to know each other," I respond steadily, for once not offended that she's compared me with our mother. After all, the reason this union exists is that we want the boys and girls to get to know each other, hoping they'll marry one day. Implicit in this is the expectation that they'll marry someone Chinese.

"She's lucky she won't have an arranged marriage." May sighs. "But even with animals, you want a thoroughbred, not a mongrel."

When you lose your home country, what do you preserve and what do you abandon? We've saved only those things that are possible to save: Chinese food,

Chinese language, and sneaking what money we can back to the Louie relatives in the home village. But what about an arranged marriage for my girl? Sam isn't Z.G., but he's a good and kind man. And Vern, forever damaged, has never beaten May or lost money gambling.

"Just don't push for marriage," May continues. "Let her get an education." (Something I've been working toward practically from the moment Joy was born.) "I didn't have what you had in Shanghai," my sister complains, "but she should go to college, like you did." She pauses, letting that sink in, as though I haven't heard this before too. "But it's nice she has such good friends," May adds as the girls cling to one another when a big wave approaches. "Remember when we could laugh like that? We thought nothing bad could happen to us."

"The essence of happiness has nothing to do with money," I say, and I believe it. But May bites her lip, and I see I've said the exact wrong thing. "We thought the world ended when Baba lost everything —"

"It did," May says. "Our lives would have been very different if he'd saved our money instead of lost it, which is why I work so hard to make it now."

Make it and spend it on clothes and jewelry for yourself, I think but don't say. Our differing attitudes about money are among the many things that aggravate my sister.

"What I mean is," I try again, hoping not to further darken May's mood, "Joy's lucky to have friends, just as I'm lucky to have you. Mama married out and never

393

saw her sisters again, but you and I will have each other forever." I put my arm around her shoulder and jiggle it affectionately. "Sometimes I think that one day we'll end up sharing a room just like when we were girls, only we'll be in the old folks' home. We'll have our meals together. We'll sell raffle tickets together. We'll make crafts together —"

"We'll go to matinees together," May adds, smiling.

"And we'll sing psalms together."

May frowns at that. I've made another mistake, and I hurry on.

"And we'll play mah-jongg! We'll be two retired ladies, fat and round, playing mah-jongg, and complaining about this and that."

May nods as she stares wistfully west across the sea to the horizon.

When we get home, we find Father Louie asleep in his recliner. I give Joy, Hazel, and Rose some straws and send them out to the backyard, where they gather peppercorns off the ground, load up their straws, and blow the harmless pink pellets at one another, laughing, squealing, and running through the yard between the plants. Sam and I go to Vern's bedroom to change his diaper. The open window does little to blow away the smells of sickness, shit, urine, and pus. May comes in with tea. We sit together for a few minutes to tell Vern about the day, and then I go back to the kitchen. I unpack and begin getting things ready for dinner, washing the rice, chopping ginger and garlic, and slicing beef.

Just before I start cooking, I send the Yee girls home. As I make curried tomato beef *lo mein*, Joy sets the table — a job that back in Shanghai had always been done by our servants under Mama's close watch. Joy lines up the chopsticks just so, making sure not to set out any uneven pairs, which would mean that the person using them will miss a boat, a plane, or a train (not that any of us are going anywhere). While I put the food on the table, Joy gets her aunt, father, and grandfather. I've tried to teach my daughter the things that Mama tried to teach me. The big difference is that my daughter has paid attention and learned. She never speaks at dinner — something May and I failed at miserably. She never drops her chopsticks for fear of bad luck, nor does she leave them upright in her rice bowl, because that's something done only at funerals and is impolite to her grandfather, who's been thinking about his own mortality lately.

When dinner's over, Sam helps Father back to his chair. I clean the kitchen, while May takes a plate of food to Vern. I'm standing with my hands in soapy water, staring out at the garden aglow in the last of the summer evening's light, when I hear my sister coming back through the living room. The sound of her steps is familiar and comforting. Then I hear her gasp — a breath so deep and sharp that I'm suddenly very afraid. Is it Vern? Father? Joy? Sam?

I rush to the kitchen door and peer around the jamb. May stands in the middle of the room, Vern's empty plate in her hand, her face flushed and with a look I can't comprehend. She's staring at Father's chair, and I think the old man must have died. I think if death has come today, then that's not so bad. He lived to be eighty-something, he spent a quiet day with his son, he had dinner with his family, and none of us can feel bad anymore about the relations between us.

I step into the room to face this sadness and then freeze, as shocked into immobility as my sister. The old man is alive all right. He sits there with his feet up on his lounger, his long pipe in his mouth, and a copy of *China Reconstructs* held in his hands so the two of us can see it. It's shocking enough to see him with this magazine. It comes out of Red China, and it's a piece of Communist propaganda. There've been rumors that the government has spies in Chinatown keeping track of who buys things like this. Father Louie, who cannot be called a supporter of the Communist regime by any measure, has told us to avoid the tobacconist and the paper goods store where the magazine is sold from under the counter.

But it's not the magazine that's the real shock; it's the front cover, which my father-in-law is displaying to us with such pride. The image is one that, even if we avoid these products, is familiar to us: the glory of New China as exemplified by two young women dressed in country clothes, their cheeks full of life, their arms loaded with fruits and vegetables, practically singing the glories of the new regime — all rendered in glowing red tones. Those two beautiful girls are instantly recognizable as May and me. The artist, who without hesitation has embraced the heightened, exuberant style favored by the Communists, is also clearly identifiable by the delicacy and precision of his brushstrokes. Z.G. is alive, and he hasn't forgotten me or my sister.

"I went to the tobacconist when Vern was sleeping. Look," Father Louie says, the pride in his voice unmistakable as he looks at the cover with May and me — not one question in my mind that it's us — selling not soap, face powder, or baby formula but a glorious harvest out by the Lunghua Pagoda, where Z.G., May, and I once flew kites. "You're still beautiful girls." Father sounds almost triumphant. He worked his whole life, and for what? He never went back to China. His wife died. His birth son is like a dried-up bedbug and about as companionable. He never had a grandson. His businesses have shriveled to one mediocre curio shop. But he did do one thing really, really well. He procured two beautiful girls for Vern and Sam.

May and I take a few tentative steps toward him. It's hard to say how I feel: surprised and stunned to see May and me looking the same as we did fifteen years ago with our pink cheeks, happy eyes, and luscious smiles, a bit fearful that these magazines are in the house, and almost overwhelmed by joy that Z.G. is still alive.

The next thing I know Sam is at my side, exclaiming, and gesturing in excitement. "It's you! It's you and May!"

My cheeks flush, as though I've been caught. I *have* been caught. I lift my eyes to May, looking for help. As sisters, we've always been able to say so much to each other with just a glance.

"Z.G. Li must have painted this," May says evenly. "How lovely that he has remembered us in this way. He made Pearl look especially beautiful, don't you think?"

"He's painted both of you exactly as I see you," says Sam, forever the good husband and appreciative brother-in-law. "Always beautiful. Forever beautiful."

"Beautiful enough," May agrees lightly, "although neither of us ever looked that good in peasant clothes."

Later that night, after everyone goes to asleep, I meet my sister on the screened porch. We sit on her bed, holding hands, staring at the magazine. As much as I love Sam, a part of me soars with the knowledge that across the ocean in Shanghai — I have to believe Z.G.'s there — in a country that is closed to me, the man I loved so long ago loves me still.

Only one week later, we realize that Father's weakness and lethargy are more than just the usual slowing of age. He's sick. The doctor tells us it's lung cancer and there's nothing anyone can do. Yen-yen's death was so sudden and it came at such an inconvenient moment that we didn't have the opportunity to prepare for her death or mourn her properly when she passed. This time each of us in our own way reflects back on the mistakes we've made over the years, and we try to make amends in the time we have left. During the coming months, many people visit, and I listen to them speak highly of my father-in-law, calling him a successful Gold Mountain man, but when I look at him during these final days, I see only a ruined man. He worked so hard, only to lose his businesses and property in China and almost everything he'd built for himself here. Now, in the end, he has to rely on his paper son for his housing, food, evening pipe, and copies of *China Reconstructs* that Sam buys from under the counter at the shop on the corner.

Father's only consolations in these final months, as the cancer eats his lungs, are the photographs I cut from the magazine and pin to the wall next to his recliner. So many times I see him with tears running down his sunken cheeks, staring at the country he left as a young man: the sacred mountains, the Great Wall, and the Forbidden City. He says he hates the Communists, because that's what everyone has to say, but he still has a love of the land, art, culture, and people of China that has nothing to do with Mao, the Bamboo Curtain, or fear of the Reds. He isn't alone in his nostalgia and desire for his homeland. Many of the old-timers, like Uncle Wilburt and Uncle Charley, come to the house and also pore over these captured images of their lost home; that's how deep their love of China is, no matter what it's become. But all this happens very fast, and too soon Father dies.

A funeral is the most important event in a person's life — more significant than a birth, a birthday, or a wedding. Since Father was a man and he lived into his eighties, his funeral is much larger than Yen-yen's. We hire a Cadillac convertible to drive through Chinatown with a large flower-wreathed photographic portrait of him propped on the backseat. The hearse driver tosses spirit money out the window to pay off malevolent demons and other lowly ghosts who might try to bar

399

the way. A brass band trails behind the hearse, playing Chinese folks songs and military marches. At the hall for the ceremony, three hundred people bow three times to the casket and another three times to us, the grieving family members. We give coins to the mourners to disperse the *sa hee* — polluted air associated with death — and candy to cleanse the bitter taste of death. Everyone wears white — the color of mourning, the color of death. Then we go to Soochow Restaurant for *gaai wai jau* — the traditional seven-course "plain" banquet of steamed chicken, seafood, and vegetables, designed to "wash away sorrow," wish the old man a long next life after this death, and launch us on our healing journey and encourage us to leave behind the vapors of death before returning home.

Over the next three months, women come to the house to play dominoes with May and me as we pass through the official mourning period. I find myself staring at the pictures I pinned to the wall above Father's recliner. Somehow I can't take them down.

Inch of Gold

"Why can't I go?" Joy demands, her voice rising. "Auntie Violet and Uncle Rowland are letting Leon go."

"Leon's a boy," I say.

"It only costs twenty-five cents. *Please.*"

"Your father and I don't think it's right for a girl your age to go around town by yourself —"

"I won't be by myself. All the kids are going."

"You're not *all* the kids," I say. "Do you want people to look at you and see porcelain with scars? You have to guard your body like a piece of jade."

"Mom, all I want to do is go to the record hop at the International Hall."

Yen-yen sometimes said that an inch of gold could not buy an inch of time, but only recently have I begun to understand how precious time is and how quickly it passes. It's 1956, the summer after Joy's high school graduation. In the fall, she'll be attending the University of Chicago, where she plans to study history.

It's awfully far away, but we've decided to let her go. Her tuition has turned out to be more than we anticipated, but Joy's received a partial scholarship and May's going to help out too. Every day Joy asks if she can go somewhere or other. If I say yes to this record hop — whatever that is — then I'll have to say yes to something else: the dance with the fifteen-piece orchestra, the birthday celebration in MacArthur Park, the party that will require a bus ride going and coming home.

"What do you think's going to happen?" Joy asks, not giving up. "We're only going to play records and dance a little."

May and I said things like that too when we were girls in Shanghai, and it didn't work out that well for either of us.

"You're too young for boys," I say.

"Young? I'm eighteen! Auntie May married Uncle Vern when she was my age —"

And already pregnant, I think to myself.

Sam has tried to pacify me by accusing me of being too strict. "You worry too much," he's said. "She's not aware of boy-girl interests."

But what girl of Joy's age isn't aware of those things? I was. May was. Now when Joy talks back, ignores what I say, or walks out of the room when I tell her to stay, even my sister laughs at me for getting upset, saying, "We did the exact same things at that age."

And look what it got us, I want to scream at her.

"I've never been to a single football game or dance," Joy resumes her complaints. "The other girls have gone to the Palladium. They've gone to the Biltmore. I never get to do anything."

"We need your help at Pearl's and in the shop. Your auntie needs your help too."

"Why should I help? I never get paid."

"All the money —"

"Goes into the family pot. You've been saving for me to go to college. I know. I *know*. But I only have two months left before I leave for Chicago. Don't you want me to have fun? This is my last chance to see my friends." Joy folds her arms over her chest and sighs as though she's the most burdened person in the world.

"You can do anything you want, but you have to do well in school. If you don't want to go to school —"

"Then I'm on my own," she finishes, reciting the line with the fatigue of centuries.

I'm Joy's mother and I see her with mother eyes. Her long black hair holds the blue of distant mountains. Her eyes are the deep black of a lake in autumn. She didn't have enough to eat in the womb, and she's smaller than I am, smaller than May. This gives her the appearance of a maiden from ancient times — lithe like willow branches swayed by the breeze, as delicate as the flight of swallows — but inside she's still a Tiger. I can try to tame her, but my daughter can't escape her essential nature, just as I can't escape mine. Since graduation, she's complained about the clothes I make for her. "They're so embarrassing," she says. I made them out of love. I made them because there wasn't a place in Los Angeles like Madame Garnet's in Shanghai for me to take her to have dresses molded to her exact shape. What upsets Joy most of all is her perceived lack of freedom, but I know the kinds of things May and I — especially May, really *only* May — did when we were young.

A lot of this wouldn't happen if Father Louie were still alive. He's been gone four years now. Sam, Joy, and I could have used Father's death as our chance to move out on our own, but we didn't. Sam had made a promise when Father took him as more than just a paper son. I may not believe in ancestors anymore, but Sam lights incense for the old man and makes offerings of food and paper clothes to him during New Year's and other festivities. But beyond that, how could we leave Vern, who's lived longer than anyone expected? Who will explain to him that his parents are gone when he asks for them, as he does every day? How could we leave May to care for her husband, run the Golden Prop and Extras Company and the curio shop, and manage the house? But it goes even past loyalty to the family and promises made. We continue to be deeply afraid.

Every day the news from the government is bad. The U.S. consul in Hong Kong has accused the Chinese community of being inclined to fraud and perjury, since we "lack the equivalent of the Western concept of an oath." He says that everyone who comes through his office looking to go to the United States is using fake papers. Angel Island has long been closed, but he's devised new procedures requiring the answering of hundreds of questions, the filling out of dozens of forms, and the procurement of affidavits, blood tests,

X-rays, and fingerprints, all in an effort to keep Chinese from coming to America. He says that almost every Chinese already in America — going all the way back to those who panned for gold more than a hundred years ago and helped build the transcontinental railroad eighty-some years ago — entered illegally and is not to be trusted. He says that we're responsible for trafficking in drugs, using fraudulent passports and other papers, counterfeiting American dollars, and illegally collecting Social Security and veterans' benefits. Worse, he claims that for decades the Communists have sent paper sons — like Sam, Wilburt, Fred, and so many others — to America as spies. Every single Chinese living in America must be investigated, he insists.

For years, Joy has come home from school with stories about her duck-and-cover drills. Now it's as though we want to live each day in that coiled position — cocooned in our houses with our families, hoping the windows, walls, and doors won't be shattered, immolated, and turned to bitter ashes. For all these reasons — love for one another, fear for one another — we've stayed together, and we've struggled to find balance and order, but with Father Louie gone, we're all slightly adrift, especially my daughter.

"You don't have to wash clothes for *lo fan*, make their meals, clean their houses, or answer their doors," I say. "You don't have to be an office girl or a clerk in a store either. When your baba and I first came here, all we could ever hope for was to have our own café and maybe one day live in a house."

"You and Dad got that —"

"Yes, but you can have and do so much more. Back when your aunt and I first arrived, only a handful of people could go into a profession. I can count them on one hand." And I do. "Y. C. Hong, the first Chinese-American lawyer in California; Eugene Choy, the first Chinese-American architect in Los Angeles; Margaret Chung, the first Chinese-American doctor in the country —"

"You've told me this a million times —"

"All I'm saying is you can be a doctor, a lawyer, a scientist, or an accountant. You can do anything."

"Even climb a telephone pole?" she asks tartly.

"We just want you to get to the top of the heap," I reply calmly.

"That's why I'm going to college. I never want to work in the café or the shop."

I don't want her to either, which is exactly what I've been saying. Still, there's a part of me that hates that our family businesses — the very things that have kept Joy fed, clothed, and housed — are so embarrassing to her. I try — not for the first time — to make her understand.

"The sons in the Fong family have become doctors and lawyers, but they still help out at Fong's Buffet," I point out. "That one boy goes to trial in the courthouse during the day. At night the judges go to the restaurant to eat. They say, "Don't I know you from somewhere?" And what about that Wong boy? He went to USC, but he's not too proud to help his father at the filling station on weekends."

"I can't believe you're telling me about Henry Fong. Usually you complain he's become 'too continental,' because he married that girl whose family came from Scotland. And Gary Wong is only trying to make up for the fact that he broke his family's heart by marrying a *lo fan* and moving to Long Beach so he can live a Eurasian life. I'm glad you've become so open-minded."

This is how Joy's last summer at home unfolds — with one petty argument after another. At one of our church meetings, Violet tells me she's experiencing the same things with Leon, who'll be going to Yale in the fall. "Sometimes he's as unpleasant as a fish left behind the couch for too many days. Here they talk about the bird leaving the nest. Leon wants to fly away all right. He's my son and my heart's blood, but he doesn't understand that a part of me wants to see him leave too. Go! Go! Take your stinkiness with you!"

"It's our own fault," I tell Violet on the phone another night when she calls in tears after her son complained that her accent means she will be forever labeled a foreigner and that if anyone asks where she's from she should answer Taipei in Taiwan and not Peking in the People's Republic of China, otherwise J. Edgar Hoover and his FBI agents might accuse her of being an undercover agent on an intelligence mission. "We raised our children to be Americans, but what we wanted were proper Chinese sons and daughters."

May, aware of the discord in the household, offers Joy work as an extra. Joy flutters with excitement. "Mom! Please! Auntie May says if I go to work with her, then I'll have my own money for books, food, and warm clothes."

"We already saved enough for that." This isn't quite true. The extra money would be welcome, but having Joy go off with May is the last thing I want.

"You never let me have any fun," my daughter complains.

I notice that May isn't saying a word, just watching us, knowing that the impish Tiger will have its way in the end. So my daughter goes off with her aunt for several weeks. Every night when she comes home she treats her father and uncle with stories of her adventures on the set, but she still finds ways to criticize me. May tells me I should ignore Joy's rebelliousness, that it's just part of the culture these days, and that she's only trying to fit in with American kids her age. May doesn't understand how confused I feel. Every day I have an inner battle: I want my daughter to be patriotic and have all the opportunities that being an American will give her. At the same time, I worry that I've failed to teach Joy to be filial, polite, and Chinese.

Two weeks before Joy leaves for the University of Chicago, I go out to the screened porch to say good night. May's in her bed at one end of the porch, flipping through a magazine. Joy sits on top of the covers of her bed, brushing her hair and listening to that awful Elvis Presley on her record player. The wall above her bed is covered with pictures she's cut from magazines of Elvis and James Dean, who died last year.

"Mom," Joy says, after I kiss her, "I've been thinking."

I know by now to beware this opening.

"You always said that Auntie May was the most beautiful of the beautiful girls in Shanghai."

"Yes," I say, glancing at my sister, who looks up from her magazine. "All the artists loved her."

"Well, if that's so, why is your face always the main focus on those magazines Dad buys, you know, the ones that come from China?"

"Oh, that's not true," I say, but I know it is. In the four years since Father Louie bought that issue of *China Reconstructs*, Z.G. has designed another six covers in which May's and my faces are absolutely recognizable. In the old days, artists like Z.G. used beautiful girls to advertise the luxurious life. Now artists use posters, calendars, and advertisements to communicate the Communist Party's vision to the illiterate masses, as well as to the outside world. Scenes in boudoirs, salons, and baths have been replaced by patriotic themes: May and me with our arms outstretched as though reaching for the bright future, the two of us with kerchiefs in our hair, pushing wheelbarrows filled with rocks to help build a dam, or standing in a shallow paddy, tending rice shoots. On every cover, my face, with its rosy cheeks, and my body, with its long lines, is the central figure, while my sister takes the secondary position behind me, holding a basket into which I put vegetables, steadying my bicycle, or bending her head from the burden she carries while I gaze skyward. Always there's some hint of Shanghai in the painting: the roll of the Whangpoo outside a factory window, the Yu Yuan Garden in the Old Chinese City for uniformed soldiers to practice their rifle drills, the glorious Bund made drab and utilitarian for marching workers. The subtle hues, romantic poses, and soft edges that Z.G. once loved have been replaced by everything outlined in black and filled with flat color — especially red, red, red.

Joy hops up and walks the length of the porch. She examines the magazine covers that May has on the wall next to her bed.

"He must have really loved you," my daughter says.

"Oh, I hardly think that's possible," May says, covering for me.

"You should look at these more closely," Joy says. "Don't you see what the artist has done? Thin, pale, and fashionable girls, like you must have been, Auntie May, have been replaced by robust, healthy, strong working women, like Mom. Didn't you tell me that your father always used to complain that Mom had a face like a peasant — ruddy and red? Her face is perfect for the Commies."

Daughters can sometimes be cruel. They sometimes say things they don't mean, but that doesn't mean her words don't sting. I turn away and stare out to the vegetable patch, hoping to hide my feelings.

"That's why I think he loves you, Auntie May. Surely you see it."

I take a breath, one part of my brain listening to my daughter, the other part reinterpreting what she said

410

before. When she said, "He must have really loved you," she didn't mean me. She meant May.

"Because look," I hear my daughter say. "Here's Mom, all peasant-perfect for the country, but look how he painted your face, Auntie May. It's beautiful, like you're a fairy goddess or something."

May doesn't say anything, but I sense her examining the pictures.

"You know, if he saw you now," my daughter continues, "he probably wouldn't recognize you."

Like that, my daughter manages to wound both her mother and her aunt, poking at our softest, most vulnerable, parts. I press my fingernails into my palms to bring my emotions under control. I lift the corners of my mouth, exposing my teeth, and then spin around and put my hands on my daughter's shoulders.

"I came out here to say good night. You should climb in bed. And, May," I say lightly, "can you help me with the books from the café? I can't seem to make the numbers work."

My sister and I have had a lifetime together of false smiles and escaping things we don't like. We leave the porch, acting as if Joy hasn't hurt us, but as soon as we get to the kitchen, we hold each other for strength and comfort. How can Joy's words be so painful after all these years? Because inside we still carry the dreams of what could have been, of what should have been, of what we wish we could still be. This doesn't mean we aren't content. We are content, but the romantic longings of our girlhood have never entirely left us. It's like Yen-yen said all those years ago: "I look in the mirror and I'm surprised by what I see." I look in the mirror and still expect to see my Shanghai-girl self — not the wife and mother I've become. And May? To my eyes, she hasn't changed at all. She's still beautiful — Chinese-beautiful, ageless.

"Joy's just a girl," I tell my sister. "We said and did stupid things when we were that age too."

"Everything always returns to the beginning," May responds, and I wonder if she's thinking about the original meaning of the aphorism — that no matter what we do in life, we will always return to the beginning, that we will have children who'll disobey, hurt, and disappoint us just as we once disobeyed, hurt, and disappointed our own parents — or is she thinking about Shanghai and how in a sense we've been trapped in our final days there ever since we left, forever destined to relive the loss of our parents, our home, Z.G., and carry the consequences of my rape and May's pregnancy?

"Joy says these mean things so you and I will come together," I say, repeating something Violet said to me the other day. "She knows how lonely we'll be without her."

May looks away, her eyes glistening.

The next morning when I go out to the porch, the covers of *China Reconstructs* have been taken down and put away.

We stand on the platform at Union Station, saying good-bye to Joy. May and I wear full skirts fluffed by petticoats and cinched with little patent leather belts.

412

Last week we dyed our stiletto heels to match our dresses, gloves, and handbags. We went to the Palace Salon to have our hair curled and teased to impressive heights, which we now protect with gaily colored scarves tied smartly under our chins. Sam wears his best suit and a somber face. And Joy looks . . . joyful.

May reaches into her handbag and pulls out the pouch with the three coppers, three sesame seeds, and three green beans that Mama gave her all those years ago. My sister asked if she could give it to Joy. I didn't object, but I wish I'd thought of it first. May loops the string around Joy's neck and says, "I gave this to you on the day you were born to protect you. Now I hope you'll wear it when you're away from us."

"Thank you, Auntie," my daughter says, clasping the pouch. "I'm not going to squeeze another orange or sell another gardenia as long as I live," she vows when she hugs her baba. "I'm never going to wear atomic fabric or one of your felt jumpers," she promises after she kisses me. "I never again want to see another back scratcher or a piece of Canton ware."

We listen to her giddiness and respond with our best advice and final thoughts: we love her, she should write every day, she can call if there's an emergency, she should eat the dumplings her baba made first and then switch to the peanut butter and crackers packed in her food basket. Then she's on the train, separated from us by a window, waving and mouthing, "I love you! I'll miss you!" We walk along the platform next to the train as it leaves the station, waving and crying until she's out of sight.

413

When we go home, it's like the electricity has been shut off. Only four of us live in the house now, and the quiet, especially during the first month, is so unbearable that May buys herself a brand-new pink Ford Thunderbird and Sam and I buy a television set. May comes home after work, eats a quick dinner, says good night to Vern, and then goes out. Remembering Joy's love of cowgirls when she was younger, the rest of us sit in the main room and watch *Gunsmoke* and *Cheyenne*.

"Dear mom, dad, Auntie May, and Uncle Vern," I read aloud. We sit on chairs around Vern's bed. "You wrote and asked if I'm homesick. How can I answer this question and not make you feel bad? If I tell you I'm having fun, then I'll hurt your feelings. If I say I'm lonely, then you'll worry about me."

I look at the others. Sam and May nod in agreement. Vern twists his sheet in his fingers. He doesn't completely understand that Joy is gone, just as he hasn't completely understood that his parents are gone.

"But I think Dad would want me to tell the truth," I continue reading. "I'm very happy and I'm having a lot of fun. My classes are interesting. I'm writing a paper on a Chinese writer named Lu Hsün. You probably haven't heard of him —"

"Ha!" This comes from my sister. "We could tell her stories. Remember what he wrote about beautiful girls?"

"Keep reading, keep reading," Sam says.

414

Joy doesn't come home for Christmas. We don't bother to put up a big tree. Instead Sam buys a tree no more than eighteen inches high, which we put on Vern's dresser.

By late January, Joy's initial enthusiasm has finally given way to homesickness:

Why would anyone live in Chicago? It's so cold. The sun never comes out and the wind always blows. Thank you for the long underwear from the army surplus store, but even it doesn't make me warm. Everything is white — the sky, the sun, people's faces — and the days are too short up here. I don't know what I miss most — going to the beach or hanging out with Auntie May on film sets. I even miss the sweet-and-sour pork Dad makes in the coffee shop.

This last is really bad. That sweet-and-sour pork is the worst kind of *lo fan* dish: too sweet and too breaded.

In February, she writes:

I've been hoping to get a job with one of my professors during spring break. How can every single one of them not have work for me? I sit in the front row in my history class, but the professor gives handouts to everyone else first. If he runs out, too bad for me.

I write back:

People will always tell you that you can't do things, but don't forget you can do whatever you want. Make sure you go to church. You'll always be accepted there and you can talk about Bible times. It's good for people to know you're a Christian.

Her response:

People keep asking me why I don't return to China. I tell them I can't return to a place I've never been.

In March, Joy suddenly cheers up. "Maybe it's because the winter is over," Sam suggests. But that's not it, because she still complains about the endless winter. Rather, there's a boy . . .

My friend Joe asked me to join the Chinese Students Democratic Christian Association. I like the kids in the group. We discuss integration, interracial marriage, and family relationships. I'm learning a lot and it's nice to see friendly faces, cook together, and eat together.

Quite apart from this Joe, whoever he is, I'm happy that she's joined a Christian group. I know she'll find companionship there. After reading the letter to everyone, I write our reply:

Your dad wants to know about your classes this semester. Are you keeping up? Auntie May wants to know what the girls are wearing in Chicago and if she can send you anything. I don't have much to add. Things are the same or nearly the same. We closed the curio shop — not enough business to hire someone to sell that "junk," as you always called it. Business at Pearl's is good and your dad's busy. Uncle Vern wants to know more about Joe.

Actually, he hasn't said a thing about Joe, but the rest of us are itching with curiosity.

And you know your auntie — always working. What else? Oh, you know the kind of things that go on around here. Everyone's afraid of being called a Communist. During troubles in business or rivalries in love, one person can find a solution by labeling the other a Communist. "Did you hear so-and-so's a Commie?" You know how it is, people gossiping, chasing the wind and catching shadows. Someone sells more curios; he must be a Communist. She spurned my affections; she must be a Communist. Fortunately, your father doesn't have any enemies, and no one is wooing your aunt.

This is my around-the-corner-and-down-the-block way of trying to get Joy to write more about this Joe. But if I'm Joy's mother, then she's definitely my daughter. She sees right through me. As usual, I wait to read the letter until everyone's home and we can gather around Vern's bed.

"You'd like Joe," she writes.

He's in premed. He goes to church with me on Sundays. You want me to say my prayers, but we don't say them at my Christian association. You'd think that Jesus would be all we'd talk about at those meetings, but we don't talk about Him. We talk about the injustices that were done to people like you and Dad, Grandma and Grandpa. We talk about what happened to the Chinese in the past and what's continuing to happen to black people. Just last weekend we picketed Montgomery Ward because they won't hire blacks. Joe says that minorities need to stick together. Joe and I have been getting people to sign petitions. It's nice to think about other people's problems for a change.

When I come to the end of the letter, Sam asks, "Do you think this Joe speaks Sze Yup? I don't want her to marry someone outside our dialect."

"Who says he's Chinese?" May asks.

That sets us to twittering like birds.

"They're in a Chinese organization," Sam says. "He has to be Chinese."

"And they go to church together," I add.

"So? You always encouraged her to go to church outside Chinatown so she could meet other kinds of people," May says, and three accusatory pairs of eyes glare at me.

"His name is Joe," I say. "That's a good name. It sounds Chinese."

As I stare at the name written in Joy's even hand and try to decide exactly what this Joe might be, my sister — forever my devilish little sister — ticks off other Joes. "Joe DiMaggio, Joseph Stalin, Joseph McCarthy —"

"Write her back," Vern interrupts. "Tell her Commies are no-good friends. She'll get in trouble."

But that's not what I write. What I write is not at all subtle: "What's Joe's family name?"

In mid-May, I receive Joy's reply.

Oh, Mom, you're so funny. I can just imagine you and Dad, Auntie May, and Uncle Vern sitting around and worrying about this. Joe's family name is Kwok, OK? Sometimes we talk about going to China to help the country. Joe says we Chinese have a saying: Thousands upon thousands of years for China. Being Chinese and carrying that upon your shoulders and in your heart can be a heavy burden but also a source of pride and joy. He says, "Shouldn't we be a part of what's happening in our home country?" He even took me to get a passport.

I worried about Joy when she left us. I worried about her when she got homesick. I worried about her hanging out with a boy when we had no idea who or what he was. But this is something different. This is truly scary.

"China's not her home country," Sam grumbles.

"He's a Commie," Vern says, but then he thinks everyone's a Commie.

"It's just love," May says lightly, but I hear worry in her voice. "Girls say and do stupid things when they're in love."

I fold the letter and put it back in its envelope. There's nothing we can do about any of this from so far away, but I begin a chant — something more than a prayer, something more like a desperate plea: *Bring her home, bring her home, bring her home.*

Dominoes

Summer arrives and Joy comes home. We bask in the soft music of her voice. We try to stop ourselves from touching her, but we pat her hand, smooth her hair, and straighten her collar. Her auntie gives her signed movie magazines, colorful headbands, and a pair of purple ostrich mules. I make her favorite home-cooked foods: steamed pork with salted duck eggs, curried tomato beef *lo mein*, chicken wings with black beans, and almond tofu with canned fruit cocktail for dessert. Every day Sam brings her one treat or another: barbecued duck from the Sam Sing Butcher Shop, whipped-cream cake with fresh strawberries from Phoenix Bakery, and pork *bao* from the little place she likes so much on Spring Street.

But how Joy has changed these last nine months! She wears pedal pushers and sleeveless cotton blouses that nip in at her tiny waist. She's lopped off her hair and styled it into a pixie cut. Inside she's changed too. I don't mean that she challenges us or insults us as she

421

did in her last months before she left for Chicago. Rather, she's come back believing that she's more knowledgeable than we are about travel (she's been to Chicago and back on the train, and none of us have been on one in years), about finances (she has her own bank account and a checkbook, while Sam and I still hide our money at home, where the government — or whoever — can't get it), but most of all about China. Oh, the lectures we hear!

She slaps her paws at the gentlest among us, her uncle. If the Boar — with its innocent nature — has a fault, it's that he trusts everyone and will believe almost everything that's told to him, even by strangers, even by swindlers, even by a voice on the radio. Years of listening to anti-Communist broadcasts have forever colored Vern's opinions about the People's Republic of China. But what kind of a target is he? Not a very good one. When Joy proclaims, "Mao has helped the people of China," about all her uncle can do is say, "No freedom there."

"Mao wants the peasants and workers to have the very chances that Mom and Dad want for me," Joy presses adamantly. "For the first time, he's letting people from the countryside go to colleges and universities. And not just boys. He says women should receive 'equal pay for equal work.' "

"You've never been there," Vern says. "You don't know anything about it —"

"I do so know about China. I was in all those China movies when I was a little girl."

422

"China isn't like the movies," her father, who usually stays out of these disagreements, says. Joy doesn't smart-tongue him. It's not because he tries to control her as a proper Chinese father should or that she's an obedient Chinese daughter. Instead, she's like a pearl in his palm — forever precious; to Joy, he's the solid ground on which she walks — forever steady and reliable.

Sensing a momentary lull, May tries to put a final stop to Joy's line of thinking. "China isn't like a movie set. You can't leave it when the cameras stop rolling."

This is one of the harshest things I've ever heard my sister say to Joy, but this most mild of reprimands acts like a nettle in my daughter's heart. Suddenly her attention focuses on May and me — two sisters who have never been apart, who are the closest of friends, and whose bond is deeper than Joy could ever imagine.

"In China, girls don't wear dresses like you and Auntie May want me to wear," she tells me a couple of mornings later as I iron shirts on the screened porch. "You can't wear a dress when you're driving a tractor, you know. Girls don't have to learn how to embroider either. They don't have to go to church or Chinese school. And there's none of that obey, obey, obey stuff that you and Dad are always bugging me about."

"That may be so," I say, "except that they have to obey Chairman Mao. How is that different from obeying the emperor or your parents?"

"In China, there are no wants. Everyone has food to eat." Her response is not an answer, just another slogan that she picked up in one of her classes or from that Joe boy.

"Maybe they can eat, but what about freedom?"

"Mao believes in freedom. Haven't you heard about his new campaign? He's said, 'Let a hundred flowers bloom.' Do you know what that means?" She doesn't wait for me to answer. "He's invited people to criticize the new society —"

"And it's not going to end well."

"Oh, Mom, you're so. . ." She stares at me, considering. Then she says, "You always follow the other birds. You follow Chiang Kai-shek, because people in Chinatown do. And they follow him because they think they have to. Everyone knows he's no better than a thief. He stole money and art as he fled China. Look at how he and his wife live now! So why does America support the Kuomintang and Taiwan? Wouldn't it be better to have ties to China? It's a much bigger country, with a lot more people and resources. Joe says it's better to talk to people than to ignore them."

"Joe, Joe, Joe." I sigh wearily. "We don't even know this Joe and you're listening to him about China? Has he ever been there?"

"No," Joy grudgingly admits, "but he'd like to go. I'd like to go too one day to see where you and Auntie lived in Shanghai and go to our home village."

"Go to mainland China? Let me tell you something. It's not easy for a snake to go back to Hell once he's tasted Heaven. And you are not a snake. You're just a girl who doesn't know anything about it."

"I've been studying —"

"Forget that classroom business. Forget what some boy told you. Go outside and look around. Haven't you noticed the new strangers in Chinatown?"

"There will always be new *lo fan*," she says dismissively.

"They aren't the usual *lo fan*. They're FBI agents." I tell her about one who's recently been walking through Chinatown every day and asking questions. He makes a loop that starts at the International Grocery on Spring, passes Pearl's on Ord, and goes along Broadway to the Central Plaza in New Chinatown, where he visits General Lee's Restaurant. From there he continues to Jack Lee's grocery on Hill, then over to the newest part of New Chinatown across the street to visit the Fong family's businesses, and finally back downtown.

"What are they looking for? The Korean War is over —"

"But the government's fear of Red China hasn't gone away. It's worse than ever. In your school haven't they taught you about the domino theory? One country falls to Communism, then another, and another. These *lo fan* are scared. When they're scared, they do bad things to people like us. That's why we have to support the Generalissimo."

"You worry too much."

"I said the same thing to my mother, but she was right and I was wrong. Bad things are already happening. You just don't know about them because you've been gone." I sigh again. How can I make her understand? "While you were away, the government started something called the Confession Program. It's all across the country, probably in your Chicago too. They're asking, no, trying to scare us into confessing who came here as paper sons. They give people citizenship if they report on their friends, their neighbors, their business associates, and even their family members who came here as paper sons. They want to know who earned money bringing in paper sons. The government talks about the domino effect. Well, here in Chinatown, if you give one name, that also creates a domino effect, which touches not just one family member but all the paper partners and papers sons and relatives and neighbors you know. But what they want most are Communists. If you report that someone is a Communist, then you'll get your citizenship for sure."

"We're all citizens. We aren't guilty of anything."

For years Sam and I have been torn between the American desire to share, be honest, and tell the truth to Joy and our deeply held Chinese belief that you never reveal anything. Our Chinese way has won, and we've kept Sam's and my status, as well as that of her uncles and her grandfather, a secret from our daughter for two very simple reasons: we haven't wanted her to worry and we haven't wanted her to say the wrong thing to the wrong person. She's much older than she was back in kindergarten, but we learned then that even the smallest mistake can have bad consequences.

I put Sam's ironed shirt on a hanger and then sit next to my daughter. "I want to tell you how they're looking for people, so you'll know in case anyone approaches you. They're looking for people who sent tea money back to China —"

"Grandpa Louie did that."

"Exactly. And they're looking for people who've tried — legally — to get their families out of China since it closed. They want to know where people's loyalties lie — in China or in the United States?" I pause to see if she's following me. Then I say, "Our Chinese way of thinking doesn't always apply here in America. We believe that being humble, respectful, and truthful will give us a better understanding of every situation, prevent others from being hurt, and result in an all-good end. That way of thinking could hurt us and many other people now."

I take a deep breath and tell her something I was afraid to write to her. "You remember the Yee family?" Of course she does. She was great friends with the oldest girl, Hazel, and spent plenty of time with the other Yee kids at our union gatherings. "Mr. Yee is a paper son. He brought Mrs. Yee in through Winnipeg."

"He's a paper son?" Joy asks, surprised, maybe impressed.

"He decided to confess so he could stay here with his family, since the four children are American citizens. He told the INS he had brought in his wife using his false status. Now he's an American citizen, but the INS has started deportation proceedings against Mrs. Yee, because she's a paper wife. They still have two children at home who are not yet ten years old. What will they do without their mama? The INS wants to send her back to Canada. At least she won't be going to China."

"Maybe she'd be better off in China."

When I hear this, I don't know who's talking — a silly parrot who must repeat everything this Joe has told her or from somewhere deep inside an eruption of her blood-mother's deliberate childish stupidity.

"That's Hazel's mother you're talking about! Is that how you would want them to feel if *I* was sent back to China?" I wait for an answer. When she doesn't give me one, I get up, fold and put away the ironing board, and go check on Vern.

That night Sam carries Vern out to the couch so we can have dinner and watch *Gunsmoke* together. The evening's hot, so dinner is cool and simple — just big wedges of watermelon made as cold as possible in our Frigidaire. We're trying to follow what Miss Kitty is telling Matt Dillon when Joy starts up about the People's Republic of China all over again. For nine months her absence felt like a hole in our family. We missed the sound of her voice and her beautiful face. But during that time we filled that hole with the television, with quiet conversation among the four of us, and with little projects that May and I did together. After Joy's been home for two weeks, it's like she takes up too much space with her opinions, her desire for attention, her need to tell us how wrong and backward we are, and the practiced way she has always divided her auntie and me, when all we want to do is find out if the marshal is ever going to kiss that Miss Kitty or not.

Sam, usually accepting of whatever comes out of his daughter's mouth, finally can't take any more and asks in Sze Yup in his quietest and calmest manner, "Are you ashamed of being Chinese? Because a proper Chinese daughter would be quiet and let her parents, auntie, and uncle watch their show."

It is the absolute wrong question, because suddenly terrible things pour out of Joy's mouth. She mocks our frugality: "Being Chinese? I don't see why being Chinese means having to save gallon-size soy sauce containers to turn into waste bins." She makes fun of me: "Only superstitious Chinese believe in the zodiac. Oh, Tiger this, Tiger that." She hurts her aunt and uncle: "And what about arranged marriages? Look at Auntie May, married forever to someone who . . . who . . ." She hesitates as we all have from time to time until she settles on "never touches her with love or affection." Her face rumples into an expression of distaste. "And look at how you all live together."

Listening to her, I hear May and me twenty years ago. I'm sad for how we treated our parents, but when Joy starts hurting her father . . .

"And if Chinese means being like you . . . The food you cook in the café stinks your clothes. Your customers insult you. And the dishes you make are too greasy, too salty, and have too much MSG."

These words hit Sam hard. Unlike May and me, he's loved Joy without regret, without conditions, without once holding back his heart.

"Take a look in the mirror," he says slowly. "What do you think you are? What do you think the *lo fan* see when they look at you? You're nothing but a piece of *jook sing* — hollow bamboo."

"Dad, you should speak to me in English. You've lived here for almost twenty years. Can't you speak it yet?" She blinks a few times and then says, "You're just so . . . so . . . so FOB."

The silence in the living room is cruel and deep. Realizing what she's done, she tilts her head, ruffles her pixie cut, and then smiles in what I immediately recognize as May's from long ago. It's a smile that says, *I'm naughty, I'm disobedient, but you can't help but love me.* I see, even if Sam can't, that all this has less to do with Mao, Chiang Kai-shek, Korea, the FBI, or how we've chosen to live our lives these last twenty years than it does with how our daughter feels about her family. May and I once thought Mama and Baba were old-fashioned, but Joy is embarrassed by and ashamed of us.

"Sometimes you think you have all of tomorrow ahead of you," Mama often said. "When the sun is shining, think of the time it won't be, because even when you're sitting in your house with the doors shut, misfortune can fall from above." I ignored her when she was alive and I didn't pay enough attention as I got older, but after all these years I have to accept that Mama's foresight is what saved us. Without her hidden savings, we all would have died right there in Shanghai. Some deep instinct motivated her and kept her going when May and I were nearly paralyzed with fear. She was like a gazelle who, under hopeless circumstances, still tried to save her calves from the lion. I know I have to protect my daughter — from herself, from this Joe boy and his romantic ideas about Red China, from making the kinds of mistakes that so dampened May's and my choices — but I don't know how.

I'm going to Pearl's to pick up takeout for Vern when I see the FBI agent stop Uncle Charley on the sidewalk. I pass the two men — with Uncle Charley ignoring me as though he doesn't know me — and enter the café, leaving the door wide open. Inside, Sam and our workers go about their business while listening as hard as they can to what floats through the door. May comes out of her office, and we linger by the counter, pretending to talk but watching and listening to everything.

"So, Charley, you went back to China," the agent says suddenly in Sze Yup in a voice so loud I look at my sister in surprise. It's as though he wants not only to have us hear what he's saying but also to let us know that he's fluent in the dialect of our district.

"I went to China," Uncle Charley admits. We can barely hear him, his voice quavers so. "I lost my savings, and I came back here."

"We hear you've said bad things about Chiang Kai-shek."

"I haven't."

"People say you have."

"What people?"

The agent doesn't answer that question. Instead he asks, "Isn't it true you blame Chiang Kai-shek for losing your money?"

Charley scratches at his rash-covered neck and sucks on his lips.

The agent waits and then asks, "Where are your papers?"

Uncle Charley glances through the plate-glass window, looking for help, for encouragement or possible escape.

The agent — a big *lo fan* with sandy-colored hair and freckles on his nose and cheeks — smiles and says, "Yes, let's go inside. I'd like to meet your *family*."

The agent enters the café, and Uncle Charley follows with his head hung down. The *lo fan* walks right up to Sam, flashes his badge, and says in Sze Yup, "I'm Special Agent Jack Sanders. You're Sam Louie, right?" When Sam nods, the agent goes on. "I always say there's no point in wasting time on these things. Someone told us you used to buy the *China Daily News*."

Sam stands absolutely still, measuring the stranger, thinking about his answer, emptying his face of emotion. The few customers, who can't possibly understand the words but certainly know that the flashing badge can't mean anything good, seemingly hold their breath to see what Sam will do.

"I bought the paper for my father," Sam says in Sze Yup, and I see the disappointment on our customers' faces that they aren't going to be able to follow this as closely as they'd like. "He died five years ago."

"That paper is sympathetic to the Reds."

"My father read it sometimes, but he subscribed to *Chung Sai Yat Po*."

"Seems like your father was sympathetic to Mao though."

"Not at all. Why would he support Mao?"

"Then why did he buy *China Reconstructs* too? And why have you continued to buy it after his passing?"

I have a sudden desire to use the toilet. Sam can't possibly answer with the truth — that his wife's and sister-in-law's faces have appeared on the covers of those magazines. Or does the FBI man already know that those are our faces? Or does he look at the pretty girls in the drab green uniforms with red stars on their caps and think all Chinese look alike?

"I'm told that in your living room above your couch you have pages from the magazine taped to the wall — pictures of the Great Wall and the Summer Palace."

This means someone — a neighbor, a friend, a competitor who has been inside our home — has reported this. Why didn't we take the pictures down after Father died?

"In his last months, my father liked to look at those attractions."

"Maybe he had so much sympathy for Red China he wanted to go back home —"

"My father was an American citizen. He was born here."

"Then show me his documents —"

"He's dead," Sam repeats, "and I don't have them here."

"Then perhaps I should pay a visit to your home, or would you prefer to come to our office? That way you can bring your documents too. I want to believe you, but you have to prove your innocence."

"Prove my innocence or prove I'm a citizen?"

"They are the same, Mr. Louie."

When I get home with Vern's lunch, I don't say anything to him or to Joy. I don't want them to worry. When Joy asks if she can go out that night, I say as lightly as I can, "Fine. Just try to be back by midnight." She thinks she's finally triumphed over her mother, but I want her out of the house.

As soon as Sam and May come home, we strip the pictures the agent talked about off the walls. Sam bags up every copy of the *China Daily News* that my father-in-law saved because of some article or other. I order May to go into her drawer and pull out the magazine covers that Z.G. painted of the two of us.

"I don't think this is necessary," May says.

I respond sharply: "Please, for once, don't argue with me." When May doesn't move, I sigh impatiently. "They're only pictures on magazine covers. Now if you won't get them, I will."

May purses her mouth and turns to go out to the screened porch. Once she's left, I look for photographs that I think might be — and here's a word I never thought I'd use — incriminating.

While Sam makes another tour through the house, May and I take what we've gathered to burn in the incinerator. I set fire to my pile of photographs and wait for May to throw in the magazine covers, which she hugs to her chest. When she doesn't move, I wrest them from her arms and drop them in the fire. As I watch the face — *my* face — that Z.G. so beautifully and perfectly painted curl in the flames, I wonder why we let any of these things creep into the house. I know the answer.

Sam, May, and I are no better than Father Louie. We've become American with our clothes, our food, our language, our desire for Joy's education and future, but not once in all these years have we stopped missing our home country.

"They don't want us here," I say softly, my eyes on the flames. "They've never wanted us. They're going to try to trick us, but we need to trick them in return."

"Maybe Sam should confess and get it over with," May suggests. "That way he'll get his citizenship and we won't have to worry about any of this."

"You know it's not enough for him just to confess his own status. He'll have to expose others — Uncle Wilburt, Uncle Charley, me —"

"You should all confess together. Then you can all get your legal citizenship. Don't you want it?"

"Of course I want it. But what if the government is lying?"

"Why would the government lie?"

"When *hasn't* it lied?" And then, "What if they decide to deport us? If Sam is proved to be illegal, then I'll be eligible for deportation too."

My sister considers that. Then she says, "I don't want to lose you. I promised Father Louie that I wouldn't let them send you away. Sam has to confess for Joy, for you, for all of us. This is a chance for amnesty, to bring the family together, and to rid ourselves finally of our secrets."

I don't understand why my sister doesn't — won't — see the problems, but then she's married to an actual citizen, came here as his legal wife, and isn't facing the same threat that Sam and I are.

My sister puts an arm around my shoulder and pulls me close. "Don't worry, Pearl," she reassures me, as if I'm the *moy moy* and she's the *jie jie*. "We'll hire a lawyer to take care of things —"

"No! We've gone through this before, you and I, at Angel Island. We won't let them do anything to Sam, to me, to any of us. We're going to work together to turn their accusations against them, like we did on Angel Island. We've got to confuse them. What's important is to keep our story straight."

"Yes, that's true," Sam says, stepping through the darkness and feeding another stack of newspapers and memories into the incinerator. "But more than anything we have to prove we're the most loyal Americans who ever existed."

May doesn't like this, but she's my *moy moy* and a sister-in-law, and she has to obey.

Joy — whom we've told as little as possible, believing her ignorance helps hold our story together — and May aren't called in for questioning, and no one comes to the house to interview Vern. But over the next four weeks, Sam and I — often together, so I can translate for my husband when we're transferred from Special Agent Sanders to Agent Mike Billings, who works for the INS, speaks not one word of any Chinese dialect, and is about as friendly as Chairman Plumb all those years ago — are called in for numerous interrogations. I'm questioned about my home village, a place I've never been. Sam's questioned about why his so-called parents left him in China when he was seven. We're questioned about Father Louie's birth. We're asked — with condescending smiles — if we're acquainted with anyone who earned money selling paper slots.

"Someone profited from this," Billings says knowingly. "Just tell us who."

Our responses don't help his investigation. We tell him we collected tinfoil during the war and sold war bonds. We tell him I shook hands with Madame Chiang Kai-shek.

"Do you have a photograph to prove it?" Billings asks, but of all the photos we took that day, that's the one we missed.

At the beginning of August, Billings changes direction. "If your so-called father was actually born here, then why did he keep sending funds back to China even after he should have stopped?"

I don't wait for Sam's response but answer this myself. "The money went to his ancestral village. His family has fifteen generations there."

"Is that why your husband has continued to send money out of the country?"

"We do what we can for our relatives who are trapped in a bad place," I translate for Sam.

At that Billings comes around the table, pulls Sam up by the lapels, and shouts in his face, "Admit it. You send money because you're a Communist!"

I don't have to translate this sentence for Sam to understand what the man is saying, but I do in the same even voice I've used all along to show that nothing Billings says will throw us from our story, our confidence, and our truth. But suddenly Sam — who has not been himself since the night Joy made fun of him for his cooking and his English and has not slept well since the day Agent Sanders entered Pearl's Coffee Shop — jumps up, sticks his finger in Billings's face, and calls *him* a Communist. Then they're shouting back and forth — No, you're a Communist! No, *you're* a Communist! — and I'm sitting there echoing the accusations in both languages. Billings gets angrier and angrier, but Sam is steady and firm. Finally, Billings clamps his mouth shut, collapses in his chair, and glares at us. He has no evidence against Sam, just as Sam has no evidence against the INS agent.

"If you don't want to confess," he says, "and you won't say who's sold false papers in Chinatown, then perhaps you can tell us a little something about your neighbors."

Sam serenely recites an aphorism, which I translate: "Sweep the snow in front of your own doorstep, and do not bother about the frost on top of another family's house."

We seem to be winning, but in twisting and in struggle, thin arms will not win out over thick legs. The FBI and INS question Uncle Wilburt and Uncle Charley, who refuse to confess, say anything about us, or rat out Father Louie, who sold them their papers. *Those who don't push the drowning dogs are already the decent ones.*

When Uncle Fred brings his family to the house for Sunday dinner, we ask Joy to take the little girls outside to play so he can tell us about Agent Billings's visit to his home in Silver Lake. Fred's stint in the service, his college years, and his dental practice have nearly erased his accent. He's lived a good life with Mariko and their half-and-half daughters. His face is full and round, and he has a bit of a belly.

"I told him I'm a veteran, that I served in the Army and fought for the United States," he recounts. "He looks at me and says, 'And you got your citizenship.' Well, of course I got my citizenship! That's what the government promised. Then he pulls out a file and invites me to take a look at it. It's my immigration file from Angel Island! Remember all that stuff from our coaching books? Well, it's all in the file. It has information about the old man and Yen-yen. It lists all of our birth dates and outlines our whole story, since we're all connected. He asks me why I didn't tell the truth about my so-called brothers when I enlisted. I didn't tell him anything."

He takes Mariko's hand. She's white with the fear we all feel. "I don't mind if they pick on us," he continues. "But when they go after my children, who were born here . . ." He shakes his head in disgust. "Last week Bess came home crying. Her fifth-grade teacher showed a film to the class on the Communist threat. It showed Russians in fur hats and Chinese, well, looking like us. At the end of the film, the narrator asked the students to call the FBI or the CIA if they saw anyone who looked suspicious. Who looked suspicious in the class? My Bess. Now her friends won't play with her. I have to worry about what's going to happen to Eleanor and little Mamie too. I remind the girls that they're named after the First Ladies. They don't have to be afraid."

But of course they have to be afraid. We're all afraid.

When you're held underwater, you think only of air. I remember how I felt about Shanghai in the days after our lives changed — how streets that had once seemed exciting suddenly stank of nightsoil, how beautiful women suddenly were nothing more than girls with three holes, how all the money and prosperity suddenly rendered everything forlorn, dissolute, and futile. The way I see Los Angeles and China-town during these difficult and frightening days couldn't be more different. The palm trees, the fruits and vegetables in my garden, the geraniums in pots in front of stores and on porches all seem to shimmer and shiver with life, even in the heat of summer. I look down streets and I see promise. Instead of smog, corruption, and ugliness, I see magnificence, freedom, and openness. I can't bear that the government is persecuting us with its terrible — and God help me, true — accusations about our citizenship, but I can bear even less the thought that my family and I might lose this place. Yes, it's only Chinatown, but it's my home, our home.

In these moments, I regret the years of homesickness and loneliness I've felt for Shanghai: the way I turned it into so many golden-hued remembrances of people, places, and food that, as Betsy has written me so many times, no longer exist and will never again exist. I berate myself: How could I not have seen what was right in front of me all these years? How could I not have sucked in all the sweetness instead of pining for memories that were only ashes and dust?

In desperation, I call Betsy in Washington to see if there's anything her father can do for us. Although he's suffering from his own persecution, Betsy promises he'll look into Sam's case.

"My father born San Flancisco-ah," Sam says in his badly accented English.

Four days have passed since we had dinner with Fred, and now Sanders and Billings have come unannounced to our house. Sam perches on the end of Father Louie's recliner. The other men sit on the couch. I'm seated on a straight-backed chair, wishing that Sam would let me speak for him. I have the same feeling I did when the Green Gang thug gave May and me his ultimatum in my family's salon all those years ago: *This is it*.

"Then prove it. Show me his birth certificate," Agent Billings demands.

"My father born San Flancisco-ah," Sam insists firmly.

"*San Flancisco-ah*," Billings repeats in a mocking tone. "Of course it would be San Francisco, because of the earthquake and fire. We aren't stupid, Mr. Louie. It's said that for there to be so many Chinese born in the United States before 1906, every Chinese woman who was here back then would have had to have given birth to five hundred sons. Even if by some miracle that could have happened, how is it that only sons were born and no girls? Did you kill them?"

"I wasn't born yet," Sam answers, switching to Sze Yup. "I didn't live here —"

"I have your file from Angel Island. We want you to look at some photographs." Billings puts two photos on the coffee table. The first is of the little boy that Chairman Plumb tried to trick me with all those years ago. The other shows Sam upon his arrival at Angel Island, in 1937. With the two images side by side, it's clear that the people in them can't possibly be the same. "Confess, and then tell us about your fake brothers. Don't let your wife and daughter suffer because of loyalty to men who won't come forward to help you."

Sam examines the photographs, leans back in the recliner, and says, his voice shaking, "I Father's real son. Brother Vern will say you."

It's as if his iron fan is collapsing before my eyes, but I don't know why. When I get up, move to behind his chair, and put my hands on the backrest so he'll know I'm there, I understand why. Joy stands in the kitchen doorway directly in Sam's line of vision. He's afraid for her and embarrassed for himself.

"Daddy," Joy cries as she scurries into the room. "Do what they ask. Tell them the truth. You have nothing to hide." Our daughter knows not one thing about what the truth actually is, but she's so innocent — and here, I'll say it, stupid like her auntie — that she says, "If you tell the truth, good things will happen. Isn't that what you taught me?"

"See, even your daughter wants you to tell the truth," Billings prods.

But Sam doesn't waver from his story. "My father born San Flancisco-ah."

Joy continues to cry and plead. Vern whimpers in the other room. I stand there helpless. And my sister is out working on a movie or shopping for a new dress or I don't know what.

Billings opens his briefcase, pulls out a piece of paper, and hands it to Sam, who can't read the English words. "If you sign this paper saying you came illegally," he says, "we'll take away your citizenship, which isn't real to begin with. Once you've signed the paper and confessed, we'll give you immunity, new citizenship, *real* citizenship, on condition that you tell us about *every* friend, relative, and neighbor you know who came illegally. We're particularly interested in the other paper sons your so-called father brought in."

"He dead. What it matter now?"

"But we have his file. How could he have so many sons? How could he have so many partners? Where are they now? And don't bother telling us about Fred Louie. We know all about him. He got his citizenship fair and square. Just tell us about the others and where to find them."

"What you gonna do to them?"

"Don't worry about that. Only worry about yourself."

"And you give me papers?"

"You'll get legal citizenship, like I said," Billings says. "But if you don't confess, then we'll have to deport you back to China. Don't you and your wife want to stay with your daughter, so you can keep her out of trouble?"

Joy's shoulders pull back in surprise as she hears this.

"She may be an A student, but she goes to the University of Chicago," Billings goes on. "Everyone knows that's a den of Communism. Do you know the kind of people she's been seeing? Do you know what she's been doing? She's a member of the Chinese Students Democratic Christian Association."

"That's a Christian group," I say, but when I glance at my daughter, a shadow crosses her face.

"They say they're Christian, Mrs. Louie, but it's a Communist front. Your daughter's connection to that group is why we looked into your husband's case in the first place. She's been picketing and getting people to sign petitions. If you help us, we can overlook these infractions. She was born here, and she's just a kid." He looks over at Joy, who weeps in the middle of our living room. "She probably didn't know what she was doing, but if the two of you are sent back to China, how will you help her? Do you want to ruin her life too?"

Billings nods to Sanders, who stands. "We're going to leave you now, Mr. Louie, but we can't let these discussions go on much longer. Either you tell us what we want to know or we're going to take a closer look at your kid. Understand?"

After they leave, Joy runs to her father's chair, sinks beside it, and sobs in his lap. "Why are they doing this to us? Why? Why?"

I kneel next to my daughter, put my arms around her, and search Sam's face, looking for the hope and strength he's always carried there.

"I left home to earn a living," Sam says, his voice far away, his eyes peering into the darkness of despair. "I came to America to make a chance for myself. I did the best I could —"

"Of course you did."

He looks at me in resignation. "I don't want to be deported back to China," he says hopelessly.

"You won't have to go back." I put a hand on his arm. "But if it comes to that, I'll go with you."

His eyes shift to mine. "You're a good woman, but what about Joy?"

"I'll go with you too, Daddy. I know all about China, and I'm not afraid."

As we huddle together, something Z.G. said long ago comes into my mind. I remember him talking about *ai kuo*, the love for your country, and *ai jen*, the emotion you feel for the person you love. Sam fought fate and left China, and even after everything that's happened he hasn't stopped believing in America, but he loves Joy above all else.

"I okay," he says in English, patting his daughter's head. Then he switches back to his native Sze Yup. "You two go see about Uncle Vern. Hear him in there? He needs help. He's scared."

Joy and I stand up. I wipe my daughter's tears. As Joy starts for Vern's bedroom, Sam grabs my hand. One of his fingers loops up and through my jade bracelet, holding me in place, showing me how much he loves me. "Don't worry, Zhen Long," he says. When he releases me, he stares at his hand for a second, rubbing his daughter's tears between his fingers.

Vern is terribly upset when I get to his room. He mumbles incoherently about Mao's Let a Hundred Flowers Bloom and how the Chairman's now condemning to death everyone he encouraged to criticize the government. Vern's so confused he can't separate that from what he overheard in our living room. As he rambles and rails — and he's so distressed that he's messed his diaper and every time he squirms or pounds his fists on the bed, a disgusting odor fills my nostrils — I wish my sister were here. I wish for maybe the ten thousandth time that she would take care of her husband. It takes Joy and me a long time to calm Vern and get him cleaned. When we leave the room, Sam's gone.

"We need to talk about this group you're a member of," I say to Joy, "but let's wait until your father returns."

She doesn't defer to me or apologize. She says with the absolute certainty of youth and being raised in America, "We're all citizens, and it's a free country. They can't do anything to us."

I sigh. "Later. We'll do this later with your father."

I head to my bedroom bathroom to get the smell of Vern off me. I wash my hands and my face in the basin, and when I lift my head I see in the mirror's reflection over my shoulder into the closet . . .

"Sam!" I scream.

I run to the closet, where Sam hangs. I put my arms around his swaying legs and lift them to take the weight off his neck. Everything turns black before my eyes, my heart scatters like light dust, and my ears buzz with my horrified screams.

The Boundless Human Ocean

I don't let go of Sam until Joy gets a stool and a knife and cuts him down. I don't leave his side when the people come and take him to the funeral parlor. I give Sam's body as much care as possible, touching him with all the love and tenderness I couldn't show him when he was alive. Then May picks me up from the funeral parlor and takes me home. In the car, she says, "You and Sam were like a pair of mandarin ducks, always together. Like a pair of chopsticks, evenly matched, always in harmony." I thank her for the traditional words, but they don't help me.

I stay up all night. I hear Vern tossing in the next room and May quietly comforting my daughter on the screened porch, but eventually the house and everyone in it stills. *Fifteen buckets drawing water from the well, seven moving up and eight going down*, meaning I'm filled with anxiety, doubts, and an absolute inability to fall asleep, where my dreams will haunt me. I stand at the window, a slight breeze ruffling my nightgown. The moonlight feels as though it shines on me alone. It has been said that marriages are arranged by Heaven, that destiny will bring even the most distantly separated people together, that all is settled before birth, and no matter how much we wander from our paths, no matter how our fortunes change — for good or bad — all we can do is accomplish the decree of fate. This, in the end, is our blessing and our heartbreak.

Regrets scorch my skin and burrow into my heart. I didn't do enough of the husband-wife thing with Sam. I looked at him too often as a mere rickshaw puller. I let my longing for the past make him feel that he was never enough, that our life together was never enough, that Los Angeles was never enough. Worst, I didn't help him enough in his final days. I should have fought harder against the FBI, the INS, and this whole immigration mess. Why didn't I see that he could no longer carry the weight of our burdens across his iron fan?

In the early morning, avoiding the screened porch, I go out the front door and around to the back of the house. I know that too many suicides haunt our community, but it feels like Sam's death has added a new grain of salt to the boundless human ocean of misery and sorrow. Beyond my rose-covered chain-link fence, I imagine my neighbors languishing and expressing the sorrows of the ages. In that moment of quiet and grief I know what I have to do.

I go back to my room, find a photograph of Sam, and take it to the family altar that he cared for in the living room. I place his picture next to those of Yen-yen and

Father. I look at the other things Sam placed on the altar to represent the others we've lost: my parents, his parents, brothers and sisters, and our son. I hope for Sam that his version of the afterworld exists and that he's with all of them now, looking down from the Viewing Terrace, watching me, Joy, May, and Vern. I light incense and bow three times. No matter what I feel about my one God, I promise that I'll do this every day until I die and I meet Sam either in his Heaven or in mine.

I'm a one-Goder, but I'm Chinese too, so I follow both traditions for Sam's funeral. A Chinese funeral — that most significant of rites — is the last time we show respect to the person who's left us, give him the honor to save face, and tell the young about the accomplishments and deeds of their newest ancestor. I want all that for Sam. I choose the suit he'll wear to rest in his coffin. I place photographs of Joy and me in his pockets, so he'll have us with him when he goes to Chinese Heaven. I make sure that Joy, May, Vern, and I all wear black — not Chinese white. We say prayers of thanks for the gift of Sam, blessings and forgiveness for the living, and mercy for all. There's no brass band, just Bertha Hom at the organ, playing "Amazing Grace," "Nearer, My God, to Thee," and "America the Beautiful." Then we have a simple, modest, mournful banquet at Soochow of five tables — just fifty people, minuscule compared with Father Louie's funeral, even smaller than Yen-yen's memorial, all a result of the fear our neighbors, friends, and customers feel. *You can always count on people to crowd your party when you are in glory, but you should never dream of people sending you charcoal in the snow.*

I sit at the main table between my sister and my daughter. They do and say all the right things, but both of them ooze guilt: May for not being there when it happened, Joy for believing that she caused her father's suicide. I know I should tell them not to feel these things. No one, *no one*, could have predicted Sam would do this crazy thing. But in doing it, he released Joy, the uncles, and me from further investigation. As Agent Billings told me when he came by the house after Sam died, "With your husband and father-in-law gone, we can't prove anything one way or the other. And it turns out we may have been wrong about that group your daughter joined. This has to be good news for you, but a little advice: when your daughter goes back to school in September, tell her to stay away from *all* Chinese organizations, just to be on the safe side." I looked at him and said, "My father-in-law was born in San Francisco. My husband was always a citizen."

How could I be so clear with the INS man but not know how to talk to my sister or console my daughter? I know they're both in pain, but I can't help them. I need *them* to help *me*. But even when they try — by bringing me cups of tea, by showing me their red and puffy eyes, by sitting on my bed as I weep — I find myself filled with immense sadness and . . . rage. Why did my daughter have to join that group? Why didn't she show her father proper respect in his last few weeks? Why did my sister always encourage Joy's American side about clothes and haircuts and

451

attitudes? Why didn't my sister help Sam and me more during these difficulties? Why didn't she take care of her husband — for all these years but especially on the day of Sam's death? If she'd been taking care of him, as a proper wife should, then I would have been able to stop Sam. I know this is just my grief speaking. It's easier to feel anger at them than agony at Sam's death.

Violet and her husband, also at our table, pack up the leftover food for me to take home. Uncle Wilburt says good-bye. Uncle Fred, Mariko, and the girls go home. Uncle Charley lingers for a long time, but what can he say? What can any of them say? I nod, shake their hands in the American way, and thank them for coming, doing my best to be a proper widow. A widow . . .

During the mourning period, people are supposed to visit, bring food, and play dominoes, but just as with the funeral, most of our friends and neighbors stay away. The gossips smack their lips, but they don't understand that my troubles could become their troubles at any time. Only Violet dares to visit. For the first time in my life I'm grateful that there's someone besides May to comfort me.

In so many ways Violet — with her job and her house in Silver Lake — is more assimilated than we are, but she's taking a risk coming here, since she and Rowland have more to be afraid of than Sam and I ever did. After all, Violet and her family were trapped here when China closed. Violet's and Rowland's jobs — which once seemed so impressive — now make them targets.

Perhaps they're spies left here to collect the United States' technology and knowledge. And yet she overcomes her fear to see me.

"Sam was a good Ox," Violet says. "He had integrity and bore the burdens of righteousness. He followed the rules of nature, patiently pushing the wheel of fate. He was not afraid of his destiny. He knew what he had to do to save you and Joy. An Ox will always do whatever is needed to protect his family's welfare —"

"My sister doesn't believe in the Chinese zodiac," May cuts in.

I don't know why she says this. Sure, there was a time when I didn't believe in these things, but that was a long time ago. I know in my heart that my sister is forever a Sheep, that I'm forever a Dragon, that Joy is forever a Tiger, and that my husband was an Ox — dependable, methodical, calm, and, as Violet said, the bearer of so many burdens. This comment, like so much of what comes out of May's mouth anymore, shows how little she knows about me. Why haven't I seen it before?

Violet doesn't react to May. Instead, she pats my knee and recites an old saying. "All things light and pure float upward to become Heaven."

In my life, no three miles have been flat and no three days have had sun. I've been brave in the past, but now I'm beyond devastated. My grief is like dense clouds that cannot be dispersed. I can't think beyond the blackness of my clothes and heart.

Later that evening — after Vern has been fed and his lights turned out and Joy has gone out with a couple of the Yee girls to talk and drink tea — May knocks on the door to my room. I get up and answer it. I'm wearing a nightgown, my hair is a mess, and my face is splotched from mourning. My sister wears a slim sheath of emerald green satin, her hair is teased into an improbably high bouffant, and diamond and jade earrings dangle from her ears. She's going somewhere. I don't bother to ask where.

"The second cook didn't show up at the café," she says. "What do you want me to do?"

"I don't care. Whatever you decide is fine."

"I know this is a hard time for you, and I'm sorry about that. I really am. But I need you. You don't understand the pressure I have now with the café, Vern, the responsibility for the house, and my business. Things are so busy right now."

I listen as she wonders aloud how much to charge a production company for extras, costumes, and props like wheelbarrows, food carts, and rickshaws.

"I always base my rentals on a ten percent value of the article," May continues. I understand she's trying to get me to come out of my room, reconnect with life, help her as I always have, but truly, I don't know one damn thing about her rental business, and right now *I don't care*. "They want to rent some pieces for several months, perhaps as much as a year, and some of what they want — like the rickshaws — is irreplaceable. So how much do you think I should charge to rent them? They each cost about two hundred and fifty dollars, so I could charge twenty-five dollars a week. But I'm thinking I should charge more, because where will we buy replacements if something happens to them?"

"Whatever you want to do is fine with me."

I start to close the door, but she grabs it and pulls it open. "Why don't you let me in? You could take a shower. I could do your hair. Maybe you could put on a dress and we could take a walk —"

"I don't want to upset your plans," I say, but I'm thinking, *How many times in the past did she leave me at home with our parents in Shanghai, in the apartment with Yen-yen, and now with Vern so that she could go out to do . . . whatever it is she does?*

"You need to rejoin the living —"

"It's only been two weeks —"

May gives me a hard stare. "You need to come out and be with your family. Joy will be going back to Chicago soon. She needs you to talk to her —"

"Don't tell me how to mother my daughter —"

She takes hold of my wrist, wrapping her hand around Mama's bracelet. "Pearl." She gives my wrist a little shake. "I know this is terrible for you. A great sadness. But you're still young. You're still beautiful. You have your daughter. You have me. And you've had *everything*. Look how Joy loves you. Look how Sam loved you."

"Yes, and he's dead."

"I know, I know," she says sympathetically. "I was trying to be helpful. I didn't think he'd kill himself."

Her words hang like elegantly calligraphed characters in the air before my eyes, the silence thick as I read

455

them again and again, until finally I ask, "What do you mean?"

"Nothing. I didn't mean anything."

My sister has never been a good liar.

"May!"

"All right! All right!" She lets go of my wrist, raises both of her hands, and shakes them in frustration. Then she pivots on one of her high heels and sways into the living room. I'm right behind her. She stops, turns, and quickly spills the words. "I told Agent Sanders about Sam."

"You did what?" My ears refuse to understand the depth of her betrayal.

"I told the FBI about Sam. I thought it would help."

"Why would you do that?" I ask, still not willing to believe what she's saying.

"I did it for Father Louie. Before he died, he seemed to sense what was coming. He made me promise to do whatever was necessary to keep you and Sam safe. He didn't want the family separated —"

"He didn't want Vern to be left only with you," I say. But this is far off the point. What she's saying about Sam can't be true. Please let it not be true.

"I'm sorry. Pearl, I'm so sorry." And with that, May lets the rest of her confession fall from her lips in a jumble. "Agent Sanders used to walk with me sometimes when I was coming back to the house after work. He asked about Joy, and he wanted to know about you and Sam too. He said this was an opportunity for amnesty. He said if I told him the truth about Sam's paper-son status, then we could work together to get his citizenship and yours. I thought if I could show Agent Sanders I was a good American, then he would see that you were good Americans too. Don't you see? I had to protect Joy, but I was also afraid of losing you, my sister, the only one in my life who's loved me for who I am, who's stood by me and taken care of me. If you'd just done as I'd said — hired a lawyer and confessed — then the two of you could have become citizens. You never again would have had to be afraid, and you and I never again would have had to worry about being separated. Instead, you and Sam continued to lie. The idea that Sam would hang himself never entered my mind."

I've loved my sister from the moment she was born, but for too long I've been like a moon spinning around her entrancing planet. Now I whirl away as the anger of a lifetime boils out of me. My sister, my stupid, stupid sister.

"Get out."

She stares at me in that Sheep way of hers — complacent and uncomprehending.

"I live here, Pearl. Where do you want me to go?"

"Get out!" I scream.

"No!" It's one of the few times in our lives that she's so directly disobeyed me. Then, in a heavy but raspy voice, she repeats, "No. You're going to listen to me for once. Amnesty made sense. It was the *safe* thing to do."

I shake my head, refusing to listen. "You've ruined my life."

"No, Sam ruined his life."

"That's so like you, May, placing fault on someone other than yourself."

"I never would have spoken to Agent Sanders if I'd thought there was any danger to Sam or you. I can't believe you'd think that about me." She seems to gather strength, standing there in her emerald satin. "Agent Sanders and the other one gave you every chance —"

"If you call intimidation a chance."

"Sam was a paper son," May goes on. "He was here illegally. For the rest of my life I'm going to blame myself for Sam's suicide, but that doesn't change the fact that what I did was right for the both of you and for our family. All you and Sam had to do was tell the truth —"

"Didn't you consider what the consequences of that would be?"

"Of course I did! I'll say it again: Agent Sanders said that if you and Sam confessed, then you'd receive amnesty. *Amnesty!* Your papers would have been stamped, you would have become legal citizens, and that would have been that. But you and Sam were too stubborn, too country-Chinese and ignorant to be Americans."

"So now you're blaming me for everything that's happened?"

"I don't want to say that, Pearl."

But she just did say it! I'm so angry I can't think straight. "I want you to move out of my house," I seethe. "I never want to see you again. Not ever."

"You've always blamed me for everything." Her voice is calm, *calm.*

"Because everything that's been bad in my life *is* because of you."

My sister stares at me, waiting, as if she's ready to hear what I have to say. If that's what she wants . . .

"Baba loved you more," I say. "He had to sit next to you. Mama loved you so much she had to sit right across from you, so she could stare at her beautiful daughter and not the one with the ugly red face."

"You've always suffered from red-eye disease." My sister sniffs, as though my accusations are insignificant. "You've always been jealous and envious of me, but *you* were the one who was cherished by Mama and Baba. Who loved who more? I'll tell you. Baba liked to look at *you*. Mama had to sit next to *you*. The three of you always spoke in Sze Yup. You had your own secret language. You always left me out."

This freezes me in place for a moment. I've always believed they spoke to me in Sze Yup to shield May from this or that, but what if they'd been doing it as an endearment, as a way of showing I was special to them?

"No!" I say as much to her as to myself. "That's not how it was."

"Baba cared enough about you to criticize you. Mama cared enough about you to buy you pearl cream. She never gave me anything precious — not pearl cream, not her jade bracelet. They sent you to college. No one asked if I wanted to go! And even though you went, did you do anything with it? Look at your friend Violet. She did something, but you? No. Everyone wants to come to America for the opportunities. They came your way, but you didn't take them. You preferred

459

to be a victim, a *fu yen*. But what does it matter who Baba and Mama loved more or whether or not I had the same opportunities as you? They're dead, and that was a long time ago."

But it isn't to me, and I know it isn't to May either. Just consider how our competition for our parents' affection has been repeated in our battle for Joy. Now, after our whole lives together, we say what we truly feel. The tones of our Wu dialect rise and fall, shrill, caustic, and accusatory as we empty all the evil we've stored up on each other's heads, blaming each other for every single wrong and misfortune that's happened to us. I haven't forgotten about Sam's death and I know she hasn't either, but neither of us can help ourselves. Maybe it's easier to fight about the injustices we've carried for years than to face May's betrayal and Sam's suicide.

"Did Mama know you were pregnant?" I ask, voicing a suspicion I've harbored for years. "She loved you. She made me promise to take care of you, my *moy moy*, my little sister. And I have. I brought you to Angel Island, where I was humiliated. And since then I've been stuck in Chinatown, taking care of Vern, and working here in the house while you've been in *Haolaiwu*, going to parties, having fun, doing whatever you do with those men." Then, because I'm so angry and hurt, I say something I know I'll regret forever, but there's enough truth in it that it flies out of my mouth before I can stop it. "I had to take care of your daughter even when my own baby died."

"You've always been bitter about having to care for Joy, but you've also done everything possible to keep me away from her. When she was a baby, you left her in the apartment with Sam when I took you out for walks —"

"That wasn't the reason." (Or was it?)

"Then you blamed me and everyone else for making you stay home with her. But when any of us offered to take Joy for a while, you turned us down."

"That's not true. I let you take her to film sets —"

"And then you wouldn't allow me even that happiness anymore," she says sadly. "I loved her, but she was always a burden to you. You have a daughter. I have nothing. I've lost everyone — my mother, my father, my child —"

"And I was raped by too many men to protect you!"

My sister nods as though she was expecting me to say this. "So now I get to hear about *that* sacrifice? Again?" She takes a breath. I can see she's trying to calm down. "You're upset. I understand that. But none of this has anything to do with what happened to Sam."

"But of course it does! *Everything* between us has to do with either your illegitimate child or what the monkey people did to me."

The muscles in May's neck tighten and her anger roars back, matching mine. "If you really want to talk about that night, then fine, because I've been waiting a lot of years for this. No one asked you to go out there. Mama very clearly told you to stay with me. She wanted *you* to be safe. You're the one she talked to in Sze Yup, whispering her love to you, as she always did, so I wouldn't understand. But I understood that she loved you enough to say loving words to you and not to me."

"You're changing the truth, like you always do, but it won't work. Mama loved you so much she faced those men alone. I couldn't let her do that. I had to help her. I had to save you." As I speak, memories of that night fill my eyes. Wherever Mama is now, is she aware of everything I sacrificed for my sister? Did Mama love me? Or had Mama in her last moments been disappointed in me one final time? But I don't have time for these questions when my sister is standing before me, her hands on her hips, her beautiful face contorted in exasperation.

"That was one night. One night out of a lifetime! How long have you used it, Pearl? How long have you used it to keep distance between you and Sam, between you and Joy? When you were in and out of consciousness, you told me some things you obviously don't remember. You said that Mama groaned when you stepped into the room with the soldiers. You said you thought she was upset because you weren't protecting me. I think you were wrong. She must have been heartbroken that you weren't saving yourself. You're a mother. You know what I say is true."

This hits me like a slap to my face. May's right. If Joy and I were in the same situation . . .

"You think you've been brave and given up so much," May continues. I don't hear condemnation or taunting in her voice, just relentless anguish, as though she's the one who's suffered. "But really you've been a coward: afraid, weak, and uncertain all these years. Never once have you asked what else happened in the shack that night. Never once have you thought to ask me what it was like to hold Mama in my arms as she died. Did you ever once think to ask where, how, or if she was buried? Who do you think took care of that? Who do you think got us away from that shack when the sensible thing would have been to leave you behind to die?"

I don't like her questions. I like the answers that run through my mind even less.

"I was only eighteen years old," May goes on. "I was pregnant and terrified. But I pushed you in the wheelbarrow. I got you to the hospital. I saved your life, Pearl, but you're still carrying resentment and fear and blame after all these years. You believe you've sacrificed so much to take care of me, but your sacrifices have only been excuses. I'm the one who sacrificed to take care of you."

"That's a lie."

"Is it?" She pauses briefly and then says: "Have you ever once thought what life has been like for me here? To see my daughter every day but always be kept at a distance? Or do the husband-wife thing with Vern? Think about that, Pearl. He could never be a real husband."

"What are you saying?"

"That we never would have ended up here in this place that seems to have caused you so much misery if it hadn't been for you." As the fight falls from her voice, her words dig deep into me, unsettling my blood and

463

bones. "You let one night, one terrible, tragic night, make you run and run and run. And I, as your *moy moy*, followed. Because I love you, and I knew you were forever damaged and would never be able to see the beauty and fortune in your life."

I close my eyes, trying to steady myself. I never want to hear her voice again. I never want to see her again. "Won't you please just leave?" I beg.

But she comes right back at me. "Just answer me honestly. Would we be here in America if it hadn't been for you?"

Her question thrusts into me sharp as a knife, because so much of what she's been saying is true. But I'm still so angry and hurt that she turned Sam in that I respond with the one thing that will be most spiteful. "Absolutely not. We wouldn't be here in America if you hadn't done the husband-wife thing with some nameless boy! If you hadn't made me take your baby —"

"He wasn't nameless," May says, her voice as soft as clouds. "It was Z.G."

I thought I'd been hurt as much as I could and still survive. I was wrong.

"How could you? How could you hurt me that way? You know I loved Z.G."

"Yes, I know," she admits. "Z.G. thought it was funny — the way you stared at him during our sittings, the way you went begging to him — but I felt terrible about it."

I stagger back. Betrayal upon betrayal upon betrayal.

"This is another of your lies."

"Really? Joy saw it: Who had the red face of a peasant on the covers of *China Reconstructs* and whose face was painted with love?"

As she speaks, images from the past tumble through my mind: May resting her head against Z.G.'s heart as they danced, Z.G. painting every last strand of her hair, Z.G. placing peonies around her naked body . . .

"I'm sorry," she says. "That was cruel. I know you've held him in your heart all these years, but that was a girlish crush from long ago. Can't you see that? Z.G. and I . . ." Her voice catches. "You had a lifetime with Sam. Z.G. and I had a few weeks."

"Why didn't you tell me?"

"I knew you had feelings for him. That's why I didn't say anything. I didn't want to hurt you."

And like that I understand what's been before me for the last twenty years. "Z.G. is Joy's father."

"Who is Z.G.?"

It's the one voice that neither my sister nor I want to hear. I turn and there's Joy, standing in the kitchen doorway, her eyes like black pebbles at the bottom of a bowl of narcissus. Her look — cold, expressionless, and unforgiving — tells me she's been listening far too long. I'm devastated by Sam's death and my sister's version of our lives, but I feel absolute horror that my daughter has heard any of this. I take two steps toward Joy, but she edges away from me.

"Who is Z.G.?" she asks again.

"He is your real father," May answers, her voice gentle and filled with love. "And I am your real mother."

465

The three of us stand in the living room like statues. I see May and me through Joy's eyes: a mother — who has tried to teach her daughter to be filial in the Chinese way and brilliant in the American way — wearing an old nightgown, with a face red from tears, sorrow, and anger; and another mother — who has indulged her daughter with treats and exposed her to the glamour and money of *Haolaiwu* — looking radiant and elegant. Freed from two decades of secrets, May seems at peace, despite everything that's happened tonight. My sister and I have fought over shoes, over who's had the better life, and over who's smarter and prettier, but this time I don't have a chance. I know who will win. For so long I've wondered about my destiny. It wasn't enough for me to lose my baby son and my husband. Now the tears of the greatest loss of my life roll down my cheeks.

When Our Hair Is White

I lie on my bed, a huge hole in my chest where my heart used to be. Destroyed, that's how I feel. I listen to May and Joy murmur together. Later, I hear raised voices and doors slam, but I don't go back out there and fight for my daughter. I don't have any fight left in me. But then maybe I never did. Maybe May was right about me. I am weak. Maybe I've always been afraid, a victim, a *fu yen*. May and I grew up in the same home with the same parents, and yet my sister has always been able to look out for herself. She grabbed at opportunities: my willingness to take Joy, Tom Gubbins's offer of a job and what that turned into, her constant striving to go out and have fun, while I accepted the bad as merely my unlucky fate.

Later still, I hear water running in the bathroom and the toilet flush. I hear Joy opening and shutting her drawers in the linen closet. As silence finally settles over the house, my mind goes to deeper and darker places. My sister has made me think about things in a whole new way, but none of that changes what happened to Sam. I'll never forgive her for that! Except . . . except . . . maybe she was right about seeking amnesty. Maybe not voluntarily stepping forward was a dreadful mistake on Sam's and my parts, which resulted in terrible tragedy for Sam. But why hadn't May told us she was going to report us, even if it was for our own good? I know the answer too well: Sam and I were always afraid of anything new. We were afraid to leave the family and go out on our own, afraid to leave Chinatown, afraid to let our daughter become what we said we wanted her to be: American. If May had tried to tell us, we wouldn't have been able to hear her.

I know that, in the worst of my Dragon aspects, I can be stubborn and proud. Cross a female Dragon and the sky will fall. Indeed, tonight the sky has fallen, but I need to tell Joy that she is and will always be my daughter and that no matter what she feels about me or Sam or her auntie, I will love her forever and ever. I will make her understand how much she's been loved and protected and how much pride I have in her as she begins her life. I have ten thousand hopes that she'll forgive me. As for May, I don't know if I can find a way to absolve her or even if I want to. I don't know if I want to have a relationship with her at all, but I'm willing to give her a chance to explain everything to me again.

I should go out to the screened porch, wake them up, and do all this right now, but it's late and it's quiet out there and too much has happened on this terrible night.

"Wake up! Wake up! Joy is gone!"

I open my eyes to my sister shaking me. Her face is frantic. I sit up, fear pulsing through my body.

"What?"

"It's Joy. She's gone."

I'm up, out of the room, and running to the screened porch. Both beds look to me like they've been slept in. I take a breath and try to relax.

"Maybe she's gone for a walk. Maybe she went to the cemetery."

May shakes her head. Then she looks down at a piece of crumpled paper she holds in her hand. "I found this on her bed when I woke up."

May smoothes the paper and hands it to me. I begin to read:

Mom,

I don't know who I am anymore. I don't understand this country anymore. I hate that it killed Dad. I know you'll think I'm confused and foolish. Maybe I am, but I have to find answers. Maybe China is my real home after all. After everything Auntie May told me last night, I think I should meet my real father. Don't worry about me, Mom. I have great belief in China and everything Chairman Mao is doing for the country.

Joy

I take a breath, and the pounding in my heart slows. I know that Joy can't possibly mean what she's written.

She's a Tiger. It's her nature to flail and strike out, which is exactly what she's done in her note, but there's no possible way she's done what she's written here. May seems to believe it though.

"Has she really run away?" May asks when I look up from the letter.

"I'm not worried and you shouldn't be either." I'm irritated with May for starting the day with more drama when I hoped to talk things through, but I put a reassuring hand on her arm, trying to keep some semblance of calm between us. "Joy was upset last night. We all were. She probably went over to the Yee's house to talk to Hazel. I bet she'll be home for breakfast."

"Pearl." My sister swallows and then inhales before continuing. "Last night Joy asked about Z.G. I told her I think he still lives in Shanghai since his magazine covers always show something about the city. I'm pretty sure that's where she's gone."

I wave off the idea. "She's not going to China to look for Z.G. She can't just get on a plane and fly to Shanghai." I tick off the reasons on my fingers, hoping logic will soothe May's concerns. "Mao took over the country eight years ago. China is closed to Westerners. The United States doesn't have diplomatic relations —"

"She could fly to Hong Kong," May cuts in haltingly. "It's a British colony. From there she could walk into China, just like Father Louie used to hire people to walk tea money in to his family in Wah Hong Village."

"Don't even think that. Joy is not a Communist. All that talk has been just that — talk."

May points to the note. "She wants to meet her real father."

But I refuse to accept what my sister is saying. "Joy doesn't have a passport."

"Yes, she does. Don't you remember? That Joe boy helped her get one."

At that, my knees buckle. May grabs me and helps me to the bed, where we sit down. I begin to weep. "Not this. Not after Sam."

May tries to comfort me, but I'm inconsolable. It's not long before guilt takes over.

"She hasn't just gone to find her father." My words come out ragged and broken. "Her whole world has been split apart. Everything she thought she knew was wrong. She's running away from us. Her real mother . . . and me."

"Don't say that. You are her real mother. Look at the letter again. She called me Auntie and you Mom. She's your daughter, not mine."

My heart throbs with grief and fear, but I grab on to one word: *Mom.*

May dabs away my tears. "She is *your* daughter," she repeats. "Now stop crying. We have to think."

May's right. I have to regain control of my emotions, and we have to figure out how to stop my daughter from making this terrible mistake.

"Joy will need a lot of money if she wants to get to China," I say, thinking aloud.

471

May seems to understand what I mean. She's been modern for a long time and has kept her money in a bank, but Sam and I followed Father Louie's tradition of keeping our earnings nearby. We hurry to the kitchen and look under the sink for the coffee can where I keep most of my savings. It's empty. Joy's taken the money, but I don't lose hope.

"When do you think she left?" I ask. "The two of you stayed up talking —"

"Why didn't I hear her get up? Why didn't I hear her pack?"

I have these same self-recriminations, and a part of me is still angry and confused about everything I learned last night, but I say, "We can't worry about things like that right now. We have to concentrate on Joy. She can't have gone far. We can still find her."

"Yes, of course. Let's get dressed. We'll take two cars —"

"What about Vern?" Even in this moment of terror and bereavement, I can't forget my responsibilities.

"You drive to Union Station and see if she's there. I'll get Vern situated, and then I'll drive to the bus station."

But Joy isn't at the train station, and she isn't at the bus station either. May and I meet back at the house. We still don't know for sure where Joy has gone. It's hard to believe that she'll really try to go to China, but we have to act as though that's what she's doing if we're to have any chance at stopping her. May and I make a new plan. I drive to the airport, while May stays at home and makes phone calls: to the Yee family to see if

Joy said anything to the girls; to the uncles on the chance she sought their advice about getting into mainland China; and to Betsy and her father in Washington to check if there's an official way to catch Joy before she leaves the country. I don't find Joy at the airport, but May receives two distressing pieces of information. First, Hazel Yee said that early this morning Joy called in tears from the airport to say she was leaving the country. Hazel didn't believe Joy and didn't ask where she was going. Second, May learned from Betsy's father that Joy can apply for and receive a visa to Hong Kong upon landing.

Since we haven't eaten, May opens two cans of Campbell's chicken noodle soup and begins to heat them on the stove. I sit at the table, watching my sister and worrying about my daughter. My beautiful, wild Joy is running headlong to the one place she shouldn't go: the People's Republic of China. But Joy — as much as she thinks she's learned about China from the movies, that boy Joe, that dumb group she joined, and whatever her professors might have taught her in Chicago — doesn't know what she's doing. She's followed her Tiger nature, acting out of anger, confusion, and misplaced enthusiasm. She's acted out of last night's passions and confusions. As I told May, I believe that Joy's rushing off to China is as much a flight from us — the two women who have fought over her from birth — as it is about finding her real father. And Joy can't possibly understand how traumatic — not to mention dangerous — finding Z.G. could be.

But if Joy can't avoid her essential nature, then I can't escape mine either. The pull of motherhood is strong. I think of my own mother and all she did to save May and me from the Green Gang and protect us from the Japanese. Mama may have agonized over her decision to leave my father behind, but she did it. Surely she was terrified to step into the room with the soldiers, but she didn't hesitate then either. My daughter needs me. No matter how perilous the journey or how great the risks, I have to find her. She needs to know that I'll stand by her, unconditionally, without question, whatever the situation.

A small smile comes to my lips as I realize that for once not being a U.S. citizen is going to help me. I don't have a U.S. passport. I have only my Certificate of Identity, which will allow me to leave this country that has never wanted me. I have some money tucked in the lining of my hat, but it isn't enough to get me to China. It will take too long to sell the café. I could go to the FBI and confess everything and more, say I'm a rabid Communist of the worst kind, and hope to be deported . . .

May pours the soup into three bowls, and we go to Vern's room. He's pale and confused. He ignores the soup and nervously twists his bedsheets.

"Where is Sam? Where is Joy?"

"I'm sorry, Vern. Sam died," May tells him for what I know must be the twentieth time today. "Joy has run away. Do you understand, Vern? She isn't here. She's gone to China."

"China's a bad place."

"I know," she says. "I know."

"I want Sam. I want Joy."

"Try to eat your soup," May says.

"I need to go after Joy," I announce. "Maybe I can find her in Hong Kong, but I'll go into China if I have to."

"China's a bad place," Vern repeats. "You die there."

I put my bowl on the floor. "May, can you lend me the money?"

She doesn't hesitate. "Of course, but I don't know if I have enough."

How could she when she's spent her money on clothes, jewelry, entertaining, and her fancy car? I shove those feelings aside, reminding myself that she also helped buy this house and pay for Joy's tuition . . .

"I do," Vern says. "Bring me boats. Lots of boats."

May and I look at each other, not understanding.

"I need boats!"

I hand him the closest one. He takes it and throws it on the floor. The model shatters, and inside is a roll of bills held together with a rubber band.

"My money from the family pot," Vern says. "More boats! Give me more!"

Soon the three of us are smashing Vern's collection of ships, planes, and race cars on the floor. The old man had been stingy and cheap but always fair. Of course he gave Vern a portion of the family pot, even after he became an invalid. But Vern, unlike the rest of us, never spent his money. I can remember only one time I saw him use money: when he took May, Sam, Joy, and me

475

to the beach on the streetcar our first Christmas in Los Angeles.

May and I gather up the wads of cash and count the money on Vern's bed. There's more than enough for a plane ticket and even bribes, if I need them.

"I'll come with you," May says. "We've always done better when we're together."

"You need to stay here. You need to take care of Vern, the coffee shop, the house, and the ancestors —"

"What if you find Joy and then the authorities won't let you leave?" May asks.

She's worried about this. Vern's worried about this. And I'm terrified. We'd be stupid if we weren't. I allow myself a wan smile.

"You're my sister, and you're very smart. You're going to start working from this end."

As my sister absorbs this, I can practically see her forming a list in her mind.

"I'm going to call Betsy and her father again," she says. "And I'll write Vice President Nixon. He helped other people get out of China when he was a senator. I'll make him help us."

I think but don't say: *This isn't going to be easy.* Again, I'm not a U.S. citizen, and I don't have a passport for any country. And we're dealing with Red China. But I have to believe she'll do everything she can to get Joy and me out of China, because she got us out once before.

"I spent my first twenty-one years in China and my last twenty in Los Angeles," I say, my voice as steady as my resolve. "I don't feel like I'm going home. I feel like

I'm losing my home. I'm counting on you to make sure Joy and I have something to come back to."

The next day I pack the Certificate of Identity I was given on Angel Island and the peasant clothes May bought me to wear out of China. I take photos of Sam to give me courage and of Joy to show to people I meet. I go to the family altar and say good-bye to Sam and the others. I remember something May said a few years ago: *Everything always returns to the beginning.* I finally understand what she meant now as I begin this new journey — not only will mistakes be repeated but we will also be given chances to fix them. Twenty years ago I lost my mother as we fled China; now I'm returning to China, as a mother, to make things — so many things — right. I open the little box where Sam placed the pouch Mama gave me. I put it around my neck. It protected me in my travels once before, just as I hope that the one May gave Joy before she went away to college is protecting her now.

I say good-bye and thank you to the boy-husband, and then May drives me to the airport. As palm trees and stucco houses drift past my window, I go back over my plan: I'll go to Hong Kong, put on my peasant clothes, and walk across the border. I'll go to the Louie and Chin home villages — both places Joy has heard about — to make sure she isn't there, but my mother's heart tells me she won't be there. She's gone to Shanghai to find her real father and learn about her mother and her aunt, and I'm going to be right behind her. Of course I'm afraid I'll be killed. But more than that, I'm afraid for all the things we still could lose.

I glance at my sister, who sits behind the wheel of the car with such determination. I remember that look from when she was a toddler. I remember it from when she hid our money and Mama's jewelry on the fisherman's boat. We still have so much to say to each other to make things right between us. There are things I'll never forgive her for and things I need to apologize for. I know for sure that she was dead wrong about how I feel about being in America. I may not have my papers, but after all these years, I am an American. I don't want to give that up — not after everything I've gone through to have it. I've earned my citizenship the hard way; I've earned it for Joy.

At the airport, May walks me to my gate. When we get there, she says, "I can never apologize enough about Sam, but please know I was trying to help the two of you." We hug, but there are no tears. For every awful thing that's been said and done, she is my sister. Parents die, daughters grow up and marry out, but sisters are for life. She is the only person left in the world who shares my memories of our childhood, our parents, our Shanghai, our struggles, our sorrows, and, yes, even our moments of happiness and triumph. My sister is the one person who truly knows me, as I know her. The last thing May says to me is "When our hair is white, we'll still have our sister love."

As I turn away and board the plane, I wonder if there was anything I could have done differently. I hope I would have done *everything* differently, except I know everything would have turned out the same. That's the meaning of fate. But if some things are fated and some people are luckier than others, then I also have to believe that I still haven't found my destiny. Because somehow, some way, I'm going to find Joy, and I'm going to bring my daughter, our daughter, home to my sister and me.

Acknowledgments

Shanghai Girls is an historical novel. Pockmarked Huang, Christine Sterling, and Tom Gubbins were real people. But Pearl, May, and the rest of the characters are fictional, as is the plot. (The Louie family didn't own the Golden Pagoda, the rickshaw stand, plus a café and various other shops, although many families did own multiple businesses in China City. May didn't buy the Asiatic Costume Company from Tom Gubbins; the Lee family did.) However, some people may read these pages and recognize particular details, experiences, and anecdotes. Off and on during the last nineteen years — and maybe my entire life — I've been fortunate to get to talk to people who lived in some of the places and through some of the events that I wrote about in *Shanghai Girls*. There were countless happy memories, but for some, sharing their stories took incredible bravery, because they were still unsettled by what had happened to them in China during the war years, embarrassed by the humiliations of Angel Island or the Confession Program, or ashamed of the poverty and hardship they had experienced in Los Angeles Chinatown. Some of them have asked to remain nameless. To them and to everyone else who helped me, I say, this book wouldn't exist without your stories and your devotion to the truth.

Many thanks to Michael Woo for giving me a copy of the handwritten remembrances of his mother, Beth Woo, of teaching English to Japanese military men, the written marriage terms they showed her, and what it was like to escape from China on a fishing boat and live in Hong Kong during the war. Beth's husband, Wilbur Woo, who was separated from his wife here in Los Angeles, shared with me many stories of those days and introduced me to Jack Lee, who told me about the FBI agent who used to hang out in Chinatown during the Confession Program era. Phil Young introduced me to his mother, Monica Young, whose memories of being an orphan sent back to China during the Sino-Japanese War were invaluable. She also lent me a copy of Alice Lan and Betty Hu's reminiscence, *We Flee from Hong Kong,* in which the two missionaries described the cold cream and cocoa powder concoction that served as part of their disguise while they and their charges tried to stay ahead of the Japanese.

Ruby Ling Louie and Marian Leng, whose families each had businesses in China City, shared with me maps, photographs, brochures, and other memorabilia, including Paul Louie's excellent slide show on China City. An extra thank-you to Marian for her discussion of the difference between *fu yen* and *yen fu.* Others who graciously shared their time and stories include Dr. Wing and Joyce Mar, Gloria Yuen, Mason Fong, and Akuen Fong. Ruth Shannon allowed me to use her dear husband's name. (On the surface, my Edfred couldn't be more different from Ruth's, but they were both kind in heart.) Eleanor Wong Telemaque and Mary Yee told me stories of what happened to their families during the Confession Program.

I also went back to interviews I did years ago when I was researching *On Gold Mountain*. Two sisters, Mary and Dill Louie, both gone now, reminisced about the Chinese in Hollywood. Jennie Lee talked to me about the years her husband worked for Tom Gubbins and what it was like to own the Asiatic Costume Company after the war. I wish, once again, to acknowledge the National Archives in San Bruno. The interrogation scenes in *Shanghai Girls* are taken almost verbatim from the entrance examinations of Mrs. Fong Lai (Jung-shee), the wife of one of my great-grandfather's paper partners, and from hearing transcripts belonging to my great-grandfather Fong See and his brother Fong Yun.

I owe a deep debt of gratitude to Yvonne Chang at the Chinese Historical Society of Southern California for giving me access to the transcripts from an oral history project about Los Angeles Chinatown conducted between 1978 and 1980. Some of the participants have now passed on, but their stories have been captured and saved. The CHSSC is currently collaborating with the Los Angeles Chinatown Youth Council to create the Chinatown Remembered Community History Project, a filmed oral history project focusing on the 1930s and 1940s. I would like to thank the CHSSC and Will Gow, the project director, for giving me a first peek at those transcripts. The CHSSC's publications — *Linking Our Lives, Bridging the Centuries,* and *Duty and Honor* — greatly contributed to my creation of time and place for this story. Suellen Cheng, of the Chinese American Museum and El Pueblo de Los Angeles Historical Monument, has once again given me encouragement, advice, and insights.

Since I am neither a historian nor an academician, I have relied on the works of Jack Chen, Iris Chang, Ronald Takaki, Peter Kwong, Dušanka Miščević, and Icy Smith. Amy Chen's documentary, *The Chinatown Files,* helped to illustrate the lingering bitterness, guilt, and sadness that resulted from the Confession Program. Special shout-outs to Kathy Ouyang Turner of the Angel Island Immigration Station Foundation, for taking me to the island; Casey Lee, for guiding us on the island; Emma Woo Louie, for her research on Chinese-American names; Sue Fawn Chung and Priscilla Wegars, for their work on Chinese-American death rituals; Theodora Lau, for her brilliant examination of the Chinese horoscope; Liz Rawlings, who now lives in Shanghai, for a bit of fact checking; and Judy Yung for *Unbound Feet,* for her family's personal stories, for collecting the stories about Angel Island and the war years from so many others, and for answering my questions. I'm grateful as well for Ruthanne Lum McCunn's friendship, recommendations, and advice. Him Mark Lai, the godfather of Chinese-American studies, answered numerous e-mails and proved to be thoughtful and thought-provoking, as always. *Island,* written and compiled by Him Mark Lai,

Genny Lim, and Judy Yung, and *Chinese American Portraits* by Ruthanne Lum McCunn inspired me in the past and continue to inspire me.

I've been to Shanghai several times, but the works of Hallet Abend, Stella Dong, Hanchao Lu, Pan Ling, Lynn Pan, and Harriet Sergeant also contributed greatly to this novel. In a series of e-mails Hanchao Lu also clarified some lingering questions I had about Shanghai's geographic boundaries in the 1930s. The character of Sam, although he has a much different destiny and outlook on life, was influenced by Lao She's proletarian novel *Rickshaw*. For the history of Shanghai advertising, poster girls, and dress, I'm indebted to the works of Ellen Johnston Laing, Anna Hestler, and Beverley Jackson. I also immersed myself in the works of Chinese writers active between 1920 and 1940, particularly those of Eileen Chang, Xiao Hong, Luo Shu, and Lu Xun.

I wish to acknowledge Cindy Bork, Vivian Craig, Laura Davis, Mary Healey, Linda Huff, Pam Vaccaro, and Debbie Wright — who participated in a monthlong Barnes & Noble online discussion with me — for their insights and thoughts; the 12th Street Book Group for reminding me that sisters are for life; and Jean Ann Balassi, Jill Hopkins, Scottie Senalik, and Denise Whitteaker — who won me in a silent auction and then flew to Los Angeles, where I gave them a tour of Los Angeles Chinatown and introduced them to various family members — for helping me find the emotional heart of the novel.

I am extraordinarily lucky to have Sandy Dijkstra as my agent. She and all the women in her office fight for me, encourage me, and push me into new worlds. Michael Cendejas has helped me navigate the movie world. Across the pond, Katie Bond, my editor at Bloomsbury, has been filled with bright good cheer. Bob Loomis, my editor at Random House, has been kindness itself. I love our conversations and his crazy dots. But I'd also like to thank everyone at Random House who has made these past few years so extraordinary, with special appreciation to Gina Centrello, Jane von Mehren, Tom Perry, Barbara Fillon, Amanda Ice, Sanyu Dillon, Avideh Bashirrad, Benjamin Dreyer, and Vincent La Scala.

A few final words of gratitude and thanks to Larry Sells, for help with all things Wikipedia, website content, and for running my Google Group; Sasha Stone, for managing my website so professionally; Susan M. S. Brown, for her astute copyediting; Suzy Moser at the Huntington Library, for arranging for me to have my photograph taken in the Chinese Scholar's Garden; Patricia Williams, for taking that beautiful photograph; Tyrus Wong, now ninety-eight years old, for still making and flying Chinese kites; my cousin Leslee Leong, for living in the past with me; my mother, Carolyn See, for her keen eye and judgment; my sisters — Clara, Katharine, and Ariana — for all the reasons you can think of and so much more; my sons, Christopher and Alexander, for making me proud and supporting me in so many ways; and finally my husband, Richard Kendall, for giving me strength when I'm struggling, humor when I'm down, and boundless love every single day.

Becoming Madame Mao

Anchee Min

From the author of Empress Orchid

Madame Mao is almost universally known as an ambitious, vindictive and cruel woman, whose bid to succeed her husband led to the death of millions. But her story begins with her childhood self, Yunhe; the daughter of a concubine, she refused to have her feet bound in a first act of rebellion.

She later fled the miseries of her childhood, first joining a provincial opera troupe then making a name for herself on the Shanghai stage. She married Mao Zedong, but the revolutionary leader proved to be an inattentive husband with an appetite for infidelity. Despite this, the couple stayed together throughout the Communist victory and the Cultural Revolution.

A complex portrayal of one of history's most vilified women, Becoming Madame Mao is a startling and moving achievement.

ISBN 978-0-7531-8236-9 (hb)
ISBN 978-0-7531-8237-6 (pb)

Binu and the Great Wall

Su Tong

In Peach village, crying is forbidden. But as a child, Binu never learnt to hide her tears. Shunned by the villagers, she faced a bleak future, until she met Qiliang, an orphan who offered her his hand in marriage.

Then one day Qiliang disappears. Binu learns that he has been transported hundreds of miles and forced to labour on a project of terrifying ambition and scale — the building of the Great Wall.

Binu is determined to find and save her husband. Inspired by her love, she sets out on an extraordinary journey towards Great Swallow mountain. What follows is an unforgettable story of passion, hardship and magical adventure.

ISBN 978-0-7531-8062-4 (hb)
ISBN 978-0-7531-8063-1 (pb)

Peony in Love

Lisa See

Peony is the cherished only child of the first wife of a wealthy Chinese nobleman, and is betrothed to a man she has never met. As her 16th birthday approaches, she has neither seen nor spoken to any man other than her father and never ventured outside the cloistered women's quarters of the Chen Family villa. She is trapped like a good-luck cricket in a bamboo and lacquer cage, and the romantic lyrics from the Chinese epic opera The Peony Pavilion, mirror her own longings.

When her father engages a small theatrical troupe to perform scenes from The Peony Pavilion in their own garden, her mother objects: "Unmarried girls should not be seen in public." But Peony's father prevails. As the women watch the opera from behind a screen to hide them from view, Peony catches sight of an elegant, handsome man through a crack, and she is immediately bewitched by him. So begins Peony's unforgettable journey of love, desire, sorrow and redemption.

ISBN 978-0-7531-8032-7 (hb)
ISBN 978-0-7531-8033-4 (pb)